OFF THE RAILS

George Hudson rose from farmer's son to the rich and powerful Lord Mayor of York – friend of royalty and owner of half of the railways in the kingdom. But Hudson was driven by greed as well as ambition and a dark secret lurked within his past – a youthful indiscretion ... and an illegitimate child. That child, Milly, has been brought up by her mother Jane, who dreams of taking revenge on her careless begetter. By a quirk of fate, both Jane and Milly work in the Hudson household. Will Jane's revenge be sweet? Or will life – and unexpected love – get in the way?

OFF THE RAILS

OFF THE RAILS

by

Beryl Kingston

Magna Large Print Books
Long Preston, North Yorkshire,
BD23 4ND, England.

British Library Cataloguing in Publication Data.

Kingston, Beryl
    Off the rails.

    A catalogue record of this book is
    available from the British Library

    ISBN   978-0-7505-3706-3

First published in Great Britain in 2011 by Robert Hale Limited

Published in Large Print 2013 by arrangement with
Robert Hale Ltd.

Magna Large Print is an imprint of Library Magna Books Ltd.

Printed and bound in Great Britain by
T.J. (International) Ltd., Cornwall, PL28 8RW

1

The farmhouse kitchen was seething with anger, reddened faces creased and twisted, mouths roaring, the flagstones loud with the stamp of furious boots, the air a storm of furious movement. The three littl'uns had retreated to the safe corner by the dresser the moment the row began and were crouched together on the long stool, keeping out of harm's way, and the farm dogs were cowering too, in their case under the kitchen table, their ears laid back and their eyes upturned and watchful, ready to make a bolt for it if the fight got too hot.

'How *could* you have been such a stupid, gormless fool?' John Hudson shouted at his brother. 'You beggar belief.' At twenty-six he'd been head of the family for seven years, ever since his father died, and although there were times when the burden of running the farm and looking after nine brothers and sisters felt as heavy as a millstone, until that day he'd thought he was doing rather well. But this was beyond a joke. 'You're fifteen, for heaven's sake, George. Fifteen. Old enough to know better. What were you thinking of?'

'He weren't thinking at all,' brother Robert said, glaring at George but speaking to John. 'He were drooling an' rutting like some great fool ram wi' the ewes. That's what he were doing. He should have his breeches sewed up wi' cobbler's thread. That'ud stop him.'

'What happened to the sixth commandment?' brother William wanted to know. 'Thou shalt not commit adultery. Remember? You'll burn in hell-fire, George. Think of that.' He was the smallest and palest of the brothers and very aware of the need for obedience.

'Since when has he ever obeyed anyone?' Thomas said, sneering at his brother from his superior height. He was a strong, thick-set seventeen-year-old with a ready pair of fists. 'He don't know t'meanin' of t'word. He thinks he may go his own way and damn the rest of us. Allus has. 'Tis what comes of being a spoilt brat. Ma's dear little pet, what may do as he pleases and take what he wants an' leave the rest of us to pay the piper.' His mother's blatant favouritism still rankled, even now, nine years after her death.

''Twere nobbut a farm gel,' George said, standing his ground. Fifteen he might be and the fifth son, which wasn't the best position to be in, especially when the other four were rounding on him and Tom looked ready to punch him in the face, but he squared up to them nevertheless. They needn't think they could bully him. 'She were willing. 'Tweren't a matter of commandments. We were doing what were nat'rul. Same as anyone would. That's all.' Talking about it was opening his mind to memories, to the baked-bread smell of the harvest and the way they'd sung as they scythed, to the warmth of the sun on the back of his head as he pushed up her skirt, the tang of salt on her skin, the harshness of the straw scratching them as they rolled over and over together in the haystack, closer and closer.

Oh, 'twere gradely. He couldn't quite bring her name to mind but he could remember the smell of her as if she were still lying underneath him.

'All!' John said, throwing his hands in the air in exasperation. 'All, he says! He gets a girl into trouble, he's fined for bastardy – bastardy I ask you, in this family; Pa must be turning in his grave – and 'tis writ in Howsham Poor Book for all the world to see and he says *all*. Twelve an' sixpence you've cost us, I hope tha knows. Twelve whole shillings and sixpence!'

'I'll pay it back,' George said.

'Aye, tha will. Every brass farthin'. I'll make sure tha does.'

Their big sister Philadelphia was sitting at the kitchen table with her younger sister Ann beside her, both of them busy shelling peas into a cooking pot, with a pile of empty pods between them ready for the compost heap. Now she looked up at John in anxiety. 'They won't see it, though, will they?' she said.

John looked distracted. 'Who won't see what?' he said.

'The neighbours,' Philadelphia explained. 'I mean to say, they won't go looking in t'Poor Book, will they? An' if they don't look in t'Poor Book, they'll not know, will they.'

'In a place this size?' John said. 'Oh come, Philly. Think on it. Three farms and a handful of cottages wi' a gossip in every which one of 'em. Course they'll know. Everyone'll know, if they don't know already. It'll only tek one to get wind of it an' it'll be round the village like wildfire.'

Philadelphia wiped the sweat from her forehead

9

with her apron. 'Oh, Georgie, Georgie,' she said, wearily. 'Look what tha's done to us.'

'It's not a matter of what he's done to us,' Robert told her grimly. 'It's a matter of what we're to do wi' him. That's the gist of it. What we're to do wi' him.'

'Thrash him within an inch of his life,' Tom said, flexing his fists. 'That'ud show him.'

'We'll not take that road,' John told him, asserting his authority. 'I'll not have fisticuffs. We're not savages.'

'Well, he can't stay here an' that's flat,' Robert said. 'They'll think we condone what he's done if we let him stay here an' I'll not have that. I don't condone it nor never will.'

Outside in the fields it was noonday and the ewes were calling their lambs into the shade, their bleating clear and tender in the summer air; green corn rippled like silk under the softest southwest breeze; the gnarled boughs of the apple tree beside the kitchen window were a-twitter with fledgling finches calling to be fed; farm horses cropped the grass in the long meadow while the labourers took their ease and their cheese beside the barn; and somebody was slowly pumping water in the garden of one of the nearby cottages, the pump handle squeaking in a steady rhythm as the water plashed into the wooden bucket. It was a gentle summer's day and the life of the village was easy-running as a stream.

'We can't throw him out,' Philadelphia said, returning to her peasecods. 'He's our brother when all's said and done.'

'We can't do nowt,' John told her. 'Rob's got the

right of it. We can't be seen to condone a lecher. We've a standing in this place, a name.'

George's memories seeped away like water on soil. There was nothing for him now but the need to fight back and his own growing and desperate anger at the way they were treating him. If they thought he'd stay a minute longer in their stupid farmhouse listening to their hateful talk, they were very much mistaken. 'There's no need to throw me out,' he said. 'I'm going anyroad. I'd not stay if you paid me to. I'll make shift somewhere else, don't you worry. I'll find myself a job wi' good pay an' I'll make my fortune an' damn the lot of you.' And he turned away from their hateful, hating faces and headed for the kitchen door and the stairs.

'Tha can't leave now,' Philadelphia protested. 'Tha's not had dinner.'

He turned, paused and faced her. 'Dinner!' he said with all the scorn he could muster. 'I don't want tha dinner. 'Twould choke me.'

'Georgie, don't!' Philly said, holding out her hand towards him as if she were going to pull him back. 'Tha must have summat to eat.' But he was already out of the door and bounding up the stairs.

'Let him go,' Thomas advised. 'There's nowt to keep him here.'

John looked round the room at his family and dusted his hands on his breeches. 'Time we were back at work,' he said.

Although he was clumsy with anger, it only took George Hudson a matter of minutes to scrabble

11

his few belongings together and push them into a pillow case. Then, still in a fury, he knotted the ends together to make a bundle, tied them with a length of rope so that he could carry it on his back, stamped down the stairs and left the house. Once outside, he made sure he keept his head high, in case any of the neighbours were watching, and he didn't look back. The farm had been his home since he was born but it was no home to him now.

It didn't take him any time at all to walk through the village for there was so little of it, just a narrow path that wound uphill, with woods to his right and a cluster of small stone cottages to his left. His life here was over and done. Now he must head for a new life in the city of York. He had no idea what he would do when he got there but what of that? It was a ten-mile walk and something would occur to him before it was over. Hadn't Ma always told him he could do anything if he put his mind to it. Very well then. He would put his mind to this and he'd get himself a job and work hard and make his fortune and one day he'd be rich and famous and they'd all have to eat their rotten stinking words and serve them right.

'They've thrown him out then,' Mother Hardcastle observed to her neighbour. The two women were out in the front gardens, sitting side by side in the sunshine, their chores temporarily forgotten. Mrs Hardcastle had been up all night birthing a baby in a neighbouring village and now she was weary and needed a rest.

'Good job an' all,' her neighbour said. 'That's

my opinion. Serve him right. Lecherous little varmint.'

'Poor Jane,' Mrs Hardcastle sighed. 'What'll become of her?'

'She'll make out,' her neighbour said. 'Her ma'll take care of her. You'll see. Bound to.'

'Ruined for life,' Mrs Hardcastle said, in her lugubrious way, scowling at George's retreating back. 'That's the size of it. An' that poor father-less brat along with her. She'll not find herself a husband now. Never in a thousand years. Ruined for life. Poor Jane.' She gave an elaborate sigh. 'Ah well,' she said, 'he's gone now. Good rid-dance to bad rubbish, that's what I say.'

Her neighbour sighed too. 'I'd best be getting back indoors,' she said. 'I've a pudden to make and if I don't start soon, I shall be all behind like the cow's tail.'

It wouldn't have surprised either of them to know that poor Jane was weeping. She sat in her familiar wooden chair in the dingy kitchen of her father's tied cottage by the footpath to Scraying-ham, with her feet on the earth floor, her hands folded protectively across her swollen belly, and cried with despair. Her face was blotchy with tears and long damp strands of her dark hair had tangled out of her cap. 'I can't bear it,' she wept. 'I can't bear it.'

Her mother was bending over the fire stirring the stew. 'That's a fool thing to say,' she said, giv-ing the spoon a sharp tap against the side of the pot. 'Tha's a labourer's child and tha'lt bear what tha has to. Tha should have thought a' this when tha said yes to him in t'first place. There's no earthly use a-cryin' over spilt milk. What's done is done. Aunt'll take care of 'ee. Tha's got tha things. Tha can write to us.' It had been a matter of such pride that she'd taught her Janey to read and write. She'd thought it put her a cut above the others. And now look where they were. Minutes away from being parted and more unhappy than they'd ever been in their lives. She knew she was being too brusque with this poor child of hers but it was the only way she knew to avoid weeping herself.

Jane looked down at the ancient carpet bag that stood beside her chair and sobbed again. Her 'things' were few and limited: her old skirt and her mother's old shawl, a brush and comb, a prayer book, a pad of writing paper and a quill pen, a parcel of baby clothes. But things were just things. What she wanted was her home. Small, impoverished and dingy as it was, it had been the only home she'd ever known, and now she had to leave it and go and live with an aunt she scarcely knew in a place she didn't know at all and she wouldn't see her mother again until Christmas. She couldn't bear it.

Her mother put down the spoon and came to stand beside her. 'It can't be helped, Janey,' she said, lifting the girl's head and wiping her face with the corner of her apron the way she'd done so many times in the last fraught months. 'You can't keep the child here, you know that, poor little scrap. 'Twould be made mock of an' spat at an' called names an' I don't know what-all. Folk can be mighty cruel. You'd not like that, now would you? No. You'll do well enough with Aunt Tot. She'll not tell anyone. She's given her word. You've got a wedding ring to show to folks. You know what to say. You're a sailor's wife an' his name's John Smith an' he's been lost at sea. They'll not press you for more than that.'

Jane made one last useless plea. 'Let me stay, Ma,' she begged. 'One more night. Just one. I'll go tomorrow, good as gold. I promise.'

'The cart's coming tonight,' her mother said, turning away from her. 'Soon as it's dark. It's no earthly use weeping. 'Tis arranged. Now dry those eyes like a good girl an' help me peel these tatties or we shall have no supper for your father.'

Peeling potatoes was no comfort to Jane Jerdon at all. It just reminded her that this would be her last meal at home. But it was a chore and she had to do as she was told. And when the meal had been eaten and she heard the cart trundling up to the door, she had to obey that too. She listened as the carter eased his horse to a halt, calling 'Whoa my sonny' the way he always did, and then her father went out to greet him, and the moment had come. She picked up her bag, kissed her mother and drooped after him. She felt utterly defeated.

'Now then, young Janey,' the carter said. 'Let's have 'ee up here alongside a' me. That's the style of it. Soon be there. I'll get her there safe an' sound, Mrs Jerdon, don't 'ee fret. I'll make sure she don't see a soul.'

Jane climbed into the cart obediently and sat where she was told but she was lost in misery. Everything was out of her hands now. What was to come would come, whether she would or no.

A night jar was calling in the copse in its flat booming way and a flock of starlings were settling for the night in the nearby oak. Everything was as she'd always known it. Then the horse snorted and farted and they were off.

It was an uncomfortable journey because the path was rough and heavily rutted so every jolt threw them about quite violently and every sudden movement made the baby squirm and wriggle. Worse than that, she gradually realized that they were travelling through a landscape grown horribly unfamiliar, for although the moon was up, the fields were black shadowed, the trees were whispering eerily in the evening breeze and the hedgerows, caught in the light of the carter's lantern, were grey as though they'd been burnt to ashes. She turned her body sideways and looked back over her shoulder, straining to keep the cottage in sight for as long as she could, but it wasn't long before the night enveloped her and she had to sit straight and look ahead of her into the darkness, willing herself not to cry.

'Soon be there,' the carter said, and he gave the reins a little shake, which the horse ignored.

It took nearly an hour and every dark minute of it was miserable and uncomfortable. I hate you for doing this to me, George Hudson, Jane thought, as the cart jolted and her back ached and the baby kicked its feet against her ribs. I thought I loved 'ee back in the harvest time, but I never did. I thought tha loved me an' all, but tha never did neither. 'Twas all nonsense an' sweet talk what tha never meant a word of, all *'let me, let me'* an' now I'm paying the price for it, an' I'm to be a stranger in a strange place an' shall never see my home again, nor live with my ma. I hate you with all my soul, an' one day I'll be even with 'ee. I swear to God I will. I'll make you wish you'd never been born. Such black thoughts for such a black night but she went on thinking them, over and over again, until the horse plodded round a bend in the path and she saw the dark shape of a farmhouse ahead, the faint glimmer of candlelight marking its windows, and she knew she'd arrived and that her life as Aunt Tot's scullery maid was about to begin.

The carter urged his horse to the side of the house and clicked him to a halt beside the kitchen door. There was a dark figure standing in the doorway, silhouetted against the candlelight, and as soon as the cart stopped moving, it stepped forward and became Aunt Tot.

'You took your time,' she said to the carter.

'Couldn't go no faster, missus,' he told her amiably, 'an' that's the truth of it. Not this time a' neet. He's a good hoss, my old sonny, but nor as young as he wor.'

'Ah well,' Aunt Tot said, 'you're here now.' And she handed him a grudging coin. Then she turned her attention to Jane. 'Tha'd best come in out t'cold then,' she said. 'I daresay tha'll have had tha supper.' And she led the way into the kitchen, leaving Jane to struggle after her with her bag and her burden, blinking in the sudden brightness that starred from the candlestick on the kitchen table.

Now that they were indoors, Jane could see that her unknown aunt was a formidable woman and an extremely bulky one, with arms like a prize fighter and a jaw to match. Her eyes were small and close set and so very dark brown they looked black in the candlelight, especially under those heavy black eyebrows, and whatever hair she had was hidden under a severe Holland cap that looked as if it had been glued to her head. Jane wilted at the sight of her, wishing herself anywhere but in this cold, horrible kitchen among the smells of congealing grease and overcooked cabbage and missing her mother so much it was making her chest ache. She looked at the dirty pots and dishes piled together on the kitchen table and knew it would be her job to scour them.

As it was. 'You can do those,' Aunt Tot said, as if she were granting her a favour, 'whilst I put the dining room to rights. Set the candle on the window sill. Tha'll not need more than the one. That'll give 'ee light enough. Soda's in pot. Water's in kettle.' And she was gone before Jane could put down her bag.

It took a very long time and a great deal of backache and soda before the dishes were clean, the pots scoured and the dish-clout hung across the sink to dry, and then Aunt Tot steamed back into the room on a strong smell of sweat to say that the kitchen table had to be scrubbed too.

By that time, Jane was so weary and miserable that all she wanted to do was crawl away into a corner somewhere and go to sleep. Knowing there was even more work to be done made her feel weak and sick and, greatly daring, she opened her mouth to ask if the table couldn't wait till morning. But she'd barely spoken the first word before Aunt Tot descended on her, striding across the kitchen until they stood nose to nose. The candlelight cast long dark shadows under her eyes and her scowl was horrible to see.

'Now look 'ee here, Jane Jerdon,' she said, 'an' get this straight in tha mind. If I says tha art to do a thing, tha jumps to and does it. Is that clear?'

Jane bit her lip, feeling suddenly afraid, and dropped her eyes to avoid that awful gimlet glare. 'Yes, Aunt.'

'Tha's got a millstone round tha neck, what'll make tha life impossible, and don't 'ee ever forget it.'

Jane kept her eyes down and her voice was little more than a whisper. 'No, Aunt.'

'Very well then,' Aunt Tot said. 'Get that table scrubbed clean and riddle out the stove ready for the morning.'

'Yes, Aunt.'

'I'm off to my bed then,' Aunt Tot said and she took up her candlestick, found a new candle for it, and lit it ready to light her way upstairs.

She was almost out of the door before Jane dared to speak again. 'If you please, Aunt,' she asked, 'where am I to sleep?'

'Why, in the cupboard, child,' Aunt Tot said. 'Where else?' And she carried her light and her disapproval out of the room.

Left on her own, Jane sat on the kitchen stool and cried for a while because she simply couldn't help it. Then she got on with her chores. The hall clock was striking midnight before she'd finished. She pushed the hair wearily out of her eyes and looked round the dark kitchen for the cupboard.

19

There was a door in one corner alongside the dresser, which looked possible, and sure enough, it led into a large walk-in larder and underneath the slate counter, where the cheese, milk and eggs were kept, was a small truckle bed with a straw mattress, a pillow with a rough ticking cover and a single blanket. She pulled the little bed out into the room and set it by the remaining warmth of the fire. Oh to lie down and sleep, she thought, as she blew out the candle. She was so tired her bones ached and she hated George Hudson with a passion.

It was late evening when that worthy arrived outside the city of York, for he'd stopped at the inn at Claxton for a supper of lamb chops and kidneys and a good sustaining tankard of ale, and when his plate was clean, he'd sat on by the fire supping his ale and thinking. By the time he set off on his walk again, the city was just a dark presence brooding below him, speckled by the flicker of rush lights and candles but impossible to see in any detail. He could just about make out the shape of the Minster looming over the roofs huddled below it, grey against the dark sky, but the city walls were shadows. He could smell the place, of course – he'd been smelling it for over a mile and very nauseating it was – because the local farm labourers were out with their dung carts collecting the night soil. But the stench and the lack of light didn't trouble him at all. He'd thought until he knew what he was going to do and that was what mattered. First he was going to find himself a bed for the night and then tomorrow morning he was going to visit his rich Uncle Matthew and throw himself on his mercy. It wouldn't be easy, he was well aware of that, for the man didn't know him from Adam, but he had a good tongue in his head and he was sure he could do it. He was George Hudson and nobody was going to put him down.

2

The next morning dawned fair and fresh. The streets of York had been swept clean as soon as day was breaking, most early-morning faces washed, horses newly groomed, their tails combed and plaited and their brasses polished to catch the sun, doorsteps scrubbed white, bed linen hung from the upper windows to air. In short, it was a sweet-smelling, purposeful day when anything was possible and George was full of food and high spirits, whistling as he walked along Goodramgate towards Monkgate and his uncle's fine house.

The central arch of Monk Bar was clogged with carts and horses, and the two side arches, being smaller, were a-jostle with people all trying to shove their way through to one side or the other, so it took a while before George could squeeze through the crush and emerge into the wide roads on the other side of the wall. It was like stepping into another world, for the houses here were new, built of brick and beautifully proportioned, with grand doors and elegant windows.

And Uncle Matthew's house was the finest of them all. Although he knew very little about this distant uncle of his, one thing was obvious. The man was rich. He walked up to the front door and knocked firmly.

The door was opened by a servant in green livery and a white wig, a very haughty man and disconcertingly tall. 'Yes?' he said, looking down at George.

'Name of Hudson,' George said, speaking boldly and determined not to be put down. 'George Hudson. I am Mr Bottrill's nephew.'

'You have a calling card no doubt, sir?' the servant said. No card had been offered, as it should have been, so he was fairly sure this young person didn't possess such a thing. Especially given the way he was dressed. His shirt was clean enough, to give him his due, but, really, those rough breeches and that waistcoat were the sort of things one saw on a farm hand.

'Not at t'moment, no, sir, I've not,' George said, trying to sound as though it didn't matter and knowing how much it did – now that it was too late. 'I've just come to town and my family gave me instructions I were to pay my respects afore I did aught else. Common politeness, they said.'

'If you will just wait here,' the servant said. What a sneering voice he had! 'I will consult with Mr Bottrill.' And he shut the door and left George on the step.

It seemed like a very long wait, standing there on his own, but at last the door was reopened. 'If you will come this way,' the servant said, 'Mr

Bottrill will see you.'

Into an elegant hall, with a tiled floor, a carved staircase and a huge chandelier that held more wax candles than he could count, up the easy tread of the stairs to a landing on the first floor, where closed doors lined the walls, then a discreet knock and a muffled cough outside the furthest one and a querulous voice calling, 'Come in, come in.' And then he was in the presence.

It wasn't the sort of presence he was expecting at all. For a start he was in a bedroom and an extremely musty one, smelling of sweat and used chamber pots, and his illustrious uncle was in his nightshirt with a crumpled nightcap on his grey hair and a decidedly grubby dressing gown swathed about his body. His feet were long and bony and the slippers he wore might have been red velvet once but were now so scuffed and discoloured that they looked more like mud than cloth. For a rich man he was downright disreputable. He was also really rather rude, for he was reading a newssheet when George entered the room and he didn't look up or stop reading for as much as a second.

If there's going to be a conversation, George thought, I shall have to start it myself. 'I trust I see you well, sir,' he said.

His uncle grunted.

''Tis a grand day.'

Another grunt.

Happen he's deaf, George thought, and repeated his observation in a louder voice. 'A grand day, sir.'

'Stow your row,' his uncle said, without looking

up from the paper. That was disconcerting but George could see that there was nothing for it but to wait until he was noticed. So he waited.

After what seemed an extremely long time, Uncle Matthew gave the paper a shake and threw it on the carpet. 'So what's all this about?' he said. 'Come on the scrounge, have you?'

George assumed an expression that he hoped would convey shock and outrage. 'No, sir,' he said hotly. 'I have not. The idea. I wonder at you, sir, that you should think such a thing. I were sent to enquire after your health, sir. That's the sum and total of it. After your health.' And since the old man looked disbelieving, he contrived to bristle. 'I see I'm unwelcome, sir.' He turned as if he were about to leave.

'Keep your wool on,' his uncle said. 'If you ain't after money, you're the only one. Rest of 'em are at it night and day. There's no end to 'em. Sit 'ee down.'

There was only one other seat in the room and that was a low armchair upholstered in pink velvet to match the curtains. It looked too delicate to be used by a farmer's son, but George sat in it nevertheless, although cautiously. Then he put his hands on his knees and waited.

His uncle was re-lighting a pipe that was half full of tobacco and decidedly evil-smelling. 'Nephew you say, I believe,' he observed, puffing thick fumes into the room.

'Yes, sir. My mother was your niece. Name of Elizabeth.'

'Ah!' Matthew said. 'A good woman. Married some fool of a farmer, as I recall.'

'My father, sir.'

'Had a sight too many children.'

'Ten, sir.'

'Total folly,' the old man said, sucking his pipe. 'So why ain't you working on t'farm?'

It was time to feed him a spoonful of truth and see what came of it 'I'm the fifth son, sir. I've to fend for myself seemingly.'

'Ah!' his uncle said and smoked his pipe for a few minutes, nodding his head from time to time as if he was thinking. 'They've thrown you out, is that the size of it?'

'Aye, sir.'

'That's families for you,' the old man said. 'Not a heart atween the lot of 'em. So you've come to York?'

'Aye, sir.'

'What's brought 'ee here to me then,' his uncle asked, 'if it ain't money? And don't give me all that malarkey about how you were asking after my health for I don't believe a word of it. My family ain't the least bit interested in my health. Not a one of 'em. They're all waiting for me to die so they can get their greedy hands on my money. So come, and tell me t'truth, mind. What's brought 'ee here? There's bound to be a reason.'

'I need a job, sir,' George confessed. 'If I'm to fend for myself I've to find a job. That's t'truth of it. I thought you might know someone who were looking for a worker, being as you live here. I'm willing, sir. I'll turn my hand to anything. And strong. Strong as a carthorse, Ma used to say.'

'Um,' the old man said and fell to puffing his pipe again, his long face creased with thought.

There was so much smoke in the room that George began to feel quite dizzy but eventually his uncle took the pipe out of his mouth, shot him a shrewd look and gave his advice.

'Nicholson and Bell's is what tha wants,' he said. 'Drapers. Looking for a 'prentice boy. Not in a good way of business since Mr Bell died, to tell 'ee true, but beggars can't be choosers. They might take to you. Corner of Goodramgate and College Street, opposite Bedern Hall. Tell 'em I sent you.' And he went back to his pipe.

It was a very short walk to the shop and an even shorter trot and, although the place was dark, dusty and insignificant, it was easy enough to find. George wasted no time deploring its appearance; he simply walked straight in. A job was a job and the sooner he landed this one the better.

It was extremely dark inside, for the ceiling was low, the walls were painted dark green and the windows were so grimy that they let in very little light. There were dark counters on either side of the room and shelves behind them holding various rolls of dark cloth, and sitting behind the right-hand counter, chewing the end of a quill pen, was a most unprepossessing woman. She looked dowdy and none too clean and she had such a long narrow face and such lank, greasy hair under her grubby cap that for a few seconds, while he got his breath back, George wondered whether she was some relation of Uncle Matthew's. Then she looked up, took the pen out of her mouth and spoke to him.

'Was it for breeches or a jacket?' she asked.

He was rather pleased to be mistaken for a customer. 'Neither,' he told her.

The answer seemed to puzzle her. 'Beg pardon.'

'I've come for t'job,' he explained. "Prentice boy. Sent by Mr Bottrill. Am I speaking to Mrs Bell?'

'Oh no,' she said and giggled as if he'd made a joke. 'Nowt like that. Wish I were. No such luck. She's my sister. Wait there till I get her.'

She looked even more ungainly standing up than she'd done sitting down, for now he could see that she was wearing dull, brown, old-fashioned clothes, that although her black lace collar had once been fine – it was prettily embroidered – it was faded and frayed at the edges, that her brown boots were down-at-heel and that there was nothing soft or rounded or feminine about her. He watched as she walked towards an inner door, moving in a slummocky way like a surly boy, her shoulders humped and her long feet splayed. I wonder whether she's any good at her work, he thought, and walked across the room to see what she'd been doing. Writing up the accounts, apparently, they didn't look at all healthy and were full of mistakes. She's no beauty, he thought, she can't add up and, if this is all the trade they do, there'll not be much work for me.

But he could hear feet approaching so he had to stand back and pretend to be looking out of the window at the street. Two sets of feet, one slum mocking, the other brisk.

'You've come to apply to be our – um – apprentice, I believe,' the newcomer said. Very much like her sister to look at but better dressed and with a chatelaine at her belt.

'Yes, ma'am.'

'Have you – um – worked with a draper before?'

'No, ma'am.'

'Can you – um – read?'

'Yes, ma'am. And write a fair hand and add my figures and subtract 'em. I kept accounts on t'family farm for the last three years.' That wasn't strictly true. He'd kept the accounts for a week three years ago when brother John had been ill of a fever and couldn't do it. But it sounded well and he could see that it impressed both his listeners.

'Did you so?' Mrs Bell said. 'Well – um – that could be an advantage, I daresay.' Then she seemed to be at a loss for words and stood silent, fingering the lace on her left sleeve and looking into space. Good lace, George noticed, and unlike her sister's, clean and starched, and she was wearing a good stout pair of boots too. Why don't she say summat? he wondered. There was nowt for it, he must make some sort of offer for this job if he wanted to get it.

'I could keep your accounts,' he said, smiling at the lady, 'if you'd like me to.'

'Oh yes,' her sister said. 'We would like you to, wouldn't we, Rebecca?'

'Well, as to that,' Mrs Bell said, looking stern, 'that's as maybe. 'Tis not a thing to be rushed at. You must – um – walk before you can run, young man, if you take my meaning. I might permit it once you're 'prenticed. We shall – um – need to see. There's a lot to be learnt. For the moment you must – um – learn how to keep the shop and

– um – sweep it and clean it and – um – so forth and bring in new cloth when 'tis needful and – um – attend to the customers, what has to be done delicate and respectful. And acquaint yourself with the cloth and the prices and how 'tis to be wrapped.'

'Yes, ma'am,' George said, in what he hoped would be a dutiful voice. 'I could do all that and willing.' And he wondered if this was the point at which he ought to ask whether an apprentice could expect any wages.

She answered him before he could ask. 'I would pay you – um – sixpence a day,' she said, 'and all found. When you've worked a month and we've seen how you do and providing you're – um – satisfactory, I will draw up articles for you to sign.'

What does she mean, *all found?* he thought. He couldn't ask her. That would make him look stupid. He couldn't argue about the wage she'd offered either. It was far too little but this wasn't the time to say so. Uncle Matthew was right: beggars can't be choosers. He could edge it up later when they'd found out how good he was. The main thing was to have something settled. 'Yes, ma'am.'

She paused again, as if she were wondering what to say next. Then she looked at her sister. 'Show him where the – um – brooms are, Lizzie,' she ordered and walked out of the shop, the keys at her belt rattling.

He swept the shop and dusted the shelves while Lizzie bit her pen. There were no customers so he stood in a patch of sunshine and waited and got

29

bored. Finally he asked Lizzie if he could have a bucket of water with a good splash of vinegar in it and set to and cleaned the windows. Then he took the bucket back to the kitchen and settled to wait again. There were still no customers.

'Is it allus this quiet?' he asked.

Lizzie put down her pen to look at him. 'People come in from time to time,' she said and confided, 'It were better when Mr Bell were alive. He attracted 'em somehow. Bein' he was a man, I daresay. He had the knack of it. Making jokes wi' 'em and so forth. He were allus making jokes.' She sighed.

'Happen tha'd like me to finish the figures,' he suggested, trying to sound casual.

'Aye. I would,' she said firmly. 'They give me headache summat chronic. But she'll have summat to say if you do.'

'We won't tell her,' he said.

That made her giggle. 'Tha'rt a bad boy,' she said.

'That's me,' he agreed and winked at her.

So the figures were corrected and finished, and Lizzie sat on the newly scrubbed window sill and gazed out of the newly cleaned window and watched the people walking past. And there were still no customers.

I shall be bored stiff in this house with only these two for company, he thought. And he remembered Philly, who was all quick sympathy and ready wit and bubbling laughter, and felt homesick for the sound and sight of her.

Someone was pushing open the door, making the bell jangle as if it was an alarm. It was a young man, very tall and very fashionably dressed, in a green jacket made of fine wool, doeskin breeches, expensive boots and a white silk hat set at a rakish angel on a shock of brown hair. He was dangling four plump pigeons in his right hand and bellowing as he strode into the shop, 'Becky! Where the devil's she got to? Ain't that just like the woman! Never here when you want her. Becky!' Then he noticed George and scowled. 'Who's that?'

'New shop boy,' Lizzie told him. 'Come to be apprenticed.'

'Humph!' the young man said. 'He'd better be good, that's all. I didn't think much to the last one. Becky!' And he pushed through the inner door, waving the pigeons and shouting as he went.

George looked a question at Lizzie. It wasn't worth putting it into words because he knew she wouldn't answer it.

But she surprised him. 'My brother, Richard. Been out buying cloth.'

George grimaced. 'Funny sort of cloth.'

'Oh, that'll be delivered when it's ready,' she explained. 'He allus buys summat special when he's out and about. He likes his food.'

I wonder whether I shall get to eat any of it? George thought. *All found* could mean meals, couldn't it, and after all that scrubbing and cleaning, he'd worked up a healthy appetite, which got sharper as their empty day gradually inched towards dinner time and the smell of roasting pigeon began to drift into the shop. Then, when his belly was rumbling loud enough to be heard in the

31

street, there were trudging footsteps on the stairs and a murmur of voices in the room above the shop and a woman in a grey mob cap appeared in the doorway. She was small, short and skinny and she looked so worn and scuffed she could have been any age between thirty and sixty.

'Dinner's on the table, Miss Elizabeth,' she said. 'Miss Bell says to shut shop.' She stood aside to make way for Elizabeth, who rubbed her hands clean on her skirt and went stooping up the stairs, then she turned and looked at George. 'You're the new 'un, ain'tcher,' she said, 'what's been a-cleaning the winders. You're to come wi' me. Name a' Norridge. Mrs Norridge to you. I'm supposed to be their cook housekeeper. That's a laugh. General dogsbody more like. Look sharp or it'll get cold.' But George needed no bidding for they were heading for the kitchen and the smell of roast pigeon was growing stronger with every step he took.

The table was set with two plates and a serving dish where two roast pigeons lay side by side and steaming, on a mound of greens and potatoes. It was a feast.

'How...?' he asked, and then stopped. If she was cheating their employers, happen it were best not to know.

Mrs Norridge winked at him. 'Nipped out the back and bought two more,' she explained, 'soon as he brung 'em in. They got an account at Mr Cullen's. I often does it. Eat hearty, boy.'

He ate very hearty. The pigeons were delicious, cooked to such perfection that the flesh fell from the bones. And when they'd eaten every morsel

32

of the main course Mrs Norridge took a tray and disappeared upstairs, returning with the remains of a sizeable cherry pie with a dish of cream. I shall live well here, he thought, as he put the first spoonful of pie in his mouth. They might not be taking much trade but they're comfortable if they can dine like this.

'Good?' Mrs Norridge asked.

'Aye,' he told her, happily. 'Gradely.' He took another mouthful and savoured it. 'They don't do much in the way of trade,' he said, speaking casually.

'You can say that again,' Mrs Norridge said. 'I don't know how they make out some weeks. Course it was all different when old man Bell was alive. They had plenty a' custom then. He was up to all sorts a' tricks to bring 'em in.'

'What sort of tricks were those then?'

'Oh, all sorts,' Mrs Norridge said. 'He used to write out little cards – *Mr Bell respectfully begs to inform his customers that the new spring cottons have arrived* or *the new broadcloths* or whatever it was – an' stick 'em in the windows. That sort a' thing. An' then they'd come a-trooping in to see what was what. Knew 'em all by name he did. All their fancies. Cracking jokes and making 'em laugh. It was like a party in there sometimes. Couldn't hear yerself speak fer cackling an' laughing. Can you manage the rest 'a this pie?'

He held up his plate.

'More like a morgue nowadays,' she said, as she served him the last of the pie. 'Creeping about, never saying nothink. Mr Richard makes enough row coming home, hollering and shouting, I'll grant you that, but he never says nothink to me. An' that last boy they had was worse than useless. Never said a blind word to anyone the whole time he was here. She threw him out after six months an' I can't say I blamed her.'

So, he thought, for all her ums and ahs and that odd way of hers, Mrs Bell can be tough. ''Twill be different now I've come,' he said, licking the last of the cream off the serving spoon. 'Watch an' you'll see. I'll have the shop full in no time. I've got ideas.'

'You got plenty a' sauce,' she said, removing the spoon. 'I'll say that for you.' She lifted her head and listened. 'They're a-coming down,' she said.

There was only one more thing he needed to find out. 'Do I sleep here, Mrs Norridge?'

'In the store room,' she told him, carrying the plates to the sink. 'Now get back to the shop, for pity's sake.'

He was standing by the shelves pretending to tidy the rolls of cloth when Mrs Bell rattled her keys into the room. 'Leave that,' she said. 'Time you – um – learnt about cloth if you mean to be – um – 'prenticed. Follow me.'

He followed her into a small dusty room, where rolls of new cloth stood in line against the walls, wrapped in rough linen and carefully labelled, and piles of boxes were heaped one on top of the other in every available space, and he caught a glimpse of a truckle bed half hidden in the furthest corner, and there he was instructed, and tried to look interested, and repeated what she told him, to show that he understood her. But his thoughts were spinning away in a completely different direction. He was surprised to see how much stock they had and even more surprised to think that it was all hidden away. It seemed total folly to him. What was the point of explaining the difference between hand prints and roller prints or cottons and calicos, when so few of them were in the shop? They should be on the shelves and draped in the windows, he thought, where the customers could see 'em, then we might tempt a few of 'em over the doorstep. But he couldn't say so. She might not take kindly to an apprentice telling her what she ought to do and he didn't want to get sent packing on his first day. So he listened and looked attentive.

For the next two days, he did what little work there was – sweeping the floor, carrying two rolls of cloth down from the store room for a customer and running errands to master tailors in Stonegate and High Petergate – and thought hard about what else he could do. On his fourth morning, an elderly lady came timidly into the shop to say that she wished to choose some new ribbons for her Sunday bonnet and Lizzie, who was busy showing the lilac broadcloth to a young man, indicated with an upward nod of her head that he was to serve the lady. It took him ten minutes, as he presented her with a tray full of possibilities from the shelf under the counter and used every ounce of charm he possessed to persuade her that the most expensive would suit her complexion to perfection. After she'd gone, smiling and satisfied and surprised by her own extravagance, he stood looking at the tray and wondering whether he could say something to Lizzie.

'These should be in the window,' he said eventually, 'where folk can see 'em, not hidden away under the counter. These and the best of the cloth. That lilac for a start, and the green. Good broadcloth is that. We should make show of what we've got to offer. Let folk see it. That's my opinion. They'll not buy what they can't see. What do 'ee think?' If he could get her on his side she might be able to persuade her sister.

She was no use to him at all. She giggled. She said she didn't know what to think. It wasn't the sort of question she'd ever been asked. 'Tha'd need to talk to Mrs Bell about it,' she told him. ''Tis not up to me.'

It was the worst possible answer. How could he do that when she wouldn't allow him to say a word? It was very frustrating and, try as he might, he couldn't see a way round it.

The next day was Sunday, which at least meant there was something different for him to do. The entire family took the short walk down Goodramgate to the Church of the Holy Trinity, where the saints stood impassively in the stained glass windows, empty-faced and distant, the flagstones were jaggedly uneven, and the box pews out of alignment and black with age. Mrs Bell and her brother and sister had a pew halfway up the aisle, which showed that the family had some standing.

'There are seats for 'prentices at the back,' Mrs Bell said, putting him in his place again. 'Norridge will show you where to go.'

George took his seat feeling belittled and irritable. He bit his lip. He ignored the other people in the pew. He scowled at the saints. He frowned

36

at the pulpit. He glared at the nobs as they swept past him on their well-dressed way to their important pews. And then one of them stopped by his lowly seat and leant across towards him and spoke his name.

'Morning, George. Tha got the job, I see.'

It was his Uncle Matthew with his wife on his arm, and a gold-topped cane in his hand, dressed in the height of fashion, in a broadcloth jacket and a pair of trousers, no less, and a waistcoat of pale blue brocade.

'Yes, sir,' he said, fighting the urge to turn his head to see if Mrs Bell was noticing. 'Thank 'ee kindly.'

'Glad to hear it,' Mr Bottrill said. 'I like a boy who works for his living. Settled in well, have 'ee?'

'Yes, sir.'

'Good,' his uncle said. And he and his wife continued their progress to the front pews, greeting Mrs Bell on their way.

Has she seen? George wondered. Please God, let her have seen.

She had and made a point of asking him about it on their way back to the shop. 'You know Mr Bottrill – um – seemingly.'

Oh, what an enjoyable moment. 'Yes, ma'am,' George said.

'How did that – um – come about?'

'He's my uncle, ma'am.'

'Is he, by Jove?' Richard said, very much impressed. 'Fancy. Now he's what I call a rich man. Very rich by all accounts. A regular Croesus. Runs a coach and four, house full of servants, property all over, in Hutton and Cranswick and Newton-on-Derwent, even as far afield as Whitby and Huntington, so they say.'

'Aye, so he has,' George said with enormous satisfaction. Now, he thought, happen they'll treat me with a bit more respect.

3

That first week with Aunt Tot was the longest Jane Jerdon had ever had to endure. The work was endless. She'd no sooner cleared away one meal and scoured the dishes before she had to start preparing the next. Aunt Tot roasted the meat on the spit and made pies and pastries but as far as Jane could see everything else was down to her. She fell into her truckle bed far too late at night, too tired to think. And the baby grew heavier day by day.

'Oh, my little Milly Millstone,' she said to it, as it wriggled and kicked its feet against her ribs. 'I'll be reet glad when th'art out in t'world.'

But when she woke at first light on Monday morning to the realization that her belly was being gripped by an unfamiliar pain, she was caught in a sudden fear and prayed that this wasn't the baby coming. I've eaten summat, she decided as the pain ebbed away. That's how 'tis. I got the gripes. But the next pain was so strong there was no denying what it was. Oh my dear heart alive, she thought. How shall I make out?

She tried to remember what she'd heard about

birthing a baby and it wasn't very much. I should have asked Mrs Hardcastle afore I left the village, she thought, but it was too late to be thinking of it now. The next pain started before she'd caught her breath from the last one. It was so powerful it made her groan. And so did the next one. And the next. Soon she was groaning as the pains began. She simply couldn't help it.

After what seemed like a very long time, she became aware that there was a face leaning towards her and that someone was calling her name. 'Janey! Janey!' And she made an enormous effort and opened her eyes. It was an oddly familiar face but she couldn't place it. 'Who...?' she said.

'See if you can sit up,' the face advised, and it was speaking with Aunt Tot's voice. But this wasn't her aunt surely. Not this woman with her long brown hair tumbling out of her nightcap and her eyes looking concerned and her voice gentle. 'Audrey's here to help us,' the face said. 'Just swing your legs round, like a good girl, and see if you can stand up. Tek your time. There's no rush. We'll hold on to you.'

Another face. This time the milkmaid's. Hands supporting her under the arms. I'll never be able to stand up, she thought. And stood up.

''Tis only a few steps,' Aunt Tot said. 'Just down to my room. You'll be more private there. 'Tis all ready for 'ee.'

'I've not lit the fire,' Jane panted. 'The bread wants...'

'Don't you worry your head about fires and bread,' Aunt Tot said as they staggered out of the kitchen. 'That's all took care of. You just concentrate on birthing this baby. Just a few more steps. There's a good girl.'

They were in a quiet bedroom, with a high bed mounded with pillows. They were lifting her into it, easing her onto a thick towel, plumping the pillows to make her more comfortable. And she *was* more comfortable. The pains were still hard but they were easier to contend with now that she was sitting up and had company.

'I'll just nip back to t'kitchen for a minute, to tend to t'fire and t'bread and such,' Aunt Tot said. 'You'll manage, won't you, Audrey? You know where I am if you need me.'

The room was so quiet that Jane could hear Audrey breathing and a clock ticking somewhere nearby. She wondered what the time was and how long this birth would go on and what would happen next. She seemed to have been struggling through pains for a very long time. And then the next thing happened, with a rush of water that soaked the towel and such an urge to push that she barely had time to recognize it before she was responding to it. She didn't even notice that Audrey had run off for Aunt Tot.

Half an hour later, her little Milly Millstone was in her arms, red in the face and crying so lustily she was showing the roof of her mouth and her bare pink gums. She had a shock of damp dark hair and the prettiest hands and feet and Jane was instantly enamoured of her. 'My dear little Milly,' she said. 'Don' 'ee cry. I got 'ee. I won't let no harm come to 'ee, ever, I promise.'

Audrey was in tears. 'I never seen a babba born

afore,' she said, wiping her eyes on her apron. 'I never know'd it was so...' And then stopped, at a total loss for words.

'Nor me neither,' Jane told her, gazing at her baby. 'She's the prettiest thing I ever did see.'

'Where's her clothes?' Aunt Tot said. 'We can't have her a-lying there naked, even if she *is* a babe new born. She'll catch her death of cold.'

Jane was kissing the baby's fingers. 'Um,' she said, 'they're in my bag. All ready and waiting. I wouldn't leave 'ee naked, would I, my precious.'

Audrey was sent to fetch them and returned carrying them reverently in her rough hands and weeping again because they were so small and delicate.

'So I should think,' Aunt Tot said. 'We can't wrap our precious in linsey woolsey. That'd never do. Tha's got to give thought to materials, when it comes to a baby.'

George Hudson was giving thought to materials at that moment too but in his case it was red brocade. Now that he'd impressed his new employers by showing them that he had a wealthy relation, he was going to make capital of it. He hadn't seen Mrs Bell since he started work that morning but he'd kept himself occupied by planning exactly what he would say to her when she finally appeared. The thing was to catch her eye before she could say um and disappear.

She smoothed in at a thoroughly inopportune moment, when he was serving an elderly man who couldn't make up his mind. Damned woman. And she stood and watched him as he tried to make a

41

sale. He had to keep a smile on his face even though he was inwardly fuming, while the old man dithered and changed his mind and finally said he'd think about it and come back later. He was so cross he could have kicked the counter. But he stayed in control. 'Mrs Bell, ma'am,' he said, 'I been thinking.'

'Not to any – um – purpose, seemingly,' she said, 'else you'd have made a sale.'

'Now that, ma'am, is precisely why I was thinking,' he said, pressing on despite her disapproval. ''Tis my opinion of it that the gentleman would ha' bought the cloth if he could ha' seen it in t'window and made his mind up afore he came into the shop.'

'Aye,' she said. 'Lizzie told me you wanted to put – um – cloth in the window. Well, let me tell 'ee. It wouldn't do a happorth of good. People never look in t'windows.'

He decided to change tack slightly. 'I been considerin' our red brocade,' he told her seriously, 'and seems to me 'tis just the sort of cloth my uncle would buy, if he knew t'was on offer, so to speak. 'Tis quality is that an' he's a man for quality.'

'Well,' she said slowly. 'As to that, I'm sure I don't know.'

'It might be worth a try,' he urged. 'I could put it all up for you in no time and glad to do it. 'Twould be an experiment. That's all. And if it don't come to any good, I'll tek it down again in a day or two and no harm done.' Then he gave her the benefit of his earnest grey eyes and waited.

She was tempted. He watched her as she

42

dithered, fingering the lace on her sleeve. Oh come on! he willed her. Just say yes. That's all you've got to do. I'll do all the rest.

'Well,' she said at last. 'Happen there'll be no harm in it.'

He started work as soon she left. By the end of the afternoon the shop was transformed. There were shelves in both windows to hold the rolls of cloth and long swathes of the boldest designs and the prettiest colours were draped over the chairs he'd purloined from the kitchen, brocades and broadcloth in one window and cotton prints in the other. Better than that, he'd gathered a crowd as he worked and when they smiled and nodded at him through the glass, he'd held up the cloth for their inspection. So much for *people never look in t'windows*, he thought, as his happy audience gazed and talked. If they walk into the shop too, I'll have made my point.

His first customers came in half an hour later, three very well dressed ladies in splendid bonnets, a mother and her daughters who'd come to see the new cottons. They bought three dress lengths, which he wrapped with a ribbon and a flourish, and departed well pleased with him and themselves.

'Well, I never,' Lizzie said when they'd gone. 'Who'd ha' thought it?'

'This is just the start,' he told her happily. 'You wait and see.'

Two days later he bought two curtain poles, gave the chairs back to Mrs Norridge and changed the window ready for the Saturday trade. He was charged with energy and full of ideas. If he went

43

about things the right way he could get himself a new suit of clothes. Then he could have some visiting cards printed, which would put that snooty butler in his place, and go visiting his rich uncle. He meant to cultivate that worthy gentleman, now that he knew how rich he was, and he thought he could see the right way to do it. All he needed was the right moment.

It didn't come for nearly a month but it was worth waiting for. Mrs Bell walked into the shop after work on his fourth Saturday and actually sought him out. She had an official-looking paper in her hand and was smiling at him. Well, there's a wonder!

'If you will – um – just step into t'back parlour,' she said, 'I have your – um – articles for you to sign.'

He'd forgotten the apprenticeship. 'Yes, ma'am,' he said and smiled back.

The paper was spread out on the parlour table and held in position with a floral paperweight. He did as he was told and read it thoroughly. Articles for an apprenticeship with Nicholson and Bell Quality Drapers to the trade of draper to last seven years from the date of signature. I shall be of age afore this is served, he thought as he signed, but it was good to know that he'd passed muster. He watched as Mrs Bell added her signature. Now, he thought, for the next thing.

'One of your customers has given me an idea, Mrs Bell,' he said.

'Oh yes,' she said. She was still smiling. 'What – um – customer was that?'

'Mr Ramsbottom,' he told her. 'He was think-

44

ing of buying a length for a new jacket and he said what he really needed was to see how 'twould make up.' It wasn't strictly true. What had really happened was that Mr Ramsbottom had discussed the cloth and it was George who had wondered aloud if it might be helpful to Mr Ramsbottom if he could see it made up. But there was no need for her to know all that. It was much too complicated.

'We're not tailors,' she said and now her face was stern again.

'No indeed, ma'am,' he agreed. 'We're not. But it gave me an idea. How would it be if I were to buy a length of one of our most popular lines and have it made up – at my own expense naturally – and then we could put it in t'window as part of the display, so to speak. I would need it on Sundays to wear to church and when I go to visit my uncle.' And he looked a question at her and waited.

She was so flabbergasted she didn't know what to say. She certainly wasn't going to let him have his own way. That would do him no good at all. 'Well, as to that,' she said. ''Twill need a deal of – um – consideration. 'Tis not a thing to be rushed.'

'No, ma'am,' he said, trying not to show her what a rush he was in. 'Course not. But happen you'll think on it?'

'How would you – um – pay for it?' she asked. 'Our cloth don't come cheap.'

He had the answer to that at once. 'It could be took out my wages,' he said.

The boldness of it took her breath away. Really, there was no end to this boy. He had an answer

45

for everything. 'It would take months.'

'Yes, ma'am, I know,' he said. 'But then if we get any sales as a result, what I can't promise – we can't know, can we? – but if we do there'll be profit from that, what we could split half and half, on account of 'tis my idea an' I'll be taking the risk of it.'

That was such a preposterous suggestion she didn't know how to answer it at all. 'I will give it – um – thought,' she said, eventually, and went upstairs to the safety of her nice quiet living room before he could say anything else.

'That boy has the cheek of the devil!' she said to her brother and sister as they sat at supper that night.

'What's he done now?' Richard asked, grinning at her.

She told him, her voice querulous with disbelief, and was annoyed when he laughed. 'It's nowt to laugh at,' she told him. 'He wants to use our cloth and put a jacket in t'window for everybody to see, as if he hasn't put enough things there already. Mr Bell must be turning in his grave. He signed the articles quick as a flash and now this. In the very next breath. I thought I were hiring a workhorse – someone strong and dependable and willing and – um – obedient and so forth – but he's more like a stallion, allus goin his own way.'

'Give him his head,' Richard said. 'That's my advice. If it works, we'll get more trade, which ain't a bad thing, if it don't, he'll learn the hard way and serve him right.'

46

'But 'tis our cloth Richard.'

'Aye, so 'tis,' Richard said. 'Let him earn it and wear it. He might have the cheek of the devil, I'll grant you that, but he's handsome enough in all conscience. 'Twill look well on him. And what looks well will sell. He's got the right of it there.'

So George got his cloth, which was a bold sky blue in a lightweight wool and found a tailor to make it up at a fair price – *bein' as 'tis a good advertisement for you, sir.* He put it in the window as soon as it was ready to wear, carefully arranged on one of the tailor's borrowed dummies and, sure enough, it attracted interest and trade just as he'd known it would. And the next Sunday, having borrowed a new white cravat from the stock and prevailed on Mrs Norridge to wash his best shirt for him when she had a copper full of hot water, and iron it ready for the occasion, he took his coat from the window and wore it to church.

It was much admired, especially by the maidservants in the back pews, and there was much smiling and bobbing of heads and eye-signalling in his direction. And then just as he was beginning to wonder whether his illustrious uncle was actually going to come to church that morning, there he was, striding down the aisle with that quiet wife of his holding his arm and a new grey silk hat on his head.

'Getting on, I see, young George,' he said as he reached his nephew's pew. 'That's the style.'

'Yes, sir,' George agreed. 'I do my best, sir.'

'Good lad,' his uncle said and made a heavy joke. 'Now all you need's the breeches, eh?'

'Yes, sir,' George said again, but he was thinking *and* the hat and the boots and a calling card. Oh, he'd a fair way to go yet.

It took him till the beginning of July and it needed all his skills as a salesman and considerable manipulation of Mrs Bell's profit figures before he'd amassed enough money to be kitted out as he wished. And then he had to wait a week for the next early closing day before he could wear it. But the result was so satisfactory he was preening all the way to Monkgate. And what a happy moment it was when he handed his card to that snooty butler and told him that Mr Bottrill was expecting him. Now sneer if you dare, he thought.

This time he was admitted straightaway and led in due and proper style to the drawing room on the first floor, where his uncle was waiting for him.

'We'll have our coffee now, Joshua,' he said, and when the butler had bowed and left them. 'Still doing well, I see, young George.'

'We've trebled our trade in the last two months,' George told him happily.

'Aye. I don't doubt it,' his uncle approved. 'I've been watching. And all your doing if I'm any judge.'

'Yes, sir,' George said, trying to look modest and making a poor fist of it.

'You're a good lad,' his uncle said. 'A worker. Which is more than can be said for the others. Been here with their begging bowls only last week, so they have. Not that it'll do 'em any good. I've got their measure, don't you worry.'

George had no desire to hear about the others

but there was no stopping Uncle Matthew once he'd started and his complaints against his avaricious family went on and on until the coffee was borne steaming into the room and he had to pause from his diatribe to drink it. George watched his disagreeable face as he scowled and sneered, and those bony hands clutching the cup and that long nose dipping towards the coffee, and decided that he would endure being bored and try to look as though he were interested. If this was the price he had to pay for being the favoured nephew then he would pay it. He'd be rewarded in the long run.

He stayed with his uncle for nearly an hour and parted with him in apparent good humour, even though he was inwardly twitching to get away. But it was a job well done, he thought, as he walked back to Goodramgate and he was eased and pleased when he began to gather admiring glances again.

'Well, bless my soul,' a familiar voice said as he emerged from the crowded arch of Monkgate, holding onto his hat. 'If it's not George Hudson. You do look well. Quite the swell.'

'Mrs Hardcastle, ma'am,' he said, giving her a courteous bow. 'I trust I see you well.' It was always sensible to keep in with the local gossip.

'Visiting my cousin,' she said.

'Ah!'

'Do 'ee work hereabouts?'

'At the drapers,' he told her. 'Nicholson and Bell's.'

'And doing well, I see.'

He laughed at that. 'Aye, ma'am, but give me a

year or two and I shall do even better.'

She gave him her shrewd look. 'Aye,' she said. 'Happen so.' They were heading in opposite directions or she would have walked with him and discovered more.

'Pray give my regards to my family,' he said as he turned to stride away from her. And that was such a happy moment he was grinning all the way back to the shop.

Mrs Hardcastle went straight to Home Farm as soon as the carter had set her down by her own gate. This was too good a piece of gossip not to be spread and besides she wanted to see how Philadelphia was because the poor girl had been quite ill these past few weeks.

She was sitting in her chair by the kitchen fire darning stockings and looking extremely pale and tired but she greeted her visitor in her usual gentle way and when Mrs Hardcastle asked her how she was she smiled and said she was 'fair to middling' even though it was plain to the midwife's experienced eye that she was no such thing. But she was visibly cheered when she heard how well her brother was doing.

'Fallen on his feet, sithee,' Mrs Hardcastle told her. 'Allus knew he would. Great strong boy like that.'

Philadelphia covered her mouth with a kerchief and coughed into it for a worryingly long time. But her mind was still on her brother and when she'd recovered her breath she questioned her visitor again. 'He looks well, would 'ee say, Mrs Hardcastle?'

'Blooming,' Mrs Hardcastle said, but she was thinking, which is more than can be said for you, poor girl. 'Great strong boy!'

4

Little Milly Smith was a very good baby and by the time she was four months old she was delectably plump and pretty. Jane had almost forgotten that her eyes had been dark blue when she was born. Now they were pansy brown and her original mop of straight dark hair had been replaced by a head of thick fair curls.

'Th'art the dearest little thing what ever was,' Jane told her and the baby smiled as if she quite agreed. But the smile brought sad thoughts. She was still a fatherless child, however dear she was, and she still hadn't seen her grandmother. Don't 'ee fret, Jane thought, kissing her dear little curled fingers. I'll be mother and father to 'ee both so I will. Tha'lt want for nowt, I swear to 'ee. And that vile George Hudson can rot in hell, what I hopes and prays he will. But what she really wanted was to see her mother.

She'd written a letter to her on the day the child was born, naturally, but it was weeks before the carter arrived and could be asked to deliver it. And now a fourth letter was being written and there were times when despite all the good things that were happening to her, Jane wept private tears of anguished homesickness. If only Milly wasn't such a very little baby and if only it wasn't such a very long way to Scrayingham Church.

September came in that year with gales and driving rain and October was no better, for now they had to endure mists and fogs. Scrayingham Church seemed even further away than ever, even though Milly was now sitting up on her mother's knee before the fire, looking about her and as warm and sturdy a child as you could hope to see. The others weren't faring so well in the colder weather; Audrey's hands were so chapped and raw she said she was ashamed to put them *near our precious* and Aunt Tot had a rheumy cold that wouldn't go away.

'That dratted wind goes straight to your chest,' she said. 'You must take care our babba's wrapped up good an' warm if you means to take her to church come Sunday. I'll look out a little blanket for her. We don't want her to take cold. That'ud never do.'

Jane was thinking fast. Was this the chance she'd been hoping for? With a blanket, the long walk might be possible. 'Well now, Aunt,' she said carefully, 'as to that, I been a-thinking.'

'Oh aye,' her aunt said. 'And what great thoughts have come to 'ee?'

'What I been thinking,' Jane confessed, 'is I would like to go to church at Scrayingham one Sunday, if 'ee were so minded, to see my ma. I do so want to see my ma. 'Twould be a fair old trudge but I don't mind a long walk and if Milly's wrapped in a blanket I can keep her out of t'cold. 'Tis five months now since I saw Ma and that's a mortal long time.'

The longing on her face was so extreme that Aunt Tot was torn with pity for her. 'You'll have to face bad looks if you're a-going there,' she warned. 'Scrayingham's a different parish to ours. You're known there.'

'Aye,' Jane said sadly. 'I know. But I do so want to see my ma.'

'I tell 'ee what I'll do,' Aunt Tot said. 'I'll see if old Jem'll take you. He might well. He's a good man and one church is as good as another, when all's said and done. You'll be warmer in t'cart than on foot, and that way you can be took straight to t'church gate and brought straight back again after t'service so there'll be less time for t'gossips to put their knives in.'

So two Sundays later, at long last, Jane was driven to Scrayingham Church with the baby in her arms, wrapped up snug in her shawl and her blanket. It was a lovely moment. When Jem clicked to the horse and set off, she was tremulous with excitement but after a while her heart began to crumple into misgiving. What if her old neighbours sneered at her and called her names? Aunt Tot had thought it likely. Well, if they did, she thought, trying to be valiant, she would have to face it. She did so want to see her ma and if this was the only way it could be done, then so be it.

Luckily, she arrived a matter of minutes before the service was due to begin and only just had time to sneak into the church and scuttle into the pew beside her mother before the rector made his entrance. And oh it *was* so good to be with her again and to pull back the shawl and show her

Milly's dear little smiling face and watch as she kissed her dear little warm fingers.

'She's a pretty child,' Mary Jerdon said under cover of the first hymn. 'She looks as if she feeds well.'

'All day long,' Janey told her proudly. 'Don't 'ee, my darling.'

'Lovely fat cheeks,' her mother approved, gazing at her granddaughter. 'Oh, it *is* good to see you, Janey.'

Neither of them paid very much attention to the service and when the rector cleared his throat to begin the sermon, they simply let him get on with it and gave themselves up to baby worship and the joy of being together. It was the happiest, easiest time. When the service was over they slipped out together as quietly and unobtrusively as they could and found a hidden corner behind the cart where they could talk more freely until Jem arrived. At last Jane could tell her mother how much she missed her.

'They treat you well, though,' Mary Jerdon prompted.

'Aye, well enough,' Jane told her. 'But they're not you. Oh, Ma, I've been wanting and wanting to see you.' She was in tears by then. She simply couldn't help it.

Her mother held her and kissed her and told her that they were back together now and there could always be another time; Scrayingham Church wasn't all that far and happen she could get home for Christmas, there was always Christmas. And Jane promised to come to Scrayingham again as soon as she could and to see what could be done about Christmas. But they parted in tears despite all their commiserations because Jem was walking towards them and the rest of the congregation had begun to leave the church. The sight of them all, so gathered together, walking down the path towards her, put poor Jane into a panic and she scrambled into the cart before they could see her and nodded to Jem to start the horse. But once they were round the first bend and travelling steadily, she calmed down, comforting herself that she'd been quiet and behaved very sensibly, not gone up to take communion, nor spoken to anyone other than her parents, and only whispered to her ma at that, and they'd left the church very quickly, slipping away like shadows, so happen no one would have noticed her.

She was wrong, of course, for there'd been one pair of eyes in the congregation that never missed a face or a trick. One very sharp pair of eyes and they belonged to Mrs Hardcastle.

'Was that your Janey I saw in church?' she said to Mary Jerdon, as they walked towards the Howsham road.

Mary admitted that it was.

'I trust she's keeping well.'

'Fair to middling.'

Even though Mary was turning her head away and looking as discouraging as she could, Mrs Hardcastle persisted with her interrogation. 'She brought the baby with her, I think.'

'Aye, she did,' Mary said, looking at her fiercely, 'and let me tell 'ee, she's a very pretty baby and a very good one. We never had a peep out of her the whole time. Not one peep.' She looked at her husband for support but he was far too much in awe of Mrs Hardcastle to venture a word on such a delicate subject and merely nodded.

'I'm uncommon glad to hear it,' the midwife said. 'Good babies are worth their weight in gold, as I should know. I'll not judge a child by the sins of its parents.'

'I'm glad to hear you say it,' Mary told her, even more fiercely. 'For I tell 'ee, ma'am, if I ever hear so much as one bad word bein' spoke against my granddaughter, I shall have summat to say what'll roast ears. And now as we've reached our footpath, I give 'ee good day, ma'am.'

But Mrs Hardcastle didn't seem to be aware how close they were to a quarrel and stood in her way, blocking their path with her bulk. 'You've heard the news about Philadelphia Hudson, no doubt,' she said.

Hudsons again, Mary thought. Don't she know how we feels about 'em? But it was obvious that Mrs Hardcastle wasn't going to move until she got some sort of answer, so she offered, 'We heard she was poorly.'

'Aye, so she is,' Mrs Hardcastle told her. 'She has the coughing sickness mortal bad, poor woman. Mortal bad. Fading away afore our eyes she is. I doubt she'll last till Christmas.'

Mr Jerdon ventured an opinion as one seemed called for. 'She's wore herself out a-runnin' that farm,' he said. 'All those great girt boys to care for. 'Tis no wonder she's poorly.'

'You've the right of it there, Mr Jerdon,' Mrs Hardcastle told him. 'She's wore out, poor woman, and that's the truth of it.'

'We must be getting on,' Mary Jerdon said. And, as the midwife was finally standing aside, she strode off along the path, leaving her husband to come puffing after her. She was so cross she could hardly contain herself.

'Hudson! Hudson! Hudson!' she cried. 'I'm sick of t'sound of the name. What makes her think I care two pins about them? They can all take ill an' die for all I care. Pernicious critters every which one of 'em, from that vile George on down, and he ought to come to a bad end if there's any justice in the world. Treating our Janey so. A thoroughgoing bad family. All tarred with t'same brush. How dare she make us talk of them and my Janey in tears for not seein' us, poor child. 'Tis cruel, so 'tis, and she should know better than to burden us. I hopes that George burns in hellfire so I do.'

'Soon be home, Mother,' Mr Jerdon tried to comfort. ''Tis no distance now. Soon be home.'

'Don't keep saying that!' she shouted at him. ''Tis no help to anyone. Damned Hudsons.'

He followed her meekly. When a fury was on her, what else could he do?

The damned Hudsons were in the middle of a family argument.

'We must tell him,' Ann was urging. 'He's her brother when all's said and done.' She might be a mere nineteen and so skinny she looked as if the slightest wind would blow her over, but now that Philly was ill someone had to mother the family and see that the meals were cooked and try to calm the brothers when they were angry, as they

57

were at that moment, torn by fury that their sister was so ill and that they were powerless to help her, shamed by the memory of how they'd parted with their feckless brother and angry because he'd made this so difficult for them by not writing to them.

'Five months he's been in York,' John said, 'and we've not had a single word out of him. Not one single word. Oh, I know our Philly's fond of him but fondness cuts both ways. He should've written.'

'He's been too busy feathering his nest,' Thomas sneered. 'That's my opinion on it. Looking after hisself. Same as allus. What was it Mrs Hardcastle said? Dressed to the nines.'

'Philly wants to see him,' Ann said, standing her ground, although their anger was making her feel shaky. 'We ought to tell him and that's *my* opinion on it. How is he to know if we don't tell him? And what if she were to die and he didn't even know she were ill. What would we say then?'

'She won't die,' William told her fiercely, his face strained with grief. 'I won't allow it.'

'And how will 'ee stop it, tha great blamed fool,' Robert roared at him. 'Tell me that. No one can stop it. There's nowt we can do. Nowt. Not one blamed thing.'

William pressed his palms against the table top to steady himself and leant across towards his brother. 'Don't,' he begged. 'Don't say such things. I can't bear it.' He was close to tears, his face distraught and his eyes red-rimmed.

Ann was so upset she couldn't find any words either to stop them or to comfort them. She

58

stood twisting the hem of her apron in both hands as if she could wring an answer from it until John came to their rescue.

'I will write him a short letter and tell him she's ill,' he said. 'In Christian charity I can do no less.'

'And he'll go his own sweet way,' Thomas warned. 'I doubt you'll even get an answer.'

The letter was delivered just as George had started to serve a prestigious customer. It couldn't have been a worse moment. He glanced at it, recognized his brother's handwriting and put it under the counter to be dealt with later. Then he turned his attention to his customer and, in the satisfaction of an excellent sale, well earned, he forgot all about it. It wasn't until the end of the day when he went to the counter to take out the account book that he found it again and this time opened the seal and read it, quickly. The news didn't trouble him. He assumed it was a rheum of some kind or a winter chill and it didn't occur to him to wonder why John should have written to him about something trivial. Poor old Philly, he thought, and took the account book into the office.

During the last three months he'd organized the back parlour into a workplace where accounts were written up every evening, deliveries noted as soon as they arrived and wages paid out on a Saturday. It pleased him to see how well ordered it was and preened to think it was all his doing. Trade was good that autumn and, on the strength of it, he'd persuaded Mrs Bell and Richard to raise his wage to five shillings a week. Now he had two good suits of clothes, several fine shirts, two pairs of fashionable boots and more than a dozen cravats, and with money in his pocket he could spend his evenings in the local hostelries enjoying a drink or two with his new cronies, and could pay for a whore when the itch grew too troublesome.

And of course there was always Uncle Matthew to visit and flatter into good humour. He was doing extremely well with that gentleman. He'd found out how to make him laugh and how to tease him into a good humour when he'd grown maudlin with too much grumbling. If he played his cards right, there would be money in this acquaintance. And he meant to play his cards to perfection. He was so happy dreaming the way into his future that he forgot all about John's letter. So it was rather a shock when another one was delivered to him three weeks later.

Poor old Philly, he thought as he opened the seal, she must be worse. I ought to go and see her.

But it was too late for visiting. The second letter had been written to tell him that his sister had *'passed away'* and to inform him that the funeral was arranged for the following Thursday. It was a cold, formal letter and at the close of it, John said stiffly that he *'expressed the hope'* that George would find himself able to attend. It seemed harsh and uncaring. Does he imagine I would stay away? George thought. She was the best of the bunch. We all knew that. As much of a mother to us as Ma herself. Of course I'll be there. I'll hire myself a horse and ride there. Then I can ride back to York when it suits me.

It was a dark, sad day and the wind out there in Scrayingham churchyard bit through to their

60

bones. Both Philly's sisters wept throughout the committal and her brothers were red-eyed. 'Best of the bunch,' they said to one another when the burial was over. 'We'll not see her like again.'

George stood a little apart from the rest of them. He felt uncomfortable and not at all sure that he ought to have been there and being ignored was making him feel worse. Eventually Ann looked across at him and, after a few words with her brothers, she walked across the church-yard and put her arms round him. She was crying so much she couldn't say anything but that made it easier for him. All he had to do was hold her and make soothing noises into her hair. And then William came over and asked him if 'wor all reet' and they spoke for a few minutes.

'It don't seem fair that she should die,' George said. 'Not so young and not when she was allus so good.'

'Best of the bunch,' William said.

And as they were in a churchyard, George said 'Amen!'

It was a matter of honour with him not to weep until he was riding back to York. Then he cried so much he couldn't see the road. But it didn't matter because there was nobody there to see *him* and luckily his horse knew most of the bridle paths round York and was entirely sure of his way back to the stables.

5

When Milly was twelve months old, she took her first staggering steps from chair to chair in the kitchen to the delight of everyone in it. Aunt Tot, who'd quite forgotten that she'd ever described the child as a millstone and would have been mortified to have been reminded of it, declared that she was the prettiest little dear and so entertaining you'd never believe it.

'You never know what'll happen next,' she said happily to Jane. 'Not with this one.'

What actually happened was that Jane had a visitor and one she didn't expect.

She and Milly were out in the kitchen garden, picking the first of the lettuces to make a green salad, when they saw her stomping up the garden path towards them. Milly looked up at once and smiled but Jane was puzzled.

'Mrs Hardcastle, ma'am,' she said, pausing in her work. 'Give 'ee good day.'

The midwife sat on the garden seat and took off her bonnet to mop her forehead with a kerchief. 'I've come here in such a rush, you'd never believe,' she explained. 'Your aunt said you were out here. Oh my stars! I was in the carriage and on my way afore I could so much as catch my breath. You'll see why when I tell 'ee. Baby's coming on well, I see.'

'Yes, ma'am,' Jane said, wondering what this

was about. 'Very well.'

'And you've plenty of milk?'

'Yes, ma'am.'

'Well now,' Mrs Hardcastle said, donning her bonnet and folding the kerchief neatly on her lap. 'I've come to ask a favour. A very great favour it has to be said. You are still feeding the baby, I trust and believe.'

'Indeed, ma'am.'

'I'm glad to hear it,' Mrs Hardcastle said, 'for that's the gist of my errand. I've just this minute come from Foster Manor at Scrayingham, where I've been all night. A difficult birth. Sir Mortimer ordered his own carriage to bring me here so you can see how urgent this is.'

There didn't seem to be anything for Jane to say so she waited.

'The long and short of it,' Mrs Hardcastle said, 'is that Lady Fitzwilliam died, early this morning. God rest her soul! The child survived and seems healthy enough, but he needs feeding. In short he needs a wet nurse. I thought of you directly. 'Twould be a fine position. The Fitzwilliams are a wealthy family and would treat you well. You would have your own rooms and a serving maid to assist you and so forth. What do 'ee say?'

The answer was immediate and direct. 'I'd rather not, Mrs Hardcastle. I'm settled here, ma'am, and my Milly knows her way about and has friends in the household and plenty of folk to pet her and talk to her. Besides which, I might not have enough milk for two babies and I wouldn't want her to go short. I'm beholden to 'ee for thinking of me, but no, ma'am, I'd rather not.'

'Now let's not be hasty,' the midwife advised. "Tis worth consideration. As I'm sure you'll agree when you starts considering. The Manor would be a very fine place for a child to grow up. They eat well there. They have a kitchen garden and a park for exercise and a stable full of horses and ponies for the children and a library where the family children learn to read and write, which would be a very great advantage to your little Milly. I can understand you not wanting to leave your friends, but it could be the chance of a lifetime. Besides which it's a mere half mile from your mother's cottage, happen even less. Your parents live on the Fitzwilliam land, do they not?'

That was an argument to give Jane Jerdon pause. To be near her mother was something she'd wanted all year long. 'Well...' she said. 'There *is* that.'

Mrs Hardcastle pressed home her advantage. 'Indeed there is,' she said, 'and not to be sniffed at. I daresay they'd allow you one of their carriages to take you visiting. Then you could take Milly along and your ma could see the both of you.'

Jane was torn. It would be a wonderful thing to be able to see her ma whenever she wanted to but she didn't want to take on the care of another baby – and somebody else's baby at that – nor to be at the beck and call of a family of strangers. She noticed that Milly had taken one of the lettuces from the trog and was busy tearing one of its leaves into small pieces but she couldn't summon up the energy to take it from her. Not when she had all this to think about.

'I'll have to ask Aunt Tot,' she said, thinking, if she says she can't spare me, which she well might, then the matter will be settled and I won't have to go.

'Of course,' Mrs Hardcastle said and stood up at once. 'That child is eating the lettuces,' she said. 'It won't do her digestion any good.'

That child allowed her mother to remove the half-chewed leaf from her mouth and was delighted to be lifted onto her hip. Then they all walked into the farm so that Aunt Tot could settle their fate.

It was rather a disappointment to Jane that her aunt had no doubt about it at all. 'Of course tha must go,' she said. ''Twould be folly not to.' And when Jane made a grimace, 'You'll never regret it, believe me. It could be the making of you. And think of that poor baby with no one to nurse him. Oh no, you go, child. You're just the right one. We shall miss you, there's no gainsaying that, but you must take your chance.'

So Jane had to pack a bag with her belongings and Milly was given a sugar plum from Aunt Tot's jar so that she would have something to keep her happy during the journey and Audrey came running up from the dairy to kiss them goodbye and then they were climbing into the carriage, which was very grand and gave Jane second thoughts about the advisability of that sugar plum, and they were off, trotting through the green fields in the warmth of the summer sunshine towards their new lives.

George Hudson was walking through the sunshine that morning too, only in his case it was a decidedly unpleasant experience for he was in a foul temper and an unpleasant place. At that moment, he was passing the Shambles, where the butchers had been particularly busy. The air around the stalls was nauseous with the smell of spilt blood and raw meat, the gunnels were clogged with blood and offal and the narrow street was crawling with flies and bluebottles from one end to the other. 'Foul!' he said to himself and it wasn't just the butchery that was annoying him.

Mrs Bell had insinuated herself into the shop that morning to make an announcement. 'I want you – um – both to know that I am considering the um – possibility of taking Richard into partnership.'

George couldn't trust himself to say anything. To give that silly boy a partnership was just plain stupidity. Can't she see what a simpleton he is? He knows nowt and thinks he knows everything, and that's the mark of a fool if ever I saw one. If you need a partner, he thought, trying not to glare at his employer, you should have took me. I've got the ideas and the energy for it. I work. I'm making summat of this shop. Not that fool Richard. Very well then. If you make him a partner, you can pay me a guinea a week from that moment on, what I'm well worth. And I'll see exactly how it's done and the day I'm twenty-one I'll make you take me into the firm too. I'll not be overlooked, not when I work so hard and make so much money for 'ee. Damned fool woman!

He carried his grudge all round the city, scowling at passers-by and kicking at corners. It wasn't until he saw one of the town's worthies approaching that he controlled himself and changed his expression. He was beginning to cultivate the men in high places for one day they were going to be useful to him. One day he was going to be as rich and powerful as they were – or even richer.

Jane Jerdon was overwhelmed by her first sight of Foster Manor. It was the grandest building she'd ever seen, all that dazzling white stone and those long rows of great tall windows and that huge front door framed by those great white columns, standing up so tall as if they were guarding the place. They must be very rich, she thought, as she followed Mrs Hardcastle through the side door, for there seemed to be servants everywhere, all of them in different uniforms. They were greeted by the housekeeper who wore a spotless grey gown and a snow-white cap and looked like someone who had to be obeyed.

Mrs Hardcastle spoke to her politely and softly. 'How has he been, ma'am?' she asked.

'About the same,' the housekeeper said, 'as you will see. We've moved the crib to the night nursery. This way.'

They climbed the stairs to the second floor and walked along a corridor hung with pictures of beautifully dressed men and women until they came to a white door which opened into a wide, high-ceilinged, handsome room. Jane had an impression of a lot of white and gold, of long white curtains at the window and a long column of sunlight that looked almost solid enough to touch. Then she became aware that there was a maid-servant in the room sitting on a low chair beside a small white crib and that she was weeping.

He's dead, she thought, looking at the cradle, and she felt sorry for the poor little thing to have lived such a short time.

'He is Sir Mortimer's only son,' the housekeeper was saying, 'so you will understand that he is very precious to the entire family. If you can help us, Mrs Smith we would be extremely grateful to you.' And she pulled back the embroidered coverlet to give Jane her first glimpse of the baby. Such a small, pale, delicate, little thing he was and he seemed more dead than alive, with his eyes tight shut and his hands curled against the covers. But they were all looking at her, waiting to hear what she would say.

'If someone will take my Milly for me,' she said, looking at the servant, 'and bring me a nursing chair, I will see what I can do. He's very weak, mind, I can see that, but I will do what I can.'

The servant stepped forward to take Milly, the nursing chair was moved into the sunlight, and Jane took the child out of the cradle, sat in the chair, loosened the kerchief that she wore at her neck for modesty's sake and eased her nipple from her bodice. The baby didn't react to it at all, but lay on her lap without moving.

'Put a little milk on his lips,' the midwife advised. 'Give him a taste of it.'

It was done. The baby moved his head once and slightly. It was done again with the same lack of result. He needs more than a drop, Jane thought. He's too far gone for that to wake him. He needs a gush. And this time she gave her breast a good squeeze and released a stream of milk all over the baby's face. He stirred, sneezed, put out the tip of a small pale tongue and licked his lips.

'There then, my little man,' Jane said to him, 'tha liked that. Try a bit more.' And she smeared his lips with the milk that was rolling down his face. For several long seconds he lay without moving, then he licked his lips again and pursed them as if he might be ready to suck. The silence in the room was intense. The three watching women were holding their breath and even Milly was still and quiet on the maid's lap. Jane eased her nipple towards that little moving mouth, very, very gently, and the baby gave a sudden lurch of his pale head and latched on.

'Praise the Lord,' the housekeeper said.

It took four days of peace and patience before Jane was satisfied that her new charge was feeding as he should and by then she'd settled into the house and her new life. On that first morning a bed was moved into the nursery for her – a proper bed, what luxury! – and that was followed by a pretty little cot for Milly, then a meal of cold meats, bread and cheese was brought up to her on a tray with a tankard of beer and, late in the afternoon, the housekeeper reappeared to introduce herself as Mrs Denman and to report that Sir Mortimer was very pleased to hear what good progress she'd made with little Felix.

'I was wondering if he had a name yet,' Jane said. 'I didn't like to ask.'

'Oh indeed he does,' Mrs Denman told her, looking down at him. 'It's a family name. It's been given to the first son for generations. Sir Mortimer was the second son. His brother Felix died when he was four, which is another reason why Sir Mortimer is so concerned for this baby. It was remiss of me not to tell you that earlier.'

'We had other things on our minds, ma'am,' Jane excused them, and was rewarded with a wide smile.

'Now as to details,' Mrs Denman said. 'Mr Glendenning wishes me to tell you that your wages will be eight shillings and sixpence a week and all found. You will have your own maid to assist you, of course. It will be her job to wash the baby's clothes and fetch hot water when you need it and clean the room and look after your little one when you are otherwise engaged with young Felix. You will find she will do everything you ask of her.'

Jane's thoughts were spinning with such amazement she didn't know what to say. First a bed of her own and that great platter of food and now this. Eight and six was a fortune, and having a servant to wait on her was something out of a dream. She gulped and struggled and eventually managed an answer, 'Thank 'ee kindly, ma'am.'

'Her name is Polly,' Mrs Denman said, 'but of course she might have told you that already.'

'No, ma'am.'

'You will dine in this room for the time being,' Mrs Denman said. 'But when little Felix is settled, I trust you will join us in the servants' hall.'

How polite she is, Jane thought. 'Yes, ma'am,' she said. 'I shall be happy to.'

The next day the baby was waking every two or

three hours and she fed him whenever he woke, feeling that the more milk she got inside him the better he would be. By the afternoon of the third day, he was sleeping for several hours between feeds and Jane was beginning to feel she'd made rather a good job of mothering him. And on the morning of the fifth day, he filled his stomach so full it was as tight as a drum, fell asleep as soon as he'd finished feeding and slept soundly. It was blissfully quiet and after a little while, since she had nothing else to do, Jane picked Milly up, settled her on her lap and sang her some of her favourite nursery rhymes. She'd just nibbled at *'this little finger on the right'*, to Milly's chortling delight, when she heard someone howling.

'Now what's that, Milly?' she said. It sounded as though it was coming from the next room and, as there was a communicating door between them, she set Milly on the floor and the two of them went to see if they could find out what was happening – not that there was much doubt what it was, given that there'd been a death in the house. The door opened easily and beyond it was another white and gold room, carpeted, curtained and full of delicate furniture. There was a small pale girl in a crumpled white dress, lying on the carpet crying bitterly, and another one, slightly older but equally pale, kneeling beside her, weeping silently with tears rolling down her cheeks.

'It ain't fair,' the little one wept. 'Why did she have to go away, Sarah? They could have kept her. It ain't fair.'

'Try not to cry, Emma,' the older one said.

71

'You'll make your eyes red.'

'I don't care,' the little one said and howled again. 'I won't eat here. It ain't fair!'

Then the one called Sarah became aware that they had company and gave her sister's arm a shake. 'Hush, Emma,' she said, in a commanding voice. 'Sit up.' And the child sat up and stopped crying.

Jane didn't know what to say. She'd never had to cope with any grieving children before and especially two who had just lost their mother. The little girls stood and looked at her for what seemed an uncomfortably long time.

Then the older one spoke. 'There's nobody here,' she said. 'They're all at the funeral.' She was quite calm now and spoke sensibly.

Of course, Jane thought. That's why the house is so quiet. 'I'm so sorry,' she said.

'Why should you be sorry?' the child asked. 'It ain't your fault. You didn't tell them to go.'

'No,' Jane said, thinking what an odd conversation this was to be having with a child.

'They sent her away,' the little one told her in an aggrieved voice. 'I don't think that's fair. We didn't ask them to.' Her lip was trembling as if she was going to cry again.

'No. I'm sure you didn't,' Jane said.

'They don't ask us when they send people away,' the older girl told her. 'You know that, Emma.'

'Yes,' Emma said sadly. Then she leant forward towards Jane. 'It was because she married that horrid man,' she confided. 'I didn't like him.'

She's not talking about her father, surely to goodness? Jane thought.

72

'He frightened the horses,' Emma went on, 'didn't he, Sarah?'

'Yes,' Sarah confirmed. 'It was because he was so ugly. Papa said so.'

Jane was completely lost now. If they weren't talking about their father and mother, then who was the lady who'd been sent away? 'Would you like to come and see your baby brother?' she offered. At least she'd be on safe ground there.

'Not particularly,' Sarah said. 'Babies ain't very interesting. I've seen one. They don't talk or anything. They just lie there. I'd rather have a dog.'

Milly had been following the conversation, turning her head from speaker to speaker and smiling at them all. Now she caught at the last word and joined in. 'Dogga-dogga-dogga,' she said.

'Heavens!' Sarah said. 'Is she talking to me?'

'She talks to everybody,' Jane explained. 'It's her new trick.'

'Um-mum-mum,' Milly said, clapping her hands.

'Heavens!' Sarah said again.

It's about time I started looking after them, Jane thought. 'Are you on your own in here?' she asked.

'Polly's gone to get our breakfast,' Sarah told her. 'She'll bring it up in a minute. Emma won't eat it. She wants to go to the breakfast room.'

'I always go to the breakfast room,' Emma said stubbornly.

'No you don't,' Sarah said. 'Not now.'

'I do too. Miss Timmons takes me.'

'Who's Miss Timmons?' Jane asked her.

'She takes me.'

'We told you,' Sarah said. 'They sent her away.' Light shone. 'She was your nurse.'

The door was opening. Someone was pushing a trolley into the room. Polly had arrived with the breakfast. But before she could say anything, Emma threw herself face downwards on the carpet and began to howl again. 'I won't!' she cried. 'It's not fair. I won't. Oh! Oh! Oh! It's not fair. I don't want you! I want Miss Timmons. It's not fair.'

Polly's face grew more anguished with every shriek. Milly was intensely interested. Sarah tried to pat her sister's arm and was flung violently aside.

I can't let this go on, Jane thought, she'll wake the baby. 'How would it be if we all had our breakfast together in the nursery?' she said. 'We could set the table in there, couldn't we, Polly, and I could tell you stories while you ate.'

'Yes,' Sarah said firmly. 'That is a very good idea. Get up, Emma. We're going to have breakfast in the nursery.'

So the table was set and chairs were carried in for the sisters and a pretty little highchair was found for Milly and they all sat round the table in the sunshine and breakfasted together and Jane told them all the story of Goldilocks and the three bears, which Emma pretended she wasn't the least bit interested in – but enjoyed very much, especially when Milly echoed 'Bear, bear, bear' and clapped her hands.

From then on they breakfasted together every day and Jane told them every fairy story she could remember, and after that they spent their time gossiping. She found out more about her fellow servants from her two outspoken guests than she would ever have done simply from her own observation – that Mrs Denman was firm but fair, that the house steward was called Mr Glendenning, that their governess was horrid, 'the sooner they get rid of her, the better,' that grooms were always larking about and gardeners touched their forelocks. 'That's how you know they're gardeners.'

Now and then, they mentioned their parents but they seemed to know far less about them than they did about the servants. They said they rode to hounds and had lots of parties, that their mother had had a good seat and had worn beautiful dresses and their father went to parliament and rode a white stallion, but that was all. They showed no sadness at their mother's death, which Jane found most peculiar. But they were entertaining company and Milly loved them, clapping her hands and shouting 'Umma, dumma dumma dumma' when they appeared.

Towards the end of August, when Felix was three months old, had learnt to smile and chuckle and to recognize that Jane's arrival by his crib meant food and cuddles, she had a sudden visit from her employer, the great Sir Mortimer himself. He arrived like royalty, with Mr Glendenning attendant at a discreet distance from his elbow and Mrs Denman three paces behind him. Jane was so overawed by the sight of him that she dropped an instinctive curtsey.

He was the tallest man she'd ever seen and

handsome in a foreign sort of way, with the same thick fair hair as his daughters, dark, shrewd eyes, a long nose, a protruding chin and a decidedly haughty manner, polite but distant, as if he were looking at her from a long way away. He wore the most beautiful clothes, his coat and waistcoat all-over embroidery, and his boots were a wonder to behold. But it was his voice that made her aware of what a great man he was, for the English he spoke was nothing like the Yorkshire accent she heard all around her and spoke herself. It was quiet, firm, and very definitely superior. She noticed that he seemed to drawl, that he dropped the Gs on the end of his words as if he was swallowing them, that he used words she'd never heard before.

'I trust you are settlin',' he said, 'Mrs...' And he looked at Mr Glendenning to supply him with her name.

'Smith.'

She curtseyed and thanked him kindly at which he inclined his head towards her. Then he walked over to the cradle and looked at the baby.

'He is a deal less pale than he was the last time I saw him, Mrs Denman,' he observed. 'Looks strong enough. Feedin' well, is he?'

As the question seemed to be addressed to her, Jane answered it. 'Yes, sir.'

'No sickness or incapacity of any kind, I trust?'

'No, sir.'

The great man walked to the window and gazed out at his estate. 'You have been carin' for my daughters too, I believe,' he said, without turning his head.

The question was courteous and seemed kindly but she was suddenly afraid he was going to tell her she shouldn't do it. 'Yes, sir. I hope that was in order, sir.'

'They speak of you warmly,' he told her, still looking out of the window. 'Uncommon warmly for gels so young.' Then he turned away from the view and began his stately walk towards the door, signalling to his two attendants that they should make way for him, which they did. But as he passed the rocking horse he suddenly stopped. 'What's this?'

Milly was standing very still beside the horse, holding on to its mane and sucking her thumb.

'If you please, sir,' Jane confessed. 'She's my little girl, sir.'

'Ah,' he said. 'Yes, yes. Of course. Is she healthy?'

'Oh yes, sir.'

'Um,' the great man said and turned to Mrs Denman, 'should there be any sickness in her whatsoever,' he instructed, 'you will remove her from the nursery forthwith. I trust that is understood.'

'Of course, sir.'

The progress towards the door continued. It was opened for him. He paused. He looked back at Jane. 'Pray tell Mrs Denman should there be anythin' that you require for any of the children,' he said. 'She will attend to it, will you not, Mrs Denman? This is all quite satisfactory, Mr Glendenning. I leave my family in your capable hands, Mrs Smith.' Then he nodded at Jane as if he were giving her permission to continue.

She curtseyed without speaking. It seemed the

proper thing to do. Then he was gone.

'Well, well, well,' she said to Milly when the door had closed behind him. 'What do 'ee think of that, Pumpkin?'

Milly gave her rapturous smile. 'Pum, pum, pum,' she said.

6

'Families are the very devil,' George Hudson said to Mrs Norridge as they sat over their dinner one cold Friday afternoon in late October. 'They throw you out soon as look at you. They're forever standing in your way. They choose the wrong man to be a partner when the best one's staring 'em in their damned stupid faces. Blamed fools the lot of 'em. Don't talk to me about families.' He was more than a little drunk and hideously annoyed.

'Never thought much to 'em mesself,' Mrs Norridge confided, filling her tankard from the beer jug. 'Not if my ol' man was anything to go by. All sweetness an' light an' heart a' my heart an' give us a kiss when he was sober. But when he was tight, you should ha' heard him. Hollerin' an' roarin'.'

'What does that fool know about running a shop?' George said. 'I could run it wi' one hand tied behind my back.' His speech was slurred but what did he care? 'One hand tied behind my back. And what do I get? We're keeping it in

78

t'family. In t'family! I ask you. That won't get 'em any trade.'

'Gives you a headache summat chronic does hollerin',' Mrs Norridge complained. 'No good tellin' 'im. Cos why? Cos 'e never listened to a word I said. Not one blamed word.'

'They needn't think they're going to keep me down,' George said. 'I'll be their equal one of these days, if it takes forever.' And he slid slowly off his chair. 'I'll show 'em,' he said to the table leg. Then he fell asleep.

Mrs Norridge left him where he was. She was used to drunks and he was much too solid to be hauled into another position. 'I'll jest finish off that beer,' she said to his boots. 'Be a shame to let it go to waste.'

Although he regretted his drunkenness, because he had such a thick head the following morning, George was not going to be put down. Mrs Bell was a fool to have given her stupid brother a partnership, but a fool can be outwitted and, once his head was cleared, he knew how he was going to do it. If she'd made up her mind that she'd only take a partner if he were a member of the family, he would have to become a member of the family. And the obvious way to do that was to marry Lizzie. She was the most unattractive woman he'd ever seen and almost as stupid as her sister but she was the means by which he could get what he wanted. And of course, her stupidity could be used to his advantage. He would start courting her that very afternoon, as soon as he got back from visiting the local tailors to see the

79

new pattern books.

It was growing dark by the time he turned into Goodramgate and his intended had lit candles in the shop and was outside in the half light closing the shutters. Time for a little chivalry.

'Let me do that for 'ee,' he said, stepping forward and putting his hand on the nearest shutter.

She didn't seem to understand that he was offering her a favour. 'I allus does the shutters,' she said. ''Tis no hardship.'

It was offputting to be rebuffed and for a few seconds while she finished her task he stood where he was, wondering what to offer next. 'I'll sweep the shop then, shall I?'

'All done,' she said, walking through the door. 'There's only the accounts.'

But there was nothing special about the accounts. Nobody could see them as a love offering. He did them all the time.

She had the candlestick in her hand. 'I'll give 'ee good night then,' she said, and stomped towards the stairs.

Damned stupid woman, he thought. Why can't she pay attention? Well, I shall just have to think of something else, that's all. Sweetmeats or summat.

Over the next few days he tried a seed cake – but she said she didn't like caraway seeds and gave it to Richard – a marzipan frog – she didn't like that either and gave it to Becky – even a liquorice stick – which she left under the counter until it went hard. It was all a waste of time. She simply didn't see that he was trying to court her. Any other woman would have taken his gifts and encouraged him. But then any other woman would have jumped at him. He was a good catch, God damn it. Handsome – no one could deny that – clever, well dressed, quick-witted, and he knew how to make money, which was more than could be said for her fool of a brother. If he could just get his feet on the ladder with a partnership, he'd end up a very rich man. Any other woman would be glad to get him.

He was in a fury of impatience and frustration and spent several evenings making brutal use of the local ladies of the night. But nothing he said, thought or did made any difference to the courtship he couldn't begin.

When Christmas came, he hung a sprig of mistletoe in the shop – which she ignored. On Christmas Day they all dined together upstairs in Mrs Bell's dining room and Mrs Norridge roasted a goose with a plum pudding to follow and the pudding gave him another opportunity because he was the one who found the lucky charm. He made a great to-do over it, explaining to them all that he only had one thing in his life he really wanted and making eyes at Lizzie all the time he was holding it in his fist and wishing.

''Twill be for money, sure as fate,' Richard said.

'That's where you're wrong,' he told his rival happily. 'It's nowt to do wi' money. There's more to life than brass.'

'Is there any more cream?' Lizzie said.

In January the snows began and went on for weeks. Their customers stayed indoors by the fire telling one another it was no weather to be thinking of new clothes, nor anything else for that matter. Mrs Bell and her brother and sister all had heavy colds and were red-nosed and miserable. Even George succumbed to the sniffles for a day or two. There was nothing to be done but to get on with his work, feed his dreams and pray for spring.

Jane Jerdon was praying for the spring too; in her case with an ever-present anxiety that kept her wakeful by night and watchful by day. It had been a bad winter, for fever had come to Foster Manor with the chilling weather and the governess had been struck down with the shaking sickness even before the snows began to fall. Sir Mortimer had dismissed her and sent her home as soon as he heard of it, naturally, but now they were all living in fear in case any of the children had taken it. Infections hopped from child to child as quickly and silently as fleas, as they knew only too well, and what could any of them possibly do to prevent it? This was the moment Jane had been dreading ever since Sir Mortimer had given his stern instructions to Mrs Denman. His voice had been echoing in her head ever since. '*Should there be any sickness in her whatsoever, you will remove her from the nursery forthwith.*' My poor Milly Millstone, she thought, as she brushed the child's pretty hair. How would she make out if they took her away from me? She's only three and a half, poor little mite. No age to be taken from her ma. And no age to take the shaking sickness either.

But in the event it wasn't Milly who caught the fever. It was Felix. Sir Mortimer was distraught with worry, sending for one physician after another, keeping fires lit in the nursery day and night, so that everyone in the room, Felix included, was uncomfortably overheated, ordering medicinal syrups to be made, which the poor child couldn't swallow and which Jane threw in the chamber pot as soon as she could, and visiting the nursery two or three times a day to check on his progress and to complain that not enough was being done. Luckily, after ten days of incessant fussing, he had letters from Westminster requesting his presence there *'at your earliest convenience'* and so he had to leave, explaining to Mr Glendenning that it would only be for a day or two and that he would be home again as soon as it was possible.

Jane was heartily glad to see the back of him. Now she could nurse the poor infant in her own way, by following her instincts, giving him sips of water and letting him suck whenever he wanted to, keeping him warm but not too hot, sponging his poor little sweating head and keeping his poor, sore bottom clean and dry. It took her a long time and so many sleepless nights she lost count of them, but gradually and very, very gently, she eased the little boy back to health. By the time his father was being driven home for Easter and the daffodils were shaking their trumpets in the gardens, he was crawling about the nursery again and even riding the rocking horse – with Milly sitting up behind him to hold him steady – pale and skinny but happily alive.

Sir Mortimer declared himself well pleased and explained to Mr Glendenning that this was proof, if any were needed, that the most efficacious way to ensure a good outcome to a child's illness was to insist that the physicians did as they were told. Then, having satisfied himself that the family line was secure, he ate a large supper and took himself off to bed, where he slept soundly until mid morning. But Jane was awake all night.

She lay on her back in her comfortable bed, watching the full white moon as it rose serenely and carelessly from pane to pane in her window and listened to the soft soughing of her babies' breathing and worried her way through the night. While she'd been nursing Felix she'd had no time to think of anything except how to cure him; now she was wondering what would become of her and Milly when her services as a wet nurse were no longer required. She'd seen how ruthlessly Sir Mortimer had got rid of that poor governess, for all his gentlemanly ways. She would be feeding Felix for another year at least, possibly more, but after that there would be no job for her. If the worst came to the worst, she could probably go back to Aunt Tot and work in the scullery but she'd had a taste of a richer life now and wanted something a bit better than that – and besides it would take her too far from her mother and she'd grown used to seeing her regularly. I think I could make a good housekeeper if I set my mind to it, she thought. Happen Mrs Denman would teach me, if I asked her politely. I could learn a lot by just watching how she goes on. I've a year's grace and I could learn a lot in a year. I'll start today, she thought, as the dawn chorus began.

The great thing is to be ready and prepared to take anything that offers.

George was taking delivery of a new batch of ribbons ready for the spring trade and was examining them carefully for flaws.

'They're pretty,' Lizzie observed, as she passed his counter. 'That yellow's like daffodils.'

The comment was so unexpected it sent his thoughts spinning. He'd never heard her say anything about the stock, not once in all the time he'd been there. Happen the spring's getting to her, he thought. Is this the chance I been waiting for all this time? A ribbon?

'Come and have a look,' he said, holding up a handful of assorted colours. 'There's nowt to do in t'shop.' Which was true enough for it was early morning and the customers hadn't started arriving.

She stood beside him at the counter and took the ribbons rather daringly into her hand. 'We're not supposed to handle the goods,' she said.

'I won't tell her,' he said, giving her the full beam of his smile. 'Which do 'ee think is the prettiest?'

She considered them, taking it very seriously. 'The green,' she said.

''Tis yours,' he said and cut off a length with a flourish. 'Your first sale of the morning.' And he took the coins from his waistcoat pocket and laid them on the counter. 'An excellent choice, madam, if I may be permitted to say so. Exactly the colour of your pretty eyes.'

She blushed. Progress at last. 'My eyes aren't

pretty,' she said, gathering up the coins.

'They are,' he told her earnestly, putting his right hand over hers, coins and all. 'You should have a new gown all in green to match 'em.'

'That wouldn't look right at all,' she said.

''Twould look gradely,' he assured her, still wearing his earnest expression, 'and so would you.'

Her blush deepened into a really ugly red. She pulled her hand away. 'Where would I wear it?'

'At t'theatre for a start. 'Twould be just the thing.'

'I don't go to t'theatre,' she protested.

'You could though. You could come with me.'

She was so surprised her mouth fell open. 'Well, I don't know,' she said. 'What would Becky think?'

'Don't tell her.'

She was shocked. 'I couldn't do that.'

'Why not?' he said, teasing her. 'What the eye don't see the heart can't grieve over. Anyroad, why shouldn't 'ee see a play once in a while? There's nowt like it. An evening out wi' your young man.'

'You're not my young man.'

Why did she have to make everything so difficult? 'But I could be.'

'You're an apprentice.'

'I shan't always be,' he told her. 'Give me another two years and I shall run my own company. I'm going to be a rich man.'

Her eyes widened but she didn't argue.

'Tell 'ee what,' he said. 'I'll get the fashion books down for you and you can chose the style and the cloth and I'll get it made up for you.

86

You'll feel quite different about the theatre if you've got the clothes for it.'

It took her two weeks to decide that she would actually quite like a new dress and another two to persuade her sister to let her have it and to choose the pattern for it. By the time it was made and ready for her to wear, the summer had come, the city gardens were full of roses and songbirds and the walls of the Minster were creamy with sunlight. It was the perfect time for courting.

But it was all wasted on Elizabeth Nicholson. The first time he took her to the theatre she fell asleep in the middle of the second act and although she told him it had been 'reet gradely' she hadn't seen more than a third of it. The second time she was certainly snoring before the interval. So he stopped wasting his money on tickets, abandoned theatre-going as a bad job and started to take her out for long walks in the country, usually on Wednesday afternoons when Richard was in charge of the shop. At least she couldn't fall asleep if she was walking about. But being alone with him made her speechless and although it was pleasant enough to tell her of his ambitions and brag a little, it didn't give him the chance to edge towards any sort of proposal.

It wasn't until October, when they were walking along High Ousegate towards the river, that he finally got his opportunity. They were passing the Church of All Saints when a wedding party came chattering and giggling out of the door, the bride very grand in a blue silk gown and an elaborately feathered hat, and all the men in top hats and carrying canes. To his great satisfaction,

Lizzie paused in her walk to watch and admire.

'What do 'ee think a' that bride?' he prompted her.

'She looks lovely,' she said, her eyes shining.

'You'd look better,' he told her. 'A sight better.'

She sighed, still gazing at the bride. 'Chance 'ud be a fine thing,' she said, sadly. 'I can't see anyone wanting to marry *me*.'

It was the perfect opportunity. He leant towards her until their cheeks were touching. 'Heart of my heart,' he said, remembering Mrs Norris, *'I do.'*

She was so confused she could barely catch her breath and she was blushing so furiously her cheek was quite hot. 'You're never proposing,' she said.

'I am,' he told her, adding with a flourish, 'Name the day.'

'My dear heart alive,' she said, turning her head to look at him. 'I do believe you mean it. Whatever will Becky say?'

'Damn Becky,' he said, and that much at least wasn't feigned. 'It's nowt to do wi' her. 'Tis what you say what counts.'

'Well, as to that,' she admitted, 'I'd say yes if 'twere possible.'

'That's all tha needs to say,' he told her. *'I'll* make it possible.'

She touched her hot cheeks with her fingers. 'My dear heart alive,' she said and looked up at him hopefully.

He *had* to kiss her as she was so plainly expecting it. It wasn't too unpleasant, which was rather a surprise given how unattractive she was. The great thing was that they were engaged and now Becky would have to accept him as family and take him into partnership. I'll give Lizzie time to get used to the idea, he decided, a week or two should do it, and I'll put a ring on her finger, what'll please her, and then we'll tell her brother and sister.

In fact he waited until Christmas Day and told her when he and the family were sitting at table replete with roast goose and wine and Mrs Norridge had gone down to the kitchen to fetch the pudding. Richard was surprised but obviously pleased.

'What a lark!' he said. 'Our Lizzie a bride.'

But Rebecca was very definitely not pleased. 'Engaged?' she said. 'What sort of nonsense is that? You're – um – an apprentice, let me remind you. Apprentice boys don't get wed. I never heard of such a thing.'

Lizzie was squirming on her chair with embarrassment but George had seen this coming and was wonderfully cool. 'Quite right,' he said. 'No more they do. But I've finished my apprenticeship to all intents and purposes. I've learnt nowt new since Michaelmas. Fact of it is, I doubt there's any more I *can* learn. Very well then, 'tis time for me to move on, get me a partnership and take me a wife, what'll move on with me.'

Rebecca looked at him shrewdly. He was a good worker, there was no doubt about that. He knew the ropes and he'd brought in a lot of trade. And Lizzie was useful too. She wouldn't want to lose them both. Not when she could keep them both with a bit of bargaining. 'We'll not quarrel over our – um – Christmas dinner,' she said. 'I tell you what I'll do. Serve out another six months, what'll finish your apprenticeship. Then we'll talk again. How would that be?'

It was agreed, as the pudding came steaming into the room and the first snow of winter swirled against the windows.

But by the time the summer sun was shining and George had served out his apprenticeship, Rebecca had thought of another and more formidable obstacle.

The articles had been signed and sealed, his apprenticeship was formally completed and he and the family were sitting round the table in the back parlour, Lizzie in her green gown, smiling happily, Richard looking pleased with himself as though the ceremony had been all his idea, Rebecca thoughtful, fingering the lace on her sleeve.

'Now,' George said, 'we'll need to fix the wedding, eh, Lizzie?'

'Well, as to that,' Rebecca said, 'there's a little matter of – um – earning your living. I can hardly let my – um – sister marry a man who couldn't support her.'

'Quite right too,' George said, giving Lizzie the benefit of his grey eyes. 'You'd be no sort of a sister were you to allow that. So I'll tell you what I intend to do. I intend to apply, here and now, for a partnership in this business, what I could handle easily, you got to allow. Keeping it in the family like, all fair and square and above board.'

'Well, as to that,' Rebecca countered. 'There's a matter of money to be considered. If you were to enter into a deed of – um – partnership with us, you would have to be prepared to pay a considerable – um – equity.'

He was all boldness now, for he knew what was coming and how he would answer it. 'Name your figure,' he said.

She told him with the air of a magician pulling a rabbit out of a hat, 'Six thousand pounds.'

Lizzie drew in her breath with surprise and shock. It was a parlous amount of money. He'd never find that, surely, clever though he was. He patted her hand reassuringly. 'I will see my uncle about it at the first opportunity,' he said.

He saw him on Sunday after church and told the old man the whole tale – with happy embellishments. The two of them were out in the garden where the air was a good deal sweeter than it would have been in that musty bedroom and Uncle Matthew was in rare good humour.

'The woman's a fool if she thinks she can outwit my nephy,' he said, grinning.

'My sentiments entirely,' George told him. 'I've had her measure for years. She don't like it seemingly but there's nowt she can do about it. She'll just have to lump it.'

The old man chuckled. 'Aye so she will. So I tek it you'll marry the wench?'

George laughed too. 'Aye, now she's willin', and I'll tek half the firm into the bargain. The old gel thinks she's stopped me wi' her talk of money. She don't know I've a friend at court. And afore you starts calling me a vulture, let me tell 'ee I'll pay it all back, every last farthing, and with interest.'

'I don't doubt that neither,' his uncle said.

'You're a good lad, George. Hard worker. I likes a worker. You'll go far. I've allus said so. That other lot ne'er do nowt except come at me with their hands out ready to pick my pockets. Oh, I've got their measure, don't you worry.'

So the bargain was made and the two men shook hands on it. And later that day Rebecca was forced to accept that her future brother-in-law was going to be her business partner too. She delayed until February, when the deed of partnership was drawn up, and made sure that George would agree to pay her £35 a year to rent the flat above the shop, but by 17 February the document was signed and George was on his way to riches at last.

Now nothing else remained to be done but to arrange his wedding, which took place five months later, in the Church of the Holy Trinity in Goodramgate, with Richard Nicholson, looking extremely elegant, and his own brother William and his sister Mary as witnesses.

The bride wore a Turkey red gown printed with sprigs of yellow and green that didn't suit her at all and she was so happy and flustered that her cheeks were as red as her dress. The groom was in a new suit of clothes that were very well cut and suited him to perfection. He smiled when he thought the occasion demanded it and looked serious while he was making his vows but as he stood at the altar rail, watched by the impassive saints in the altar window, bright and ancient in their strawberry pink and cobalt blue and their saintly touches of gold, his thoughts were elsewhere, spinning with ambition and the certainty of a rich life. As he and Lizzie were pronounced man and wife, he looked down at the tombstone under his feet and read it idly. 'Here lyeth Wm Richardson Lord Mayor of York 1671 died 1679,' it said. Just you wait, William Richardson, he thought. I'll be Lord Mayor of York too, you just see if I won't, and I'll be a sight more powerful than you've ever been.'

7

Being dismissed came as a shock to Jane Jerdon even though she thought she'd prepared herself very well for it. Mr Glendenning told her kindly enough that he'd found her a position as house-keeper to one of the richest men in York but his courtesy only made things worse. She'd accepted that Felix would soon be sent away to school and it had been obvious for some time that the girls would be whisked off to London for the next social season but now that the moment of parting had actually come she was miserable with loss, for during the last six years, as she dried their tears and shared their dreams, nursed them through coughs and colds and patched up their quarrels, she'd grown to think of these three children as her family.

Sarah and Emma had no qualms about leaving her at all. They'd been chirruping with excitement ever since their father announced that they were to have their first season.

'They say that London is a splendid place,' Sarah confided and Jane agreed that she was sure it must be.

'Do you think I shall find a husband straightaway?'

'You might well, my lovey,' Jane said, 'but I wouldn't rush if I were you.'

'Oh, I mean to marry as soon as ever I can,' Sarah told her, tossing her ringlets. 'You just see.'

'Then be sure you choose a gentleman,' Jane said.

But Sarah was seventeen and in no mood for caution.

When the dressmaker arrived to measure them for their new city clothes and their mantuas and petticoats and ballgowns, Jane was there to help them in and out of their clothes and, when the gowns were finally finished and carried carefully into the nursery to be fitted for the last time, she was there to admire. And truly they both looked very fine in their pretty muslins and their grand silks, even if the sight of them made her heart ache because it showed how soon she would be parted from them.

But if she grieved to think of losing the girls, she wept when she had to say goodbye to her poor little Felix, for he had nothing to look forward to except the rigours of a school he didn't want to attend for, although his father told him it would be a fine thing to be a scholar at Eton, which was the best school in the land, it made him withdrawn and unhappy to think about it. He was such a little chap even if he *was* nine and he looked so frail, standing there in the nursery saying goodbye.

Milly wept and hung about his neck and made him promise 'see it wet, see it dry' to write to her 'every every day' and he promised valiantly, struggling to play the man and be controlled. But when he put his little thin arms round Jane's neck and kissed her, his tears overwhelmed him and he cried for a very long time and was still sobbing when Mr Glendenning arrived to tell him that his carriage was ready for him.

'I will see you again, won't I?' he said, turning to look at her for one last time as he left the room.

'Yes,' Jane said. 'Of course.' But she knew it was an empty promise for he was off to another life and it was one she couldn't share.

Then Mrs Denham arrived with last-minute instructions for her and her trunk was being carried downstairs and she and Milly were climbing into the dog cart and waving goodbye.

'I hate York,' Milly said, as the cart rattled through Sir Mortimer's imposing acres. 'I shall hate it for ever an' ever an' ever.'

Jane tried to be reasonable because she was none too pleased to be going to the city either. 'There's a daft thing to go a-sayin', Millikins,' she said. 'How can 'ee know? Nanna says 'tis a fine place wi' shops an' theatres an' all sorts. She were tellin' me only last Sunday. We shall have a fine ol' time there. You see if we don't.'

'I shan't be with Felix,' Milly said doggedly, 'and there'll be no pony for me to ride and I shan't see Sarah and Emma ever again, and it'll all be horrid. I don't care *what* Nanna says.'

'Oh well,' her mother sighed, 'if tha's made tha

95

mind up to it there's nowt I can say.'

'And it'll be a horrid house. You just see.'

Jane was beginning to get cross. 'How can 'ee possibly say such a thing?' she said. 'Tha knows nowt about it.'

'I do so,' Milly said haughtily. 'Sarah told me. She says there are no proper houses in towns. They're all nasty and pokey and they don't have any grounds or proper stables or anything, except in London.'

'Now look 'ee here, miss,' Jane said, sternly. 'I'll not have 'ee speak so. You're repeating tittle-tattle, that's what you're doing, what's a fool's trick an' I'll not have it. Mr Bottrill is the richest man in the city and he'll have one of the richest houses, you can depend on it. Rich men don't live in pokey houses. Anyroad, we're to live in his house now, whether you like it or not. We're not in the great house no more, so if you've any sense, you'll mind your manners and keep a civil tongue in your head.'

Milly made a face and didn't answer.

They were so cross that they didn't speak to one another until the cart stopped in front of Mr Bottrill's undoubtedly fine house in Monkgate and by then the weather had changed and it was beginning to spot with rain. They jumped down onto the cobbles and scampered into the house as quickly as they could, leaving the driver to carry their trunk in after them. There was a man in imposing green livery and an old-fashioned white wig waiting for them in the hall.

'Name of Josh,' he said to Jane, 'and you'll be Mrs Smith, I daresay. Follow me and I'll show you to your rooms.'

There were two of them, right at the top of the house, a bedroom with a high bed, a linen press and a washstand, and a parlour that could be a cosy place with a bit of rearrangement. There was a sizeable fireplace there and a dresser and two comfortable chairs on either side of the fire. We shall do well enough here, Jane thought. But before she settled in, she must go down to the kitchen and meet her staff.

'You stay here,' she said to Milly, 'and unpack the bed linen and hang the clothes in t'cupboard. When I've had a bit of a look round I'll come back and we can make up the bed. They're good-sized rooms.'

Milly put her hand on her mother's arm. 'I'm sorry I was ratty, Ma,' she said.

'We were both ratty,' Jane said. ''Tis a hard thing to leave home.' She was remembering how unhappy she'd been when she'd had to go and live with Aunt Tot. She put her arms round her poor woebegone child and gave her a hug and kissed her. 'I'll not be long,' she promised.

But in fact it took her the entire morning to check how the house was run and what she discovered didn't please her at all. She started in the kitchen, which was a large room and well equipped but none too clean and very untidy. She would have to do something about that. The cook, who said she was called Mrs Cadwallader, was a rather slatternly woman in a dirty apron. She told Jane that Mr Bottrill dined at three but that she never asked him what she was to cook 'not since Mrs Bottrill died, poor lady, on account of the housekeeper done that – the one what was here afore you, ma'am. I jest does as I'm told.'

'Has he been asked today?' Jane said, brisk and businesslike.

'No fear!' the cook said. 'She was up an' gone yes'day art'noon and you wouldn't catch me upstairs with old Curmudgeon, not for all the tea in China.'

'Then I will do it,' Jane said, 'and I will do it now or you'll not have time to send someone out to market. Get the scullery maid to scrub that table while I'm away. It looks overdue for a good clean. Now where would I find him?'

Then cook sniffed. 'Don't ask me,' she said. 'I got enough to do wi'out wondering where the master is. Let sleeping dogs lie. That's my opinion of it. You'll have to ask Josh.'

Jane kept her patience with an effort. 'Then where would I find Josh?'

'Don't ask me,' the cook said again. 'Could be anywhere.' But when Jane gave her an Aunt Tot scowl, she offered, 'You could try the butler's pantry, I suppose. He offen in there.'

Josh had tossed his wig onto a row of empty bottles and was helping himself to a large glass of red wine – and he wasn't the least bit abashed to be caught in the act. ''Tis to keep out t'damp,' he explained. 'I suffers chronic with damp. An' when I suffers I'm neither fit for God nor man. What can I do for 'ee?'

She scowled at the wine glass to show that she didn't think much of his behaviour. 'You can tell me where Mr Bottrill is, for a start.'

'I'll just finish this,' he said, swirling the wine in

98

the glass. 'Be a pity to waste it. Then I'll tek 'ee there. Be warned though. He's in a rare ol' paddy this morning.'

He was also still in his nightclothes, slumped in a musty bedroom – don't they ever clean anything in this house? – squinting at his newspaper. He didn't look up and he didn't speak.

'Give 'ee good day, Mr Bottrill, sir,' she said, carefully polite. 'I am your new housekeeper.'

'Speak up,' he said tetchily and without looking at her. 'Can't hear a word if you mumble.'

She repeated her message in a louder voice. 'I've come to see what you would like for your dinner.'

He looked up at her sideways. 'What's it to me what I have?' he said. 'I shan't eat it.'

'A meat pie,' she suggested. 'Or a little pork chop. I could serve it with a dish of baked apples, being they're in season.'

'Cook what you please,' he said. 'I shan't eat it. All this nonsense in the papers. Have 'ee seen it?'

'No, sir,' she told him. 'I've not had time for reading papers this morning. I've only just arrived from Foster Manor.'

'We're to rush about the country in carriages on rails, if you ever heard such nonsense,' he said, shaking the paper at her. 'Railways, they call 'em. All crammed in together, whether we will or no. All going the same way at the same time. I never heard the like. Some mad man called Stephenson wi' a bee in his bonnet. That's how 'tis. Invented an engine, so they say, what'll pull carts and carriages instead of horses. And what's wrong wi' horses? You tell me that. Good strong reliable beasts if you treats 'em right. We don't need engines. But we're to have 'em, seemingly, whether we will or no. Bad enough when they were planning to use the dratted things a-pulling coal – I didn't think much to that but t'government thought different – but now, look 'ee here, they've lost their senses. I never heard such folly. Engines carrying human beings. Human beings I ask you. Men and women – and children, for all we know – carted about from place to place like corn sacks or coal or barrels of ale. And do 'ee know what speed they'll be travelling at in their damn fool contraptions? Twenty miles an hour! Twenty miles! Did 'ee ever hear the like? We shall all be shook to kingdom come. I don't know what t'world's coming to, I truly don't.'

'Meat pie with egg custard to follow then,' Jane said and left him to grumble on his own.

It took her until three o'clock that afternoon before the kitchen was cleaned to her satisfaction, the meat had been purchased and the meal cooked. She climbed the back stairs to her parlour feeling decidedly weary and not a little guilty, for now that she had a minute to think about it she knew she'd been unkind to have left her Milly for so long, especially when she'd been so upset at leaving the Manor, poor girl. Ten was no age to have to leave home. But she needn't have worried. Milly had been busy too and was well pleased with what she'd done. The bed was neatly made up, both rooms had been swept and dusted and, when her mother came into the room, she was cleaning the windows.

'What do 'ee think?' she said.

'I think you're a dear good girl,' Jane told her, 'an' you'll need a good nourishing meal inside you after all this work, what we've got all cooked and ready. And after that we'll have a fire set, being it's so cold, and we'll sit beside it in our nice comfy chairs and read stories to one another.'

Milly made a sad face. 'We haven't got any books now,' she said.

'Then we will buy some,' Jane told her. 'There are bound to be book sellers hereabouts, given the size of the place. We'll go a marketing on my first afternoon off and see what we can find. Now how about that meal?'

'I'll just wash my hands,' Milly said, and beamed at her.

They walked down the stairs arm in arm, telling one another about their morning. 'We've made a good start,' Jane said.

They made a good meal too for despite her untidy appearance the cook was a dab hand at meat pies and egg custards, as Jane was happy to tell her, and as the entire staff was gathered about the kitchen table, she had a chance to meet and observe them as they ate. There weren't very many of them for a place this size: a man smelling of horses who said he was 'groom, coachman and God knows what besides', a stable lad, four maids of all work, a scullery maid, Josh, Mrs Cadwallader and a small pale boy, who made her think of Felix, who said he 'done the boots, ma'am'.

'Does Mr Bottrill entertain much?' she asked as Mrs Cadwallader served the custards.

'Don't entertain at all,' Josh told her. 'Not since his wife died. He has plenty of company though.

101

We're never short of that. There's nepheys and nieces in and out all the time. After his money so he reckons. He complains about 'em non-stop. You'll hear him. But they don't get entertained. They just comes in and smarms all over him – "Uncle this and Uncle that" – and goes away again.'

'Except for that Mr Hudson,' Mrs Cadwallader said. 'He gets tea sometimes. Or a glass of Madeira wine.'

The name gave Jane an unpleasant cramping sensation in her chest as if someone was squeezing her heart. 'Mr Hudson,' she said, keeping her voice as noncommittal as she could. It couldn't be George, surely. 'Who's he?'

'Another nephey,' Mrs Cadwallader told her. 'Very attentive he is. In and out all the time. Worse than all the others put together.'

'Does he live hereabouts?' Jane fished.

'He's the draper in Goodramgate,' Josh told her. 'Hudson and Nicholson. What used to be Nicholson and Bell afore he took it over.'

Jane went on fishing.

'What's he like?'

'A deal too full of hisself,' Josh said. 'Jumped up. Thinks he's God's gift to the town.'

That sounded like George. She had a sudden painful memory of him holding her face between his hands, urging her, *Let me. Let me. Tha knows tha wants it.'* A deal too full of hisself. Allus were. Happen it *was* him. 'Twould be a rare piece of luck if it were. George Hudson delivered up to her all neat and unknowing, ready for her revenge.

'You'll see him in church a' Sunday,' Mrs Cadwallader told her, 'up in t'front pews with t'nobs, a' course. He's very grand when he goes to church. No one can miss him. I'll point him out to you, if you like, bein' as you're interested.'

'That would be kindly,' Jane said, and she smiled as she passed her empty plate to the scullery maid. And sitting there in her warm, newly cleaned kitchen, surrounded by all these people who were going to be her staff, she wondered whether this pushy man really would turn out to be George Hudson and, if he was, whether he would remember her.

Lizzie Hudson was in the little room that was now the nursery trying to coax her son into his petticoats ready for church. It was a difficult job because although he was only fifteen months old he had a will of his own and was making it just a little too clear that he didn't want to be dressed. She'd had a terrible tussle with him and she was beginning to feel cross and weary. If only they could hire a nursemaid they could leave him at home to play with his toys and go off without him, which would be the sensible thing to do. She'd tried to suggest it to George but he'd been quite brusque with her and told her they couldn't afford it, not when they'd only the one child, which had hurt her feelings terribly – for, after all, it wasn't her fault that her poor little James had taken ill and died – although of course she couldn't say so. There were times when it wasn't sensible to say anything much to Mr Hudson, particularly when he was busy with business matters. As he was that morning. He'd been sitting at the breakfast table reading the paper for over an hour. About the new railways, of course. He was passionately interested in railways and forever telling her that someone was going to make a mint of money out of them. But railways meant nothing to her. Her life was babies and praying to keep them alive.

'Is that child still not dressed?' George said, suddenly appearing beside her. 'He'll mek us late.'

Lizzie tried to explain that the child was fractious but his father wasn't interested. 'I'll give you five more minutes,' he said, 'an' if he's not ready by then I shall go without you. I'm to walk home with Uncle Matthew after service and he'll not tek kindly if I'm not there to greet him. Five minutes.' And he was gone.

'Tha'lt not let me dress 'ee, will 'ee, Dickie,' Lizzie sighed, hanging the petticoat on the towel rail.

And the baby, sensing that he had won, clapped his plump hands and babbled at her.

Matthew Bottrill strolled through the gate into the churchyard of Holy Trinity two minutes after his nephew. The two men greeted one another with their customary handshake and stood together for a few minutes exchanging pleasantries like the old friends they had now become before they entered the building and progressed up the aisle together towards their respective pews. Jane and Milly and Mrs Cadwallader, waiting humbly for their turn to enter the building, had a clear and revealing view of the meeting.

Well, well, well, Jane thought, as the two well-dressed backs disappeared into the shadows of the porch, so it is him and Mr Bottrill does think well of him. And she wondered when she would see him at Monkgate.

But the months passed and Jane and Milly settled into their new lives and, true to her promise, Jane bought two books of fairy tales to amuse them, one collected by a man called Charles Perrault and translated 'from the French' and the other 'translated from the German', both of which they enjoyed very much, and although Mr Hudson was a frequent visitor, it was late November before he and Jane finally came face to face.

At the end of September the Stockton and Darlington Railway had been officially opened for the carriage of freight and Mr Bottrill had been grumbling at the folly of it ever since. He and George were sitting by the fire in the drawing room that afternoon while he held forth about it. Outside the window, the city was dank with fog, which rose from the river to clog the narrow lanes and choke anyone foolish enough to venture out in it. George had been coughing ever since he arrived, despite the fact that he'd covered his nose and mouth with a muffler before he set out, and when half an hour had passed and he'd got no better, his uncle paused in his complaint, rang the bell and ordered a dish of tea to ease his lungs.

Jane made the tea but there was no maid free to carry it up to the drawing room and Josh had disappeared, probably to 'keep out the damp', so she picked up the tray and carried it upstairs herself. She set it carefully on the table before the fire and then closed the curtains to keep out the worst of the fog. She was turning to leave when the visitor stood up. For a few seconds she stood quite still before him, disturbed to realize that her heart was racing. Seen close to, he was very much changed. The boyish good looks that had charmed her so easily when she was fifteen were quite gone. Now the man who stood before her was portly and self-satisfied and had a fat face. What was worse, it was plain from the way he was looking at her that he didn't have the slightest idea who she was. It was hurtful to have to accept that she'd been used and forgotten but that was clearly what had happened. She bobbed a quick curtsey and left the room, holding her head high and her spine straight, cursing George Hudson in her heart.

After that, she avoided the drawing room whenever her one-time lover was in the house. One day she would be revenged, she knew that even more clearly now, but in the meantime there was no necessity for him to see her. If he wanted to visit, let him. It was no concern of hers. So the months passed and became a successful year. New staff were hired; Milly celebrated her eleventh birthday and started work as an under housemaid; Felix sent them the occasional letter to tell them about the games he was playing and what a lark he was having with the other chaps; Sarah wrote to say that she was engaged to be married and would soon be Lady Livingston; and Jane saw her mother every other Sunday and had a visit from her every single week all through the summer. And although she often thought of George Hudson, she never saw him at all.

But then something happened that would change her decision and her life.

A little before Christmas, Josh went into his master's bedroom one dark morning with his customary pot of hot chocolate and found him lying on the floor unconscious. He fled to the kitchen in a panic, demanding to know what he was to do, and naturally it was Jane who took command, ordering one of the housemaids to run out and fetch a surgeon and another to bring her lint and a bandage in case the master was hurt. Then she and Josh and the boot-boy went back to the bedroom to see what was to be done. Mr Bottrill was still where Josh had left him but now he was groaning.

'Lift him on t'bed and let's take a look at him,' Jane said to the two men and when they'd done as they were told she sat on the edge of the bed and examined his head and arms, checking him for bruises and looking in his hair for cuts, neither of which she could find. While she was checking him over, he gave a long shuddering groan and opened his eyes.

'Where am I?' he said and his speech was slurred. 'Wha's going on?'

Jane explained that he'd had a fall but that made him tetchy. 'I don't fall,' he said crossly. 'I ain't a man to fall. Never been known to fall in all me life. Never.'

There was no point in arguing with him. With luck the surgeon would be there presently. Let him explain. He'd be better at it.

He was a very small man and a very subservient one but he was firm in his diagnosis. Mr Bottrill had taken a fit and now he must be bled. He would see to it immediately. Mr Bottrill was *not* pleased to hear it but he wasn't well enough to refuse. He groaned a great deal but he submitted to a vein in his arm being opened and to the blood being collected in a cup.

'Now Mrs Smith,' the surgeon said to Jane, 'he must take plenty of rest and light nourishing food, if you please. I will do myself the honour of calling again tomorrow.' Although his patient complained that he felt a great deal worse for having been bled, the next day the surgeon applied his scalpel for the second time, drew off another cupful of blood and left well pleased with himself.

The old man grumbled and swore and said the surgeon was making him ill and that evening he took another fit and was unconscious for an alarmingly long time. That Sunday, prayers were said at The Holy Trinity Church for his recovery, and after the service George Hudson waited for Jane and Milly to emerge from the porch and approached them, hat in hand. He was sorry to hear of Mr Bottrill's illness, he said. Would Mrs Smith be so kind as to carry his respects to his uncle and tell him he would visit on Monday.

He called on Monday and Thursday and Saturday, bringing titbits to tempt his uncle's appetite. Josh said he wondered he didn't bring his bed and set up residence. At Christmas he arrived with a jar of calves' foot jelly, in January he brought a pot of shrimps, in March two jars of honey, in April, when his uncle was feeling too weak to leave his bed for more than an hour at a time, it was marzipan.

'Tha'rt a good lad,' Matthew said, looking at the sweetmeats.

'I do my best,' George told him. 'You *are* family, when all's said and done. We have to look out for family.'

'Try telling t'others,' the old man growled. 'They're in here night and day. I don't see *them* bringing gifts. Not even at Christmas time. They only come on account of the money. They don't fool me. I tell 'ee, George, you're the only one with any heart at all.'

It was time to make a play for preferment. 'It'ud serve em right,' George said, 'if you were to leave it all to someone else.'

The idea made the old man look devilish, despite his weakness. 'Aye, so twould.'

'Cut 'em off wi'out a penny,' George said, pressing home. 'That'ud show 'em.'

The old man giggled. 'I've a mind to do just that.'

'Why not?' George urged. 'Think how they've hurt your feelings all these years, plaguing and pestering. Show 'em who's boss, eh?'

'Aye. I've half a mind.'

'I'd like to see their faces if you do.'

'Aye. And so you shall, boy. So you shall. I shall see to it. What sport, eh?'

The next day he sent Josh with a letter summoning his lawyer to his bedside. Six weeks later he was dead.

8

For a funeral it was a very jolly occasion. The nephews and nieces arrived in force, wearing their best clothes and in a state of barely concealed excitement, as though they had arrived for a party. George had taken care to be soberly dressed and had his own hopes under tight and private control. He watched them as they greeted one another and admired the act they were putting on but they didn't fool him for a second. They might be saying the right things but their greed burst through the seams of their fine clothes and shone from every pore of their caring faces.

The funeral breakfast was held in the drawing room at Monkgate where they nibbled at pastries and drank a considerable amount of wine until the lawyer arrived in his sober clothes with a black bag tucked under his black arm and that housekeeper following quietly behind him. Then they took up positions in the row of chairs that had been set out for the purpose and waited with avid impatience to be told how much of the Bottrill fortune they were going to be given. It was so large that, even if the old man had divided it up between them, they would still be taking away a comfortable income.

'This should not delay us for long, ladies and gentlemen,' the lawyer said. 'Mr Bottrill was admirably precise in his instructions.' He took the will from his black bag and began to read. '...last will and testament of the late Mr Matthew Bottrill, written and witnessed before me on the twelfth of April in the year of Our Lord 1827.' Then he cleared his throat while they all waited. 'There are two small bequests,' he said, and began to read again. 'I leave my gold watch to Richard Hudson, infant son of Mr George Hudson. I leave the clothes and wearing apparel of my late wife Ann to my housekeeper Mrs Jane Smith in token of her faithful service.'

The cousins turned in their seats to nod approval at Jane, who was sitting quietly at the back of the group. It was rather a waste to bequeath his gold watch to a child, but leaving clothes to a housekeeper was only right and proper and she was a nice quiet body and not like to give herself airs.

When Jane had left the room, the lawyer spoke again. 'After deducting such sums as have been spent on funeral arrangements,' he said, 'Mr Bottrill left his entire estate in land, property and capital, to one person.' Then he paused because there was a shiver of excitement in the room as the nephews and nieces realized what an enormous fortune that one person was going to receive and each of them hoped to be the lucky one. All eyes turned to the lawyer and held him gimlet-fixed until he spoke again. The tension in the room was so strong it was as if the air was singing with it.

'One person,' the lawyer said, looking round at them all and smiling benignly, 'and that one person is his nephew Mr George Hudson.'

There was an uproar. 'How could that possibly be?' they shouted, waving their arms. 'There must be some mistake.' 'He would never have passed us by in this way. Never. Never. Not our dear Uncle Matthew.' 'We are his nearest relations. Nearest and dearest.' 'You've got it wrong, sir.'

George was so happy he was grinning fit to split his face in half. He left his seat and walked across to the lawyer to shake him by the hand and thank him for his services. His relations were still shouting, red in the face with the heat of their anger and disappointment. One of the nieces had had her bonnet crumpled by a flailing arm, another was weeping. Two of the nephews were striding about the room. It was a triumph.

They were making such a noise that Jane and Mrs Cadwallader and the maids could hear them in the kitchen, where they were now setting the table for their dinner.

'What on earth's going on up there?' Jane said, lifting her head towards the sound. 'I thought this was supposed to be a funeral.'

'Don't sound much like a funeral, and that's a fact,' Mrs Cadwallader said sourly.

'Where's Josh?' Jane asked her. 'If anyone'll know, he will. Nip upstairs, Sally, and see if you can find him.'

He was standing outside the drawing room door listening to the outburst. 'Shush!' he said, putting his finger to his lips. 'They're going at it hammer and tongs. Come to blows I shouldn't wonder.'

At that moment the door was pushed open with

112

such violence that the handle hit the wall and two of the nephews rushed out and shouted their way downstairs, so he had to leave Sally standing and go off and attend to them.

'Tell Mrs Smith I'll be down presently,' he said as he sprinted off.

He was in the kitchen and spreading the news ten minutes later. 'We're to have a new master,' he said.

'Which one?' Jane asked. Not that it mattered. A master was a master and anyone would do as long as he paid your wages. But when she heard his name, she was horribly taken aback. Was she really going to be a servant to the man who had treated her so badly? The very idea was horrible, crushing, unfair, not to be borne. I shall just have to find another position, she thought. I can't stay here and work for *him*. I'll go to the next hiring and see what's on offer.

But George Hudson was too quick for her, just as he'd been thirteen years ago. By the end of the afternoon, he and his wife and his chubby little boy had arrived to take up residence and he hadn't been in the house for more than an hour before he called all his servants together in the drawing room and told them how he intended to run the place. First of all he announced with a broad smile that he was thinking of increasing their wages.

'I've took a look at t'books,' he said, 'and 'tis my opinion you could be worth a deal more than my uncle paid you. So I tell you what I propose to do. You will work for me at the old rate for a week or two, so's I can see how you get on, and then

I'll reconsider. Can't say fairer than that but then I'm a fair man. You play fair by me and I'll play fair by you.'

He's charming them, Jane thought, recognizing the persuasive talk and the smiling face, and they're taking it in and believing him. Well, you don't fool me, George Hudson. I shan't be charmed a second time, no matter how much you might be offering. I've got your measure. But the offer had put her in a difficult position. I can't hand in my notice now, she thought. Not right this moment anyroad. 'Twould look ill. I shall have to stay here and see it out for a week or two at least. But I'll make enquiries at t'hiring just to be on t'safe side and I'll go as soon as ever I can.

Their new master had finished telling them what he intended to do. He was looking at the door, patting his belly in a self-satisfied sort of way, saying, 'That'll be all for now.' But as they began to leave, he added, 'Follow me to the parlour will you, Mr Timmins,' and looked at Josh.

'What's all that about?' Mrs Cadwallader said when she and Jane were back in the kitchen. 'Singling *him* out. I hope he don't mean to give him more'n the rest of us. Not the way he goes on in that ol' pantry of his, what I don't approve of and neither should he.'

Jane didn't care. She had enough to think about without concerning herself with Josh and his drinking habits. 'We shall know soon enough,' she said.

They knew ten minutes later when Josh banged into the kitchen red-faced with temper and threw his wig onto the dresser with such force that he knocked over a candlestick.

'He's told me to find another job,' he said. 'Another job! Did 'ee ever hear the like? It beggars belief. Twenty years I've been here, man and boy. Twenty years of faithful service. And now this! He says he don't need a valet. Don't need a valet, my eye! I never *seen* a man what needs one more. Well, he won't get far wi'out one and that's a certainty. He's got no taste at all. Not that he gave me the chance to tell him. I couldn't get a word in edgeways, he kept saying I was *free to seek better employment elsewhere*. You'd ha' thought he was offering me a favour.'

'Oh dear,' Mrs Cadwallader said, righting the candlestick to hide the fact that she was grinning. 'And here's me thinking you were going to get some special offer.'

The parlour bell was jangling against the wall. 'Now what?' Josh said, as one of the housemaids went to answer it.

It was the mistress, the girl said on her return, 'a-wantin' to see you, Mrs Smith, ma'am. Only the thing is...' she hesitated, 'the thing is, it looks as if she's been a-weeping.'

Lizzie Hudson was sitting on one of the dingy old chairs in the parlour window. Her long nose was quite red and her cheeks were blotched and drawn. But the most noticeable thing about her was not her unhappy face but the fact that she was heavily pregnant.

'Oh!' she said. 'It's Mrs Smith, isn't it? Yes, of course. What am I thinking of? I know you are.

115

Mr Hudson told me. What I means for to say ... the thing is...' And then she was crying again, the tears running down her long nose. 'Oh, oh!' she sobbed. 'What must you think of me?'

Her distress was too great not to be answered. 'Is there owt I can do for 'ee, ma'am?' Jane asked. 'Do you want for summat? You've only to say.'

'It's this baby,' Lizzie grieved, looking down at her belly. 'I'm so afraid. What if I lose this one as well?'

It was time to be practical. 'Have you booked a midwife, ma'am?'

Lizzie shook her head, scattering teardrops from the end of her nose. 'I don't know of any,' she admitted. 'Not the kindly sort anyroad. Not what I'd call kindly. The one who came when my Richard was born was the hardest sort of woman you ever did see.' And she whispered, 'I think she drank.'

'Would you like me to find one for you?' Jane offered, thinking of Mother Hardcastle.

There was such relief on Lizzie Hudson's face it was pitiful to see it. 'Oh, I would. I would.'

'I'll write this very afternoon,' Jane reassured her, 'and I'll ask her to attend on you just as soon as she can. Don't fret, ma'am. She's a gossip but she's allus kindly.' But even as the words were in her mouth she was thinking how foolish she was being. Now she would have to stay until this was settled, which wasn't at all what she'd been planning when she walked into the room. But she could hardly turn away from this poor woman and do nothing for her, not when she was in such a state.

She wrote to Mrs Hardcastle as soon as she was back in her parlour and sent the letter by what was now the Hudson dogcart so that she was sure it would be delivered that day. The midwife was equally quick, appearing on the doorstep at Monkgate early the next morning in her best bonnet and shawl. She spent the entire morning with her new mother, talking her through her worries, calming and soothing and finally telling her that her baby would be born safe and well 'on account of I shall see to it'.

'Such a relief,' Lizzie said to Jane that afternoon. 'I'm so grateful to 'ee, Mrs Smith. You've no idea. I was at my wits' end afore you came along. Right at my very wits' end. And now...Your Mrs Hardcastle is a splendid woman. Absolutely splendid. But I don't need to tell 'ee that, do I? First rate and so kindly. She says I've got a fine healthy baby and 'twill be born wi' no problem at all, bein' the third like. She hasn't any babies booked for August, so that's a mercy. I'm to send the carriage for her when I have my first pains and she says she'll be here within the hour. Oh, you've made all the difference to me. All the difference. You truly have. I tell 'ee, when we came here 'twas like the end of t'world, leaving home and the shop and all, but now... I'm so glad you're our house-keeper. Now I shall have you *and* Mrs Hardcastle when the baby comes. I shall, shan't I?'

'Aye,' Jane said. 'Of course.' She knew her promise was tying her feet to the ground but what else could she say?

'Oh an' afore I forget,' Lizzie said. 'Mr Hudson said to tell 'ee he wants to see thee. In his office, so he said. Anyroad, I think that's what he said. He's so full of plans for this house, I can't keep pace with him. We're to have a new nursery and I don't know what-all. He'll tell 'ee.'

So Jane left her grateful mistress and went off to find her graceless master. He was sitting at the desk in the office, reading letters. There were several rolled-up plans standing in a long vase at one end of the desk, obviously waiting for his attention, and a pot full of sharp quills ready at the other. 'Aye,' he said, without looking up. 'Mrs Smith. I'll be with 'ee shortly.'

She stood in the sunlight and waited as patiently as she could although her brain was seething. In two days all her sensible plans had been overturned and now she was stuck here in a house where she certainly didn't want to be, with a master she certainly didn't want to serve. The minute that baby's born, she thought, I shall be off out of here like a shot.

'Now then,' George said, looking up at her. 'What do 'ee say to the number of servants I've got in this house? Is there a sufficiency, d'you think?'

She answered him seriously. 'It depends on what use you means to mek of the place,' she said. 'There are enough of us to run it day to day but if you were thinking of having company or entertaining...'

'Oh, I shall be entertaining a great deal,' he told her, 'so there'll be a deal of company. I mean to have the house redecorated to a more suitable style for it. So what sort of household would you need to manage all that?'

118

She gave him a generous estimate which he accepted without argument. 'See to it,' he said. 'Tell 'em they can start on the old wages till I see if they suit.'

Not a word about his wife, Jane thought, as she took the back stairs to the kitchen. And not a word of thanks to me for helping her either. I don't believe he pays any attention to either of us. He doesn't see us. It's just him and what he wants, him entertaining, him having a deal of company, him redecorating the house, what'll be hard work whichever way you look at it.

She was right, for it wasn't so much redecorated as stripped bare and redesigned. First all the old furniture was removed. Then the painters and decorators arrived. Within a week, the place was so clean that even Jane couldn't fault it, a new bed had been installed in the master bedroom, there were bright new curtains at the windows, a new Turkey carpet on the floor and two fine new chairs where the master and mistress could sit at their ease. Then he set about reorganizing the dining room and the drawing room and planning a nursery. He bought sumptuous new furniture for all three rooms, and an expensive bone china dinner service for the dining room, a table big enough to seat eighteen people, a canteen of silver cutlery, linen tablecloths, dozens of napkins. No expense was spared and no detail overlooked.

'I'm a rich man now,' he told his dizzied wife, 'an' I must live according. Rich men live well. What's the point of having brass if you don't use it? I tell 'ee, Lizzie, this might be a windfall and unlooked for, but I mean to mek it work for me night and day. Night and day. You see if I don't. For a start, I mean to build a railway from York to the Midlands, an' when I've built one, I shall build another and another. There'll be no stopping me. And every one'll mek me money. This inheritance is just the start. It'll be doubled in a twelvemonth if I have my way. I'm the richest man in York today, there's no doubt about that, but give me a year or two and I'll be the richest man in England. That'll show 'em back in Howsham.'

Lizzie would have been quite content to be married to the richest man in York and had no national ambitions at all, but she only said, 'I'm sure you will, dear,' and smiled at him because she'd learnt by then that it wasn't wise to disagree with Mr Hudson when he'd set his heart on something. Besides which she didn't want to risk upsetting herself with an argument, not while she was carrying.

Another two weeks of ceaseless preparation followed and then her rich husband invited all his cronies to a splendid dinner, where roast beef was served in copious quantities, a great deal of excellent wine was consumed and raucous songs were sung. The guests didn't leave until past midnight, by which time they were so drunk they had to be lifted into their carriages and were declaring that 'old Hudson' was a stout feller, 'be dammed if he wasn't'. It was all extremely satisfactory and successful and the best thing about it was that when his guests were stupid with drink, old Hudson had told them about the new railways and explained what a wonderful idea they were and what a lot of money they would bring to the town, and they'd been so well oiled they'd been happy to agree with him. Of course he knew that it would take time to really persuade them. They were too set in their opinions to change overnight. But they would be persuaded eventually. He would win them over with rich food and fine wine and enthusiasm. He'd made up his mind to it. Sooner or later he would build a railway between York and the coal mines and the prosperous manufacturing towns of the Midlands, just as he'd promised Lizzie, and these men would help him do it.

Meantime he had to find a way to meet George Stephenson and persuade him that he should be the principal engineer of that railway. And he also had to find his workforce, the first of whom had to be the engineers who'd learnt their trade on the Stockton and Darlington. Nothing less than the most experienced would do. His head was so full of plans he could barely sleep at night. Change was coming to his ancient city and he was the man who was going to bring it there. Even if it took years to raise the capital and to persuade the government to pass a bill to legalize the venture, his railway was going to be built. He hadn't the slightest doubt of it.

Jane Jerdon had to admit that living in a house that was being revitalized was an exciting business. It wasn't at all what she expected but that's how it was. There wasn't time to sit and brood over the injustice of having to work for George

Hudson, she was too busy working – and being surprised. For not only had her life quickened to a head-spinning extent but surprises followed one after another.

The Hudsons had been in the house for two months when Lizzie Hudson sent a maid down to the kitchen one hot afternoon to ask if Mrs Smith would come to see her in the parlour and bring a jug of lemonade for two, which Jane duly did. It had become a habit to take tea or lemonade with Lizzie and one she rather enjoyed. The first time it happened she'd been rather surprised because the lady of the house never took tea – or lemonade for that matter – with one of her servants but as the days passed she'd become accustomed to it. After all, they were rather more than lady and housekeeper now. In fact, if it hadn't been for the great wealth that occasionally opened a chasm between them, they could have been friends.

'I got a question to ask 'ee,' Lizzie Hudson said, when they were settled. 'Well, more of a favour, if truth be told. What I means for to say is ... I got a question to ask you about your Milly.'

Jane was alarmed. Has she done summat wrong? she thought. But surely not. I'd have known if she had. Someone would have told me.

'Aye,' she said, speaking pleasantly, and waited.

'The thing is,' Lizzie said, 'I need a nursemaid to help me with my little Richard. He can be a right little terror when he likes, I got to admit, and now that I'm carrying... Well, tha knows how it is. Anyroad, t'long and short of it is, Mr Hudson says I may choose whomever I like, what is kindly done, uncommon kindly, don't 'ee think, I mean for to say when you consider what a lot he has on his mind, what with the shop and the house and all his properties and everything. He's such a kind man. So what I mean for to say, I mean the thing is...' She gulped and took a deep breath and went on, her words tumbling from her as if she couldn't wait to get them out of her mouth. 'The thing is, I wondered whether your Milly would care for the – um – position.'

The surprise of it was so extreme that Jane didn't know what to say. I can't possibly agree to this, she thought. 'Twould be downright wrong. Horrible. She'd be nursemaid to her brother. But she could hardly say so without appearing rude and ungrateful.

Outside the window, the world was carrying on in its usual way. A fine carriage was being driven towards Monkgate and three young women in very pretty bonnets were chattering past, arm in arm in the sunshine. She drank her lemonade to give herself a pause in which she could think, while Lizzie went babbling on.

'She's such a very good girl,' she said. 'So willing. I saw it at once. And so good with my Richard. He took to her on that first day – do 'ee remember? – what a day that was! He fell over and grazed his poor little knee – do 'ee remember? – I felt so sorry for him, falling over in all that muddle. He set up such a roar, 'twas a wonder I didn't fall over myself, there was so much going on – anyroad she picked him up and rubbed it better and stopped him crying, what I was so grateful for you couldn't begin to imagine. I'll never forget it. I was at my wits' end, what with the move and worrying about the shop and coming into all that money, what I never expected for a minute – not for one blessed minute – and Mr Hudson so excited an' all, and then for him to fall over, poor little soul. 'Twas the last straw.' Then she realized that Jane hadn't answered her and she stopped and looked at her hopefully. 'Tha'lt say yes, won't 'ee, Jane?' she said, leaning forward. ''Twould mean a great deal to me to have it settled.'

In her artless way, she had babbled Jane into a corner and somehow or other an acceptable answer had to be found. To refuse wasn't possible. How could she explain it? Even to say nothing would look ill-mannered. 'I shall have to talk to Milly about it,' she temporized.

'Oh yes, pray pray do,' Lizzie said eagerly. 'Such a good girl. I couldn't want for a better. Shall we order more lemonade? I've a parlous thirst.'

Jane offered to fetch more lemonade herself and made her escape before any more pressure could be put on her. But her thoughts were spinning. How could she possibly let her daughter act as nursemaid to her brother? It was a ridiculous, impossible situation to be in but she was in it now and she would have to ride it out as best she could. With luck Milly would say she didn't want the job and the problem would be solved.

But Milly thought it would be a very good idea. 'I'm just the one for it,' she said. 'She's got no idea how to handle a baby, poor lady, and I know all about it. Anyroad, I'm tired of being a housemaid an' being bossed around all day an' traipsing up and down stairs emptying stinking chamber pots an' all. I'd make a first-rate nursemaid.'

'How can 'ee possibly know that?' her mother asked, laughing at her earnestness, despite her misgivings.

'On account of I been watching you all these years,' Milly said, 'and what I've not learnt at your knee, Ma, isn't worth knowing.'

It was a flattering answer but it didn't help Jane to come to terms with what was being proposed. 'Wouldn't 'ee rather I found 'ee some other job?' she said. 'I can see tha'd not like being a housemaid. No one does. 'Tis mortal hard work. But I could ask at the next hiring if tha wanted a change.'

'This'll be change enough for me,' Milly told her. 'Tell her yes, Ma. I'd love to do it. When do I start?'

She began her new job the next morning, to Jane's continuing misgiving and Lizzie's relief, and she settled into her new position without a qualm. Within a week Richard was eating out of her hand, Lizzie was declaring that she couldn't imagine how she'd ever managed without her and Jane had come to accept the arrangement, partly because she'd seen that her daughter was confident enough to handle anything and partly because she'd had another – and this time a very pleasant surprise.

At the end of July, George Hudson informed her that he was leaving for Filey to inspect his properties there and would be away for some time. 'You'll hold the fort for me, I don't doubt, Mrs

Smith,' he said. And she agreed almost carelessly that she would.

The weather was warm and soporific. York dozed under a hazy sky, Lizzie dozed in a hammock in the garden, Mrs Cadwallader dozed in the open doorway of her kitchen. Even the birds were asleep. And it was the day of the hirings.

'I think I might stroll into town and tek a look round the market,' Jane said to Lizzie when she brought out her lemonade. 'If there's nowt tha needs for the moment.' And as Lizzie opened her eyes and nodded sleepily, which was permission of a sort, she put on her new straw bonnet and left the house.

There was a strange man standing on the doorstep with his hand outstretched towards the door knocker, an unfamiliar, stocky man dressed almost entirely in brown, breeches, jacket, hat, boots and all, except for an expensive blue cravat.

'Ah!' he said. 'I give 'ee good day, ma'am. I was just about to knock. Name of Cartwright. Come to see Mr Hudson.'

'He's not here at the moment, sir,' she told him, looking up at him. He had a very strong face and the most extraordinary blue eyes. They were almost the same colour as the sky over their heads, and that was a most peculiar shade that morning, having been softened by the incessant heat to a smoky mixture of blue and grey. And his eyelashes were as long and dark as Milly's.

'Happen I might come in and wait for him,' Mr Cartwright said. 'He was most particular that I should see him.'

That made her smile. 'You'll have a long wait,'

126

she said. 'He's gone to Filey.'

'Do you know when he'll be back?'

'It could be any time,' she told him. 'He doesn't tell us his plans. He just ups and goes.'

'Then I'd better find myself some lodgings until he returns,' he said, 'being as he was so particular I should see him. Happen you could recommend me a place. Somewhere clean and comfortable.'

'I could show you where the best inns are,' she offered. 'I'm heading into town myself, but as to how comfortable they'll be, that I couldn't say, never having been inside a one of 'em.'

He smiled straight into her eyes and she was surprised and confused to realize that the smile made her feel as though he was lifting her off her feet. 'That's uncommon kindly,' he said. 'I'm most grateful.'

How direct he is, she thought, as they set off towards Monk Bar together, and how honestly he speaks. There's no deceit or false charm about *him* at all.

'Have you come far?' she asked.

'From Darlington,' he said. 'I've been working on the Stockton and Darlington Railway. You may have heard of it. 'Twas in all the papers. I'm a railway engineer. Which is why Mr Hudson wants to see me.'

She noticed the pride in him and was touched by it. A worker, she thought, and good at his trade. 'I'll take you to Mrs Tomlinson's first,' she said. 'It's nobbut a step and it might suit.'

'I'm beholden to you,' he said and gave her that smile again, 'but I mustn't put you out of your way.'

'It's my afternoon off,' she told him, 'and I meant to take a walk in town anyroad.'

'Well, then, if that's the case,' he said, 'and always providing you will take a cup of coffee with me when the job is done, I will accept your kind offer.' And he offered her his arm.

She took him to five different inns, where he read the menus and inspected the dining rooms and went upstairs to see the bedrooms while she waited in the entry halls. And when they'd finished their tour, he decided that the Star and Garter would suit him very well and they went back to book a room there.

'Now for our coffee, I think,' he said, rubbing his hands together.

It was a real pleasure to sit in the coffee house with his pleasant voice filling her ears and the scent of coffee filling her nose and the taste of it rich on her tongue. She couldn't remember when she'd ever felt so happy.

'I will call again tomorrow,' he said, when he'd escorted her back to Monkgate. 'Perhaps Mr Hudson will be returned by then.'

That made her smile, knowing Mr Hudson. 'What if he's not here?' she asked.

'Then we will take another cup of coffee together and I will call again the next day.'

And the next, and the next for five happy sun-filled days, until their daily walk around the town had almost become a habit and her staff were beginning to wonder why she was always out at the market.

9

It was a magical summer. The long easy days floated past like thistledown, the city drowsed, the River Ouse sunned itself silky, church bells sang like birds, sunsets were evening enchantments. It was the best possible season for falling in love.

Jane and Mr Cartwright took a walk in one direction or another every afternoon as soon as she was free to take a pause from the work of the day. Lizzie didn't seem to mind and there was no George Hudson to chivvy her about. Sometimes they strolled through the city along the banks of the Ouse, when it wasn't too evil-smelling, but more often they followed the little River Fosse through the fields beyond the city walls, where the sky was china blue above their heads, ripe corn breathed out a wholesome scent of baked bread and skylarks rose from the fields around them to trill and bubble in their spiralling upward flight. And they talked about themselves, for what is sweeter in a young summer time than the mutual revelation of hopes and dreams.

On their fifth afternoon, she told him about her life in Scrayingham with her mother and father and how happy they'd been, 'although to tell 'ee true, most of the time we were that poor we didn't have two happence to rub together.' And he told her he'd been born and bred in Leeds,

129

'which was a rough sort of place, or at least some of it was, though I never saw it that way when I was living there' and that he had been an only child, with a widowed mother.

'My father was a jeweller,' he said with obvious affection. 'A very patient man and very skilled. I can remember him sitting at his bench, turning a diamond round and round until he could understand how to cut it. We used to live in the flat over the shop in those days and I would tiptoe into the workshop sometimes and watch him. I had to be very quiet and not interrupt him, because if he made one false move the stone would be ruined, but that was no hardship. It was wonderful to see him working. He made some beautiful rings.' And he sighed, his face full of sadness.

'You miss him,' Jane said, understanding completely. For wouldn't she miss her own parents if they were to die.

'I do,' he said. 'He was a good man. If it hadn't been for him I wouldn't have gone to school and if I hadn't gone to school I wouldn't have been an engineer and worked on the railway. I've a lot to thank him for.'

Fancy going to school, Jane thought, and she had a sudden sharp memory of her little Felix as he turned to say goodbye to her and wondered how he was. 'Did you go away to school?' she asked.

'No,' he said. 'I'm very glad to say. I would have found it hard if I'd had to leave home. No, I went to the old grammar school. They've built a new one now but I went to the old one.'

So she told him about Felix and how sad he'd

been when he'd had to leave home and go to Eton. 'Poor little thing. He was no age and he *did* cry.'

''Tis a mortal hard thing for a child to leave home,' he said.

The sympathy in his answer raised another sudden memory and this one was even sharper than the first. She was fifteen again and anguished, begging to be allowed to stay just one more night, with her unborn baby kicking at her ribs and the carter waiting at the door. Tears welled into her eyes before she could prevent them and she had to duck her head and try to hide under the brim of her bonnet before he could see them.

But he was a much keener observer than she knew and was touched by the sight of her remembered distress. Until that moment she'd seemed so sure of herself, neat and assured and capable in her grey gown, like most of the housekeepers he'd met – only prettier with those thick dark curls escaping from under her cap and those dark eyes watching him as he spoke. Now her vulnerability pulled at his heart and that was something that had never happened to him before.

'Time for our coffee, I think,' he said. 'This heat is a rare thing for provoking a thirst.'

By the time they reached the coffee house she had recovered her poise but he decided to change the subject of their conversation so as to be quite sure he didn't provoke her tears again and spent a little while telling her about some of the towns and villages he'd passed through when he was working on the railway. And she listened and admired, thinking how wonderful it must have been to have travelled so far and seen so much. That's why he's got such a strong face, she thought, and such a smile.

Her admiration was so open he could hardly avoid noticing it and after a while he knew he was basking in it. Being admired wasn't something he was used to but every moment he spent with this delectable woman was opening him up to unfamiliar emotions. He'd never been one to brag or to think particularly well of himself. He did his work, to the best of his ability, enjoyed the company of the work-gangs, ate well, drank deep, took his pay and thought no more about it. Now he was bragging and he knew it. He wanted her admiration, that was the truth of it.

It was a sad moment to both of them when their afternoon together had to come to an end. As usual he escorted her back to Monkgate and, as usual, stood on the river bank with his hand resting on the garden gate, admiring her pretty face in the sunshine.

''Tis Sunday tomorrow,' he observed.

'Aye. So 'tis.'

'Happen I shall see you at church,' he said, trying to make the suggestion sound casual and failing. ''Tis Holy Trinity, is it not?'

'Aye,' she said and wondered if he would be able to find her in that little crowded place.

He not only found her, he squeezed into the pew beside her, so that they sat thigh touching thigh, which was a delicious private pleasure, and shared the same hymn sheet and said the same prayers and then when they were saying *'Peace be with you'* he took both her hands in his and held them for a wonderfully long time. And while the sermon droned on, he turned his head and winked at her as if they were conspirators, which was another pleasure, for it was a secret moment between them and it gave her the now familiar sensation of being lifted off her feet. It really was amazing how he could do that simply by looking at her.

After the service he walked her back to Monkgate and asked, as usual, if she would walk with him again the next day, always providing Mr Hudson wasn't returned. But they both knew the answer now. It had become a routine.

That afternoon she asked him what it was like to build the railway.

''Twas laborious,' he said, which wasn't bragging for it was nothing more than the truth. 'We were out in the open country in all weathers, you see, which was easy enough when 'twas warm and dry as it is today but not so pleasant when 'twas wet or cold, for we slept in tents and there's not much comfort in a tent when it's cold. But if you're cutting your way through a hillside, there's no stopping for the weather. We work come rain or shine.'

'Did you really cut through a hillside?' she asked. It sounded too amazing to be true.

'We cut through several hillsides,' he told her. 'We had to. The one thing a steam train can't do is climb a steep hill – they can manage a gradual incline but not a hill – so we either have to cut out an embankment to make way for them or tunnel through it. 'Tis a rare old job.'

She was impressed. 'It sounds it,' she said.

'Mr Stephenson says we're driving an iron road into the future,' he told her, 'and that's my opinion of it too. Nothing will ever be quite the same once the railways are built. There'll be no toiling away in some old stagecoach or riding horseback in the rain. We shall ride in carriages and we shall ride at speed. Give us a year or two, and I tell you the world and his wife will be riding rails from one end of the kingdom to the other.' His face was flushed by the thought of it. 'They'll get up in the morning and leave their homes and ride off for a day beside the sea or out in the nearest market town. Think of that. Working men and women who've never travelled more than a few miles in the whole of their lives, riding down to London to see the sights.'

'All that way!' she said, wondering at it.

'All that way.'

'I've never been further than York,' she told him rather wistfully. 'And I'd not have come here had it not been for work.'

He beamed at her, too full of the importance of what he'd been saying to be properly cautious. 'When the tracks are down, I will take you to London,' he promised. And when she raised her eyebrows in disbelief, he thought he'd better add, 'If you will permit me and you would like to go there.'

'I would love to,' she said, and then blushed, realizing how forward that sounded. It was one thing to walk out with him of an afternoon but quite another to suggest that she would like to travel all the way to London with him. She must find some way to put this right. 'Howsomever,' she said, attempting a jest, 'I can't imagine it ever coming about.'

He wasn't deterred in the slightest. 'Oh, 'twill come about,' he told her. 'As sure as sunlight. I'll lay money on it.'

Neither of them slept very well that night. The heat was oppressive and the smell of the night soil being gathered was so nauseating that they had to keep the windows shut until the work was done. But it wasn't the heat or the stink that kept them wakeful, bad though they were. In Jane's case it was delighted disbelief, in Nathaniel Cartwright's it was the resurgence of a dream.

While he'd been working on the railway he'd sustained himself through the long cold nights and the back-breaking days by indulging in a daydream. One day, when the railway was built, he would take his pay and find a house of his own and settle down there with a good woman. The details were usually vague because he really didn't have very much idea what sort of house he would like and as to the woman he would marry, she was nothing but a shadow for he was too shy to go courting and found that most of the marriageable women he'd met, in church or at the playhouse or in various coffee houses, were either sharp and witty and decidedly offputting or as shy and tongue-tied as he was. But the dream had gone on notwithstanding its lack of detail and it had been a steadying comfort to him. Now, when he wasn't expecting it at all, he knew he had met the woman he wanted to marry. And just at the right time, for he had sufficient pay to buy a house and he'd met his delectable Mrs Smith. She was the very flesh of his dreams: pretty, gentle, quick-witted without being offputting in the least, a good housekeeper, practical – look at the way she'd found him an inn – and yet with that touching vulnerability about her that made him want to protect her and look after her. He'd never felt that way for anybody except his mother, which was different, and yet here he was dreaming of throwing his cloak at her feet. He could barely believe his good fortune.

I mustn't rush this, he told himself. I came close to it this afternoon when I told her I'd take her to London. He remembered how she'd blushed. Was that pleasure or confusion? Thinking back on it, he couldn't tell. But now that he knew what he wanted, his senses were roaring for speed. If only he knew a bit more about how a courtship should progress. He knew so little. For instance, how long do you have to walk out together before you can speak? It had been six days since they met. Was that long enough? How will I know when it's the right time? And what should I say? It was all very strange and puzzling but undeniably exciting.

He could hear the sound of brooms being used very vigorously, somewhere near at hand, and realized that the street cleaners had arrived which meant that the night soil men must have finished their work and gone, so he walked across to the window and flung it wide. The moon was full and the roofs of the town were silvered with its light. This is a beautiful world, he thought, I have money in my pocket and work a-plenty and I've found the woman I'm going to marry. Everything is possible.

Jane Jerdon was standing at her window too, leaning on the sill and enjoying the moonlight. Her attic bedroom was a lonely place now that Milly slept in the nursery but, for once, she was glad of her solitude. Her emotions were in such turmoil she needed time and peace to make sense of them. A week ago, she was diligently getting on with her work, glad of Milly's company about the house, sorry for poor Lizzie because the baby was making her so uncomfortable, accepting that this was all her life had to offer but more or less happy with her lot, sustained by good food, good ale and her private dream of revenge, now she dreamed of walking through the warm fields with Mr Cartwright and woke in the morning in a rush of happiness because she was going to see him again. They might even go to London together and that was something she would never have imagined a few short days ago – nor agreed to so easily. It was as if she'd become a different person, as if her life had been turned inside out, as if she was walking in her sleep. It couldn't be love, could it? And yet, if she was honest, she knew she would like it to be. No, it was stronger than that. She wanted it to be. He was the kindest man she'd ever met and the most interesting and as unlike George Hudson as it was possible for him to be. I don't know where you are, Mr horrible Hudson, she thought, but I hope you stay there for a very long time.

It was a decided disappointment to her when the horrible Mr Hudson returned a mere two days later. He arrived full of bustling importance and hadn't been in the house more than five seconds before he was ordering everybody about, giving orders to Jane and Mrs Cadwallader about a grand supper party he intended to host, and as soon as he heard that Mr Cartwright had arrived in town, sending the boot boy to 'tell the gentleman to call this afternoon'. That turned out to be another disappointment, because although Mr Cartwright arrived very promptly, she didn't get a chance to see him because the horrible Mr Hudson took him over at once and completely.

'Must apologize for not being here to greet you, Mr Cartwright,' he said, holding out his hand to his guest as he was ushered into the parlour. 'A deal too much needing my attention, that's the trouble. But all in the line of business, d'ye see, so all to t'good. Property and so forth. Where are you staying?' And when he was told it was the Star and Garter, he approved at once. 'Capital place. Get 'em to send the bill here to me. Have you dined?'

'No, sir.'

'Then you must dine wi' me. No, no, I'll not tek no for an answer and anyroad you'll be doing me a kindness for otherwise I shall dine on my own, what I can't abide. Mrs Hudson needs a deal of rest nowadays, d'ye see, being in the family way. We can talk railways over the roast.'

Which they did, at considerable length and to the accompaniment of large quantities of red wine, followed by a bottle of excellent brandy. Mr Cartwright felt as if his head was slipping sideways off his shoulders by the time the meal was over and he staggered as he rose from the table.

George was delighted. It always pleased him when he found someone who couldn't hold his liquor as well as he could himself. It made him feel superior. He slapped his guest between the shoulder blades and roared with laughter at him. 'We'll take a turn in t'garden,' he said. 'Clear our heads. You can meet the wife. She's allus in t'garden.'

She was lying in the hammock embedded in a mound of cushions, red in the face, hugely fat and taking lemonade with her dear Jane who had carried it out into the garden not two minutes since. As George walked towards her along the path, she was squealing and flapping her hands at a swarm of wasps that were climbing up the side of her glass and buzzing round her head.

''Tis the plums!' she cried as the two men drew near. ''Tis allus the same this time of year. They won't leave me alone, dratted things.' And she flapped her hands again as the wasps darted towards her. 'Oh, go away do, for pity's sake.'

George ignored her plight. 'My love,' he said, giving her his stern look and flicking a wasp away from his shirt front, 'allow me to present Mr Cartwright, who has come to be my railway engineer and work on my railway.' And when she'd recovered herself sufficiently to say that she was pleased to meet him, he then introduced Jane to Mr Cartwright, adding as an afterthought, 'And this is my housekeeper, Mrs Smith.'

Mr Cartwright turned his head and gave Jane a decidedly conspiratorial smile as she looked up from the lemonade jug. And again that extra-

139

ordinary sensation of being lifted off her feet. 'Aye,' he said. 'We've met.'

Lizzie caught the intonation and saw the smile and understood that something significant was going on between this new acquaintance and her Jane. She looked up at her husband to see whether he'd seen it too but he was much too full of himself to notice anything if it didn't immediately concern him and had already turned away from her.

'We'll tek a turn through town, when you've cleared your head,' he said, leading his guest towards the river at the end of the garden, 'and I'll show you the parcel of land I've bought for my railway. I'll be glad of your opinion on't.'

So they walked across the city, keeping up a brisk pace despite being jostled by the crowds, past the looming towers of the Minster and the higgledy-piggledy shops in Goodramgate, through Thursday market where the stalls stood empty, across the river and finally out through Micklegate Bar into the fields beyond the wall.

'There 'tis,' George Hudson said. 'What do 'ee think?'

It was a large patch of scrubland that stretched west from the grass banks below the city wall and north to the towpath alongside the river and they had it almost entirely to themselves apart from a pair of black and white goats who were grazing the rough grasses and lifted their heads briefly to glare at them.

''Tis a good site,' Mr Cartwright said. 'Room for manoeuvre. Where do you intend your first railway to run to?'

'South Milford for starters,' George told him. 'To give 'em a taste for it. And when that's up and running profitable, Leeds and Selby.'

'South by south-west to start with then.'

'Aye. I'll need a survey done and maps drawn up and such.'

'When would you want me to start?'

The goats, sensing trouble, were walking away from them, dropping pellets of dung from under their flicking tails.

'Next week. Would that suit 'ee?'

Mr Cartwright wanted to shout his delight at the question but he managed to answer it sensibly. 'Yes,' he said. 'That sounds reasonable. 'Twill take time though. It's not a job to be rushed.'

'Tek all t'time you need,' George said expansively. 'I've to find myself some shareholders afore we can start laying track.'

'And then there's the matter of my remuneration,' Mr Cartwright said.

'Double what the Stockton and Darlington Company paid 'ee,' George said easily. 'Would that suit?' If his reputation was true, this man knew what he was about and was worth paying well.

It would suit admirably. 'With a good wage I might rent myself a house of some kind,' Mr Cartwright ventured, 'while I'm at work hereabouts.'

'Ask my housekeeper if that's what you want,' George advised. 'She knows t'town like the back of her hand and she's a sensible woman. Got a good head on her shoulders.'

'Yes,' Mr Cartwright said, finding it even more difficult to control his feelings, thinking of that

141

good head and those sturdy shoulders. 'I might do that.'

'Or there's my brother-in-law, a' course,' George said. 'Not the brightest of young men, if truth be told, but he's obliging and he's grown up in the town since he wor a lad. Works at t'drapers in Goodramgate. Hudson and Nicholson. Tha can't miss it.' He pulled his fob watch from his waistcoat pocket and squinted at it in the sunlight. 'Time to have us some tea, I think.' And he looked up from his watch to grin at his new engineer. 'Unless tha'd like summat stronger.'

10

Jane Jerdon was floating above the river in the sunshine, her feet barely touching the ground, her body as light as thistledown, as if she were flying, and Mr Cartwright was floating beside her, holding her hands, smiling into her eyes – oh so tenderly – and telling her how much he loved her. 'Yes,' she was saying to him. 'Yes, oh yes!' It was a perfect, joyous moment, to love and be loved in return, but just as she was enjoying it, feeling full of wonder and happiness, never wanting it to stop, she became aware that there was somebody pulling at her arm. She twisted away, irritated by the intrusion. 'No. Not now,' she said. 'Later.' But the tugging went on and on. She couldn't shake it off and the sun was right in her eyes, dazzling her, and Mr Cartwright was beginning to melt as though he was made of ice. 'No. Not now. Please.'

'Ma!' Milly said, urgently. 'Wake up. 'Tis the baby.'

Baby, Jane thought. What baby? There's no baby here. Nor like to be. 'Twould fall in the river, poor little thing, and be drowned. But the river was disappearing and so was the sky and the grass was sliding from under her feet and swirling the last drifting shadow of her dear Mr Cartwright away and away and away. And she knew she was in bed and that there was a lighted candle on her bedside table shining into her eyes and that her daughter was shaking her arm.

'She's frightened to death, Ma,' Milly said. 'She's been asking for 'ee this last half hour.'

Common sense returned. There was work to be done. She got up, put on her dressing gown and her slippers, lit her candle. 'Have 'ee sent for Mrs Hardcastle?' she asked.

'Long since.'

'Then go and wake Mrs Cadwallader and tell her we need a dish of gruel and a pot of good strong tea. There's the key to the caddy. Plenty of sugar, tell her. She'll need sustenance, poor woman.'

As they reached the second floor she could hear Lizzie sobbing. 'I'm coming,' she called. 'Hold on! I'm coming.' And she strode into the master bedroom on a breeze of urgency and compassion.

The bedclothes were tossed all over the floor, there was no sign of Mr Hudson, and Lizzie was rolling about on the bed, her face streaked with tears. ''Twill die,' she wept. 'I know it. As sure as fate. 'Twill die. I shall lose it.'

'Die?' Jane said trenchantly. 'What sort of nonsense is that, wi' me here to look out for 'ee and Mother Hardcastle on her way? 'Twill be a fine strong baby. You heard what she said. A fine strong baby. Now let me get 'ee comfy afore we have her here.'

'Coming along lovely,' the midwife said when she arrived. 'Get this nice gruel inside you and build up your strength, for we shall have this one here in no time at all.'

In fact it was born a long two hours later when the sun had risen and the room was washed with light, and it was another boy, small and extremely pale, but full of life, with a cap of very fair hair and a comically pained expression.

'Where's his father?' Mrs Hardcastle wanted to know.

'He went to the blue room,' Lizzie said, not looking up from her new son's now contented face. 'He needs his sleep, do y'see, on account of all the important work he does.'

'Does he so?' Mrs Hardcastle said grimly. 'Well, he can wake up betimes this morning, on account of we got summat even more important to tell him. Mrs Smith'll rouse him, I'm certain sure. Won't 'ee, Jane?'

''Twill be a pleasure,' Jane said equally grimly. 'Why should he slug-abed when his poor wife's been labouring all night? 'I'll do it now.'

She could hear her master snoring as she stood outside the blue room door. The sound irritated her, so she gave the door a sharp rap and walked in. He was lying on his back with his belly mounded before him and his mouth fallen open. Not a pretty sight, she thought, and spoke to it loudly.

'Mr Hudson, wake up.' And when he didn't stir, she shouted her message again. 'Wake up. You have a son. Which is the third you've fathered besides a daughter you don't give a fig about.'

He turned on his side, grunting. 'Whassat?'

'A son,' she told him firmly. 'Just born, what I've no doubt you want to come and see.'

He groaned. 'Is that all?' he said. 'Tell her I'll be along presently – oh, and tell Cook to bring me up a pot of tea. Well, don't just stand there. That'll be all.' Then he turned on his back again and closed his eyes.

Heartless pig, Jane thought, glaring at him. You don't care about that poor little baby nor about my poor Lizzie. It's just you, you, you all the time. Your sleep. Your money. Your railway. Your tea. And her long-held need to be revenged on him roared up in her as strong as it had ever been.

Nathaniel Cartwright arrived on Mr Hudson's imposing doorstep at a little after ten o'clock that morning. He was clean shaven, dressed in his best clothes with a new cream-coloured cravat to set off the russet brown of his jacket and full of cheerful determination. As always, now that he'd made up his mind to do something, he couldn't wait to get on with it. And what he was going to do was buy a house and propose to his delectable Mrs Smith. The sun was warm on the nape of his

145

neck, there was a blackbird singing in the may tree in a garden across the street and no doubt in his mind at all.

'Mr Cartwright,' he said happily to the house-maid when she opened the door, 'come to see your housekeeper.'

'If you'll just step inside and wait, sir,' the housemaid said, opening the parlour door, 'I'll go up and tell her.'

He waited as patiently as he could, but it seemed an age before she arrived and then he was disappointed to see that she was hard at work for she wore a Holland apron and long Holland sleeves over her grey gown.

'I've only got a minute,' she said rather breath-lessly. 'I promised to be straight back.'

'I've come at a bad time,' he said, his heart sinking a little, and he gave her a slight bow by way of apology.

'No, no,' she said, reassuring him. 'Quite the reverse. 'Tis the best of times. Mrs Hudson has just had her baby and what could be better than that? I would spend more time with you if I could, but I promised to stay with her.'

'Naturally,' he said, smiling at her. 'That is quite understood. In that case I will call again this afternoon, if I may.'

'I shall look forward to it,' she said, which was nothing less than the truth.

And so will I, he thought, as he walked out of the house. It was a disappointment but only a temporary one. If she couldn't advise him, there was always Mr Hudson's brother-in-law.

He found the draper's shop with no difficulty,

for he vaguely remembered seeing it on his way to Monkgate, and there was the name helpfully printed above the window. Hudson and Nicholson. The door was open so he ducked his head under the lintel and went in.

There were two people in the shop, a fair-haired young man in a very well-cut blue jacket and an apprentice boy in poor-quality breeches and a crumpled waistcoat who was staggering towards the nearest counter carrying three fat rolls of cloth and grimacing as if the weight was too much for him.

'How can I help you, sir?' the young man said, ignoring the grimace.

'Mr Nicholson?'

The young man gave a slight bow. 'The same, sir.'

Nathaniel explained what he wanted.

'I say,' Richard Nicholson said. 'What sport! And what luck! You've come at just the right time. I know just the place. Old Mr Melly's got it. Been on his books for ages. It's right by Bootham Bar. Lovely house. Spanking new. Just the style. Come and see it.' And he turned to his apprentice, saying, 'You can keep the shop, can't you, Sam?' and without waiting for an answer, disappeared into the office to collect his hat and cane. 'That's more like it,' he said as he stepped through the door into the sunshine. 'To tell 'ee true, a shop can be too much of a good thing when the sun's shining. There are days when I can't be doing with it.'

They strode off together along Goodramgate towards Low Petergate, scattering passers-by with their onrush, visited Mr Melly's little office above the corn chandlers and were given the key. And then they were off again, this time heading for Bootham Bar, where the stones of the city wall were honeyed with sunshine and the Bar stood before them, humping its elderly shoulders as if it was disgruntled. Then through the archway and out into a grassy field and a quiet road, where there were three new houses, two in occupation and one plainly empty.

Nathaniel was taken with Shelton House as soon as he saw it. It was so modern and upright, with its fine door and its well-balanced windows. This new style is so elegant, he thought, as he approached it, and he was prepared to like it even before he'd set foot in the place. They explored it from the kitchen to the attic, telling one another what a fine place it was, admiring the dining room with its marble mantelpiece and its beautifully moulded ceiling – as good as Mr Hudson's any day of the week – and climbing the easy rise of the stairs to the upper rooms, where the master bedroom was just right for his delectable Mrs Smith and then up again to the three small attic rooms that were the servants' quarters. And they were just right too, for he was a gentleman now and his wife should have servants in a house this size.

'I shall take it,' he said as the two of them stepped out into the sunshine.

Richard Nicholson was locking the door. 'What sport!' he said, beaming at his new friend. 'I say! Never thought I'd sell a house when I got up this morning an' that's a fact. This beats drudgery any day. Take my tip though. Don't give him the asking price. You could beat him down by several pounds, if I'm any judge of it. Fifty at least.'

'I shall bear that in mind,' Nathaniel said, admiring the elegant frontage again.

'You'll be needing a solicitor,' Richard told him. 'I know just the man. Name of Leeman. George Leeman. Fine feller. He'll see you right.'

Nathaniel knew his new friend was talking sense. He would certainly have to find a solicitor, but he couldn't think about it at that moment. He was too busy trying to imagine how the face of his lady love would look when she heard what he'd done.

When Lizzie Hudson had fed her baby for the second time and had satisfied herself and Mrs Hardcastle that he really was taking enough milk to sustain him, she settled into her pillows and fell asleep, her plump arms lying heavily on the counterpane and her face smoothed with content. Jane stayed on in the room for a quarter of an hour just in case she woke again but by then it was plain that this was going to be a long sleep and that she could leave the midwife on watch while she went back to the kitchen to attend to her own affairs. There was plenty to attend to, the soiled bed linen waiting in the copper for the laundry maid, fresh food to buy at the market, the usual evening meal to be cooked. And as if that weren't enough, there was also the possibility that Mr Cartwright would come to see her again. While she'd been busy with the mistress and the baby she hadn't given his morning visit much thought; now it pricked her mind with curiosity. He'd arrived because of something important. That much was obvious. The subdued excitement in him had been proof of that. Now she was itching to know what it was.

As she walked towards the larder to check supplies, her peculiar early-morning dream inched back into her mind and she was reminded that she'd been extremely foolish while she was asleep, thinking she could fly and that Mr Cartwright was telling her he loved her, and she told herself quite sharply that she really ought to take her thoughts in hand and try to check her stupidity. For that's what it was. Just plain stupidity and it was folly to give in to it. But scolding herself didn't help her at all, because it set her thinking. What if that odd excitement she'd noticed meant that he *was* thinking of proposing? It wasn't at all likely when they'd only known each other for such a short time but what would she say if he did? It had been the oddest sort of day, so odd that anything seemed possible, and her dream certainly seemed to be pointing in that direction, so what...? I *must* be sensible, she scolded herself, lifting the lid of the flour bin. I'm not a child. I'm a woman grown and a mother, what's more, not a silly girl full of silly dreams but twenty-seven with a daughter who's twelve and old enough to work. I ought to have more sense than to give in to fantasies. But the dream flew in and out of her head as she worked and she couldn't get rid of it. She was so preoccupied that when young Sally appeared at her elbow to tell her that she had a visitor, she jumped as if she'd been bitten by a wasp.

'Who is it?' she asked, trying to sound non-chalant about it, and failing.

''Tis that Mr Cartwright, Mrs Smith ma'am,' Sally told her. 'Him what come a-calling this morning, dratted man. D'you remember? We wor all that busy we wor fair wore out and why he should've come to plague us at a time like that I can't for the life of me imagine. I've put him in the parlour.' She was still ruffled by the un-suitability of that visit.

It was necessary to be calm and businesslike. Jane took off her apron and smoothed the skirt of her grey gown. 'Go upstairs,' she said, 'and see whether Mrs Hudson is still sleeping. Tiptoe in, mind, and don't go knocking on t'door. She needs her sleep. But if she's awake and she wants to see me, come straight to the parlour and tell me.'

Then she went up the back staircase to see the man of her dream.

There was no doubt about his excitement now. He seemed to be twice the size he'd been in the morning, like a turkey-cock with his feathers fluffed out, and he was smiling like sunshine. He strode across the room towards her as soon as she set foot inside the door and took both her hands in his and held them and gave them a little shake. While he'd been waiting for her he'd convinced himself that he was going to break this news to her gradually and calmly, like a man of sense; now he couldn't wait to tell her. 'I've bought a house,' he said. 'What do you think of that?'

'My dear heart alive,' she said, gazing up at him. He really was exceedingly handsome.

151

'Now I want your opinion of it,' he said, still holding her hands. 'Could we walk out to look at it, do you think, or are you too busy?'

'Well, as to that,' she said, trying to be sensible, which was very difficult when her heart was racing fit to leap out of her chest, ''twould depend on Mrs Hudson an' how she's feeling. If she needs me to be here, I must stay with her.'

'Happen you could ask her,' he hoped.

But there was no need, for the door was opening and Sally was making an entrance, her face bright with importance. Her expression changed to a scowl when she saw that her unnecessary nuisance of a visitor was holding Mrs Smith by both hands but she stayed perfectly proper and gave her message notwithstanding her disapproval. 'If you please, ma'am, Mrs Hardcastle said to tell 'ee, Mrs Hudson is still asleep.'

'Good,' Jane said, retrieving her hands. 'Then I shall be free to inspect this house of yours, Mr Cartwright, and give you my opinion of it. If you will just wait till I get my bonnet.'

'Standing there as bold as brass he was, holding her hands,' Sally said to Mrs Cadwallader when she was back to the kitchen. She was pink with the effrontery of it. 'Did you ever hear the like?'

'Many's the time,' the cook said. 'Happen they're courting. Don't surprise me. She's a handsome woman.'

'Courting!' Sally said in horror. 'She can't be. 'Tis unfitting.' And she was quite put out when Mrs Cadwallader roared with laughter at her.

When they were through the crush at Monkgate and out in the welter of the crowds pushing their way along Goodramgate, Nathaniel offered Jane his arm and smiled with satisfaction when she took it. There was a warmth and intimacy between them now that neither could ignore. As they stepped into the darkness under the low archway beside Mr Nicholson's shop, he put his arm round her shoulders and pulled her protectively towards him and he left it there for several happy seconds when they emerged into the sunshine of Priest Row.

'It's not very far,' he said, as they passed the dilapidated frontage of St William's College.

Jane didn't mind how far it was. There was such an extraordinary sense of unreality about this day she felt that anything could happen. A walk was nothing compared to what could be coming. They passed the humped shoulders of Bootham Bar, strolled through the central arch, were out in the quiet fields and there was the house he'd bought, warm-bricked in the sunshine, its windows gleaming. She loved it at once.

He escorted her from room to room, opening every door with a flourish and watching her face to see if she approved. And eventually, he led her out into the meadow that would one day be their garden and they stood together among knee-high grasses and looked out at the fields where they'd walked and talked together in their short, extraordinary courtship. It was time for his declaration.

Now that the moment had arrived, he was horribly nervous, afraid that he might say the wrong thing or that this was, after all, the wrong time. She was smiling in a dreamy sort of way, which might be taken as an encouragement, but on the other hand...

''Tis a fine house,' she said.

'I thought so as soon as I saw it.'

'And you've bought it,' she prompted.

'There are still some legal matters that will require attention,' he told her, 'but Mr Leeman has it in hand and, to all intents and purposes, 'tis mine.'

Then he was lost, for it wasn't the house he wanted to talk about or, at least, not in this serious businesslike way. He cleared his throat. 'What I mean to say–' he said and then stopped.

She waited, her face bright with expectation, although she was doing everything she could to keep her expression under control. Was he going to propose? Or was she being foolish? Oh do go on, dear Mr Cartwright. This waiting is too much for a body to bear.

'What I mean to say,' he started again. 'The thing is. The thing is...' And then because she was smiling at him so hopefully, the words came tumbling out. 'I knew this was the house for me the moment I saw it. I mean, I knew I wanted it to be my house. I wanted to live here. With you. I do not wish to alarm you, my dear Mrs Smith, I would not alarm you for the world, but the truth of it is, I have loved you ever since I first set eyes on you. I knew then that I wanted to marry you, that I *would* marry you if you would have me. I know this may sound unlikely – possibly not even proper – we have known one another such a very short time, but it is the truth notwithstanding. I loved you as soon as I saw you standing on the doorstep in your grey gown. You cannot imagine how much I loved you. You cannot imagine how much I love you now. More than I can possibly tell you. Oh, say you will have me, my dear, dear Mrs Smith. Say you will have me and live with me here in this house. I will make you a loving husband, I promise you.' And then he had to pause for breath for he was quite overcome.

For a few seconds she was speechless. 'My dear heart alive!' she said at last and smiled at him with such transparent happiness that he knew she was going to accept him.

He took her hands in his and looked down at her glowing face. 'Is that an affirmative or a negative?' he asked. It was a needless question.

Their troth was sealed with a kiss for they were blessedly private out there in their garden and there was no one to see them. It was as if they had the world to themselves. And naturally, after that first kiss, they took another and another, until they'd kissed one another breathless. Then they exchanged Christian names and agreed that they would marry as soon as the house was ready for them and, naturally, they had to kiss again. It wasn't until they were walking slowly back to Monkgate, arm in happy arm, that she remembered Milly and Lizzie and her mother and all the people she was responsible for.

He smiled at her happily, his mind full of plans. 'I will arrange the wedding as soon as Mr Leeman tells me that the house is mine,' he told her. 'How long will you need to prepare? You must have a wedding gown, of course, and a bonnet and they must be the best that money can buy. How if we say a fortnight from completion?'

It *was* a dream, an unbelievable, dizzying, totally delightful dream. They had barely known one another a fortnight and yet here he was planning their wedding. She held on to his warm, solid, loving arm, feeling she would turn faint and fall without his strength to support her.

He was still planning. 'We will send our invitations as soon as we have a date,' he said. 'You must give me a list of all the people you would like to be there. We shall have our wedding breakfast at the house. Now as to your daughter.'

'Milly,' she told him.

'Aye indeed, Milly. She shall come and live with us, naturally, and have a room of her own and be the daughter of the house, if that is agreeable.'

It was very agreeable.

'Then 'tis settled,' he said. 'She shall want for nothing, I promise you. I will treat her as though she were my own.'

His generosity was all-enveloping, overpowering. He seemed to have thought of everything. She could just see Milly in that elegant house. What a total change of fortune this was.

'As soon as I know that the house is mine, I will send to tell you,' he went on happily, 'and then you may hand in your notice to Mr Hudson and be the lady of your own house.'

Talk of handing in her notice made Jane remember poor Lizzie, lying abed with her newborn baby beside her. She hadn't given the poor lady a thought since she'd left her and it was a jolt to her mind to remember that the baby had been born such a short time ago. Was it really only this morning? If he means us to be married within a fortnight, she thought, I shall be leaving her just when she's up and about again. And she wondered what Lizzie would say and how she would manage without her. I must tell her as soon as I get home, she thought. I'll write to Ma first and then I'll go straight up to the bedroom.

11

Lizzie Hudson was sitting up in bed eating a sugar plum and looking stickily contented, when Jane gentled into the room. She knew at once that something significant had happened and smiled when Jane said, 'I've summat to tell 'ee.'

Her face was all encouragement. 'Aye?'

'Mr Cartwright has asked me to marry him.'

Lizzie clapped with delight. 'I knew it,' she crowed. 'I've know'd it all along. I saw it on his face when we met in t'garden that time. Clear as daylight. Do 'ee remember? All those dratted wasps after the plums and plaguing me summat cruel, crawling and buzzing all over t'place and the sun that hot I thought I were ready to suffocate, I truly did. And Mr Hudson introduced us and he looked at you with such affection – Mr Cartwright, I mean, not Mr Hudson – I knew it straightaway. Such affection. It did my heart good to see it. You'll make him a fine wife, my dear. The best. And who knows that better than I do?'

Jane's conscience was tugging in her chest. 'I shall have to leave you when I marry,' she warned.

'Of course tha will,' Lizzie agreed, 'and I shall miss 'ee, my dear, dear friend, there's no denying it for tha's been uncommon kind to me since I came to this house. Uncommon kind. But what happiness! Anyroad, I'll still have thy Milly, won't I? Such a treasure. I couldn't manage wi'out her, and that's t'truth of it.'

It was the wrong time to tell her that Milly would be leaving too so Jane kept quiet. Let her digest my news first, she thought. I can tell her all that later, when she's rested. Not that Lizzie noticed. She was still happily babbling on.

'We shall still see each other,' she said, 'for tha'lt come and visit me as often as tha can, if tha's not too far away, that is.'

'We're to live in York by Bootham Bar.'

'How splendid! That's no distance at all. Oh, how I do wish 'ee well! Have 'ee told Milly? No? Well, she's in t'garden wi' young Richard. You must go there at once.'

She was on the lawn, playing catch with Dickie, who was doing his best to hurl the ball into the bushes so that she had to go down on her hands and knees and crawl about to retrieve it. To Jane's love-dazzled eyes she looked quite delectably pretty in her blue gown and her frilled cap and apron. But when she heard her mother's news, instead of being pleased, she opened her brown eyes wide with astonishment.

158

'Married!' she said. 'What *do* you mean, Ma, married?'

'To Mr Cartwright,' Jane explained.

'But whatever for?' Milly said, tossing the ball towards the waiting child. 'Not in the bushes this time, young man.'

'Because he asked me,' Jane said, with some pride.

It was incomprehensible. Mothers didn't rush off and get married. They stayed at home and ran the house and looked after the mistress and her children. She picked up the ball that Dickie had flung rather wildly back at her. 'What about poor Mrs Hudson?' she said. 'What's she got to say about it? You can't just go haring off and getting married. Not when she's just had a baby. Hold tha hands right out, Dickie, like this. See? Then tha can catch it. Good boy! That's the way!'

'I shan't leave her just yet,' Jane said. 'Not for a week or two anyroad. Not till she's finished lying in. And I'll not leave thee at all for tha'rt to come wi' me and live in my new house and have a room all to thyself. What do 'ee think of that?'

'I think it's silly,' Milly said. 'Who'll look after Dickie during the night if I'm not here?'

'They'll find someone else,' Jane said easily.

'He'll not want someone else,' her daughter said stoutly. 'I can tell 'ee that. He's used to me.'

'Aye, well,' Jane said, amiably, 'there's no need to make decisions yet awhile. Tha's not seen the house yet. 'Tis a grand place. 'Twill be gradely there.'

But her daughter pulled a face and turned away from her. 'If tha throws yon ball in t'bushes one more time,' she said to the little boy, 'tha'lt have to get it out thassen. I'm not a-clamberin' in after it *no more*.'

'Shan't!' Dickie said.

'Oh yes tha will,' Millie told him sternly, 'or we'll not play. Now try an' throw it straight. *That's* the style! Good boy!'

How well she handles him, Jane thought, as she walked into the house, and she was full of pride in her daughter's good sense. I'm not surprised she says he'll not want anyone else. But he'll have to learn to live wi' that, once she sees the house and decides to live in it.

It seemed dark indoors after the brightness of the sunshine in the garden but the kitchen was full of light and movement for Mrs Cadwallader and the kitchen maids were hard at work preparing dinner. But everything came to an instant halt when Jane told them her news.

'Don't surprise me in the slightest!' Mrs Cadwallader said. 'What did I tell 'ee, Sally? Didn't I say 'twould be a wedding. When is it to be?'

'As soon as he can arrange it,' Jane told her.

'Well good luck to 'ee both,' Mrs Cadwallader said, and echoed her mistress. 'And if you're thinking to hire a cook when you're the lady of the house, don't forget me.'

'Would you like to work for me?' Jane asked.

'Give me half the chance,' Mrs Cadwallader said. 'We'd get on like a house a-fire.'

'I'll talk to Mr Cartwright about it,' Jane said, 'and see what he says.'

'In the matter of servants,' her beloved told her,

'I trust you to make your own decisions which I know will be wise ones. Hire whomever you think fit.'

So Mrs Cadwallader was hired and so were several other servants. Then there was furniture to buy and cloth for her wedding dress, which was to be in the latest style with a neat waist, exactly where your waist should be, instead of under your bosom where the old style had it, and a very full skirt, instead of the old straight ones, and the most elaborate sleeves topped by a collar so wide it looked like a shawl. And then it was time to send out the invitations – to her mother and father and Aunt Tot and Audrey Palmer, the milkmaid, and dear Lizzie, and dozens of his friends from the railway.

By the time George Hudson learned what was going on, the house was completely furnished, Mrs Cadwallader had taken up her new position in it, the wedding breakfast was cooked and the guests were travelling to York for the ceremony.

He and Lizzie were breakfasting late that morning. He'd been up until past three in the morning mixing with the York worthies at a prestigious dinner at the Guildhall and now he was overtired and crabby and in no mood to be served burnt kidneys and bacon that, as he complained, was 'nobbut a shrivel'.

'What's the matter wi' Cook this morning?' he said. 'Damned woman. Ring the bell. I've summat to say to her.'

'She's a new one,' Lizzie said timidly. 'Happen, she hasn't quite got the hang of things.'

161

The information put him in a temper. 'New one?' he shouted. 'What are you talking about?'

Lizzie explained as well as she could for trembling but her explanation only made him shout louder.

'Gone?' he roared. 'What's the matter wi' the woman? I pay her enough in all conscience. Allus have. Never stint any of my servants. Never have. You know that. She'll not get the same wage elsewhere, I can tell 'ee that. Where's she gone?'

Lizzie tried to dissemble. 'Well, as to that,' she said, 'I couldn't rightly say.'

'And what's that supposed to mean?' he said, his anger rising. 'Either you know or you don't. Out wi' it! A woman can't have secrets from her husband. Where's she gone?'

'Well,' Lizzie said in a very small voice, 'she's working for Mrs Smith. At Bootham Bar.'

He couldn't believe what he was hearing. 'Mrs Smith?'

'She's going to marry Mr Cartwright,' Lizzie said, nervousness making her babble. 'Such a nice house they've got – well, it would be, wouldn't it, being he's an engineer, but you know that, of course, that he's an engineer, I mean, not that he's going to marry our Mrs Smith, which he is and we must wish her well, mustn't we, George? I mean to say getting married and everything.'

'I never heard the equal!' her husband shouted. 'What does she think she's playing at? Blamed fool! There's no need for her to go running off getting wed. No need at all. She should think on't. She's got everything she could possibly want here,

162

rooms, good vittals, wardrobes full of clothes. Think of all the clothes she got when the old man died. What's the matter with her?'

Lizzie picked at her shrivelled bacon and tried to ignore him. It was no good arguing when he'd got a rage on.

George was in full, red-faced flow. 'Now we shall all be put to the fuss of finding another,' he complained, 'which is unnecessary and inconvenient. Stupid woman! I've enough to do wi'out that. Well, you'll have to do it, that's all. I haven't time for hiring and firing.'

That was alarming. 'I don't think I could, George,' Lizzie said, looking up at him anxiously. 'I mean to say, I've never hired a housekeeper, not in all my life. I wouldn't be equal to it.'

'Then you'll have to make do wi'out one, that's all,' George said. 'I've to go to Whitby. I'm off on the first stage out this morning.'

That made Lizzie's heart sink. 'Couldn't you do it afore you go?' she said. 'I mean for to say, couldn't this trip wait till...?'

He silenced her with a peremptory wave of his fat hand. 'No, it could not,' he said. 'Have you no sense, woman? This is *business* I'm talking about. Railway business. Mr Stephenson is like to be there – they said so in t'paper this morning – *the* Mr Stevenson, the one what invented the Rocket, and if *he's* there I mean to be there too and catch him. I can't hang about here hiring and firing housekeepers.' And he smoothed down his waistcoat which had been crumpled by the exertions of his tirade and marched out of the room.

Lizzie waited until he'd banged the front door

after him, then she set her plate aside and rang the bell.

'Ah!' she said when Sally came in all bright faced to answer it. 'Are you all ready?'

'Rarin' to go, ma'am,' Sally said. 'Only got to take these old aprons off an' put our bonnets on an' we'll be fine an' dandy.'

'If you'll just clear the table,' Lizzie said, heading for the door, 'while I see to t'baby, what shouldn't take more than a minute or two. What a blessing he's such a good little soul. Dear little man. We mustn't be late, whatever we do.'

'No, ma'am,' Sally agreed, starting work at once. 'Not for our Mrs Smith.' And when she saw that Mrs Hudson was looking anxiously at the clock, 'Don't 'ee fret, ma'am. We've plenty of time. 'Tis an hour yet an' Dickie's washed an' dressed an' looks quite the little man – Millie's seen to that – an' our Betsy's all ready to help 'ee to dress too. 'Tis all took care of.'

'Oh what a happy day this will be,' Lizzie said, as she opened the door.

And a happy day it indubitably was. One look at the bride as she walked along the uneven stones of the aisle on her father's arm was enough to lift every heart in the church, for her face was glowing, and when she and Mr Cartwright exchanged their vows, there were tears in every pew. Mary Jerdon, in her seat of honour in the front pew, wept freely to see her daughter so happy and so did Milly, rather to her own surprise for she hadn't expected a wedding to bring such a rush of emotion. Aunt Tot and Audrey Palmer let their tears run and didn't bother to wipe them away and so did Lizzie Hudson, who'd forgotten all about George's nasty temper and simply gave herself up to the pleasure of the occasion. Even Nathaniel's work mates from the railways, who were the toughest bunch of men it was possible to imagine, found they needed to blow their noses and blink a bit. And Jane herself was caught up in such joy and pride and excitement it was like all the good feelings she'd ever experienced all wrapped up in one.

Afterwards, as she and her new husband strolled together through the town towards their waiting feast, with the sun on their faces and their guests bubbling and chattering behind them, she held his arm and smiled into his eyes.

'Happy?' he asked unnecessarily.

'So, so happy,' she told him. 'I don't want this day to ever end.'

'There is better to come, my dearest, dearest Jane,' he said. 'This is just the beginning.'

George Hudson was standing in front of the Angel Inn by the harbour at Whitby, feeling jaded. He'd had a long wearying journey and was glad to be out of the coach. Far too many of the roads he'd travelled were in need of repair, which meant that he'd been bounced and jolted in the most painful way, and there had been far too many hills that the horses couldn't manage, which meant that he'd had to get out and walk along with the rest of the passengers. What we need in these parts, he thought, as he toiled up one steep incline after another, is a railway – and if it weren't for those blamed fools in York I could be building one

165

this very minute instead of enduring all this. It aggravated him that the wealthy men of his home city should still be dragging their feet. God knows he'd wined and dined 'em enough, and told them over and over again what fortunes they could make, yet they were still dithering and saying asinine things like ''Twill never catch on' and 'We must be cautious. There's no need for a rush'. Rush! he thought, irritably. They don't know the meaning of the word.

Whitby turned out to be a small, dishevelled fishing village, consisting of a few run-down houses clustered together on the cliffs on either side of the river Esk, the ruins of an ancient abbey looking romantic on the northern cliff-top, a harbour full of well-used fishing boats with stained and faded sails, and the Angel Inn which was where the stage set them all down.

The air was full of gulls, wheeling and screeching above their heads and dipping perilously close to their faces, and the place smelt of fish and tarred rope and the pungent smoke of coal fires and tobacco. There was a swing bridge over the river, which was the most rickety contraption he'd ever seen. It was made of sea-stained wood and seemed to be held together by ropes that were so old they were black and frayed and looked as if they would snap at the least exertion. Here's a place that needs waking up, he thought, and I'm just the man to do it. The thought cheered him. He stood at the quayside and watched as a boat set out to sea and the bridge was opened for it. It was done by pulleys and such a muddle of dangling ropes that one of them got caught in the rigging and boat and bridge were both brought to a standstill. The sight of such incompetence made him feel superior – and then laugh out loud. He left the crew struggling to disentangle the muddle and walked into the Angel, ready for ale and sustenance and feeling equal to anything.

The waiter was a burly man with a seafarer's roughened face. He wore blue breeches, a checked shirt and a clean white apron, carried a clean white cloth over his arm and recommended the sea bass.

As he seemed to be knowledgeable, George asked him if he knew when Mr Stephenson would be arriving.

'End of the week, sir,' the waiter told him. 'Very important man, is Mr Stephenson. He's a-comin' to tell us about the North Yorkshire Moors Railway. 'Tis all in the local paper, sir. Shall I bring you a copy?'

'Aye,' George said. 'That 'ud be handsome.'

It was also informative. Mr Stephenson's visit wasn't until Friday which was a long time for George to cool his impatient heels, but the meeting was taking place in the Angel, so it would be easy enough for him to attend it, and it was plain that the local worthies in this little village had a deal more sense than their cousins in York. They certainly didn't need anyone to wake *them* up. They'd already made up their minds that the North Yorkshire Moors Railway should come to their part of the world and had invited Mr Stephenson to come and tell them all about it. What was more, they seemed to have a sensible idea about what benefits a railway would bring to their village.

'The time will come,' their leader-writer said, *'when ordinary folk will be travelling abroad in the same way as the gentry do today, taking their ease in the spas and the fine towns. Some will undoubtedly come here to enjoy the sea air, which is well known to be beneficial to the senses and healing to the constitution. Let us make preparation for the changes that are coming.'*

Let us indeed, George thought, settling to his sea bass. The article had given him an idea. There was money to be made in this place and it wasn't just from the railways. When trainloads of city folk started coming here to enjoy the sea air, they'd need somewhere to stay while they enjoyed it, in boarding houses, like as not, or lodgings of some kind, happen a hotel for the most affluent. There was plenty of spare land hereabouts. He'd seen that as soon as he arrived. I will stroll about this evening, he decided, and see what's on offer.

What he found was several acres of unwanted scrubland on the hillside. Two days later he and the farmer who owned it had come to an agreement and the site was his. The next day he put an advertisement in the local paper asking for local builders – carpenters, bricklayers, plasterers and labourers – telling them to apply to him if they wished to work on a 'prestigious new development in the heart of town' and adding that he was offering a 'fair wage with bonuses to such as suit'. Then, since it was Friday, he settled himself in the bar ready to take his chance to meet the renowned Mr Stephenson.

After a few minutes he became aware that there had been a steady procession of well-dressed gentlemen walking through the bar and heading for the stairs and, as they were obviously arriving for the meeting, he finished his ale and followed them. They led him to an upstairs room, which was loud with booming greetings and neatly laid out ready for the event with several rows of chairs standing in line and, facing them, a table covered in green baize on which stood a tumbler and a carafe of water.

'Name of Hudson,' he said, as he edged his way through the first arrivals to nab a place in the front row. 'George Hudson from York. You've a good turn-out.'

'Are you into railways too, sir?' one man asked.

'Oh aye, sir,' George told him. 'Heavily. Like all men of good sense. Railways are t'future.'

That was Mr Stephenson's theme too and his audience cheered and stamped their feet to hear it. The most vociferous and obvious cheers came from Mr George Hudson. When the speech was over and the official thanks had been given, he stood up and walked to the table, holding out his hand.

'First-rate speech, if I may say so, Mr Stephenson,' he said. 'Needed sayin' did that.'

The famous man smiled his agreement.

It was encouragement enough. 'I'm one as knows, sir,' George said, 'on account of I'm a man what means to build railways, wherever there's a need of 'em.' And because he could see that Stephenson's interest was now suitably roused, he pressed on. 'Happen you'd care to join me for a drink or two, and I'll tell 'ee what I have in mind. They serve an excellent brandy here. Name of Hudson.'

By the end of a brandy-soaked evening and after considerable technical conversation, both men had established that they were two of a kind where the coming of the railway was concerned and that they should and would work together. Now, George thought, as they finally parted company, I shall get my railway company. There's nowt in t'way of it.

12

The first months of Jane's married life were so extraordinarily happy she felt she was still living in her dream. After years of being a servant in someone else's house, it was a joy to organize her home in exactly the way she wanted, to plan her own meals and eat them in her own dining room with her dear Nathaniel beside her. Her dear Nathaniel. He was everything she'd hoped and dreamed he might be and even the delights of running her own home paled into insignificance compared to the private and delectable pleasures of being his wife. Her brief affair with George Hudson had left her feeling that love was passionately urged but brutish in the act; now she was discovering what tenderness and delicacy were like and her senses were blooming.

The weeks passed in a glow of rewarding sensation. The months threaded her happiness with the heady colours of autumn. Now fires were lit to crackle in their new hearths and roar up their new chimneys and the first chills of coming winter brought hoar frost to the fields.

'We must hold a party at Christmas, Nat,' she said over breakfast one morning late in November. Outside their window a grey mist was swirling about the city walls but inside the room their fire was burning warmly.

'Indeed we must,' he agreed. 'Whom shall we invite?'

Her parents, naturally, and Milly and Aunt Tot and Audrey Palmer 'because she's the kindest girl I know and she has no family beyond the farm'.

'A family party.' He understood. 'You will need a new gown.'

'I shall wear my wedding gown,' she told him. ''Tis just the occasion for it.'

It was a surprise to her that the gown seemed to have shrunk. It was very tight about the waist and didn't fit at all well. She stood before the pier glass examining her image with some concern, aware that she'd put on rather a lot of weight since September, which was only just over ten weeks ago when all was said and done. And as she tried to adjust the dress over her burgeoning curves she suddenly realized what was happening to her. She was carrying. Of course. What a wonderful blissful thing. Oh, just wait till I tell Nathaniel. If he hadn't gone off to work she could have told him there and then but, never mind, waiting would make it sweeter.

She told him late that night when their love-making was over and they were cuddled together in their comfortable bed. It was a great surprise to her that instead of telling her how wonderful he thought it was or kissing her or doing any of the things she'd expected, he sprang from the bed, lit the candle and ran across the room to their linen press.

'Art tha not pleased?' she asked.

'Wait, wait,' he said, pulling the sheets and towels this way and that. 'I've something to show you.' And he pulled out a small brown box, much scuffed with age, carried it to the bed and laid it tenderly in her lap. 'Open it,' he said. ''Tis for you, with my love.'

It was a gold ring, set with blue stones, shaped like the petals of a flower and set about a central stone that shone so brightly in the candlelight she knew at once that it was a diamond. 'Oh Nathaniel!' she said.

'My father made it for my mother when I was born,' he explained, 'and when she died he gave it to me and made me promise I would give it to my wife when *our* first child was born. The blue stones are turquoise, which signify lifelong love, so he told me, and the one in the middle is a diamond, which signifies constancy.'

''Tis the most beautiful thing I ever saw,' she said and took his eager face between her hands and kissed him lovingly. 'Only 'twill be months afore our baby's born. Should 'ee not wait till then?'

'I couldn't wait,' he said. 'I love you too much.'

Jane spent the next morning writing invitations

172

to her Christmas party and the next afternoon she hired a pony and trap and went to visit her mother and father at Scrayingham, fidgeting with impatience all the way there because she couldn't wait to tell them her good news.

Her father said he 'wor reet glad to hear it' and her mother wept and said *she* weren't a bit surprised for she'd thought it likely last Thursday. 'What does our Milly think on it?' she asked.

'Nowt yet,' Jane admitted, 'on account of I've not told her.'

'She'll be reet happy for 'ee,' Mrs Jerdon said. 'That's certain sure.'

But Milly took the news coolly. 'I thought it like as not,' she said, 'being as you're married. 'Tis the way of it wi' married women. Look at Mrs Hudson. She has a baby every year.'

'You do exaggerate,' Jane teased. 'Every other year I'll grant but not every year.'

'I'll tell 'ee one thing,' Milly said. 'She gets cantankerous when she's in t'family way and she were short wi' my Dickie this morning. So nowt would surprise me.'

I'd get cantankerous if I were married to Mr Hudson, Jane thought, nasty bad-tempered thing, and she looked down at her new ring and was glad, all over again, that she'd chosen such a gentle loving man.

Her gentle loving man was in Tanner's Yard with Mr Hudson that afternoon examining a possible site for the start of the proposed York railway. They'd already looked at half a dozen possibilities but, in Nathaniel's opinion, this one was the

173

best. The yard was full of tanners all hard at work and it was an evil-smelling place, like all tanneries, the air rank with the stink of the raw hides that hung in rows waiting treatment, but it had one obvious advantage if they were to build a station and a railway line there and that was the long pit that had been dug out like a moat between the sheds. At that moment it was full of hideously stained water and very smelly but it lay at right angles to the city wall and was pointing in exactly the right direction for the rails that would carry Mr Hudson's trains out through the wall and off into the open countryside towards Leeds and Manchester.

'We would need to open an exit through the city wall,' he said to Mr Hudson.

George took that calmly. 'Aye. We would an' we will. Once we've got the city fathers on board 'twill all fall into line. You'll see. How soon can 'ee draw up a plan?'

As always Nathaniel was impressed by the confidence and energy of the man. 'By the end of the week,' he said.

'Mek it Thursday,' George told him. 'Now I'm off to woo the Tory Party.'

He will too, Nathaniel thought as he watched the portly figure striding purposefully out of the yard, for they both knew how important it was to have an MP onside if they were to get their proposal through the House of Commons, and even though York was a staunchly Whig town and had been for years, the Tories had friends in court.

The Tory club was in the centre of town and in

174

some disarray. The party funds were lower than they'd been in years and just at the very moment when they had the chance of an excellent candidate, the son of a baronet, Sir John Lowther of Swillington Park, no less. Sir John was a wealthy man and would undoubtedly back his son, but, in all honour, they had to match his contribution pound for pound, they could do no less, and at that moment they couldn't begin to see how it could be done. If they could persuade Mr Hudson to contribute....

Mr Hudson blew into their sober committee room like a gale, hand outstretched to greet them, the gold chain on his impressive fob-watch shining in the wintry light, loud, bold and the picture of confident wealth. Within minutes he had told John Henry Lowther he was just the man the town needed, commended the committee on the wisdom of their choice and invited them all to dine with him. They were swept along by his enthusiasm whether they would or no and, although some of them found his brashness hard to countenance, the gleam of his coin soon put such petty considerations to one side. By the end of that first dinner, they had decided that he was a strong, confident man, and one, moreover, who put his money where his mouth was. By the time they had partaken of his lavish hospitality at a party at his house in Monkgate, they had decided to invite him onto the committee.

John Henry was bewitched by him. Having been reared in the sedate and cultured environs of Swillington Park, he had never come across such a storm of a man.

'You should meet him, Father,' he said to his wealthy parent over dinner two weeks later. 'He's a rough diamond, I'll grant you, but a man of great strength and considerable vision. He saw at once that I was the man for York.'

Sir John condescended a faint smile.

'Believe me, Father,' John Henry urged, 'you really should meet him. In my opinion you would agree with him a deal more than you might imagine. He holds the soundest opinions.'

'A tradesman, I believe,' Sir John said.

'Yes, sir. A draper.'

'Does he hunt?' Sir John inquired.

'I doubt it,' his son had to admit. 'Drapers ain't huntin' men, by and large.'

'No,' his father agreed. But he had already decided that despite his shortcomings, Hudson was a man to be cultivated.

Jane's Christmas party was a much gentler and more loving occasion than the drunken feast George held at Monkgate but in its quiet, hospitable way it was every bit as successful. She and Nathaniel had made sure that their guests would be warm and well fed and when the meal was done and the servants who had stayed with them for the season were gathered in the kitchen for their own meal, she and her family gathered round the fire in the drawing room to roast chestnuts and tell one another ghost stories. At the end of the evening, when they went their separate ways to the beds Jane had prepared for them, Aunt Tot said she'd never known a Christmas so full of good things and Jane's mother and father and Audrey were so overwhelmed by those good things they all said they didn't know what to say. Only Milly found the words she needed.

She put her arms round her mother's neck and kissed her lovingly. 'Your baby's uncommon lucky to have *you* for a mother,' she said, 'as I should know.'

Jane was moved to tears. 'My dearest child!' she said, holding her close.

'Never a truer word,' Nathaniel told her, coming up beside them.

So their Christmas Day ended with happy kisses.

George Hudson's, on the other hand, ending with a bout of violent sickness. He'd drunk so much at the table he'd been feeling queasy ever since he retired to his room. Lizzie was sound asleep with her mouth open and she didn't stir as he splattered the carpet with the remains of his meal. Selfish woman.

He poured a little cold water from the ewer into the bowl and washed his face and hands, groaning and feeling sorry for himself. He was having to work far too hard to get this railway company up and running. Far too hard. Still, even if things *were* moving slowly, they were moving in the right direction. He'd discovered several very useful things during the course of the conversation that evening – most of them from John Henry, who was indiscreet when he was in his cups. The first was that Sir John was planning to set up a bank in York. He even had a name for it, apparently, the York Union Banking Company, so the plans must be well under way and, even more significantly, he'd estimated how much capital would be needed to get it established which, according to his son, was half a million pounds – a clear indication of how wealthy he was. Then, as if that weren't good news enough, he also discovered that the baronet had a powerful friend, one George Glyn, who besides being the chairman of Glyns, which was the best known bank in London, had also been appointed chairman of the proposed London and Birmingham Railway Company. Give me time, George thought, and I shall dine with the great. Meanwhile he couldn't lie here in this stink. He'd never get to sleep if he did. There was only one thing for it and that was to take himself off to the blue room. He groaned to his feet, stepped delicately round his vomit and staggered off to a cleaner bed.

The new year progressed from a very chill winter into the ease of spring and Jane began to make preparations for her baby's arrival. At the end of May she wrote to Audrey Palmer asking her if she would consider leaving her job as a dairy maid and coming to live in Shelton House with her to be the baby's nursemaid. *'You were so good to me when my Milly was born,'* she wrote, *'I can't think of anyone I would rather have to help me when this child arrives.'*

Audrey needed no urging. *'I could not think of nothing better,'* she wrote back, adding *'I could be there by Friday, that being the carter's day for York.'* And Friday it was. By the time June and the baby arrived, everything was ready and orderly.

Audrey had moved into the house and her new job, delighted to have a bed of her own in the nursery corner, and Mrs Hardcastle was making daily visits, not because there was anything amiss with either her patient or the baby but because Mr Cartwright had insisted on it.

He needn't have worried. His baby arrived with so little fuss that he was born, fed, washed and dressed within five quiet hours. Nathaniel would have named him only for some unaccountable reason Jane seemed to have taken against the name he'd chosen, which, naturally enough, given how much he admired the man, was George. She said it wouldn't do at all and her voice and her face were so fierce he gave in to her at once and tried to think of another name that would suit her better. In the end, for want of any other inspiration, he suggested Nathaniel, since that was his own name and his father's and she said that was much better and to show how well she approved of it shortened it at once and lovingly to 'my little Nat'.

He was an affable baby, and made no complaint even when he was passed from hand to hand like a sleeping parcel. Milly was very taken with him and spent more than an hour nursing him on that first afternoon, saying she'd forgotten how small newborn babies were. 'He makes Matthew look enormous.' And Audrey was totally enamoured, calling him her 'dear little duck' and waiting on him as if he were royalty. It was the happiest, easiest time.

Lizzie came to visit a fortnight later when Jane had finished lying in. She was so sorry to have taken so long to come and see them, she said, and tried to explain, getting steadily more and more flustered. 'Mr Hudson is so… What I mean to say is, he has such a lot of work to do and he does need me to be there although why that should be I can't imagine. 'Tis not as if…' But then Audrey carried the baby into the parlour and rescued her. 'Oh, what a dear pretty baby! Such big eyes! How happy you must be my dear, dear friend.'

Jane took the baby on her lap and motioned to Lizzie to sit beside her, which she did, leaning forward to slip a practised finger into the infant's small curled fist. 'They're so pretty at this age,' she said. Then she paused to take a kerchief from her reticule and held it in front of her mouth for several seconds.

'Are you not well?' Jane asked.

'A little sickness,' Lizzie said. 'Nowt to speak of. 'Twill pass.'

'You are carrying again,' Jane said.

'Aye,' Lizzie admitted. 'How quick you are, my dear. 'Tis due in January, so Mrs Hardcastle says, but I've been uncommon sickly from the word go, not that I'm complaining. I mean to say, that could be a good sign, couldn't it? I mean to say I were never sick wi' t'others an' if I'm sick this time happen 'tis a girl. I would so like a girl. Not that I don't like my boys. They're darlings all of 'em, especially my poor little James, but a girl would be so…'

'Would tea be helpful?' Jane offered.

'And then there's this dress,' Lizzie said. 'I'm sure I don't know what to wear for the best and 'tis such a worry. 'Tis such a grand occasion, you see, and up in London, what is worse, and I wouldn't want to let him down. The seamstress says blue and white are all the rage but I favour red and orange myself. Such pretty colours. What do 'ee think?'

Jane had to admit she knew nothing about the sort of gowns that would be worn at society dinners. 'But the seamstress should know,' she said. 'Happen you should be advised by her.'

Unfortunately Lizzie went her own way and chose a dress that was wildly unsuitable, being a concoction in yellow, amber and red. The next day the society gossips were busy in their parlours and salons tearing her to shreds for her lack of class. And two days later Milly had a letter telling her all about it. She read it through twice and on her afternoon off she took it to Shelton House to show to her mother.

It had come from the Lady Sarah Livingston, who was, as she invariably signed herself, *'your old friend from our nursery days at Foster Manor'*, and had been writing to her at frequent intervals ever since she started work with the Hudsons. Their letters were usually full of the latest news of their families but this one was rather different. It was bubbling with amusement at the terrible gaffs Mrs Hudson had made at a society dinner and the dreadful figure she'd cut. *'I know you work for her, my dear, but really she is quite, quite impossible. She is so fat and has absolutely no taste at all. Fat women should never wear yellow. Everybody knows that. I can't think what she was thinking of. Howsomever, poor taste one can forgive but lack of wit is*

181

something else entirely and she has no wit at all. When they asked if she would like sherry or port, she said she would have a bit of both. Can you imagine that? She was an absolute laughing stock. Emma and I have been in stitches ever since.'

Jane read it in silence, occasionally shaking her head.

'What do 'ee think of that?' Milly asked.

'She was always hoity-toity,' Jane said, 'but I'd never have thought she was spiteful. Poor Mrs Hudson.'

'Should I say summat when I write back?'

'No,' Jane said, 'you should not. There are plenty of other things to write about. Tell her about our little Nat. And ask after Felix.'

'Should I say summat to Mrs Hudson then?' Milly asked. 'To warn her.'

'No,' Jane said again.

'Will you?'

'No,' Jane said. ''Tis not for us to criticise our betters. Leave it to Mr Hudson. He was the one what took her there and exposed her to being a laughing stock and he ought to have known better. Let him deal with it.'

So they left it to George.

It was four weeks before Lizzie came visiting again and Jane half expected her to be cast down but, on the contrary, she was triumphantly happy.

'Oh, 'twere a great success,' she said when Jane asked her about the dinner. 'I can't think why I were so worried about it. I were foolish, that's the size of it. Mr Hudson were that pleased, you'd never believe. He said I were the best dressed woman there. A credit to him, he said.'

182

So Jane changed the subject and asked after her health instead. But later that afternoon, as she sat comfortably in her bedroom suckling her baby, she turned the conversation over in her mind and decided that she couldn't make any sense of it. If George had really told poor Lizzie that she was the best dressed woman there, when it was plain from what Sarah had said that everybody else had a very different opinion, he was either blind to what people were saying or he was deliberately telling her lies. Either way it didn't show him in a very good light. But she must be charitable. Happen he was so busy climbing the social ladder, he didn't notice things.

That summer was what Mrs Cadwallader called 'a mixed bag what we could well do without', with days of blue skies and strong sunshine followed by days when the sky was heavy with sodden grey clouds and the showers were sudden and drenching. Jane was glad to stay at home with her little Nat when the weather was bad and saw to it that there were always warm towels ready for his father when he came home from a day on one of Mr Hudson's railway sites because on far too many occasions he was drenched to the skin.

'We can't have 'ee catching cold,' she said, when he thanked her. *'That* wouldn't do at all.'

But in the event it wasn't Nathaniel who took harm from the rain, it was Lizzie's baby, Matthew.

Jane was in her parlour, sewing a new gown for Nat, who was rapidly growing out of his old ones, when the parlour maid arrived with a message from Mrs Hudson. It was a roughly written note, short and to the point. *'Please come dear friend. Matthew has taken a fever. I am at my wits' end.'*

What followed was painful in the extreme for both women. The fever was sharp and virulent. Within three days the little boy was so ill he couldn't keep anything down and he was losing weight visibly, lying motionless in his sour-smelling cot with his eyes tightly shut, as if he'd given up on life. Jane visited every day as soon as she'd settled Nat and she and Lizzie kept vigil and did what they could to ease his suffering. They tried coaxing him to take sips of water but that only exhausted him; they cleaned his soiled clothes but that exhausted him so much he was gasping for breath; and from time to time Lizzie eased him gently out of his cot and took him on her lap to nurse him and croon to him and tell him how much she loved him but he was too far gone to hear her. He died in the small hours of the tenth day without opening his eyes. She was inconsolable.

'I can't keep my babies alive,' she wept to Jane. 'First my poor little James and I *did* try. I tried so hard. No one will ever know how hard I tried. And now my poor Matthew. I knew he wouldn't live. I said so at the time. I did, didn't I? You remember. Oh, what's to become of me?'

Jane did her best to comfort her, pointing out that most women lost at least one baby in the course of their lives, 'that seems to be the way of it', that she still had Dickie and another child on the way and that there would be others, 'bound to be' – but nothing she said made any difference. Lizzie didn't want 'others'. She wanted James and Matthew and she wept for them both uncontrollably. It took more than two months before she could take any comfort from anything at all. And as far as Jane could see, George wasn't being any help to her at all, for he was always out at one meeting or another and seemed to be leaving her to get on with it on her own. But he was certainly climbing. By the time Christmas arrived he had become the treasurer of the York Tory Party and had befriended the Tory MP for Sunderland, who was also a London alderman and a former Lord Mayor of London, no less.

'This Christmas, we'll throw the biggest party this city's ever seen,' he told his long-suffering Lizzie. 'Make 'em all sit up, eh?'

Lizzie may have learnt to cope with her grief but she was now so heavily pregnant it was all she could do to sit still, leave alone up, as she complained to Jane when she visited her in the new year.

'Not that I can tell Mr Hudson,' she said, shifting her bulk uncomfortably on Jane's padded settee. '*That* wouldn't do at all, would it, being he's so particular to have everything just so, and of course he's right to have everything just so, when so much depends on it, but, I tell 'ee, there are times when my back aches summat cruel, specially when they go on, and they *do* go on, some of 'em. I shall be glad when this one's born. Oh, I do so hope 'twill be a girl.'

It was a private and much-wept disappointment to her when the child turned out to be yet another boy, healthy enough and really quite pretty, but a boy. His father called him George – 'What better name, eh?' – but otherwise paid no attention to him. He was too busy pushing for a post with the newly formed York Union Bank. And the push, as Lizzie discovered a few weeks later, meant that she was expected to join him at another grand party in London.

'Although,' as she confided to Jane, 'how I shall mek out wi' my poor Georgie to feed I do not know. I suppose I shall have to tek him with me and what a to-do that will be, I dread to think.'

'Then tell Mr Hudson it can't be done,' Jane said practically.

But Lizzie was shocked. 'I can't do that, Jane. Not when so much depends on it. No, no, I must mek shift somehow or other.'

So she went to London with her baby and his nursemaid and so much luggage that they were hard put to get it all in the coach.

Milly didn't think much of it. 'She should stand up to him,' she said to her mother. 'Dragging all that way with a new baby. 'Tis the most ridiculous thing I ever heard. What if he takes a fever? What will she do then?'

'I daresay they have surgeons in London,' Jane said. But she had to admit that she agreed with her daughter and didn't think her poor friend was being wise. 'Howsomever, there's nowt we can say to change her mind. That's plain and obvious. He's her husband and if he wants his own way he'll get it, on account of she'll do whatever he tells her. He's got her under his thumb.'

But the months passed and Lizzie obeyed her

husband and only complained about him very occasionally and Jane enjoyed hers and rejoiced in him every single day and their children thrived, despite Lizzie's trip to London. At the end of the year, they discovered that they were both carrying again and that their babies would be born within weeks of each other, which pleased them both. This time Lizzie didn't say anything about how much she wanted a daughter, accepting that she was doomed to produce boys and only boys. Even when July came and Jane gave birth to her third child and her second daughter, she kept quiet and tried not to show how envious she was. So it was a surprise and a reward to her when her own fifth baby turned out to be a girl too. The two babies were christened in the Church of the Holy Trinity together, Mary Cartwright and Ann Hudson, and it would have been hard to say which of the two mothers was the happiest. And ten months later, when Lizzie had yet another boy, they made a celebration of that too and took young Dickie and all four of their babies to the church to see him christened John.

And so they continued until the cholera came to York.

13

It began slowly on a bright April morning with an unobtrusive report in the *York Courant*. Two patients, both resident in Skeldergate and both *'men in poor circumstances'* had been taken to the hospital suffering from Cholera Morbus. Two days later one of them was dead, there were thirteen new cases in the town and the new Board of Health had been called to a meeting to decide what should be done.

George Hudson had no doubt about what action should be taken and demanded it forcefully. The cholera was spread by effluvia. Very well then. The first thing they should do was strip the patients of their clothes, the minute they arrived in the hospital, and take every single garment away to be burnt. If they died, their bedding should be burnt too.

'"Twill cost,' his fellow members told him.

'Aye,' he said, grimly. '"Twill. But think on't. If we allow it to spread into an epidemic, *that'll* cost a darn sight more. We need to fight this and fight it now.'

'It's all very well saying burn their clothes,' another board member objected. 'Some of 'em might not have other clothes to wear. Have 'ee thought of that?'

He hadn't but he was quite capable of thinking on his feet. 'Then we must collect old clothes from folk as can spare 'em,' he said, 'and provide replacements. We could use t'Guildhall as a collection point. If t'committee are agreeable, I will organize it.'

He was full of energy and determination, driving them as he used to drive the horses when he was a lad, allowing them to snort and balk and pull at the traces but knowing they'd give in and do what he wanted, come the finish. After all, they had no option for he was George Hudson, the man who got things done. It was a disagreeable surprise to him when he finally returned to Monkgate, a great deal later than he expected but glowingly pleased with himself, to be met with a furious attack in his own dining room.

Lizzie was standing by the window where she been watching out for him for the last hour and she was incandescent with fear and fury, her face so twisted by it that for a few seconds he didn't recognize her and thought he'd come into the wrong house.

'What are you going to do about this cholera?' she said, attacking him before he could open his mouth to tell her how successful the meeting had been. 'Tell me, why don't you. Don't just stand there. There's people dropping like flies. 'Tis no earthly good you pulling a face. I *know* and don't 'ee think I don't. Like flies. 'Twas in the paper. You must *do* summat. Oh, what are we to do? I'll not lose *another* baby. Not to the cholera. I've lost two and that's enough, I'll not lose another. I couldn't stand it. You must tek us out of here this minute. This very minute as ever is. Afore we all tek ill and die.'

He tried to bluff her into a more amiable mood. 'You'll not tek ill,' he said. 'You're safe here.' And he ventured a joke to clinch it. 'Safe as houses, you might say.' It was a waste of effort. She was scowling worse than ever. So he changed tack again. 'See sense, woman. Nobody's dropping like flies. That's all silly talk.'

'Silly talk!' she screamed at him. 'Silly talk! 'Twas in the paper. Dropping like flies.'

'One or two cases, that's all,' he said, 'and they're in the Shambles and Skeltergate. Nowt for you to worry your head about.'

'All over the meat!' she shrieked. 'What we're supposed to eat. Oh, I won't stay here. Mek up your mind to it, George. Not in this hell-hole. Not another minute. You must *do* summat. Don't you understand? You must get us out of it.'

He didn't know how to cope with her. She looked as if she'd gone lunatic, with her eyes staring and her hair falling out of her cap and her face twisted as if it was being blown sideways by some great gale.

'Do you hear me?' she shrieked.

'Aye,' he said angrily. 'The whole house can hear you. Have 'ee no shame?'

'Shame!' she yelled. 'Don't talk to me about shame. You're the one who should be ashamed. Leaving us here in this hell-hole. You're a disgrace to the universe.'

'Shut your mouth!' he yelled back at her, now thoroughly angered. 'I won't be spoken to like that in my own house. Do you hear me?'

'I'll speak as I please,' she shouted back. ''Tis my children we're talking about. Don't you understand? My children, what I love to distraction. I'll not stand here and let 'em be took by the cholera and you needn't think it. I've lost two and I'll not lose any more. 'Tis more than human flesh and blood can stand.'

Even in his anger he could see that she was lunatic. Lunatic and out of control. And although it was ridiculous and unpleasant to have to admit it, he knew he'd have to give in to her or she'd go on shrieking all night.

'Very well then,' he said, calming himself with an effort. 'Since you can't see sense and you're determined to make a scene, you can go to Whitby, and good riddance to you. I will order the carriage for you first thing tomorrow morning. But I warn you, you'll not be very comfortable. Some of the houses are finished but they're poorly furnished. They're not what you're used to.'

She wasn't the slightest bit interested in furnishings or comfort. 'Oh thank God!' she said. 'Thank God! I'll go and get packed.'

'What about dinner?' he said. But she was already out of the door.

It seemed most peculiar to be dining alone, especially when he'd had such a victory over the Board, but what else can a man do when his wife runs lunatic?

Jane Cartwright was worrying about the cholera too. She and Nathaniel were discussing what to do over their dinner.

'Should I take them to Ma's, do 'ee think?' Jane asked.

'Would she have room?' Nathaniel said. His face

was creased with concern, for really this outbreak was very worrying, especially as he would be working on the Selby–Leeds railway for the next couple of weeks and wouldn't be able to get home. He couldn't bear to have any of his darlings taken ill with the cholera. That was too dreadful to contemplate.

'She'd mek room. I'm sure.'

There was a modest knock on the dining room door and Audrey came in, very quietly because she could see they were talking.

'Which one is it?' Jane said anxiously. Audrey always came down at once to tell her if either of her babies was stirring.

'Neither of 'em,' Audrey said at once. 'Sleeping like babes, they are, dear little lambs. Not a peep out of 'em. No, no. 'Tis Mrs Hudson come. Shall I show her in here or tek her to t'parlour?'

She was ushered into the dining room and urged to sit at the table with them, flustered and dishevelled as she was. She was red in the face from her exertions and so out of breath from her rush to their house that it was several seconds before she could tell them why she'd come. But when she did, what she had to say – once they'd managed to decipher it – was the solution to their worries.

'I've had such a to-do as you'd never believe,' she said, 'what wi' packing and worriting an' all, I've been at my wits' end all day. I've not know'd where to turn, to tell 'ee true, and then Mr Hudson being... Well, you know how he can be sometimes. Not that I blame him. He works so hard he can't be expected... But really he were so late home I thought he were never coming but he did in the end, thank the Lord, although he weren't at all agreeable about it – disagreeable is more the word, truth to tell, well, you know what I mean – perhaps I shouldn't say disagreeable but anyroad I won through in the end, my dear, can 'ee imagine? – although how I did it I really cannot think – and we're going tomorrow and not a minute too soon. I thought of you in the middle of the packing, my dear, and how worried you must be – well, we all are. Who wouldn't be? And I thought, I'll go straight round and see if she'd like to come with us. What I mean to say, if *you'd* like to come with us, which I'm sure you would, what I mean to say I hope you will. This is all such a worry. You and the babies and Audrey and anyone else you need. The house will be plenty big enough. It's going to be a hotel.' At which she stopped, now being completely out of breath, and beamed at her friend.

It was Nathaniel who made sense of it. 'You are leaving York?' he said, and it was only just a question.

She nodded, puffing from her exertions.

'Tomorrow?'

Another nod.

'Where are you going?'

This time she managed an answer. 'Why, to Whitby, Mr Cartwright, where Mr Hudson has all those houses and a hotel and I don't know what all.'

''Tis a kindly offer,' he said, inclining his head towards her and smiling, 'and we thank you for it.' Then he turned to Jane. 'I think you should accept it, my dear.'

So early the next morning the two families set out, travelling in a convoy of two four-horse carriages, followed by a dray-cart carrying their luggage. They were a large company: Lizzie and Jane and their six children, Audrey and Milly with their charges and Sally, who was now nurse-maid to Georgie, Ann and little John, and very proud of her new status and her new uniform, and Mrs Cadwallader to cook for them and two of Lizzie's scullery maids to share all the other work and travel in the cart and look after the luggage, to say nothing of three Moses baskets for the babies, three picnic hampers full of food, various sunshades and umbrellas, a jar of sugar plums to placate the four-year-olds if they got fretful and Dickie's little dog, Spot, which was not impressed by being put in a coach and escaped the minute he could and barked off to spook the cart horses.

Lizzie was harassed and anxious while they were packing and clambering aboard, but once they'd left the terrible danger of York behind them and were away from the smoke and the stink and out in the clear, clean air of the countryside, she grew steadily more cheerful and by the time they'd passed a place called Norton, which the coach-man said was their halfway mark, she was quite herself again. They found a suitable field where they could stop for their picnic and they all tumbled out of the carriages and stretched their limbs while Mrs Cadwallader and Jane and Lizzie unpacked the hampers and spread the cloth on

194

the grass and handed out pies and fruit and table napkins as if it was the sort of thing they did every day of their lives.

'Isn't this fun!' Lizzie said to her eldest.

And Dickie, who was eight years old and adventurous, said it was 'the best ever'.

It got even better on the second leg of the journey for now they were climbing some extremely steep hills and had to get out and walk to help the horses, which meant that he and Spot could go running off into the fields again and although both of them were getting very grubby nobody seemed to mind. And best of all was when they'd reached the top of a particularly long climb: when they looked down, there was a blue lake shining beneath them. It was the sparkliest thing he'd ever seen and so big he couldn't see across it to the other side.

'That,' Milly told him, 'is because it's the sea.'

'Where does it end?'

'The sea don't end,' she said. 'Don't 'ee remember, I showed 'ee on the globe. All that blue. It goes round the world, round and round and round.'

Wonders would never cease.

'When we get to Whitby,' Milly told him, 'what is where we're a-going, we'll be right alongside of it and you can walk into it and get your feet wet. How will that be?'

He could barely believe it. 'Truly?' he asked.

That made her grin. 'Truly,' she said. 'An' I'll come with 'ee and get *my* feet wet an' all.'

Whitby was a revelation to all of them, all those boats in the harbour and men in great boots and knitted caps and jerseys instead of jackets, and huge baskets standing on the quayside full of fish, and great grey and white birds everywhere swooping and calling and snatching up pieces of fish in their great beaks, 'caw, caw, caw', and everything smelling salty and a rickety bridge that Milly said was like something out of a fairy tale.

'How we ever got across in one piece,' Lizzie said, when they'd left the harbour and were all safely on the other side of it, 'I shall never believe.'

And then a town that was built on a hillside, where they had to get out and climb, through narrow alleys and over higgledy-piggledy cobbles and past the oldest shops and houses they'd ever seen, even in the Shambles, until they came to Mr Hudson's wide streets and squares and the huge house that was going to be a hotel and where they were going to live. They were met at the door by Mr Hudson's younger brother Charles, who was quiet and gentle and seemed to be the caretaker. When he heard who they were he hastened to assure them that, although the hotel might look *'summat empty'*, appearances were deceptive. There *were* rooms ready furnished that he thought might suit them admirably and bowed to indicate that they should follow him and see if they agreed. What he showed them was a suite of eight rooms, a dining room that was really rather fine, a drawing room, five bedrooms and a dear little parlour overlooking the sea.

'There are servants' quarters alongside the kitchens,' he said. 'And coach houses, of course.'

''Tis all most satisfactory,' Lizzie told him, when she'd carried out a full inspection of all the rooms they would need, and she smiled at him happily. 'Thank 'ee kindly, Mr Hudson.'

'I'm glad to have been of service,' he said, smiling back. 'I live in t'house on t'corner of t'terrace, should you have need of me. I will call in t'morning and see if there's owt else in the way of furnishings you might be needing.'

Then what a flurry and a scurry there was as the boxes were carried upstairs and unpacked and the coaches eased into the coach house and the horses led to the stables to be fed and watered and the kitchen fire lit and the scullery maids sent to the harbour to buy fish for their supper. And in the middle of it all Mr Hudson returned with two loaves and a pitcher of milk and a note from his wife to tell them where the best fruit and salads could be had.

After he'd left them for the second time, Lizzie said he was so unlike George she could hardly believe they were related, leave alone brothers. 'I mean to say, such a *kind* man.' There was a lot she found hard to believe on that first day – how quickly they settled in, how delicious freshly caught fish could be, how kind it was of Mrs Hudson to send them bread and milk, how good the children were being and how obediently they'd gone to bed and, above all, how absolutely amazing it was that she'd stood up to her husband.

'If anyone had told me when I were first wed that I'd ever, ever dream of doing such a thing,' she said to Jane when the children had been coaxed to bed and they were on their own together in the parlour, 'I'd have told 'em 'twere a nonsense. And yet I *did*. Can 'ee believe it? I don't know what got into me.'

Jane was trying to make herself comfortable in the armchair, which, because it was so newly upholstered, was rather unyielding. It had been a long day with far too many new things to be absorbed and understood and she was missing Nathaniel a bit too keenly now that the rush of their journey was over and the children were settled for the night. She spoke out before she could stop to think that it might not be sensible to be so frank. ''Twill have done him good,' she said. 'High time someone stood up to him.'

Lizzie was horrified to hear her husband criticized. 'Oh, we mustn't say that,' she protested. 'I mean to say, he's a good man. Allus has been. If it hadn't been for the cholera and me being sick wi' worry, I would never have done such a thing. Never in a thousand years. I know he has a bit of a temper but that's on account of all the hard work he has to do. I mean to say, just think of what a lot he does, what with the railways and all these properties and the Board of Health and I don't know what-all. I never knew such a man for work. He has to make a stand to get things done.'

'Aye,' Jane said, pretending to agree. 'Happen. But making a stand and being a bully is two different things, don't 'ee think?'

'He's never a bully,' Lizzie said loyally.

He were a bully when he were a lad, Jane thought, and if I weren't such a coward I'd tell you so.

It would have surprised her to know that at that moment bully-boy George was visiting the sick in the most evil-smelling slums in the city and not only commiserating with them in their distress but making diligent notes about what could be done to help them.

That afternoon the chairman of the Board of Health had requested that the members of the Board should provide him with the latest inform-ation on the progress of the epidemic. There was no one to keep him at home now that Lizzie had left so, as soon as he'd finished his solitary dinner and taken a glass of brandy to sustain him, he put on his hat and set off along Goodramgate to-wards old Christ Church and the Shambles to see what was happening.

Until that evening he'd never ventured into the squalid alleys in that part of town. There'd never been anything to take him there. It was just a place where the servants went to buy meat. A place to avoid. He walked boldly into the foetid darkness like a man exploring a foreign country.

At first he found it difficult to see where he was going because there were only a couple of rush lights attached to the walls, but after a while his eyes adjusted and then he was profoundly shocked by what he saw. The cobbles of the alley were so broken and distorted that what he was stepping over was largely bare earth trodden into a mire. The houses rose crookedly from the filth, leaning against one another like drunks, their walls scabbed by occasional flakes of chipped plaster, their windows so grey with dust it was impossible to see through them, their greasy doors standing ajar. The smell of vomit and shit was overpowering. Pity rose in his throat like bile and for a second he was tempted to turn back and go home. But he'd come here to see what was happening and he could hardly run at the first difficulty. There was no honour in that. He covered his mouth with his hand and stepped through the nearest door.

He was in a dark evil-smelling hall, where two dishevelled men wearing an extraordinary combination of ancient clothes and hats that were more grease than cloth were leaning against the walls smoking clay pipes. They looked at him with undisguised suspicion for several long seconds but eventually one of them leant towards him and spoke. 'What would you be afther, sor?'

'Board of Health,' George explained. 'Name of Hudson. Come to see what help you need.'

The man took his pipe out of his mouth and bellowed towards the nearest door. 'Bridie! Bridie!' And when there was no answer, he roared again. 'Bridie, will ye come out of it dis minute, woman.'

The woman who appeared at the door was as down-at-heel as he was. She was wearing a man's jacket, a filthy flat cap, a stained shawl and an apron made of old sacking tied round her waist with a length of rope. 'Stow your row,' she said to the man. 'Who's de gent'man?'

George introduced himself again, adding, 'Happen you could show me round.'

She took him from room to overcrowded room,

each one darker and more noxious than the last. There was a family in every room and at least one sick person in every family. The sick lay on the floor on straw pallets, their vomit beside them and their children huddled in corners, bare-footed and timorous as if the horror was too great for them to believe or understand. He hadn't known until then that there were people living in his city in such utter squalor.

In the third room, Bridie confided that she was the midwife. 'I lays 'em out, may God rest deir souls.' In the fifth they found a small boy sitting in a corner howling like a dog and when George raised his eyebrows at the noise, she explained, 'Sure he's hungry, poor soul, since his ma went to glory.' Her matter-of-fact acceptance of the situation made George feel angry. Dammit, he thought, this is no way to treat an epidemic. These people need cleaning up and proper nursing. The lad needs feeding. Something must be done and done quickly. He made notes in his notebook and moved on to the next room.

The next afternoon he presented his report to the Board.

'Our first priority,' he said, 'must be to provide t'children and t'destitute with food, bread and soup and such like. That is imperative. We must open a public subscription fund to pay for it. I will personally donate £500 to start it. Then we must provide more beds in the hospital and more surgeons to attend 'em.'

'How many beds did you have in mind?' one of the more timorous members wanted to know.

His answer was immediate. 'Fifty,' he told

them. 'We're dealing with an epidemic.'

'Oh, I wouldn't say that,' his colleague demurred.

'Well, *I* would,' George said, forcefully. 'I've been there and I've seen it.'

The first soup kitchen was opened three days later.

In Whitby the sun was shining, the sky was summertime blue and Dickie and Spot and the toddlers were paddling in the sea with Milly in happy attendance with her skirts pinned up, wading up to her knees in the water. It was a daily habit and one they never tired of, even though they were now into their fifth week away from home. On that morning Jane and Lizzie had packed a picnic lunch and gone down to the beach with them and watched while they jumped in the water and splashed one another.

'This is doing them so much good,' Lizzie said, 'I've a mind to make it an annual occurrence. A holiday by the sea. What do 'ee think?'

''Twould depend on t'length of it,' Jane said honestly. 'I'd not want to be away from Mr Cartwright for too long.' This five-week separation had been very difficult and although she was grateful to Lizzie for taking them all out of danger she couldn't wait to be back in her own house.

But York wasn't pronounced clear of the cholera until the end of June so they had to stay where they were. And by then George had become embroiled in a furious row with the Board of Health. When the two families returned, the town was seething with gossip about it. Peggy,

Jane's parlour maid-cum-lady's maid, regaled her with a detailed account of it almost as soon as she got back.

'He called the chairman a blamed old fool,' she said. 'What a thing to say. A blamed old fool what wouldn't know the truth if it jumped up and bit him. And then he said he was a doddering idiot and he ought to stand down afore he fell down and mek way for someone who knew what was what. I never heard the like.'

'What brought *that* about?' Jane asked. It sounded exactly the sort of thing George would say. She'd heard worse when he'd been roaring at Lizzie. But there had to be a reason for it.

''Twas the dead bodies,' Peggy explained, as she hung Jane's jacket in the closet. 'There were so many of 'em you see, and Mr Hudson reckoned they should be buried outside t'city walls, on account of the effluvia, what he said spreads the disease, what could be right when you comes to think on it, on account of it must be summat. Anyroad, he had a plot of land what would suit, seemingly, and he meant to have 'em use it. Only t'Board stood up against him and said he were out to mek a profit and it got nasty. 'Twere all over town the next day.'

'What was the upshot?' Jane asked, although she already knew the answer.

'Oh, he got his own way,' Peggy said. 'They've been burying 'em in his graveyard ever since. But what a way to go on! Roarin' an' hollerin'.'

She was interrupted before she could tell her mistress any more for there was a sudden thunder of feet on the stairs, the door was flung open and

Nathaniel strode into the room, beaming and holding out his arms to his family.

Then there was a commotion as the children ran full tilt at their father and were caught up in his arms one after the other to be tossed into the air and caught and kissed. Audrey and Peggy shadowed tactfully away and left them to their reunion and they were all so happy they never saw them go.

'I *did* miss you, Papa,' Nat said, clinging about Nathaniel's neck.

'And I missed you, little one,' Nathaniel told him, 'but never mind, we're back together now.'

'Did you miss me?' Jane teased, smiling into his eyes.

'Aye, a little,' he teased back, but his rapturous face gave the lie to his words.

This is where I should be, Jane thought, here at home with my dear Nathaniel and my babies. Not with Lizzie Hudson, kind though she is. And as for George, he may do as he pleases and suffer the consequences. 'Tis all one with me. I'm home.

But in fact some of the consequences of George's blazing row were not what she might have expected. Although there were plenty of people who castigated Mr Hudson for his boorish behaviour, there were as many others who admired it and told one another that he might have a rough edge to his tongue but he'd been right about the cemetery and, what was more, he was plainly a man who got things done.

Early in the new year, to his personal delight and few people's surprise, he was voted onto the council and when spring came and the York Union Bank was officially opened, he bought a large number of shares and was appointed a director. Now, and at last, he had a position in the town. There was nothing to stand in the way of his railway committee.

14

The upper room in Mrs Tomlinson's hotel in Low Petergate on that crisp December evening was packed to the walls and loud with excitement. George stood behind the baize-covered table waiting to take charge of the meeting and watched and listened with enormous satisfaction as more and more men arrived to join the throng and the noise of their mutual greetings grew deafening. There was no doubt now that the wealthy lawyers and businessmen of York had finally understood that a railway would bring higher profits to the town and that *he*, George Hudson, was a man to follow. Time to call them to order, he thought, and boomed at them that they should 'pray be seated, gentlemen'.

The speeches from the floor were extremely gratifying for they began with a clear statement that a railway would be beneficial to the town and it came from one of the town's leading businessmen, a gentleman called James Meek, who was a Whig and had the ear of the local MP.

One or two voices were raised to express concern about the possibility that the trains might carry passengers. They reminded George of his Uncle Matthew, but he dealt with them patiently. He'd been sure of his success as soon as he called the meeting and the knowledge made him uncharacteristically tolerant.

'Our line will certainly carry a deal of freight,' he told them, 'that being the principle reason for bringing it into existence, as we all know, howsomever, in my humble opinion, 'twould be folly to preclude the possibility of carrying passengers. The Liverpool and Manchester Railway carries passengers already, as I'm sure you know, and is making a handsome profit out of it. If I'm any judge, and I think I can say I know as much as most on the subject, rail travel will soon be the preferred mode of transport, being, as it will assuredly be, fast, comfortable and dependable.'

There was no gainsaying him. He made sure of that. By the end of the evening, after several rousing speeches and a steady consumption of brandy, the York Railway Committee had been voted into existence, with Mr James Meek as its chairman, Mr James Richardson as its solicitor, and Mr George Hudson as treasurer. It was, George thought, as he strolled happily home to Monkgate, with a sharp frost under his feet and a sky full of bold white stars above his head, a thoroughly satisfactory outcome. And the best thing about it was that it was only just the beginning. There was more and better to come. I'm the richest man in York by a long chalk now, he thought. Just give me a few more years an' a few more railways, an' I'll be the richest man in England. There'll be no stopping me. Wait till I tell Lizzie.

It was a disappointment to find that, late though it was, Lizzie wasn't in bed and waiting for him. Fussing with one of the children, he thought, and strode off to find her.

She was in Dickie's room, sitting by the bed, looking anxious, her long face darkly shadowed by the gas light, with Milly standing beside her, demure in her dressing gown and looking even more anxious.

'Ah,' he said. 'There you are. Come to bed, woman. I've summat to tell 'ee.'

She didn't appear to have heard him. 'He's not at all well,' she said, looking at the little boy, who certainly had a very flushed face and was tossing his head from side to side on the pillows. 'Poor little mite. He's been coughing half the night, hasn't he, Milly?'

'He's in a blue funk because I told him he was going to school,' George said. 'That's all. Come to bed. I've summat to tell 'ee. Summat important.'

She didn't move. 'I'll be along presently,' she said, not even looking up. 'When I've just got him settled, poor lamb.'

'Goddamnit!' he roared at her. 'Am I not to be allowed to speak to my wife in my own house? Do as you're told, woman, and come to bed. The girl'll see to him.'

The girl glared at him but Lizzie rose stiffly and reluctantly to her feet and bent to kiss the boy's hot head. She was carrying again and her pregnancy was making her look fat and awkward. She bent her head towards Milly and whispered to her please to let her know if there was any change, then she waddled after her husband.

'He's such a bully,' Milly told her mother three days later when she was visiting Shelton House. 'He treats her like a servant.'

'Nowt would ever surprise me wi' that one,' Jane said. 'He's a brute. Allus was. Come up to the nursery and see what your brother and sister have got for Christmas.'

'Is it Christmas already?' Milly laughed.

'It *is* for Mr Cartwright,' Jane said, laughing too as she led her daughter upstairs. 'He couldn't wait to give it to them. Not even for a week. I never saw such excitement.'

It was a painted rocking horse with a leather saddle and a thick mane of grey horsehair. The sight of it took Milly straight back to the nursery of her childhood. 'Oh, Ma,' she said, 'do 'ee remember our horse at Foster Manor?'

'I've been remembering it ever since Mr Cartwright took off the wrapper,' Jane said. 'Remembering and wondering how they all are.'

'Felix is up at Oxford,' Milly said, automatically lifting her sister into the saddle. 'Sarah told me in her last letter. Enjoying it no end, she said.'

'He was such a dear little boy,' Jane said rather wistfully.

'And now you've got a dear little boy of your own,' Milly told her briskly. 'Hasn't she, Nat? And two dear little girls, even if one's not quite as little as she was.'

Outside their long window it was starting to snow, the light flakes tossing and dancing in the cold air.

'Loo'! Loo'!' Mary called, pointing at it. 'Wha's dat?'

'That's snow,' Milly told her, 'and if it settles we'll go outside and build a snowman.'

Which they did, to the children's intense excitement. Playing with them, as they wielded their spades and patted the solid sides of their creation and were lifted up to give their beautiful snowman a hat for his icy head and a carrot for his nose and two round black pebbles for his eyes, Jane knew she had never been so happy in all her life.

'If I could only get my Milly to leave Monkgate and come and live here with us,' she said to Nathaniel later that night, 'I'd never want another thing.'

'Happen she'll join us when Dickie goes away to school,' Nathaniel said.

But fate had other and more terrible plans for Dickie and his father, as they were to find out in the next three months, for the little boy was seriously ill and the racking cough and the exhausting fevers continued, despite everything Lizzie could do to ease them, like keeping a kettle steaming in the bedroom or heating coal tar in a pumice-stone saucer until it let off healing fumes, which the pharmacist promised her was 'just the thing' for coughs and rheums.

'He'll be better come the spring,' she said to Milly, her face strained with the need to hope. ''Tis just this bitter cold what does it, that's all. He'll be better come the spring, don' 'ee think so.'

But the spring came, at first tentatively but then

with encouraging warmth and strength, and the fevers continued and got worse. And then at the end of March, the child developed a rash of small red spots and when Mrs Hardcastle was called to attend him, she took one look at his labouring chest and diagnosed the measles, instructing that a sheet dipped in disinfectant should be hung across the bedroom door, that only Lizzie and Milly should enter the bedroom and that the other children should be kept well out of their brother's way. "Tis a mortal powerful infection,' she said to Lizzie, 'and you'll not want them to tek it too.'

It was indeed mortal. Five days later, in the small hours of a very chill morning, Dickie Hudson gave up his unequal struggle against the terrible combination of consumption and measles and died in his mother's arms.

Lizzie was wild with grief. 'Three of them,' she wept to Jane, when her old friend came hurrying round to comfort her. 'Three! I can't bear it. First my poor little James and he was such a pretty baby, you never saw such a pretty baby, and then my poor little Matthew just when I thought he was better and now my dear darling Dickie. Oh, what did I ever do to deserve it? I've loved them more than I can tell 'ee, much more, oh much, much more. I'd have given *anything* to keep them alive. Anything at all. I don't know how I shall go on, I truly don't.'

'No, my dear,' Jane said, putting her arms round Lizzie's pitifully bowed shoulders and holding her gently. 'I can see you don't.'

"Tis more than human flesh and blood can

210

stand,' Lizzie wept. "'Tis all very well George saying *'you'll have others'*. I don't want others. I want my dear darling Dickie and my darling Matthew and my poor little James. Oh, oh, what's to become of us? And that poor little dog howling all the time.'

It was impossible to find anything to say that would comfort her so Jane simply went on holding her and stroking her tear-damp hair until the worst of her grief was over. It was a terrible time. And it got worse when she finally said goodbye to Lizzie and went downstairs to the back door for she found Milly sitting in the kitchen, rigidly upright on one of the kitchen chairs, with a carpet bag at her feet and her face under such tight and ugly control that it hurt Jane simply to see it.

'My dear?' she said. And Milly burst into tears.

'I can't stay here, Ma,' she wept. 'Not now. Not wi' my Dickie gone. There's nowt for me to do now he's gone and everyone's so upset. I can't bear it. And with the funeral coming and everything. Why did he have to die, poor little man? It's not fair! He was such a good little boy and we all loved him. I can't stay here.'

'Quite right,' Jane said, taking charge of her. 'You must come home wi' me and let me look after you.'

'Can I bring Spot with me?' Milly asked. 'He's been howling ever since and 'tis upsetting everyone. He won't howl with us, I promise. I'll look after him.'

So it was agreed that the dog should come too and Sally was instructed to tell everybody where they'd gone.

Even in the midst of this grieving household, Jane was glad to think that her daughter was finally coming home, but she brought her grief with her and ate so little and was so quiet during their first dinner together that Jane was seriously worried about her.

''Tis a dreadful thing to see her in such a state,' she said to Nathaniel when they were on their own together in the bedroom.

'Aye,' he said, looking at her compassionately.

''Tis all so unfair,' Jane said. She was very close to tears herself. 'There's not a scrap of sense or justice in any of it. When you think of all the hard work it takes to carry a child and bring it into the world. And the weariness of those last months. And then to have to watch him die. 'Tis the cruellest thing. She was so fond of him, poor Lizzie. And so was my Milly.'

He put his arms round her and held her protectively close. 'I will look after your Milly, my dearest,' he said. 'She'll be well cared for here. I'll see to it.'

And at that, she wept.

The funeral was held in Scrayingham Church on a bright spring day. Jane and Milly were touched to tears as they watched that little white coffin being lowered into George's imposing family crypt in the churchyard. He should have been buried in his own little grave, Jane thought. That would have been much more fitting. All that expensive marble looked too heavy to be used to cover a little boy and his tender wreath of daffodils, although she noticed that George seemed pleased by it and was standing with one hand resting on it in a proprietorial way. She also noticed that he wasn't paying any attention at all to poor Lizzie. He could at least have offered her an arm to lean on. 'Tis all money with him, she thought, hateful man, and she walked across to put a comforting arm round her old friend's shoulders.

'Time for me to be off,' George said, throwing the words in their direction. 'Tha'lt be fine wi' Mrs Smith, will 'ee not.'

Lizzie tried to dry her eyes. 'When will 'ee be back?' she asked, huskily. He was already striding through the churchyard to where his groom stood patiently holding his horse. 'No idea!' he called. 'Don't wait up.'

Jane was appalled. 'Where's he going?' she said.

'Oh, 'tis business,' Lizzie told her, as if that explained it.

Jane was too cross to be cautious or even polite. 'Business!' she said. 'At his son's funeral?'

Even in the terrible depths of her grief, Lizzie knew she had to defend her husband and struggled to rouse herself to do it. 'People depend on him,' she said. 'He's a great man, Jane. We must mek allowances. He wants to link his railway up with another one in Leeds. Or was it Derby? Anyroad, one or t'other, 'tis important. He were telling me only t'other evening. Linking two railways, you see. You *do* see, don't you, Jane?' And then she looked down at the little grave and cried again.

He's a heartless beast, Jane thought, but she

didn't say anything more. Lizzie was too upset for that and if George wouldn't look after her, *she* would. She put her arm round her friend's shoulders and held her while she cried. But she carried her anger in her heart and by the time she got home it had hardened into the old familiar hatred.

'He left her standing at the graveside,' she said to Nathaniel, as they were getting undressed ready for bed. 'I ne'er saw owt so cruel. And she with her son just buried and barely able to walk for the weight of the next baby and weeping so much 'twas a wonder she could see. There are times when he beats cock-fighting.'

'But she had *you* to look after her,' Nathaniel said easily, hanging his jacket in the closet. 'She was in good hands.'

'That,' Jane said, stepping out of her petticoat and giving it a cross little shake, 'is beside the point. 'Twas *his* job to look after her. He's her husband.'

'He's a great man,' Nathaniel told her, patiently, as he took off his shoes. 'A man with a vision. You can't expect a great man to play nursemaid to his wife. He has other things to do.'

Jane snorted.

'He means to build railways from one end of the kingdom to the other,' Nathaniel went on, 'and when 'tis done, 'twill change the entire country. There's no doubt on it. As I told you, he's a great man.'

Being opposed made Jane dogged. 'Aye, I daresay,' she said, pulling her nightgown over her head, 'but that don't give him leave to be cruel to

214

his wife.'

'Don't exaggerate, Jane,' Nathaniel said and now his voice was stern. ''Tis unbecoming. He wasn't cruel, he just didn't have time to stay with her. That's all it was and that's business, I'm afraid. The merger with the Leeds and Derby project is an important matter. If he's to make it work he has to act quickly. She'll have understood that.'

We're quarrelling, Jane thought, and the thought made her shrink for they'd never quarrelled, not once in all the time they'd been married. But she couldn't back down, not now, and especially as she knew she was right. 'She shouldn't have been asked to understand it,' she said, standing her ground, her heart pounding. 'He should have stayed with her and given her a bit of comfort. But no, he had to go rushing off the minute the service was done, when she was still weeping at the graveside. He couldn't spare her five miserable minutes. You'd not leave me standing at a graveside, now would 'ee?'

'That,' he said crossly, 'would be an entirely different matter. I am not Mr Hudson.'

'That,' she told him hotly, 'would be exactly the same matter.'

'Now look 'ee here,' he said and now there was no doubt that he was angry with her for his face and his voice were hard. 'This is a nonsense and it's got to stop. You don't know what you're talking about.'

'I know Mr Hudson every bit as well as you do,' she said, fighting hard. 'You seem to forget I was his housekeeper.' And she was thinking, Besides being the mother of his child, although of course she couldn't tell him that.

'Housekeepers have most of their dealings with the mistress, not the master,' he told her far too coldly. 'I hardly need to tell you that. In any case I can't have you going about saying detrimental things about Mr Hudson.'

'I don't go about...' she tried. But he was pressing on, his anger growing as he spoke.

'Even if you can't accept that he's a great man and above mere domesticity – although why that should be beyond you I can't imagine and it does you no credit – you must remember that he is my employer. He pays me my wages – generously as you well know. He keeps this roof over our heads. You will oblige me by keeping a civil tongue in your head when you speak of him.'

'But you don't work for him now, do you?' Jane said, trying to fight back, for really it was hideous to be scolded. 'You work for the Leeds and Derby.' But the words brought her up short and shamed. If Mr Hudson bought the Leeds and Derby, he *would* be their employer again. She put her hands over her mouth, acknowledging her mistake and not knowing what to say.

'*Now* do you understand?' he said.

She was crushed, defeated by her own lack of thought as much as his anger, lost in a sudden terrible misery because they were quarrelling and she didn't know how to put things right. There was nothing she could do but creep into bed and lie with her back towards him and pretend to go to sleep. But her thoughts were seething with the injustice of it and sleep was impossible, although

216

she noticed that Nathaniel was asleep and breathing deeply and easily within minutes of getting into bed. In the end, she got up, put on her dressing gown and slippers and tiptoed out of the room, using the light of the moon to guide her as she didn't think it would be sensible to light the gas in case she woke him up. Then she felt her way down the dark stairs until she reached the parlour, where she lit the gas, turned it down low and settled to think and brood in her own armchair before the empty hearth. It was all so unfair. She knew George Hudson a great deal better than Nathaniel, a great deal better than Lizzie, come to that, knew him better and understood him better and couldn't say so, because that would mean explaining how and why and she'd lost the right to do that on the day she agreed to her cock-and-bull story about a husband lost at sea.

There was a soft shuffling noise outside the door and for a second she thought Nathaniel had woken and come down to find her and wondered what on earth they were going to say to one another. But the door opened, very gently, and the person who was standing in the doorway was Milly, bearing a candlestick, her face full of sympathy.

'Couldn't you sleep either?' she said, walking to the fireside. 'I been a-tossing and a-turning for hours thinking of him, poor little man.'

'What time is it?' Jane asked.

'Half past three. Would 'ee like me to light the kitchen fire and make a pot of tea?'

Tea suddenly seemed a most agreeable, normal

idea. So they went down to the kitchen warmly arm in arm, and Milly lit a taper from her candle and set fire to the kindling and they sat side by side waiting for the coal to take and the kettle to boil.

'I've had a letter,' Milly said, just a little too casually.

Jane was alerted by her daughter's careful tone but she stayed calm. 'Have 'ee?'

'From Sarah,' Milly said. 'Lady Livingston as now is. I wrote to tell her about our Dickie and how sad we all were and she wrote back that very day. Wasn't that kindly? I know you said she was catty about Mrs Hudson but she's got a loving heart. Anyroad, I got her letter this morning only what with the funeral and everything I couldn't tell 'ee about it. We had no time to talk, did we? 'Twere all weeping.'

'Aye,' Jane agreed sadly.

'Howsomever,' Milly said, 'the letter brought me some good news. Leastways *I* think it's good news and I hope you'll think so too. We need some good news, don't 'ee think?' She paused and looked at her mother for confirmation, her pretty face earnest in the firelight. 'The long and the short of it is she's offered me a job as governess to her two little girls. The boys are at Eton but she thinks the girls should have some schooling too. She says she thought of me as soon as she and Sir James started to discuss it, and he's agreeable to it. What do 'ee think to that?'

Jane's heart felt as if it was being crushed but she was careful to say the right thing because it was obvious that Milly liked the idea and wanted to accept. After all, she was eighteen now and a woman grown. She had a right to live her life in her own way. 'I think you'd make a first-rate governess,' she said, 'if you're sure that's what you want to do. When would she want you to start?'

'As soon as I can, so she said. She said she'd send the dog cart for me. They're at Longfield Hall for the summer and 'tis no distance.'

The kettle began to whistle so Jane was rescued from having to say anything more and could busy herself mashing the tea. And by the time the tea had drawn and they'd poured that first sweet cup, she was in full control of herself and told Milly she thought it was a splendid idea and promised that they would go into town that afternoon, as ever was, and buy the material for a couple of new gowns. 'You'll need better clothes in Longfield Hall.'

Their shopping kept them happily busy – and out of Nathaniel's way – all the next day. By dinner time the cloth had been bought, the patterns chosen and the seamstress instructed *and* they'd bought a reticule and ordered a fine pair of button boots.

'Now,' Jane said as they walked happily home in the sunshine, 'we can tell Mr Cartwright your good news, what I'm sure he'll be pleased to hear.'

As he was, and not only because it was a step upwards for this stepdaughter of his but also because it gave them all something neutral to talk about over the mutton and made it possible for him to be kindly towards his poor Jane. Although

219

he wouldn't have admitted it, their row had upset him very much and he'd been worrying about it off and on all day while he worked at his plans and maps, trying to think of a way to put things right, for truly it was terrible to think how bitterly they'd spoken to one another. Now they could smile and agree, which was a first step, wasn't it?

In fact it took them two days before they could recover from the blows they'd dealt one another and then their reconciliation came about more by instinct and accident than judgement. They were late to bed that night because they'd been hosting a supper party for four of Nathaniel's workmates and the talk went on until well after midnight. By the time they finally reached their bedroom, Jane was so tired she was drooping and yawning. Her weariness touched Nathaniel to gentleness and when she started to struggle with the buttons on the back of her dress he walked across the room and almost automatically began to undo them for her as he often did when she was tired. It was the first time he'd touched her since their quarrel and his touch made her feel as if she was melting. She turned in his arms and laid her head on his chest, like a child coming home. And then, of course, he could kiss her and tell her he loved her and she could kiss him back and weep a little.

But it was their first quarrel nevertheless and it left a shard of ice in her heart. From that moment on, she knew she couldn't talk to him about George Hudson, no matter what unpleasant and selfish things that hideous gentleman might get up to – as, given his character, he undoubtedly would.

But for the moment Mr Hudson's star was in the ascendant. He'd come home from his meetings with the chairman of the Leeds and Derby Railway cock-a-hoop because the merger was accomplished and all it now required was ratification by the shareholders. It was given at the end of May on the day after Lizzie's sixth and last child had been born. On his father's instructions he was called William and even though Lizzie had declared that she *knew* she would never love another baby, he was loved instantly and with her usual total passion.

So they went their separate ways, George to greater wealth, Milly to adventure in a great house, Lizzie to the renewed pleasures of motherhood and Jane to the private yearning of being parted from her firstborn.

15

Miss Millicent Smith was given such a loving welcome at Longfield Hall that she felt instantly at home there, for the moment she was ushered into the parlour Lady Sarah sprang to her slippered feet and skimmed across the room to greet her.

'Dumma-dumma!' she said, catching Milly's hands and holding them. 'How good it is to see you.' And she turned to the maid, who was watching open-mouthed. 'We will take tea now,

Robinson,' she said, and led Milly to the nearest armchair. 'You would like tea, would you not, me dear? Mr Williams will see to your luggage.'

They took tea together almost as if they were equals and were soon talking of old times and exchanging family news.

'The gels are visitin' with their cousins,' Lady Sarah said. 'They'll be here this evening for dinner, they and their cousins and Emma and Felix. It will be quite a family party, all of us together again after all these years. Sir James is in London so we can be as silly as we like. While the cat's away the little mice play, don't ye know.'

Milly thought of her mother and Mr Cartwright and how happy and easy they were with one another and wondered what sort of marriage it was that led her beautiful Sarah to say such a thing but she kept her counsel and asked no questions for that wouldn't have been her place.

The family party arrived – in a grand carriage – as she was unpacking her clothes in her own bedroom alongside the schoolroom. She heard the crunch of the carriage wheels on the gravel and ran to the window at once to see them. There seemed to be a lot of children, five as far as she could make out, although it was difficult to count them because they were all running about and darting in and out of the house. Emma was as recognizable as Sarah had been with her pretty fair curls and her beautiful gown and there was a plump lady who looked as though she was a nursemaid and three others who were carrying cases into the house and were obviously servants. And while they were all running about and laughing and teasing, a fine young man rode up on a splendid bay horse. A footman and a groom appeared at once to greet him and take charge of the horse and the children all rushed at him as soon as his feet touched the gravel path, to cling about his legs and be tossed into the air. Felix, she thought, gazing down at him. It has to be. And how very handsome he is in his fine clothes.

The dinner party was as lively and confused as the arrival had been because it seemed to be totally disorganized. Emma rushed up to Milly at once to kiss her and tell her how glad she was to see her again, but there were no formal introductions and no order of entry. The family simply walked into the dining room together, and once they were settled at the table they all began to talk at once. After a while Milly worked out that the two little girls with the dark ringlets were her pupils and that they were called Arabella and Maria and that the other one with the fair curls like her mother was their cousin, as were the two little boys, who were a great deal less boisterous than the girls, which was rather a surprise. Felix sat in the midst of them and teased them and encouraged them to say outrageous things but otherwise said very little until they were waiting for the sweet to be served. Then he leant across the table to Milly and spoke to her directly for the first time.

'My sisters are remiss not to have introduced us,' he said. 'My name is Felix. I am, as you have doubtless observed, related to these impossible children, whom I shall spank presently.'

His sisters shrieked with laughter at him. 'Oh

Felix!' Sarah said. 'My dear boy! You don't know who you're talking to, do you? It's Dumma-dumma. Our dear Dumma-dumma.'

He was startled. 'Well, I'll be blowed!' he said. 'You might've told me. How was I to know?'

At which they laughed even more.

'Is your name really Dumma-dumma?' Arabella wanted to know.

Milly sent a quick eye-message to Sarah, who rescued her smoothly. 'This lady is your new governess,' she said. 'I told you about her before you went a-visiting. And don't tell me you don't remember. Her name is Miss Smith and that is what you will call her. Is that understood? We three are the only ones who are permitted to call her by her nickname. Ah! Here comes the pudding. Now sit up straight and I might let you have a mouthful.'

Arabella pouted and gave her mother a saucy look. She obviously knew she didn't have to sit up straight or make any kind of effort to be fed to capacity and that she could do and say whatever she liked. 'Twill be a hard thing to make her mind, Milly thought. I wonder if she can read. I must consider my first move very carefully or she's like to outwit me.

She thought about it for most of the night but when she went up to the schoolroom after breakfast the next morning she still hadn't formed a sensible plan. It was a well-furnished room, with a round table and four wooden chairs where the children could work, a shelf full of books, a globe, slates and slate pencils, an abacus, even a pile of sketchbooks and box full of charcoal but the two little girls were sitting on the window seat staring down at the empty drive as if nothing in the room had anything to do with them. They barely turned their heads when she said good morning to them and the expression on their pretty faces was decidedly supercilious.

'Well now,' Milly said, sitting in one of the chairs and trying a smile, which they both sneered away from. 'What do you usually do first thing in the morning?'

'We don't do anything,' Arabella told her, speaking languidly.

'That must be dull!' Milly said, taking a sheet of paper from the pile and choosing a large stick of charcoal. She studied them carefully for a few seconds, while they went on staring out of the window, then she started to sketch them. It was completely silent in the room except for the tick of the clock and the scratch of the charcoal. Eventually Arabella was driven to speak.

'We shan't learn, you know,' she said, looking defiantly at her new governess. 'You'll not be able to teach us. You can lead a horse to water but you can't make him drink.'

She spoke so glibly that Milly knew she was quoting and that this was something she'd said to rather a lot of people. All her other governesses, like as not. 'You're learning already,' she said calmly, 'so that's a nonsense.'

Arabella was rather taken aback by such an answer but she recovered quickly. 'No, we're not,' she said stoutly. 'You can't make us.'

'I don't have to,' Milly said, drawing a swirl of ringlets. 'You're learning all the same whether you will or no.'

That was such a puzzling answer that Arabella had to think about it. 'No, we're not,' she said. And then after a pause. 'What are we learning then? Show me that.'

Milly sketched for a few seconds before she looked up. Then she gave her answer straight into the child's puzzled eyes. 'You're learning what I do when you're rude to me,' she said.

'We're ain't rude.'

'Oh, indeed you are,' Milly said calmly, keeping her eyes on the sketch, 'which is foolish, on account of I got things for you to do what you'd enjoy no end.'

Maria got down from the window seat and wandered towards the table, casually. 'What sort of things?' she said, trailing her fingers along the tabletop and looking sideways at the sketch.

'Well, for a start,' Milly said, pushing the pad towards her, equally casually, so that she could see the drawing more clearly, 'I should like to go for a walk in your park, being as the sun's a-shining.'

That was such an extraordinary suggestion that Maria's mouth fell open. 'A walk?' she said. 'Out in the park?'

'Aye. Why not?'

'We don't go for walks in lesson time. Miss Fennimore never went for walks.'

'I'm not Miss Fennimore,' Milly told her, continuing with her sketch. 'If you'd like to go for a walk that's what we'll do. All you've got to do is put your bonnets on.'

Surprised eye signals between the two girls and

then Arabella took her sister by the hand and led her through the connecting door into their nursery. They were back in no time at all with bonnets on their heads.

'Splendid,' Milly said. 'Now I'll go and get my bonnet too and we'll be off.' And she slipped through into her own room, where she took her bonnet from its peg and, as an inspired afterthought, found her book of fairy stories and slipped that into her pocket.

Two minutes later they were running down the back stairs towards the kitchen garden and the sunshine.

Milly was very impressed by the Great Park and the girls enjoyed themselves showing her round. It was three times as big as the park at Foster Manor, with a huge kitchen garden and an ornamental garden that was full of bright flowers and fountains, and stables and a dairy with its own herd of milking cows and fields full of sheep and a lake so big it had a wooded island in the middle of it and a wonderful wilderness where wild flowers grew in abundance. There were also several grassy knolls which would be the ideal places for listening to stories.

'I tell 'ee what,' she said. 'Let's go up there and sit under that great tree and I'll tell you a story. How would that be?'

'We won't have to read it, will we?' Maria asked and her face was anxious.

'No,' Milly told her, gently. '*I'm* going to read it. All you've got to do is sit alongside of me and listen. 'Tis a fine old story.' And she took her much-thumbed book of fairy tales from her pocket and opened it at 'Sleeping Beauty'.

'*Once upon a time,*' she read, '*there lived a king and a queen who lacked but one thing to make them entirely happy. The king was young, handsome and wealthy, the queen had a nature as good and gentle as her face was beautiful.*'

'Like Mamma,' Maria said.

'*And they adored one another, having married for love – which among kings and queens is not always the rule. Moreover they reigned over a kingdom at peace, and their people were devoted to them. What more, then, could they possibly want?*'

They were caught, hooked in by the old easy magic of the tale, their eyes wide.

'Go on,' Maria urged and then, remembering her manners, she added, 'if you please.'

So they sat in the shade and absorbed the story and were happy. And when it was finished and Milly had closed the book and put it back in her pocket, they stayed where they were.

'You ain't a bit like our other governesses,' Arabella said at last.

'Course not,' Milly said. 'On account of we're all different. And I'm more different than most.'

'They used to hit us with the ruler,' Maria confided. 'When we couldn't read.'

Which accounts for a lot, Milly understood. 'I don't hit anyone,' she said, smiling at the child, 'ever, and certainly not a little girl. The idea!'

'Not ever?' Maria wanted to know.

'Not ever.'

'They never read us stories,' Arabella told her.

'Like as not,' Milly said. 'I wager they didn't play Bears either.'

Her pupils were so surprised they spoke with one voice, their blue eyes wide. 'Bears?'

'I'll show you this afternoon,' Milly said, 'when you've shown me how to use that abacus. How's that for a bargain?' Much cheerful nodding. 'But now we must be getting back to the house or we shall be late for your lunch.'

They scampered happily back to the house and after a little while, to Milly's delight, Maria held her hand.

That afternoon she coaxed them to demonstrate how it was possible to add up using their abacus and then she played Bears with them for over an hour 'because you've been such good girls'.

'Shall we take another walk tomorrow?' Arabella asked when their schoolday was over.

'Oh, I think so, don't you?' Milly said.

'And read another story?'

'That too.'

'Thanks to Mr Perrault's fairy stories, I think I can be said to have won them over,' she wrote to her mother after dinner that night. She was trying to be modest about it but, really, it was a triumph.

As the weeks passed by, Jane Cartwright read all her daughter's lovely long letters twice and greedily. She was still miserable with the loss of her and seeing her writing so firm and clear on the page brought her close and made the pain of being apart less acute. When she'd read them through a second time, she passed them across the dinner table to Nathaniel, who read them attentively too, and said he was glad she was doing so well. But after he'd read the fifth letter, he set it to one side and looked at her seriously across the table.

'I think you should read *my* letter now,' he said and held it out to her.

It was from George Hudson with instructions that Mr Cartwright was to travel to Leeds at his earliest convenience where he was to meet up with the chairman of the old Leeds and Derby Railway, 'which we have now taken over', and receive instructions for the continuance of the new line.

Jane tried not to show how disappointed she was. 'How long are you like to be away?' she asked.

'That I couldn't say,' he told her, 'but how would it be if you were to accompany me?'

'To Leeds?'

'Aye.'

'All that way?'

''Tis nowhere near as far as Whitby,' he laughed. 'Not by a long chalk and you managed that safely enough as I recall.'

'But what about the children?'

'Audrey will look after them,' he said, and when she still hesitated, he decided to urge her a little. 'Come with me, my dearest. I cannot promise you sea and sand but Leeds is a fair place. 'Tis my home town when all's said and done. I should like to show you round for I know you would like it and here's the chance come for us.'

So she agreed, feeling greatly daring, and they travelled by stagecoach two days later on a misty autumn morning, while Milly was walking her two pupils in Longfield Great Park, with a basket full of breadcrumbs to tempt the ducks on the lake and her book of fairy stories in her pocket.

Their walks had now become an established part of their day and one they all enjoyed – almost as much as playing Bears, which they did every afternoon, after they'd done their sums and their sketching. That afternoon was going to be particularly special because Uncle Felix was coming to ride with the hunt and he always came early enough to play Bears too – when he wasn't talking to Miss Smith, which he did far too much, in Miss Arabella's opinion. But when they got back to the house it was obvious that some great change had occurred for there were servants rushing about everywhere in a state of obvious agitation.

Arabella knew what it was at once. 'Papa's come home,' she said. 'Now we're for it.' Her pretty face was set in its old supercilious expression and Maria looked as though she was going to burst into tears.

'He'll give us a spection,' she told Milly, fearfully. ''Tis what he does when he comes home. He gives you a spection.'

'And he'll not find us wanting,' Milly said, trying to reassure her. 'He'll be pleased with you. You'll see.'

But Maria wasn't comforted and drooped away to the nursery for her meal as if she was carrying the weight of the world on her thin little shoulders.

They're afraid of him, Milly thought, as she watched them climbing the stairs. Poor little things. Well, I'm not. I'm the equal of any bully no matter how much he roars.

231

But as she was to find out that afternoon, Sir Percival wasn't the sort of man who roared to get his own way. He simply expected unquestioning obedience and invariably got it. He made an entrance into the schoolroom just as Milly and her pupils had settled themselves round the table and the two girls sprang to their feet at once and stood perfectly still, looking down at their slippers as if they were afraid to meet his eye. Milly stood respectfully too, but she faced up to him boldly.

'Miss Smith,' he said, looking at her sternly, 'I understand from Mr Garnforth that these gels have been walkin' in the grounds every mornin'. I must say I find that hard to believe. Is he correct?'

The icy menace of the man made Milly's heart judder but she stood her ground. 'Perfectly correct, Sir Percival,' she said. 'That is where they have their reading lessons.'

'Indeed?' he said and he made the word sound sarcastic and threatening.

'Yes, sir.'

'Readin' lessons?'

'Yes, sir.'

He looked at her with open disbelief. 'Then perhaps you will be so kind as to provide them with a readin' book,' he said, 'so that I may ascertain what progress they are makin'.'

Maria was turning pale before their eyes and Arabella was wiping her hands on her skirt. You're a nasty bully, Milly thought, but I've got your measure and I'll not let you bully these girls, not if I can help it. She pulled her book of fairy stories from her pocket, turned her back on her employer, set it on the table and opened it at 'Sleeping Beauty'. 'Begin at the beginning,' she said to Arabella, smiling at her. 'She may sit down to read, may she not, Sir Percival?'

He waved a white hand at them to signify that she might. So Arabella sat down and took the book in her hand and began to read. She was already beginning to recognize words and to be able to piece them together but, as Milly knew, she was word perfect with this story because she knew it by heart.

'*Once upon a time,*' she read, '*there lived a king and a queen who lacked but one thing to make them entirely happy. The king was young, handsome and wealthy; the queen had a nature as good and gentle as her face was beautiful; and they adored one another, having married for love – which among kings and queens is not always the rule.*' Then she paused and looked at Milly to see whether she'd read enough.

'Well done,' Milly applauded. 'You read that very well. Wouldn't you say so, Sir Percival?'

'Commendable,' he said, but it didn't sound like praise. 'How of the younger one?'

'Pass the book to your sister, Arabella,' Milly said, as if reading aloud were perfectly natural to both of them. 'Start here, Maria. 'Tis when the baby has been born. You remember, don't you?' And she read by way of prompting her nervous pupil, '*Strangers meeting in the street fell upon each other's neck, exclaiming...*'

'*Our queen has a daughter!*' Maria remembered with superb fluency.

'*Yes, yes – our queen has a daughter. Long live the little princess!*'

'Well, well!' her father said. 'Very commendable. Al fresco tuition appears to have achieved somewhat.' And he patted both girls on the head, very awkwardly, as if they were wild animals that might bite him if he got too close, and left them.

Maria was so relieved she got an attack of the giggles.

'Oh hush!' Arabella said. 'He'll hear you and come back.'

'I think he's gone,' Milly told her. 'There's no sound of him.'

But Arabella was anxious. 'He could be outside the door,' she said. 'You never know with Papa.'

'Try to giggle quietly,' Milly said, 'and I'll go and see.' She tiptoed to the door as quietly as she could, inched it open and put out her head – to find herself almost nose to nose with Felix. It was the most extraordinary moment. They were so close to one another she could feel the warmth of his breath on her forehead and he was looking at her in such an extraordinary way, almost as if he was going to kiss her. It was like being caught in a spell. Then he took a step backwards and laughed and the spell was broken.

'What *are* you doing?' he said.

'Looking out for Sir Percival.'

'I passed him on the stairs,' he told her and strode into the room. 'Booba-doo gels!'

They fell on him, both talking at once. 'We've been spected.' 'And we *read* to him. Can you imagine that, Uncle Felix?' 'We didn't make *one* mistake.'

'Time for Bears,' he said, dropping to his hands and knees. 'Who's first?'

Lizzie Hudson was playing Bears with her children that afternoon too. So she wasn't pleased when the game was interrupted by the arrival of her husband. And he wasn't pleased at all.

'What are you doing rolling about on the floor?' he said. 'Get up, for pity's sake, and show a little decorum.'

''Tis only a game, George,' Lizzie tried, 'and they do enjoy it so.'

'You haven't got time for games,' he said sternly. 'We've an important meeting to attend. I need you ready and dressed in half an hour.'

Lizzie scrambled to her feet, brushing the creases out of her gown. 'What meeting is it, George?' she asked.

'Tory Party,' he said, as he opened the door. 'Best bib and tucker and wear your pearls. We're going to win t'next election. I've got it all planned. That fool Meek's too slow.' And he was gone.

'Bears 'gain, Mama?' John said hopefully.

She bent to kiss his pretty face. 'Later if you're good,' she said and went to deck herself in her finery. The orange and red, she thought, as she climbed the stairs, wi' the headpiece. That should suit.

It was a very noisy dinner and seemed to involve a great deal of drinking and shouting. At one point several of the gentlemen banged on the table with their knives and sang an interminable song, very loudly. It quite made her head ache. But George was in his element, booming and shouting and making jokes she couldn't understand. Eventually they seemed to have come to some decision because they were all nodding and clapping and George stood up and made a short speech.

'Gentlemen,' he said, 'you have made a momentous decision here this evening. Nowt but good will come of it. Of that you can be assured. I will run this campaign for you and Sir John Lowther according to the best possible principles and according to the best possible principles we will prevail. By this time next year York will have a Tory Member of Parliament.' He paused to give them time to cheer and thump the table and then went on, his voice throbbing with deliberate emotion and his eyes moist with induced tears and brandy. 'Moreover, I tell 'ee this. The highest gratification I can receive is to promote our glorious cause and to work to bring it about. My politics, gentlemen, as you all know, are simple and straightforward. You could say they are politics in a little room.' He paused to ensure that he had their full attention, standing before them with his face rose-red with drink and his thumbs hooked into his waistcoat pocket in the manner of an orator. 'They consist, gentlemen, in a sincere love of the king and the constitution and a desire to hand it down unsullied to my children.' His audience were enraptured and cheered him until they were hoarse.

Lizzie turned her orange-feathered head to admire him. Such a good man, she thought. A wonderful man. I wish Jane could have been here to hear him.

On their way home in the carriage the wonderful man fell asleep and woke when the horses stopped to complain that he'd had 'a reet skinful' and felt 'reet sick'.

'You work too hard, that's how 'tis,' Lizzie sympathized. 'Tek my arm.'

But he shook away her proffered arm and staggered off without her, blundering heavily up the stairs to their bedroom where he fell diagonally across the bed and slept again, snoring loudly.

As there was no room for both of them, Lizzie tiptoed quietly away to the blue room and slept there. Which was perhaps just as well, for later in the night her much admired husband woke and was sick all over the carpet and the armchair.

16

Despite her misgivings, Jane Cartwright was very taken with Leeds. She liked the old Talbot Inn and the fine shops in Briggate and was intrigued by the way the ancient Moot Hall stood right in the middle of the road as if it were a sentinel. On her second afternoon she discovered the linen drapers and bought so much of their fine cloth that she could barely carry it all back to the Talbot Inn.

'New clothes for the children,' she explained to Nathaniel when he got back from his meeting, 'and Christmas presents for my Milly. Not long till Christmas now. I wonder how long a holiday they'll give her. After all, it's not as though she's a servant.'

As it turned out, she was given the full twelve days and arrived home on Christmas Eve, on the four o'clock stage from Middlesbrough, laden with parcels, and with a handsome young escort to help her carry them. Jane had been waiting for nearly half an hour in the coach yard with the children beside her, all warmly wrapped up in their new coats and their new mufflers with new button boots on their feet and new beaver hats on their heads, and as soon as they saw her they rushed towards her with their arms outstretched to hug and kiss her. And the escort put down his parcels and strode towards their mother with *his* arms outstretched.

'Oh, Mrs Smith,' he said. 'How *good* it is to see you. You haven't changed a bit. I would have known you anywhere.'

It took her a second to recognize him and then it was with a shock of such pleasure it brought a flush to her cheeks. She put her arms round his elegant neck and kissed him like the son he was. 'Felix,' she said, 'my dear boy.'

'Who,' Nat said to Milly very suspiciously, 'is that?'

'That's Felix,' big sister Milly told him, 'and he's bought us a hamper full of good things.'

He wasn't placated. That was *his* mama the young man was hugging and he and Papa were the only ones allowed to do that – except for the girls, of course. 'Why?'

Milly was no help to him at all. 'Why not?' she said.

'I've got a new coat,' Mary told her, holding out

238

the skirt for her inspection. 'An' a new muffler. An' gubs an' boots an' a hat.'

'Very pretty.'

'Her name's not Mrs Smith,' Nat said, scowling at this unnecessary young man.

'It's going to snow,' Jane said, squinting up at the sky which was colourless with cold. 'Home I think and as quick as we can.'

The snow began to fall as they approached Bootham Bar and by the time they reached Shelton House their coats were flecked with it and it was curtaining around them so thickly they could barely see where they were going. Nathaniel was waiting at the door for them and rushed them inside, all talking at once – except for Nat, who was still scowling – and then settled them by the fire in the parlour, with a glass of hot punch to warm the adults and a glass of Mrs Cadwallader's nice hot lemonade for the children and Spot sitting at their feet and the shutters closed against the weather.

'Welcome home!' he said to Milly as he handed her the punch, adding courteously, 'And welcome to you too, Felix. It is good to make your acquaintance. I've heard much about you.'

'And I of you, sir,' Felix said. 'Milly never stops talking about you all.'

'How long can you stay with us?' Jane wanted to know. 'You'll not go rushing away as soon as dinner's done, will you?'

'I could stay as long as you'll have me,' Felix said, giving her that old shy smile she knew so well. 'There's no one at home in Foster Manor except the pater and, truth to tell, he don't notice

239

whether I'm there or not and Sarah's got a house full of Livingstons, which makes me a bit of a fish out of water, and Emma's house is full of Smithson Lumleys.'

'If that's the size of it,' Nathaniel told him, 'consider it settled. You can stay as long as Milly does and then escort her home again afterwards, which would please us mightily. How would that be?'

There was great satisfaction all round – except for Nat, whose scowl was enough to turn the milk sour.

When Audrey had arrived to take the two children away for their nursery tea, Nathaniel turned to his wife and made a grimace. 'What *was* the matter with our Nat?' he said to Jane. 'I've never seen such a little thundercloud and that's not like him.'

'He's jealous,' Milly told him.

That surprised him. 'Jealous?'

'Of Felix,' Milly said. 'He was fairly bristling when Ma kissed him.'

'Oh dear!' Jane said. 'I shall need to set that to rights. I can't have my poor Nat feeling put out.'

'Don' 'ee fret,' Milly said, smiling at her. 'Let me read 'em their story tonight and 'twill be right as rain in the morning. I promise.'

Jane was half impressed, half doubtful. 'How will 'ee bring that about?' she asked.

'By magic,' her daughter said, giving her a wicked grin. 'I'm a dab hand at magic.' She knew she was bragging, which wasn't very admirable, but why shouldn't she? She *was* a dab hand. Look how she'd coaxed Arabella and Maria to read.

So that evening, while the others were still dressing for dinner, she went to the nursery. Nat and Mary were bouncing up and down on their beds and Audrey was fussing beside them, begging them to 'be good children and get into bed, there's lambs'.

'I shall count to three,' their sister said sternly, in her governess voice, 'and if tha's not under the covers and quite quiet tha'll not get a story.'

They were ready as she reached two. 'Now then,' she told them, speaking in her own voice, as Audrey left the room, 'I've got a lovely story for you tonight.'

'But you've not brought your book,' Nat said.

'That's on account of this story is in my head,' Milly said. 'And all the better for being in such a good place. Now then, are you comfy?' And when they nodded, she began her tale.

'Once upon a time there was a little boy. He lived in a mighty big house and had lots of servants to wait on him and plenty of fine things to eat and fine clothes to wear and a pony to ride when he was old enough, so you'd think he was the luckiest boy alive.' Earnest and happy nodding. 'But no, I'm sad to say he wasn't, on account of on the very same day he was born, his dear mama, who loved him very much, the same as your ma loves you, his dear mama took ill and died and the poor little boy was left all alone wi'out a mother to care for him. Wasn't that the saddest thing? Now then, what could be done about it? His father thought and thought and couldn't come up with an answer, the servants thought and thought and couldn't come up with an answer, even the groom thought and thought but *he* couldn't come up with an answer either and said they'd probably have to feed the baby to the pigs, like as not.' Wide-eyed shock. 'And the poor little baby lay in his pretty cot and cried for his mama. And then, just when they were all at their wits' end and the poor little baby had cried himself to sleep on account of there was nobody there to cuddle him and feed him, a fairy flew in through the nursery window.'

The two children were transfixed, waiting in silence for the story to go on.

'She was a very sensible fairy,' Milly said. 'Some fairies can be very sensible, you know. *"Stop that caterwauling"*, she said, *"and let me think what's to be done. I can't think if you mek a row."* So they all stopped crying and stood where they were and they waited. *"'Tis plain for to see,"* the fairy said, *"that what this baby needs is another mother."* And she waved her wand, so that sparkles flew in all directions like fireflies, and a beautiful lady walked in through the door. She had lovely thick dark curls on her head, and the finest brown eyes you ever saw and the gentlest face and she was wearing a shawl made of very soft wool in every shade of pink and blue and lilac.'

'Like Mama,' Nat said. 'She's got a shawl like that.'

'And gubs,' Mary put in.

'And gloves,' Milly agreed.

'Like Mama,' Mary decided.

'Quite right,' Milly said, 'she was very like your mama, with her dark hair and her kind heart. The spit and image, you might say. And when she saw

242

the poor little motherless baby a-lying in his cot with the tears still wet on his poor little face, she picked him up straightaway and gave him the biggest cuddle ever. And so she became his mother and fed him and looked after him until he was a big boy and had to go away to school. And even though he'd had a reet bad start in his poor little life, he ended up such a happy baby that they called him Felix, what means happy. Did 'ee know that?'

'Felix?' Nat said.

'Aye.'

'The one what's come here to stay?'

'Aye. The very same. The one what's come here to stay.'

Nat considered this for quite a long time. 'Did *his* mama die, like you said?'

'She did.'

'On the day he was born?'

'She did. And then our mama, what has the kindest heart on the world, as tha knows, she picked him out of his cradle and cuddled him and looked after him, and that's why he's so fond of her. I think she's the kindest mama ever and that's the best story ever. Don't you?'

He considered again and then smiled at her. 'Yes,' he said.

And Mary echoed him. 'Yes.'

'Now settle to sleep,' Milly said, stooping to kiss them both, 'and if tha'rt good, tomorrow we'll play Bears. Felix is top-notch at Bears.'

So despite its rather precarious start, it turned out to be a very happy holiday, their easy world shining with snowfall, the Christmas goose cooked to succulent perfection, the presents splendidly successful, and Bears every afternoon. Nathaniel said he'd never *had* such a rollicking Christmas and when he said goodbye to Milly and Felix he told them he hoped he would see them both again 'very soon'.

'Oh you will, sir,' Felix assured him. 'You will.'

'I'll be back at Easter,' Milly promised as she kissed her mother. 'Save me some of the plum cake.'

'That'll be gone long afore Easter,' Jane laughed. 'We'll need to bake a simnel cake if 'ee wants cake.'

'Look after our Milly,' Nathaniel said as he shook hands with Felix.

The answer was as solemnly given as a vow. 'You may depend on it.'

And then they were both climbing into the coach and Milly was waving through the little window and the horn was sounding and the horses were snorting and the holiday was over.

'I like your Felix,' Nathaniel said to Jane as they walked back home. 'He's a gentleman.'

'He is,' Jane agreed. 'A proper gentleman.'

They crunched over the trodden snow for several happy seconds. 'If you ask me,' Nathaniel said, 'I think he's sweet on your Milly.'

'Aye,' she said. 'Quite possibly.'

'Very possibly,' Nathaniel said. 'The signs are there.'

''Twill be a boy and girl affair,' Jane told him. 'They're too young for owt else, which is just as well to my way of thinking. If they were serious, his father'd have summat to say.'

'Aye,' Nathaniel said. 'Possibly.'

'There's no possibly about it,' Jane told him. 'His father's a stickler for family alliances and obedience and that sort of thing. He'll want him to marry a duchess, at the very least, if I'm any judge of the man. He'd not tek kindly to our Milly.'

'Our Milly's the equal of any duchess,' he told her, tucking her hand into the crook of his elbow. 'Howsomever, we'll cross that bridge when we come to it. They're young yet. You've the right of *that*. Much could happen in the meantime. There are changes coming.'

Milly and Felix talked about their holiday all the way back to Cross Lanes where Felix had arranged for the dog cart to meet them and the coach stopped to put them down. But when it had rattled away and left them standing on the snow-trodden path in a desert of snow-covered fields with a keen wind blowing, there was no sign of a cart and no sound of one either.

'It will be along presently,' Felix said, with a confidence he didn't feel. 'We could walk and meet it, if you'd care to. We've only got our travelling bags and I could carry them. Easily. And we'd have the wind at our backs. What do you think?'

So they walked, with the wind at their backs, and after a while, because her hands were cold even in their gloves, she took his free arm and walked as close to him as she could get. And since they were on their own in an empty countryside, with no one to hear them, they began to talk rather more freely than they'd dared to do when they'd been in company.

'It was so good to see your mother again,' he said, 'even if it did upset young Nat.'

'He got over it,' she said happily.

'Yes,' he said. 'How did you persuade him? I didn't like to ask while we were...'

'I told him a fairy story,' she said, and explained. 'About a little boy who lost his mother when he was born and how a fairy godmother came and waved her magic wand and a beautiful lady came to look after him.'

'That accounts for his question,' he said, when she'd finished.

'What question?'

'He asked me if I'd really lost my mother on the day I was born. I told him I had but I *did* wonder why he'd asked.'

They walked on, thinking all this over. 'We have a lot in common,' he said at last, 'apart from the fact that your mother brought us both up, which is the most important thing. We're both orphans, are we not? I lost my mother on the day I was born and you lost your father even *before* you were born.'

'Aye. I did. But then there are lots of orphans. There's nowt unusual in being an orphan. Happen that's why there are so many in fairy stories.'

'You and your fairy stories,' he said.

'There's a deal of truth in a fairy story, I'll have 'ee know.'

'Yes,' he agreed. 'There is. You're right. Your mama and Mr Cartwright are like a fairy story.'

That was intriguing. 'How so?'

246

'They married for love,' he said, 'like Sleeping Beauty's mother and father, which is a rare thing.'

'Aye,' she said, thinking of the Hudsons, 'so it is.'

'It made me feel happy to see them so happy, if that's not a foolish thing to say.'

She didn't think it was.

'If I had a fairy godmother,' he said, 'to come and wave her magic wand for me, that's what I would wish for. In fact, if I tell you the truth, I can't think of anything I'd like more.' Then he was lost for words, and stood looking at her while he changed the bags from his right hand to his left, wondering whether it was a proper time to tell her other things.

'There's the cart a-coming,' she said, winding her muffler more closely round her neck.

'Ah, yes,' he said, trying to sound as though it didn't matter, although he was secretly flooded with disappointment because they were going to be interrupted at such an inopportune moment and there were so many things he wanted to say to her. However, by the time Jenkins brought the cart to a slithering halt alongside them he had recovered his balance and was back to his public persona again, handing the young lady into the cart and giving the luggage to the servant like the gentleman he was. There would be other times. He knew he would have to ride to Oxford as soon as they got back to Longfield Hall because that was arranged. But he could always write to her.

He wrote as soon as he got back to Oxford and

the letter was delivered to her at breakfast the next morning. She was careful not to open it until she was alone in her room. It would never have done to read it in front of all the others. But it was worth the wait for it began *'My dearest Milly'*. The words made her feel quite overcome. She had to sit down on the bed before she could go on reading.

'I hope you will forgive me for addressing you in such an informal way,' he wrote, *'but we are both orphans, after all, and were both raised by the same good woman and I felt I could scarcely address you as Miss Smith. It was such an enjoyable holiday I haven't digested it all yet. I do so hope we can visit with your mother and Mr Cartwright again very soon.*

'I will visit the bookshops tomorrow and see whether I can find you any other fairy stories since I know they are dear to your heart.

'Meantime, I remain your fellow orphan,
'Felix.'

She put the letter in the top drawer of her chest of drawers, hidden away underneath her petticoats. And that night, when the day's work was done and dinner was over, she sat down at her dressing table under the gaslight and wrote him a long reply. *My dearest Milly,* she thought as she settled in her bed. Oh my dear Felix. Am I truly your dearest? Really truly? The words had turned her life upside-down. I should so love to be your dearest.

17

It was the new year of 1835 and change was coming to the city of York. It wasn't just the railway – most people knew that was on the way and were either looking forward to it or deploring it – it was change of a political kind and that was a thing very few of them expected. York had been a staunch Whig town ever since most people there could remember. So when it was announced that there was to be an election for a Member of Parliament, they assumed that a Whig would be elected. But they were reckoning without Mr George Hudson, who took immediate action to ensure that, this time, young John Henry Lowther, his favoured Tory candidate, would be the one to win.

'High time the Whigs were ousted,' he said to the Tory election committee. 'They've had t'run of t'mill for a deal too long. Give me a list of all the electors and let's see if I can persuade 'em.'

He was persuasive to the tune of several thousand pounds and when some of his fellow Tories worried that what he was doing might not be completely legal, he laughed them to scorn.

'What's "legal" to do wi' it?' he scoffed. 'What counts is brass, gentlemen, brass and influence, and there's brass in t'kitty. Don't you worry about *that*. I matched old Sir John Lowther pound for pound, right back at the beginning. Now all we have to do is spend it to good purpose. Don't fret about niceties. Leave that to lesser men. Now's the time for banquets and junkets and standing a few drinks and slipping a few pennies in a few pockets. Electors are an empty-headed lot and empty heads can be swayed.'

As it turned out. To the Whigs' annoyance and amazement, it was John Henry Lowther who was returned to Westminster as Member of Parliament for the City of York. George was cock-a-hoop and threw a party to celebrate, naturally, and got splendidly and uproariously drunk, naturally. And while he was still well oiled and exuberant, he posted a sovereign to every voter he'd swayed by way of a thank-you present.

His detractors were appalled at such behaviour. 'Showing off,' they said to one another. 'Flashing his money about it. No good'll come of it.'

George let it all roll off his shoulders. They were plenty broad enough. His man had won and that was what mattered.

'Now,' he said to Lizzie as they were finishing their lunch the next day, 'I can build as many railways as I want and be sure of an Act of Parliament to support 'em instead of kicking my heels for months waiting for some blamed fool at Westminster to tek pity on me. James Meek's not an earthly bit of use. 'Tis pointless waitin' for him to do owt.'

Lizzie became aware that he was waiting for her to say something. 'I thought I might just walk down to t'shop,' she offered, 'if that's agreeable to 'ee. To have t'children measured for some new clothes. Well, the three eldest I mean, not Baby. He can manage a bit longer I daresay, being a baby. But George is such a big boy now and he's grown right out of his little jacket, you can see all his wrists, and what I can say about Ann's little dresses I really don't know. I mean for to say they don't fit at all – I mean not as they should. She can get them on, I'll grant that, but they're such a tight fit her little arms are all stuck out sideways.'

'You've not been listening to a single word I've been saying,' George said, hot with exasperation. 'Not one single blamed word.'

'Oh no, George,' Lizzie flutttered in some panic. 'I wouldn't want 'ee for to think that. I've been payin' the greatest attention. I allus do.'

'Greatest attention my aunt fanny,' her husband said and left her.

'He was that cross, you wouldn't believe,' Lizzie said to her brother half an hour later. Since their sister's death two years ago, the two of them had grown so much closer to one other that she felt she could confide in him. 'I do try to listen, tha knows that, I allus do, I'd not be much of a wife to him if I didn't, but this talk of railways and elections and whatnot is mortal hard on the ears.'

'Lift your arms up, Georgie,' Richard Nicholson said to his nephew, who was standing on the counter being measured. 'How would 'ee fancy the blue wool for his jacket, Lizzie? 'Tis all the rage this season and I could give 'ee a good price.'

They decided on the blue wool and the sprigged muslin for Ann and then Richard folded up his tape measure and put it in the drawer under

251

the counter and told them all he was taking them out for tea, as they'd been such good children.

'Actually,' he said to Lizzie when they were all settled with pots of tea and a plateful of sugar cakes, 'it's you I want to talk to.'

'What about?' Lizzie said, wiping cake crumbs from her mouth.

'I've been thinking of buying shares in the railway,' her brother said. 'What would 'ee say to that? Would it be wise?'

'Aye, it would,' Lizzie told him. 'Railways are going to mek a deal of money once they're up and running. George told me. He might get a bit tetchy wi' me when I don't listen – he's a great man and you've got to mek allowances – but he knows all there is to know about railways. None better. And money.'

'I'd like to buy one of those new houses up by Clifton Croft,' Richard said, 'furnish it all *a la mode*, sort of thing. Live easy, sort of thing.'

'Why not?' his sister approved. 'George would advise you, I'm certain sure. You have to buy at the top of the market – or was it the bottom? Anyroad there's a best time for it. He'd be able to tell 'ee. And there's a new railway a-coming. You could buy shares in that.'

The new railway was voted into existence that summer at a meeting of the Committee of the York Railway which was now such a prestigious group they held their proceedings in the Guildhall. On this occasion they agreed to link up with the Leeds–Derby project and form a new railway company, which they called the York and North Midlands Railway. And when the shares were

252

floated, one of their principle new shareholders was Mr Richard Nicholson, who naturally became one of the company's directors.

George invited him to one of his rowdy dinners to celebrate.

'Now,' he said, as they took their places one on either side of the table, 'tha's on tha way to becoming a very rich man.' And he raised his first glass to his brother-in-law. 'Your very good health, sir!'

Jane and Nathaniel were dining with Milly and Felix that evening. Dining together had become a regular event since their brief visit at Easter and one they all looked forward to. Sir Percival and Lady Livingston were in London for the season, as was Felix's father, and as term was over and Felix was officially 'home for the hols', they had plenty of free time – as well as one of Sir Mortimer's carriages in which to travel about. Persuading his father to let him have it had been quite a victory as Felix was happy to tell them.

'He thinks I'm visitin' my Oxford friends,' he said, the first time he drove to their door. 'He'd have a fit if he knew where I really was.'

'Good job he doesn't then,' Jane said, kissing her daughter. The warmth of being a conspirator and outwitting the icy Sir Mortimer was a real pleasure.

But on this occasion, Felix had arrived with a problem which was obviously worrying him, and it wasn't long before they discovered what it was. Apparently Sir Mortimer had come back to Foster Manor for a few days and had been laying down the law as to what his son was to do when he finally came down.

'He says I can holiday abroad for the summer but then I'm to go back to the Manor and learn how to run the estate ready for when I inherit.'

'You must have expected that, surely,' Nathaniel said reasonably. 'After all, that's what eldest sons always do.'

'Yes,' Felix admitted. 'I suppose I did, in a general sort of way. But...' He sighed.

'So what is the problem?' Nathaniel asked.

'It ain't what I really want to do with my life,' Felix told him honestly.

'And what *do* you want to do with your life?'

'I want to be a lawyer, sir. Always have done, as Milly will tell you.'

'Could you not do both?'

'Not according to the pater,' Felix said ruefully. 'We had words, I'm afraid. He said he wouldn't allow any son of his to join such a disgraceful profession.'

'Ah!'

'You're young yet,' Jane said, trying to comfort. 'You've got another two years at Oxford, have 'ee not? Happen he'll change his mind.'

Felix sighed even more heavily. 'The pater never changes his mind,' he said. 'He tells you what he intends you to do and leans on you until you do it.'

Yes, Jane thought, that's exactly what he does.

There was a long pause, while Milly and Felix looked sadly at each other and Jane looked hopefully at Nathaniel and Nathaniel poured more wine for them all and then considered, gazing away from them into a space of his own.

'When we're building a railway,' he said eventually, 'and we hit upon a problem – an incline too steep for a cutting, for example, or an inpenetrable hill – we sit down and ask ourselves questions and give our minds to finding another solution to it. There are invariably other solutions. It's just a matter of looking for them and asking the right questions. Happen I might ask you some questions in this case, Felix.'

Felix nodded, although both Jane and Milly could see that he had little hope that an interrogation would provide any useful answers.

'Your father appears to dislike the legal profession for some reason,' Nathaniel said.

'Yes. He does.'

'Do you know why that should be?'

'Oh yes,' Felix said. 'He makes no secret of it. In his opinion lawyers are rogues and fools.'

'Not honest men, is that the size of it?'

'Yes.'

'Does he often express such an opinion?'

'Yes. He does. Frequently.'

'Then I believe we may have hit upon a plan of campaign,' Nathaniel said. 'I would advise you to say nothing about your hopes for the time being. In fact if I were you I would avoid the subject of your future altogether, agreeing that you would, of course, be prepared to learn how to run the estate but otherwise holding your peace. Then all you have to do is wait until the next time your father is holding forth about the dishonesty of lawyers and, when he has disburdened himself of his opinion, I suggest that you ask him, very politely, whether he would allow you to provide him with a lawyer who would be more to his taste. If what you say about him is true, he will protest that there is no such thing as an honest lawyer. You can then ask him whether he might prefer a lawyer who has been raised and bred in his own house and therefore knows right from wrong and would be utterly trustworthy. What do you say to that?'

Jane clapped her hands with delight to think of this cold, powerful man being outwitted. 'I never knew you could be so artful,' she said.

But Nathaniel was still looking at Felix.

'I'm not sure, sir,' Felix told him. 'The pater ain't the easiest man for anyone to talk to. He don't listen, d'ye see.'

'Then you would have to choose a good moment,' Nathaniel said. 'You've plenty of time to think about it.'

Then the subject was dropped because their parlourmaid had come in to ask if there were owt else they needed and they decided that as the meal was finished they would walk in the garden while it was still light. And Milly and Felix asked if it would be agreeable for them to take a short walk in the fields instead, which they always did when the meal was over.

Jane watched them stroll away, very close together but being careful not to hold hands until they were out of sight. 'They do mek me remember,' she said, taking Nathaniel's arm.

'Aye,' he smiled. 'I can see that. Will he take my advice, do you think?'

'He will try,' Jane said. 'He does so want to be a lawyer.'

'He would make a good one,' Nathaniel said. 'He has the necessary virtues.'

'And what are they, pray?'

'He is patient and he listens. You brought him up well.'

The summer gentled by: Jane's garden was scented by roses and raspberries; Nathaniel worked on plans for the new railway; Sir Mortimer stayed in London and so did Sir Percival and Lady Sarah, who wrote to Milly twice a week to send her the latest gossip and to enquire after her daughters. And at the end of July, her letter was bubbling with the news that 'that dreadful upstart George Hudson' had been summoned to appear before a special committee in the Houses of Parliament to answer charges of bribery and corruption during the recent election.

'We are all agog to see how it will turn out,' she wrote. *''Twould give the wretch his just deserts were he to be sent for trial. He has always been a deal too full of himself.'*

That was the opinion of the Whigs in York, who were still smarting over the way Mr Hudson had outmanoeuvred them and still complaining about the effrontery of those sovereigns. George himself was annoyed to be summoned so peremptorily but not overly concerned. After all, both parties had bribed the electors. That was the way of the world. It was a storm in a teacup, as he told his friends in the Tory Party. Nevertheless he had to obey the summons, even though his first instinct had been to ignore it, and he duly travelled down to London on the appointed day,

257

taking his solicitor friend James Richardson to support him, and prepared himself to answer their unnecessary questions.

They were a great deal more searching than was comfortable for, as he saw at once, one member of the committee seemed to have made up his mind that he was guilty as charged before he'd had a chance to open his mouth.

'You are the treasurer of the Tory Party in York, I believe,' he said.

George agreed that he was.

'Then you would have been responsible for any monies spent by that organization.'

'No, sir. That was the responsibility of the committee as a whole.'

'But you were the treasurer?'

'Aye.'

'Then you would have paid out monies on Mr Lowther's behalf.'

That needed a denial or the wretched man would trap him. 'No, sir, I did not.'

'I find that hard to understand,' his questioner went on. Really, the man was like some ugly little terrier. 'Were you treasurer without a treasury?'

He would have to be answered, George thought. Wretched little man. 'Well,' he said, 'perhaps that admits of some explanation. The fact is that I believe in 1832 I was what they call treasurer but I received no monies; but I was told by the chairman that cheques on the city and county bank would be answered, if I drew them on account of the expenses of the election. That is the explanation.'

'The total amount drawn from the bank was

258

£3,240,' another committee member put in. 'Is that correct?'

'I believe so.'

'Was this polling money?'

'I don't know what you mean by polling money,' George said loftily, and he turned to appeal to the chairman. 'I don't like to be entrapped into an answer by a question of that sort. Let him put his question in a straightforward way.'

It was done. Instantly. 'Very well then, I ask you, do you know whether any polling money was paid on behalf of Mr Lowther?'

George drew himself up to his full pompous height. 'That question,' he said loftily, 'I respectfully decline to answer.' And he glared round at his persecutors, daring them to challenge his right to stay silent.

The questioning went on for three days but George stayed obdurately obscure about his financial dealings. In the end the meeting was adjourned and no further action was taken.

Mr Richardson was deeply impressed. As they were travelling back to York and safety, he said it was a masterly performance, 'damn if it wasn't'.

'Oh, I've got the measure of a pack of bullies, don't 'ee worry,' George said, preening himself. 'They needn't think they can tell me what I'm to do with my own money. Sod that for a game of soldiers. Oh no. I showed 'em what's what. Shout first and shout loudest. That what you do wi' bullies.' If he'd learnt nothing else back in that crowded, quarrelsome farmhouse, he'd learnt that. 'Anyroad, they can't touch me. I'm too rich for 'em. And if I'm too rich for 'em now I shall be ten times richer come the end of the year. You watch and see. My star's in the ascendant.'

It certainly seemed to be. By the end of that year he owned seven railway companies and had so much money he was a millionaire and sure enough not one further word had been said about their stupid trumped-up charge of corruption. And to set the seal on his success, by that time the local Tories held the balance of power within the Corporation and in their view, when it came to choosing the new Lord Mayor for 1837, there was only one man for the job.

It was marvellously gratifying. 'Didn't I tell 'ee I'd be Lord Mayor,' he said to Lizzie. How well he remembered standing in that little church when they were getting wed and looking down at the tombstone to another Lord Mayor, whose name he had quite forgotten, and vowing that one day he would follow him into office.

Lizzie looked up at him in admiration. He seemed to have swollen to twice his size that evening and he looked so well with his cheeks red and his eyes shining and that gold watch chain shining on his chest like a medal.

''Tis no more than you deserve,' she told him. 'I mean for to say you're just the man for the job. I've allus said so.'

'I shall have my portrait painted in my mayoral robes,' he said, admiring himself in the long mirror. 'And I shall throw a banquet. An inaugural banquet. That's the way to win hearts. Good food and champagne and plenty of it.'

18

When Princess Victoria was eighteen, the law was changed so that she could be declared to have come of age. Most people knew that the old King could die at any time and nobody in parliament wanted her mother to be regent. That wouldn't have done at all.

There was considerable celebration and anybody who was anybody threw a party. Even Sir Mortimer, who was usually too dour for parties, decided to host a large one and invited half society as well as all his children. Felix couldn't see the point of it but he attended dutifully, telling himself that he could slip away unnoticed after an hour or two because it was bound to be a crush.

As it was. The drawing room of his father's fine town house was booming with loud voices and dazzling with flamboyant diamonds, most of them, as he noticed sourly, decorating wrinkled bosoms, and it was so impossibly crowded it was really quite difficult to move around in it. But he stayed polite and asked after the health of anyone who addressed him and tried to watch where his father was, so that he could keep out of his way.

He was out of luck, for just as he was asking after the health of another drawling young man, a duchess in full sail bore down upon him, bearing his father in her wake.

'Me dear,' she said. 'I've been searchin' for you all over the room. Where have you been hidin'? You mustn't hide. 'Tain't kind, ye know, and it ain't the style. Now tell me what you mean to do with yourself now you've come down. You will come to my soiree, naturally.'

He agreed with her, giving her the slight bow that was her due. What else could he do? 'Naturally, ma'am.'

'Quite right,' she said, nodding her plumed head so that the feathers swept his father's face. 'Now tell me what you mean to do with yourself until you come into the estate. It ain't a bit of use puttin' on that face to me, Mortimer. A young man should have an occupation otherwise he runs to the bad. We all know that.'

Her words put Felix into a state of delighted shock. Had the moment actually come? Could he tell *her* what he wanted? Would she prove an ally? It probably wasn't the place or the time but, even so, he was scrabbling about in his mind to remember the words he'd planned to say.

The great lady leaned towards him and whacked him on the shoulder with her fan. 'Speak up!' she ordered. 'What do you have in mind?'

'Well now, as to that, ma'am,' he said, gaining a little time while he got his thoughts in order, 'I've been considering the law, ma'am.'

She looked at him quizzically. 'Have you now?'

'Yes, ma'am. I thought it might be helpful for Pater to have his own personal lawyer. A trustworthy one, if you take my meaning.'

'Quite right,' she said, whacking him with the fan again. 'Some of 'em are rogues. Absolute

262

rogues. That all sounds very sensible. Wouldn't you say so, Mortimer?'

Sir Mortimer had retreated into his chilly face and didn't answer but the lady sailed on in her imperious way. 'It's quite the done thing, ye know,' she said, 'dependin' on the number of sons you have available. One to the army, one to the church, one to the law. Quite the done thing and a matter of good sense to my way of thinkin'.' She gave Felix a nod as if the whole matter were settled. 'Call on me a' Friday,' she ordered. 'I will speak to the duke. He has friends in the Inns of Court.' Then she sailed away, skirts swishing as she bore down on an old friend. 'Me dear!'

Felix realized that his heart was beating uncomfortably fast and that his father was looking as if he'd been frozen into his skin. 'I wouldn't do anything against your wishes, Pater,' he hastened to assure.

'Quite!' his father said. Then he gave his son a short formal bow and left him.

Has he agreed or not? Felix wondered. How am I to find out if he will keep walking away? But there was no point in worrying about it and fortunately just at that moment he saw an old college friend so he struggled through the crush to join him and they spent the next twenty minutes making ribald comments about the various impossible people in the assembly, which was entertaining and cheering. He would know his father's decision soon enough.

He knew it five days later after he'd paid his courtesy call on the duchess and been given the address of the 'best chambers' and a letter of introduction to the head of those chambers, whom the duchess pronounced 'a stout chap'. He went back to his father's house feeling so elated that his feet were barely touching the ground and showed him the letter with some pride and considerable satisfaction.

'Ah well,' his father said. 'We can't argue with a duchess. I suppose 'twill be a convenience to have my own lawyer on hand. But I trust you will allow me to assist you in the matter of findin' a suitable wife. You will stay in London for the Season and attend such balls as I deem necessary, will you not?'

He had to agree. How could he do anything else?

'I will be back as soon as it is humanly possible,' he wrote to Milly that evening, *'which will not be until the end of the Season, I fear. I must attend these wretched balls now that I have given my word to the pater although I will tell you candidly that I am dreading them and that in any case it will all be a waste of time for there is no one else for me but you nor ever will be. Please tell Mr Cartwright that his advice has been taken at last, which will surprise him, and thank him for all his kindness towards me.'*

Milly was most upset to know that she would have to spend the summer without him, especially as she'd been looking forward to it so much, but she put a brave face on it and when she went to York for a couple of days she explained it to her mother as though it was all perfectly normal and to be expected. And Jane, who was now quite sure that this was a serious love affair, made commiserating noises but otherwise said little to her.

She told Nathaniel all about it, naturally, when they were on their own together later that night, describing how sad her poor Milly had been when she arrived and how bravely she'd tried to hide it.

"Tis such a nonsense to make him stay in London,' she said, 'when anyone with half an eye can see he wants to marry our Milly.'

'He is on the social merry-go-round,' Nathaniel said, 'like all the other eligible bachelors in London and they will find him a wife whether he will or no. He'll need to be uncommon strong-willed if he's to resist them.'

Jane thought about that for a few minutes, remembering how meek her poor Felix had been as a little boy and how easily his father had bullied him. 'We must hope love will give him strength,' she said at last.

'Now,' he said, pulling on his nightshirt, 'ask me what *my* news is.'

'I hope 'tis better than mine,' she said, climbing into the bed and smoothing the covers over her legs.

'We are invited to a party,' he said, and when she looked the obvious question at him, 'to celebrate Princess Victoria's eighteenth birthday. I met Mr Nicholson in town today on his way to buy another painting and he was telling me all about it. 'Twill be a very grand affair, so he says, which I don't doubt, seeing it's being given by Mr Hudson. He was sure we would be invited. And when I got home, there was the invitation. What do you think of that?'

She said she wasn't a bit surprised and agreed

that it was a fine thing to be invited, although she was secretly thinking how unfair it was that George Hudson should be rich and prosperous and throwing grand parties while Milly and Felix were being deliberately kept apart.

It was a very grand party indeed and, to her perverse disappointment, really quite enjoyable. Whatever else you might say about the obnoxious Mr Hudson, he certainly knew how to celebrate. It was the talk of the town for weeks afterwards. Then just as interest was dying down, the news arrived that the old king was dead and that Princess Victoria had been proclaimed Queen of England.

'There will be no hope at all of getting to Longfield to see you now,' Felix wrote dolefully to Milly, *'even for a day. London has gone wild over the new queen. There are more parties planned than ever and the pater is insistent that I attend every single one. I cannot see any end to it except the end of the Season, for which I pray.'*

He was back at Longfield Hall on 11 August and went straight to the schoolroom, where Milly and the girls were sitting together by the window, reading their fairy stories. He strode across the room and had caught his beloved by both hands and kissed her before he could come to his senses and realize what an improper thing he was doing. Fortunately his nieces were so preoccupied by their story that they barely noticed the interruption, except to scold him for it.

'Do sit down, Uncle Felix,' Maria said. 'It's "The Fisherman's Wife".'

He was still bemused by being with his darling again and quite unable to think straight. 'What?'

'Just sit down,' Arabella told him, sternly. 'You are standing in the light.'

So he took one of their chairs from the table and placed it where he had a perfect view of his lovely girl and when the story was done he persuaded them all out for a walk in the park where he managed to snatch several kisses and planned to meet his darling again after dinner. He was so happy he felt quite dizzy.

Later that evening as the day cooled and a quiet dusk descended, they walked in the grounds and he told her about the balls, 'which were uncommon dull', and the scores of young women who had been pushed his way, 'and not a pretty one among 'em' and how he had met Sir Godfrey Featherstone at the Inns of Court and been taken on as his junior and would start work in October.

'In London?'

'I fear so.'

The knowledge pinched her heart. 'You will still be able to come here?' she hoped.

'Not very often, I fear.'

Her heart flinched again but she answered him sensibly. 'Then we must make the most of the time we have,' she said.

They made the most of it until it was completely dark and they only had the light of a fitful moon to guide them back to the house. And from then on they took every opportunity that offered, even if it was in more company than they would have liked, riding with the children every morning, pretending to teach them archery, dining together *en famille* whenever Sir Percival was away and walking in the wonderfully enclosing darkness of every evening, talking of the time when they would be married and living in a house of their own, 'which will be soon, I promise you, my darling'. It was a short, sweet, tantalizing time and over far too soon.

'I will write to you every day,' he promised on their last evening together. And did. Although, as she told her mother sadly the next time she visited Shelton House, ''Tis not the same as having him beside me.'

'You will see him at Christmas,' Jane comforted.

But to her miserable disappointment, Christmas was denied them because his father wrote to say that his presence was required 'at home' over the holiday.

'It is most unfortunate,' he wrote to Milly, *'because I had hoped that I would be able to find the right moment to ask Mr Cartwright if he would be agreeable to our courtship, but it cannot be helped. I must keep the pater sweet or he will forbid our marriage, which, I promise you, is coming nearer day by day. It will not be long before I have earned sufficient to rent a house out in the country, in Mortlake perhaps or Clapham or Eltham. There are some pretty villages south of the Thames, and then we will marry, Mr Cartwright being willing, which I am sure he will be – will he not – and be together for the rest of our lives. I miss you more than I can say and am yours most unhappily until I see you again,*

'Felix.'

George Hudson spent his Christmas in the happiest frame of mind, planning his next extravagant party. Princess Victoria's birthday party had been a tremendous success but he wasn't a man to rest on his laurels – never had been – and one success simply spurred him on to want another even greater. As soon as he knew that Queen Victoria's coronation would be on 28 June he began to make plans and preparations. He had six months in which to organize his great event and six months would only just be enough for the sort of magnificence he had in mind. He started work on it as soon as the new year began.

This time Jane Cartwright paid very little attention to what he was doing, although she went to his party, having been invited, and ate his food and drank his champagne. But her mind was elsewhere, fretting over Milly's rather too obvious unhappiness and her own inability to do anything about it. Felix was in London, enduring his second 'wife-hunting' Season, and that would have been reason enough for the poor girl to be cast down but this time being kept apart from him seemed to be even more of a trial to her. On her last visit to Shelton House, she hadn't been herself at all. She'd drooped and stayed silent at table and even gone out walking on her own in a shower of rain.

''Tis so unlike her,' Jane said to Nathaniel after her poor sad daughter had climbed into the dog cart to be driven back to Long Hall.

'She's bound to be missing him,' Nathaniel said reasonably.

'Aye, she is,' Jane said. 'But there's more to it

than that. I've never seen her so cast down. Never. I tell 'ee there were times when 'twas almost as if the affair were over. Oh Nathaniel! That couldn't be the cause of it, could it? He'd not have quarrelled with her, surely. Not my Felix. He were allus such a tender heart. Oh my poor Milly! I shall have to do summat about it.'

'But not until I get back from Rugby,' Nathaniel said rather anxiously, 'and not until you know what is really happening, what I'm certain she'll tell you in her own good time.'

'Aye. Happen she will,' Jane said, but she didn't sound as if she thought it very likely. 'This is what comes of long courtships. I never did hold wi' long courtships.'

'Aye,' he laughed at her. 'So I've noticed.'

She smiled at that but her forehead was still puckered with worry.

The problem plagued her for the next two days and would have gone on troubling her for even longer if her thoughts hadn't been dramatically interrupted. On the third day after Nathaniel had left for Rugby, when she was planning the day's meals with Mrs Cadwallader, she had an unexpected visit from Mother Hardcastle, and the news she brought put all thought of poor Milly right out of her head.

'I'm so sorry to be the bearer of bad tidings, my dear,' the midwife said, as she took the seat that Jane had offered her. 'But there it is. In the midst of life we are in death.'

The word put Jane into an instant alarm so that her thoughts spun like fireflies. It couldn't be Nathaniel because Mrs Hardcastle wouldn't

270

know what was happening to him, nor Milly, but it could be Lizzie. 'Who is it?' she said, forgetting her manners in her need to know.

'I'm sorry to tell 'ee straight out,' Mrs Hardcastle said, 'but there's no way I can mek it easy. 'Tis your father.'

'Dead?'

'Aye. Dropped dead in the fields yesterday at the end of the day. Never said a word, apparently, just dropped down dead where he stood. I came on account of your Ma being in such a state, poor woman.'

Jane's thoughts were still spinning. He couldn't be dead. She'd only seen him last week and he was his usual red-faced self, stomping into the kitchen and kissing her in his usual rough way, looking every bit as strong as he always did, if a little more stooped. Then she took a deep breath and understood that her mother was in a state and needed her and that brought her to her senses and she knew she had to go to Scrayingham at once. She got up, walked briskly over to the fireplace and gave the bell-pull a sharp tug. There were things to be done. For a start, she would need the carriage and Audrey would have to be told to look after the children until she got back.

Half an hour later she and Mrs Hardcastle were on their way to her father's cottage. It was a quiet summer morning, the sky was full of gentle clouds and there were skylarks singing over the cornfields. It simply wasn't possible that her father was dead.

But one look at her mother brought reality into

271

the sharpest focus. She was sitting in her old chair beside the empty hearth and she was totally distraught, rocking to and fro, to and fro, her face so pale that even her lips had no colour. Jane strode across the kitchen at once and took her in her arms. ''Tis all right, Ma,' she said. 'I'll look after you.'

'What am I to do?' her mother said, looking down at her old patched skirt. 'Oh Janey! What *am* I to do? They'll not let me stay here, bein' tied an' all. What's to become of me?'

'Tha'rt to come home wi' me and be cared for,' Jane told her. 'I'll see to t'funeral and such. Have 'ee had owt to eat?'

'I couldn't eat,' her mother said. ''Twould stick in my throat.'

I'll coax her to eat when we're back home, Jane thought. A little bowl of gruel or summat. For the moment the important thing was to get her out of the cottage and away from the anguish.

It surprised her when her mother got up meekly and allowed herself to be led out to the carriage. 'If you'll just wait for another five minutes, Mr Morton,' she said to her coachman. 'I'll not be long.' Then she went back into the cottage to gather her mother's belongings and say goodbye to her father.

He was lying on his back on the bed with his arms folded across his chest and his familiar face looking completely empty, just as poor little Dickie's had done. 'Dear Pa,' she said to him. 'Don' 'ee fret about Ma. I'll look after her. I'll look after everything.' And she kissed his cold forehead.

She was true to her word, even though everything she did over the next few days was fraught with grief. She drove to Scrayingham Church and arranged the funeral, organized the funeral breakfast, ordered mourning clothes for her mother, sent invitations to her father's three cousins and wrote to Nathaniel, who sent a letter back by return of post to say he would be home in time for the funeral and to Milly, who came home the very next day. And then, after what seemed an endless time and no time at all, they were all standing beside the grave as her pa's simple coffin was being lowered into the ground and the priest was speaking the ritual words of farewell. And she turned her head to look at her weeping mother and her sad-eyed daughter and remembered how worried she'd been. How life and death do sweep you on, she thought. I haven't given 'ee so much as a thought since Pa died. But I'll make up to 'ee now.

It was easier thought than done. Her mother needed a lot of gentling, Nat and Mary were difficult, Nathaniel was away in Rugby again and Milly's three-day stay was over before she'd barely had a chance to speak to her, leave alone ask her about Felix. In fact nothing was said until she was packing her travelling bag and ready to leave. And then it was her mother who opened the subject.

'We'll see thee again come Christmas,' she said, as she kissed her drooping granddaughter good-bye.

Milly smiled at her. 'Aye,' she said.

'And Felix too?' her grandmother pressed on. 'He comes to stay at Christmas, en't that right?'

'Only if his pater will allow it,' Milly said sadly, 'which I doubt he will.'

'Oh, I'm sure he will,' Mary Jerdon said. 'He'll not want to keep 'ee apart at Christmas time, not bein' tha'rt so fond of each other.'

She was most upset when Milly sat down on the bed and burst into tears. 'My dear child,' she said, putting her arms round Milly's shaking shoulders. 'What is it? Tell your old nanna.'

And out it all came tumbling, how Sir Mortimer was a brute – *'tha knows that, Ma'* – and how he was determined to make Felix marry *'some awful girl from some awful family, whether he will or no'*, how Felix didn't like to argue with him and was being pushed from one party to the next and not allowed to visit anyone except his family and how unhappy she was.

'If he'd only make his mind up that he's got to say summat,' she said, looking at Jane, 'but he can't do it. He puts things off when they're difficult – what I can understand bein' how gentle he is and I wouldn't want him any other way – but that only makes 'em worse. He said he was going to ask Mr Cartwright if he could marry me, all proper like, and that was last Christmas. He promised me, Ma. You'd think that'd be the easiest thing in t'world, but no, he couldn't even pluck up t'courage to do *that*. For the life of me, I can't see how we're ever going to get married. We'll just go on and on, growing further and further apart. He used to write to me every day in the Season and now it's only every other day, and in the end he'll marry some awful girl because that's what his father wants him to do

274

and he can't stand up to him. I've lost him, Ma, an' that's the truth of it.' And she cried worse than ever.

Jane took a handkerchief from the drawer and handed it to her. 'Dry your eyes,' she said, 'and try not to fret too much. Tha's not lost, not by a long chalk. We can change things atween us, you'll see. I'll not stand by and see thee unhappy and do nowt.'

Milly mopped her eyes. 'I don't see what you *can* do,' she said.

'There'll be summat,' Jane promised. 'There allus is. For a start, I'll not let the old man bully you. I've stood up to him afore and I'll stand up to him again, if need be.'

'She will too,' her mother said. 'I've never know'd such a fighter.' And that made Milly smile.

'That's better,' Jane said. 'Now you leave it to me and don' 'ee fret. Tell your Felix he's more than welcome here whenever he wants to come.' And when Milly looked at her bleakly: 'Christmas if he can or if not Christmas some other time. 'Twill all work out, my darling, I promise.' She didn't have the faintest idea what could be done, but she knew she would do it.

19

'Gentlemen!' George Hudson said, standing before the committee of the York and North Western Railway, legs commandingly astride, thumbs in the pockets of his white waistcoat, round face beaming with self-satisfaction. 'I think I can promise you that this will be the biggest celebration our old city has ever seen. *This* will be the official opening of the York and North Western Railway, and this will top every party I've ever given. You have my word for it. And if George Hudson gives you his word, you may depend on it.'

His listeners cheered and thumped the table, for if there was one thing they knew about the ebullient Mr Hudson, besides the fact that he paid good dividends, it was that he knew how to entertain.

The news pleased Jane Cartwright too.

'Now this,' she said, handing the newspaper to Nathaniel, 'is exactly what we need for Felix.'

He read the article briefly and laughed at her. 'Is it indeed?'

'It is indeed,' Jane told him seriously. ''Tis just what I've been waiting for. A grand occasion with plenty of guests and lots of food and drink. Summat lively. He'll not have time to sit and brood if he's rattling along on a train or sitting next to our Milly at a banquet. 'Tis just the very thing.'

Nathaniel grinned at her. 'I'm sure Mr Hudson had your Felix in mind when he planned it.'

'I don't really care what Mr Hudson had in mind,' Jane said. ''Twill suit *our* purposes to perfection and that's what counts.'

'Then I suppose I must contrive to get him an invitation.'

'Of course,' Jane said. 'We can't have him drooping about not saying anything the way he did at Christmas. He'll never marry Milly if we let him go on like that. He needs a push.'

'Which you intend to give him,' Nathaniel said, laughing at her.

As the date of the official opening grew nearer, York fell into a fever of excitement. New outfits were ordered, carriages and horses were spruced up ready for the parade, the gossip was endless. Milly begged leave of absence from her two pupils for four whole days, Jane bought a new bonnet, Nathaniel treated himself to a grey top hat, and after a long three weeks while everybody in Shelton House held their breath and hoped, Felix wrote to say that he had written to Mr Hudson accepting his kind invitation and would be driving his carriage over for the great occasion and was very much looking forward to it.

'Now all we want is the weather,' Mary Jerdon said to her son-in-law.

'Which Jane will have ordered up for us,' he said.

She laughed at that. 'Even my Janey can't change the weather,' she said.

'When she's in one of her determined moods,'

Nathaniel told her, 'I believe she could turn the tides.'

And sure enough the weather was superb. As the 400 guests arrived at the Guildhall for the inaugural breakfast, the sun shone on their fine feathers and made their polished carriages gleam like new. And Jane was delighted to see that Felix handed Milly out of his own carriage in the most loving and gentlemanly way and walked into the Guildhall arm in arm with her.

'So far, so good,' she said as she and Nathaniel followed them.

It was a champagne breakfast, as everybody there expected, and as they emerged into the sunshine afterwards, replete and not a little tipsy, they found the carriages lined up and waiting for them, so the procession got off to a smooth start and looked and sounded extremely grand. Jane said it made her feel as if she were the queen. But the best moment was when she saw Mary and Nat waiting on the bridge, just as she'd arranged, with their grandmother and Audrey holding their hands and their eyes wide with the wonder of it all.

The great George Hudson was driving at the head of the procession, waving to right and left and smiling at the crowds, with his wife sitting stoutly beside him, and *he* was in his element. He *knew* he was royalty and of a real and laudable kind, for weren't folk calling him the Railway King? He heard it everywhere he went and the newspapers were beginning to use the title as if it were his name. And why not? He was every bit as rich as a king now and had quite as much power.

'A grand occasion,' he said to Lizzie with immense satisfaction. 'And nowt but what I've earned.'

But the best and proudest moment was when they turned into Thief Lane and he saw the train all ready and waiting for them, eighteen coaches long, no less, five first class and ten second class for all his guests, and three third class for the navvies who'd worked on the line, with one of Mr Stephenson's splendid locomotives at each end, one for the outward journey to South Milford, and the other to bring them all home again. It was a triumph.

It took a very long time and a great deal of excitement to get everybody aboard but it was eventually done and the engine shrieked and they were off, heading south into the open countryside at an unbelievable speed with white smoke puffing out behind them and parasols fluttering in the breeze they were causing.

'Wouldn't our littl'uns enjoy this,' Jane said to Nathaniel as they were swayed from side to side by the onrush of their journey. 'We must take *them* for a ride as soon as we can. 'Twould be such an adventure for them.'

Felix said it would be an adventure for anybody and wondered how far they were going on this particular trip and what they would do when they got there. 'Feller at breakfast was telling me Mr Hudson means to build a line from York to London.'

'Aye,' Nathaniel said. 'He does. The plans are already under way.'

'Amazing,' Felix said. 'He is truly an extraordinary man. Quite extraordinary. To have built all this is amazing enough but to build a railway all the way to London... It takes one's breath away, it truly does.'

It took their impressive train just over half an hour to reach the little wooden platform at South Milford and then half a dozen men in their new railway uniforms appeared along the platform to help the ladies to dismount and to inform the party that they had half an hour to explore the countryside and to reassure them that the train would whistle when it was time for them to return.

'He has every little detail planned,' Felix said admiringly.

'It's the nature of the man,' Nathaniel said as they walked down the little flight of steps. There were footpaths leading east and west, running alongside yet another set of gleaming railway lines, and they took the westward one, which seemed the natural choice to Nathaniel as it led them towards Leeds. He and Felix walked at a sturdy pace, talking of railways and their recent champagne breakfast while he watched until Jane and Milly had fallen so far behind that they were lost among the strolling crowd. It was time to give this young man the push he needed.

'You had something particular to say to me, I believe,' he said and smiled.

Felix blushed so much that he was rosy to the roots of his fair hair. 'Well, sir,' he said, 'as to that, I mean to say, there was something, actually there is something, only the truth of it is it's a deal more complicated than I would wish, so perhaps...'

'There's nowt so complicated but can't be cured by a little consideration,' Nathaniel said, quoting the old saying. 'If I've learnt nothing else from working on the railways I've learnt that.' And then as Felix blushed and said nothing, he prodded for a second time. 'It concerns my step-daughter, I believe.'

The hedges around them were a twitter of nestlings calling to be fed, the corn was green and promised a good harvest, and in the old lush fields beside the new straight lines of their amazing railway, white lambs snuggled against their mothers' mud-flecked sides and watched them curiously.

'Which is all in the nature of things,' Nathaniel prompted.

'The truth of it is, sir,' Felix ventured at last, 'the truth of it is, I would like to – um – ask your permission to – um – marry your Milly. However ... however, the fact of the matter is ... I would have liked to have been able to tell you that I could provide for her, I mean to say, provide for her well, that one day she would become Lady Fitzwilliam and live in Foster Manor and that she would never want for anything, but I fear that is uncertain.'

'On account of your father, I don't doubt.'

Felix swallowed painfully. 'He has made up his mind that I'm to marry a girl he approves of,' he admitted, 'which means a girl he's chosen for me.'

'And if you do not?'

'Then I fear he may disinherit me.'

'I can see that that is a problem for you,'

Nathaniel said gravely, 'and a very considerable one, however it need not concern us unduly, for the matter between is whether or not I would give my permission to your marriage. Even if you were to be disinherited you would not go penniless, that is true, is it not?'

'I could earn a living, sir. I am a barrister now that I've completed my pupillage. I take cases. Not very many at the moment, I must be truthful, but I'm building a reputation. Quite a good one, actually. I am patient and thorough and I persevere. My clients are pleased with what I do for them. Sir Godfrey speaks well of me and that's quite a feather in my cap, for he is a man who speaks his mind.' He was talking with some pride now, as Nathaniel was pleased to notice, and a great deal more easily. 'In short, sir, I am confident that my career will grow. I will earn more eventually, possibly a great deal more. I don't earn a great deal at present, I have to admit, but what I *do* earn is enough to keep us.'

Nathaniel smiled at him. 'Then you have my permission,' he said.

Felix was blushing again. 'Thank you, sir,' he said, holding out his hand, which Nathaniel shook. 'Thank you very kindly.' Then he couldn't think what else to say so perhaps it was just as well that the train gave out a long shriek to recall them to their carriages and that allowed him to run back along the path to find his beloved. And Nathaniel, walking more sedately behind him, was able to send an eye signal to Jane as she walked towards him that the deed had been done and all was well.

They rode back to York in great pomp and the happiest state, although since there were other guests in the carriage with them they couldn't talk about this great change to their fortunes, but Felix and Milly sat happily hand in hand, and Jane smiled so much, first at her daughter and then at her husband, that by the time they chuffed back into Thief Lane, her jaws were aching.

A civic banquet seemed entirely appropriate after that.

George Hudson stood at the centre of the high table in the banqueting hall, with the great George Stephenson beside him, smiling at his 400 guests. Success on such a stunning and public scale was lifting his spirits to ecstasy. It was entirely deserved, of course, which was all the more reason to enjoy it. He'd tackled things that nobody else could have tackled or even dreamed of – he, George Hudson, who'd once been mocked as a mere farmer's son and a one-time linen draper, and he'd done it all on his own, often with far too much opposition. And this was just the beginning, as he would soon be telling his guests.

The master of ceremonies was clearing his throat and calling the assembly to order. 'My lords, ladies and gentlemen, pray silence for your host, Mr George Hudson, Lord Mayor of York.' And they were applauding and turning expectant faces towards him. It was a perfect moment.

He began his speech with a graceful tribute to George Stephenson. 'If ever there is a man who deserved to be held up to the public approbation of the whole world,' he said, beaming at his

283

famous colleague, 'that man is Mr Stephenson.' His audience applauded with enthusiasm and, from that moment on, he had them agog for every word he uttered. He was cheered to the echo every time he paused to take breath and wine, and was given prolonged applause when he predicted that within a year there would be trains running from Edinburgh to York and from York to London by way of Derby and Rugby. 'They will take no more than ten hours to complete the entire distance,' he told his happy listeners, 'and they will travel at a speed of over twenty miles an hour, just as you did this morning.'

When he finally sat down they didn't just cheer, they beat the table with their fists until he was rosy with success.

The next speaker to be called upon was Mr James Meek and he seemed to be in an un-characteristically sanguine mood. 'London,' he predicted, 'will be the head of our railway, Edin-burgh the feet and York the heart.' The diners were delighted by such sentiments and waited to see what he would say next. He turned so that he was facing George Hudson and gave him a sly smile. 'I hope,' he said, 'that the head will never be afflicted with apoplexy, nor the feet with gout, and that York will continue sound at heart.'

Most of his listeners thought that this was just a pretty conceit and applauded it roundly but George was peeved. There was no need to go on about gout – that was just spiteful when the man knew how badly he suffered with it – nor to make snide remarks about the soundness of York's heart. There's nowt wrong wi' my heart, he thought, and

I can stand on my own two feet no matter how much gout I've got.

'The man's jealous,' he said to Lizzie under cover of the applause. 'This is all on account of me being Lord Mayor two years running. Won't do him a happorth of good. I've got his measure, don't you worry. Nasty sly-faced bit o' goods.'

The speeches continued, ten opulent courses were served and devoured, wine glasses were constantly refilled and by the time the great crowd rose from the table for their short stroll to the ballroom, many of them were almost too drunk to stand and the opening reel was a riot of trodden toes and cheerfully inebriated men who'd forgotten which way they were supposed to turn. Jane and Nathaniel retreated from the chaos after the first five minutes and sat peaceably at their table to watch the proceedings.

'They're so happy,' Jane said, as Milly and Felix skipped by, gazing into each other's eyes. 'If he don't propose to her now I'll eat my hat.' It was a torture to her to have to sit here and wait when her dear, dear daughter was so close to the question she wanted to hear and the answer she wanted to give. 'Oh, he *must* propose to her now, surely to goodness. Yes, look, they're going out into the grounds.'

It was dark and rather chill out in the gardens after the crush and heat of the ballroom but blissfully private. Milly and Felix strolled towards the river arm in arm still singing the tune of the reel. They were dizzy with love and wine and good food and impervious to the cold. Above their heads the stars were white pinpricks in a velvet sky, the music of the next dance drifted out towards them over the lawns and below their feet the river was a moving blackness made visible by the reflected lights from the Guildhall.

'I feel as if I'm dreaming,' Felix said, as they stood side by side leaning against the parapet. 'I shall wake up presently and none of this will be true.'

She leant amorously against his side, looked up into his face and pinched his cheek.

'Ow!' he said, jumping back from her. 'What did you do that for?'

She laughed at him. 'If you'd been asleep you wouldn't have felt it,' she said. 'Now tell me what Mr Cartwright said.'

'You know what he said,' he protested. 'I've been telling you all afternoon.'

'So why don't 'ee propose to me?' she teased. 'You're mighty slow about it.'

'I couldn't very well go down on one knee in the ballroom,' he said.

'No,' she agreed, 'possibly not. But you can do it now.'

'Is that what you want me to do?'

'Naturally. I couldn't say yes to 'ee if you were standing on your feet. Or on mine as the case may be, what you were doing in that reel, summat chronic.'

He was appalled to be told such a thing. 'I wasn't,' he said and then asked anxiously. 'Was I?'

'You were,' she said, laughing at him again, 'but I'll not scold 'ee for it. Not if you propose nicely.'

'Now?'

'Now.'

He lowered himself rather gingerly to one knee. He really *was* very squiffy. He reached for her hand and took it, more to steady himself than because it was the thing to do. 'Miss Smith,' he said, gazing up at her. 'It cannot have escaped your notice that I am very much – um – enamoured of you. Is that the right word, Millikens?'

'Aye,' she said, delighted by him but pretending to be severe. 'It is. But do get on with it, for mercy's sake. I never knew anyone so longwinded.'

'Where was I?'

'May I have the honour,' she prompted.

'Ah yes,' he said and took a deep breath. 'My dearest Dumma-dumma, may I have the honour of your hand in matrimony?'

'Yes, yes, yes,' she said, stooping to kiss him full on the lips.

At that he had a fit of the giggles. He simply couldn't help it, the relief was so ovewhelming. 'I can't believe it, I tell 'ee,' he said, between gasps of laughter. 'I simply can't believe it.'

Now and a little late in the occasion, she realized that he was kneeling in mud. 'You're getting mud all over your breeches,' she said. 'What will people think?'

'I don't care,' he said. 'Let 'em think, say I. Let the whole world think.'

There were people approaching them along the path. Rather grand-looking people.

'Get up, my darling,' Milly said. 'They're looking at us.'

He got up but he was too excited for caution. 'My dearest, darling Dumma-dumma,' he said and kissed her long and passionately.

When he lifted his head he discovered that he was being scrutinized by one of his old college friends. 'I say, Felix!' that gentleman said. 'I never thought you had it in you. You *do* go it!'

Felix recovered sufficiently to make introductions. 'Miss Smith, allow me to present an old friend of mine. Rufus de Seward. His pater's a lord, don't ye know.'

Milly had recovered her balance more quickly than her lover. 'Your servant, sir,' she said and dropped him a pretty curtsey.

'Rufus,' Felix said with splendid aplomb, 'allow me to present my darling Miss Millicent Smith who has just done me the honour of agreeing to be my wife.'

'My stars!' Rufus said. 'You *do* go it!'

They walked back into the ballroom together, giggling and laughing, and Milly and Felix ran straight to her mother's table as soon as they got in through the door because they couldn't wait to tell her they were engaged. Rufus watched them rather enviously for a few seconds, and then strolled off to find his friends and tell them the amazing news but, unfortunately for Felix, the first person he actually found was his father and his father had seen their cheerful entry and quizzed him about it straightaway.

'Was that not Sir Mortimer's son I saw coming in with you?' he said.

'It was indeed, Pater,' Rufus told him. 'Bit of a

surprise, what?'

'And who was that *person* hanging on to his arm?'

Rufus was too cheerful with drink to realize that he was treading on dangerous ground. 'Oh, she's his fiancée,' he said. 'They've just got engaged. He was telling me all about it.'

'Engaged?' his father said, eyebrows disappearing into his hair. 'Never heard the like. Most unsuitable person I ever saw. Looks like a governess. I can't imagine what Sir Mortimer will have to say about it. Does she have a name, this person?'

Rufus dithered but he could hardly disobey his father by not answering his question – not now the conversation was under way. 'Millicent,' he said 'Millicent Smith.'

The eyebrows disappeared completely. 'Smith?' the noble lord said and his voice was shrill with outrage. 'Smith?'

'She's a deuced fine gel, sir,' Rufus said, trying to make amends. 'Frightfully jolly.'

'Jolly!' his father said. 'My dear boy! She's common.' Sir Mortimer would certainly have to be told about this and the sooner the better.

20

The next morning, while most of his guests were sleeping off their excesses, George Hudson woke at first light. Despite the enormous success of the grand opening, Mr Meek's spiteful jibe still scratched in his brain and, as always when he felt he'd been unfairly put down, he needed to work to restore his sense of importance. He wrapped his dressing gown around him and strode off to the library, where he took Nathaniel's huge railway map from its long drawer and spread it out across the table. Just the sight of it restored his equilibrium, all those long dependable double lines, drawn in red ink where his railways already ran, and in pencil where the lines were being built or still in planning. It was admirable. He traced the route from York to London with his finger, through Normanton to Sheffield and Derby and then on to Rugby. I'll complete the South Milford to Altoft section as soon as it can be done, he thought, and then I can link up with the North Midland Railway. That should have been done long since. And I must send a letter to Mr Stephenson and ask him to dinner. We hardly had time to talk about anything yesterday and his proposal for a route to Scarborough and Whitby is very sound. Needs following up. A line like that would do a deal of trade.

Let Meek and his nasty-minded cronies say

what they like, he thought, as he sat down at his desk and reached for pen and ink. I'm the man who gets things done – and I'm a damned fine Lord Mayor, what's more, which nobody can deny. Why shouldn't I be Mayor two years running? All that fuss about it being unconstitutional is just a lot of rot. If you've got a good 'un, stick with him, that's what I say, and damn the constitution.

By the time the letter was written, Lizzie had come waddling in to see where he was and to tell him that breakfast would be served in half an hour and that the post had come.

It was a very satisfactory post, for the first three letters were singing his praises for throwing such an enjoyable party and the fourth was from Harrow school saying they were pleased to offer his son George a place in the school.

'There you are, George,' he said to his quiet son, who was sitting beside his mother eating bacon and kidneys as neatly as he could and concentrating hard. 'When you're thirteen, you'll be going to Harrow. What do 'ee think of that?'

George swallowed the latest mouthful, wiped his mouth with his table napkin and said he was gratified.

'And so you should be, boy,' his father boomed. 'Cost me a deal of money has that. So see you're worth it.' Then he thought he ought to pay attention to his other children. 'Sit up straight, John, I don't like to see you all a-slouch. It's bad for the spine. Then if you're a good boy I'll send you to Harrow too. And you an' all, William, when you're old enough.'

'What about me, Pa?' Ann said, tossing her newly brushed ringlets at him and flirting her eyes because she knew he liked it. 'Am I to go to Harrow too?'

'You,' he told her, making eyes back, 'are to have a rich husband what'll keep you in fine style and give you everything you want. Can't say fairer than that, can I?' Then, having distributed largesse to all four of them, he went back to spearing his kidneys and picked up the morning paper to see what they had to say about his grand opening. And it had better be good.

Over on the other side of town in the sunlit warmth of their pale green breakfast room in Shelton House, Mr and Mrs Cartwright and their now extended family were all talking at once. There was so much they wanted to say and it all had to be said that very minute. Mary wanted to know when her Milly was going to get married and scowled when Felix said he didn't know because he had to ask his father's permission first and his father was away visiting a cousin for the next two months, so she asked if she could be a bridesmaid and carry the flowers and clapped her hands when Milly said yes; Nat asked whether Felix was going to be his 'really truly brother' and clapped *his* hands when he was told he was, declaring to anyone who was actually listening that he'd always wanted a really truly brother; and Milly laughed at them and said she couldn't really believe it 'even now' and her grandmother laughed at them and said she'd never heard anything to equal it and Nathaniel begged them to speak 'one at a time' and none of them took any notice of him. Felix was in a state of such over-powering happiness that he could barely put a sentence together without blushing and Jane smiled and smiled because her two babies were so gloriously, transparently happy with one another. And wasn't that exactly what she'd said was going to happen? And as if all this weren't enough, they had three more days to enjoy themselves before Milly and Felix and her dear Nathaniel had to go back to their work.

''Tis a beautiful day,' she said, when they finally paused for breath. 'Let's take a drive out into the country and have us a picnic. What do 'ee think?'

They had two picnics, because the weather held for them, and they dined well and noisily every evening, and when the happy lovers finally kissed them goodbye and left for their short drive to Longfield Hall, Jane was still stupid with delight at what had happened. Oh, she thought, life is so good.

Milly and Felix took such a long time to say goodbye to one another when they reached Longfield Hall that Nathaniel's coachman, who was waiting on his seat, discreetly looking in another direction, was forced to dismount and remind the young gentleman that he had a stage-coach to catch and that if they didn't get back to the Star and Garter in good time it would go without him. And as he was due to appear in court the following afternoon, Felix sighed and agreed to get back into the carriage.

It was a long lonely journey back to London

and the overnight stop at Rugby only served to increase his loneliness, for the food was poor and the bed was extremely uncomfortable. He felt weary and decidedly grubby when he climbed back on the coach early the next morning. I must take a cab to Charlotte Square and get washed and changed before I go to court, he thought. It wouldn't be at all proper to appear there in his present dishevelled state.

He was surprised to be greeted at the door of the house by his father's butler, Mr Jennings.

'Sir Mortimer's compliments, Mr Felix,' Mr Jennings said. 'I am to tell you he would be obliged if you would join him in the library.'

'Now, Jennings?' Felix asked.

'As soon as you arrived, sir. Those were his instructions.'

It sounded ominous but Felix did as he was told. He could wash and dress later.

His father was sitting at his desk, busily writing. 'Yes?' he said without looking up.

'You wished to see me, Pater.'

The pen was wiped and put on its stand, the page dusted dry, the chair swivelled until they were facing one another. 'I do indeed, sir,' Sir Mortimer said. 'Sit down.' And when Felix had perched himself rather precariously on one of the chairs beside the library table, he gave him a discomforting look and went on. 'I have been hearin' some extremely disquietin' reports of you, sir.'

As an answer seemed to be expected, Felix swallowed and provided one, as politely as he could. 'I am sorry to hear that, Father.'

'I trust you are, sir, and that the matter will be remedied.'

He knows about Milly, Felix thought, and his heart shuddered. But he didn't say anything for there didn't seem to be anything he *could* say. Instead he concentrated on staying calm and not showing any emotion. His father's long nose was pinched white with anger and his expression was so cold it was turning the air to frost. It was several chilly seconds before he spoke again.

'You were seen at some vulgar celebration in York, I believe.'

'The opening of the York and North Midlands Railway,' Felix told him, speaking with deliberate calm in his gentle barrister's voice. 'It was a very grand occasion.'

'That,' his father said, 'is of no concern to me. The unfortunate matter we have to discuss is the company you were keepin'.'

Felix tried to deflect him. 'I was there as the guest of Mr Nathaniel Cartwright,' he said, 'who is one of Mr Hudson's principal engineers and a man of some standing.'

Sir Mortimer flicked that information aside with his long white fingers, as if it were of no consequence at all. 'I was told, by a reliable source,' he said, freezing the air between them, 'that you were in the company of a highly unsuitable person.'

'I was with Mr Cartwright's stepdaughter, sir.'

'In the company of a highly unsuitable person to whom you claimed to be affianced. I trust you were in your cups, sir, and unaware of what you were sayin'.'

Felix steadied himself before he answered. 'I was perfectly aware of what I was saying, Father,' he said. 'Miss Smith has agreed to be my wife, so, yes, we are affianced.'

'You will pardon me, sir, until you have asked my permission and it has been granted, you are no such thing. Let me tell you here and now, I have absolutely no intention of agreein' to an alliance with a tradesman's daughter. You will terminate this engagement forthwith.'

'I cannot do that, Father. I love her and I have given her my word.'

'Love!' his father sniffed. 'Love has nothin' to do with the case. We are talkin' about marriage, which is a matter of breedin' and society and family obligations. If you love the gel you may take her as your mistress until you tire of her, providin' you are discreet about it, but marriage, sir, marriage is quite another thing. And marriage with this "person" is out of the question. I trust I make myself clear.'

'Perfectly clear, sir,' Felix said, straightening his spine, for battle had now been joined. 'However I must tell you that I intend to marry Miss Smith no matter what you might say. I love her and mean to make her my wife.'

Sir Mortimer's anger was hard as ice. 'In that case, sir,' he said, 'you leave me no alternative. If this marriage goes ahead, I will disinherit you.'

'As you wish, sir.'

'Your folly does you no credit,' Sir Mortimer said, breathing deeply to control his anger. 'However, I am nothin' if not fair. I will make no decision for the moment. I shall be visitin' with my cousins in Norfolk probably for the rest of the Season. You have until August to come to your senses and be done with all this foolishness. Is that clear?'

Felix agreed that it was, stood up, stiffly, and left the room. He felt as though he'd been pole-axed. But there was work to be done and little time in which to prepare for it. He went to his room to wash away the dust of his journey and dress himself in his working clothes, acting automatically as if what he was doing was nothing to do with him. When he was respectably ready, he sat down at the table and wrote a short controlled letter to the one person who would know how he was feeling. Then he went out to call a cabriolet to take him to court.

Jane was rather surprised to receive such a serious letter. In fact, she had to read it through twice before she could make any real sense of it. Something had happened, that much was clear, for he said he would be coming to see her in a day or two and then went on to hope that Mr Cartwright would be at home *because I would be much obliged if I could ask his advice on a matter of some urgency*.

She wrote back at once to tell him he was welcome at any time but that Mr Cartwright would be away until a week Saturday *on account of he is working on the Altofts Junction*. Then she worried, and went on worrying until a week Saturday had arrived and Nathaniel was home and Felix had written again to tell her he would be arriving on the three o'clock stage that afternoon. She was waiting in the inn yard at the Star and Garter, fidgeting with impatience and anxiety for twenty long minutes before the coach rumbled in, and as soon as she saw him stepping down and walking towards her she knew her fears were horribly justified. He looked drawn and much too serious, almost like a different young man, as if he'd aged by several years since she last saw him.

'Oh Felix, my dear,' she said, reaching up to kiss him. 'What is it?'

He told her baldly. 'My father has forbidden our wedding.'

Thoughts crowded into her head, angry and disturbing – that Sir Mortimer was a heartless brute, that her poor Milly would be heartbroken if the engagement was broken – but she didn't give them voice. That would have been unkind. Instead she took Felix's proffered arm and walked him out of the yard. 'Let's have 'ee home,' she said, 'and we'll see what Mr Cartwright has to say.'

Nathaniel was waiting for them in the parlour and rang the bell at once for tea to be served. Then, when the kettle had been brought up and the tea made, steaming and comforting, they sat in their comfortable chairs around the empty hearth, drank their first soothing cup and listened while the tale was told.

When it was finished Nathaniel put down his cup and sat for several seconds deep in thought. 'It seems to me,' he said at last, 'that you are faced with an impossible choice. Either you obey your father and break off your engagement to our Milly or you marry Milly and lose your inheritance. We spoke of this earlier, as I daresay you remember. However speaking of a thing and having to face it are two very different matters.'

'That,' Felix agreed miserably, 'is the case in a nutshell. For the life of me I don't know what to do.'

'Have you told Milly what has happened?'

Felix winced. 'No, sir,' he admitted.

The next question was probing but kindly spoken. 'Why not?'

'I couldn't bear to,' Felix said. 'It would upset her too much.'

'But if you decide to break off your engagement you will have to tell her, will you not? Should she not be forewarned?'

The idea made Felix shudder. 'What *am* I to do?' he said.

'I cannot tell you, Felix,' Nathaniel said. 'It is your decision and yours alone. You are the only one who can make it. However, it does seem to me that if you cannot bear to forewarn our Milly, which is something that does you much credit, then you are already more than halfway to your decision. But it is your decision.'

There was another very long silence, while Jane and Nathaniel waited and Felix looked at the carpet and battled with his thoughts. Eventually he lifted his head and looked at Jane. 'I can't not marry her,' he said. '*You* know that, don't you? I simply couldn't. I love her too much.'

She got up, took the two paces between them in one stride and bent to kiss him, first on one cheek and then on the other. 'Follow your heart,' she told him. ''Tis the one thing what never lets 'ee down. All the rest is merely money and property. Here today and gone tomorrow.'

'Yes,' he said and smiled at her. It was the first time he'd smiled since his arrival. 'I will.'

'In that case,' Nathaniel said, 'I will give you a bit of advice which you are free to take or not as you wish. You say that you have until the end of the Season to tell your father what you have decided to do. Very well then. My advice to you would be to marry as soon as you can but to say nothing to your father until the day he has specified, which is to say, the very end of the Season. That way you would allow time for his temper to cool and for you and Milly to get accustomed to married life before you have to see him again.'

Felix was much easier now that he'd made his decision. 'I will go to Longfield Hall first thing tomorrow morning,' he said. 'I think I should tell her as soon as I can.'

So the carriage was ordered for him and he left to visit his darling as soon as he'd finished his breakfast. He was pale and anxious, but determined.

Milly was walking in the grounds with her two charges, a pretty straw bonnet on her brown curls and the book of fairy stories in her hand. She'd just promised them that their first story should be 'Puss in Boots' when she heard feet pounding towards her. She turned her head to see who it was and was lifted with pleasure at the sight of him.

'My dear heart alive,' she laughed as he came

300

panting up beside her. 'You're in a rush this morning, Mr Fitzwilliam.'

'I've something to tell you,' he said. 'Could the girls read their story without you, do you think?'

'No,' Maria said, pouting. 'We could not. Miss Smith reads us our story. Always.'

'Not this morning she doesn't,' Felix said firmly. 'She'll read to you in a minute but we've got something to discuss first.' And he took Milly by the elbow and walked with her until they were out of earshot. They were both tense, he because of the enormity of what he was going to propose, she because she was afraid he was going to say the engagement was over. When they finally paused under the shade of one of the great oaks, he was completely out of breath.

She waited, looking up at his anxious face, her heart struggling like a bird in a cage. 'You've spoken to your father,' she prompted.

'He has forbidden our marriage,' he said, and told her everything that had happened.

Her heart crumbled with every word he said. It was over. Hadn't she known all along that it was bound to be once his father found out? 'Have 'ee seen Mr Cartwright?'

He took both her hands and held them, grieved to see how much this was distressing her. 'Of course, my darling, of course. And he's given me some excellent advice. He thinks we should marry as soon as we can and not tell my father. If you are agreeable, I will go back to London this afternoon and find us a cottage where we can live and when that's done I will come back and we will plan our wedding.'

She burst into tears of relief and fell forward into his arms. 'Oh!' she sobbed. 'I thought it was over.'

'Dearest girl,' he said. 'I love you much too much to ever, ever let you go.'

So the cottage was found and rented, dresses were made and flowers ordered and Millicent Smith 'of this parish' and Felix Algernon Fitzwilliam 'of Foster Manor' were married three weeks later in the church of St Michael, both of them encouraged by the solemn words, 'Whom God has joined together let no man put asunder.'

'God damn it all!' George Hudson said, scowling horribly. 'What's up wi' t'man? Don't he see what an opportunity we're offering?'

'Apparently not,' George Stephenson said. The two men were in the library at Monkgate, drinking brandy and discussing their plans for the proposed York to Scarborough line. And the plans had hit a snag. 'According to his solicitor's letter, Sir Mortimer Fitzwilliam does not wish – what is it? – *"to have the peace of his country seat disturbed by locomotives"*.'

George Hudson eased his bandaged foot into a better position on the footstool. This gout was no joke. His big toe was throbbing with the most exquisite pain. 'The man's a fool,' he growled and gulped his brandy.

'Quite possibly but he seems to be adamant. Not a single acre of Foster Park is up for sale. His solicitor made that abundantly clear.'

'We could skirt round it, I suppose,' George Hudson said, scowling at the map. 'But it'll be deuced awkward. Who owns that farm to the north?'

Mr Stephenson gave a wry smile. 'He does,' he said.

'God damn it all!' George Hudson said again. 'Are we to be blocked at every turn? We'll have to find some way round this. I can't have this line gainsaid by some self-important landowner. We must see if we can sweeten him. I'll think of some inducements. Meantime we must think about a railway bridge over the Ouse. I'll get Cartwright on to it. He's got some wedding or other, today. I'll send him a *billet* about it tomorrow.'

21

The South bank of the Thames was lined by long warehouses, massive yards for brick and timber and innumerable wharves for the sea coal that the city burned by the ton day in and day out. It was always busy, for as well as black coal barges, tar-stained coasters and cargo ships from Norway, Italy, France and Germany, there were ferrymen plying an incessant trade from one bank to the other. The tracks behind the yards were usually choked with carts either being loaded or lumbering heavily away, but a hundred yards beyond the river all trade stopped and it was open country-side, where cows grazed in the water meadows and fruit and vegetables were grown for sale in the markets of the Covent Garden, and there were long tenter grounds where cloth was stretched to dry whenever there was sufficient sunshine.

Mr and Mrs Fitzwilliam's newly rented house was a small, sparsely furnished cottage fronted by bargeboards, painted white. It stood quietly beside a country road called Green Walk, facing north and a few yards away from the local church. It had a dining room, a small parlour and an even smaller kitchen downstairs, a dark staircase that rose extremely steeply through the centre of the house and two rooms upstairs. There was a very small garden in front of it, where their carter had deposited their trunk and their hamper, and a rather bigger vegetable patch behind it, where there was a shed for coal and another for garden forks, spades, trowels and plant pots. It was called Rose Cottage, even though there were no flowers anywhere in its vicinity. Milly was entirely enamoured of it.

'Our first home,' she said, when Felix had opened the door and stepped aside to let her enter first. 'Oh Felix, our very first home.' She walked from room to room, noticing everything. 'I must sew us some curtains,' she said. 'Those empty windows won't do at all. We'll have the world and his wife looking in on us otherwise. And we shall need candles for those stairs or one of us'll come a-tumble. Is there a market hereabouts?'

Felix had to admit he had no idea. The niceties of housekeeping were entirely beyond him, never having had to attend to such things in his life.

He was saved by somebody knocking on the door. It turned out to be a solid-looking young man followed by a plump young woman, in a blue gown, a mob cap and a rather grubby apron, who said her name was Polly and told him Mr Muffin had sent her to be their cook-house-keeper, 'what I daresay he's told you, if you recall, Mr Fitzwilliam'.

Mr Fitzwilliam was beginning to feel light-headed and couldn't remember anything much at all. 'Um, yes, well...' he said.

His baffled expression puzzled the young woman. 'Ain't this the day you 'ad in mind then?' she said.

'Oh yes, yes,' he hastened to reassure her. 'Indeed it is. We're very glad to see you. It's just that I can't recall a gentleman called Mr Muffin.'

'Lord love yer,' Polly said. 'Everybody knows Mr Muffin. He's the man what lets the 'ouses. Now you'll want this trunk a-bringin' in an' un-packin', fer a start. Harry'll see to it, won'tcher, my duck. I'll bring the 'amper.'

It was fun unpacking, as if it was Christmas and they'd been given a huge bran tub full of presents. The hamper had been packed by her mother and Mrs Cadwallader and it was full of good things – a sugar loaf and tongs, a large jar of sugar plums, a twist of tea, a good half pound of butter in a covered dish, a quartern loaf wrapped in a cloth to keep it moist, even a large ham swathed in butter muslin. And the trunk was a revelation for there weren't just clothes and linens in it, which she expected, but saucepans and wooden spoons, a good stout frying pan, a cloth full of cutlery, and even two candlesticks and a bundle of wax candles.

305

'Dear Ma!' Milly said, when the trunk was finally emptied and had been carried out into the back garden and put in the shed. 'She's thought of everything. I must write and thank her.'

'But not tonight,' Felix hoped. They'd stayed virginal and sensible all last night in that uncomfortable inn. Now he wanted to take her into their own bed and love her.

'I'm starving hungry,' she said. 'What do you say we have supper?'

The disappointment on his face was so intense that even Polly noticed it.

'I'll be off then,' she said. 'You've got all you need, ain'tcher? I'll be in termorrer to light the stove and get yer breakfast. Don't you worry about nofink, ma'am. I'll get in through the back an' it'll all be done afore you wakes up.' She bobbed them a little curtsey and Harry touched his forelock and they were gone.

Now and at last the newlyweds were alone together in the privacy of their own home.

'Come to bed?' he hoped. And was answered by a kiss so long and rapturous that within seconds there was nothing in their enclosed world except the tempest of their love for each other.

It was very quiet in Shelton House when the wedding was over, even with young Nat and Mary to fill it with their chirruping voices, and Jane was pale-faced and fidgeting.

'She'll write to you soon,' Nathaniel said, trying to comfort her.

'London's such a long way away,' she said. 'Anything could happen to her there and I'd

306

never know.'

'Nothing's going to happen to her,' Nathaniel said reasonably.

That made her tetchy. 'You don't know.'

He decided to change his approach. 'I've been thinking,' he said.

She wasn't very interested in what he was thinking but she said 'Yes' as he seemed to expect it.

'How would it be if we gave a dinner party?' he said. 'It's high time we did. We've lived here long enough.'

She looked surprised. 'We don't give dinner parties.'

'We haven't done until now,' he allowed, 'but that's no reason why we shouldn't.' His face was all concern and urging.

She noticed the concern and was touched by it but she tried to be practical. 'Who would we invite? We don't know enough people.'

'I tell 'ee what,' he said, sensing victory, 'I will write the invitations and you provide the meal. How would that be?'

He's doing this to cheer me up, she thought, understanding him, and although she had niggling doubts about her ability to host such an event, she decided to agree with him. 'When would you want it to be?' she said.

They held their party ten days later and by that time she'd had three letters from Milly and was much cheered by how well she and Felix seemed to be getting along in their faraway city. And despite her initial doubts, the party was a success. They sat eight to table and Mrs Cadwallader and her newly enlisted helpers cooked an excellent meal and served it with aplomb. But it was the conversation that made the evening, for their guests talked about so many things and were so unexpectedly entertaining and knowledgeable it was a revelation to Jane just to sit at the table and listen to them.

Old Mr Greer, who was the manager of the York Union Bank and looked so dry and crumpled that Jane thought he would have nothing to say, started the conversation off by talking about what York had been like when he was a child living in Coppergate and reminding them all what a small place it had been.

'All of us contained within the walls,' he said. 'There were no buildings in the fields in those days. 'Twere more like a village than a town. Mrs Patterson will tell you.'

Their next-door neighbours, the Pattersons, were a jolly pair, he with a set of fine mutton-chop whiskers adorning his pale face and a gold watch chain hung across his red waistcoat, she round and rosy and dressed in the latest style with ringlets bobbing on either side of her cheeks. She beamed at Mr Greer and told him he was right in every particular, adding that she remembered what it had been like before they built the pavements in the Thursday market.

''Twere ruination to boots,' she said, 'even if you wore pattens, if you tek my meaning. On account of the mud. You never saw so much mud as there were in that old market.'

That set the entire table off and Jane was glad to see that even her mother joined in. The mud was remembered and the crush in the markets and the rush lights.

'And now we have gas light,' Mrs Leeman said, 'which to my way of thinking is an absolute blessing. No more creeping about with candles that blow out as soon as look at you. My night candle always blew out when I was halfway up the stairs. Now all you need is a tinder box and one little taper and you have a nice dependable light for as long as you need it.'

Jane was pleased that Nathaniel had invited the Leemans, for she knew from what Nathaniel said of him that Mr Leeman had been extremely helpful when he was buying the house and, even though he looked rather stern, he was plainly a gentleman and she'd liked Mrs Leeman as soon as she saw her.

The talk streamed on as the second course was served. They discussed the daily newspapers and that took them on to books.

Mrs Anderson and her husband were great admirers of a new young writer called Charles Dickens and she set the table laughing with tales of the exploits of his hero Mr Pickwick, who seemed to be a bumbling, well-meaning, rather pompous man who got into extraordinary scrapes.

'You *must* read it,' she said to Jane and appealed to the others round the table. 'Must she not? I never was so agreeably entertained in all my life. I tell 'ee I just couldn't wait for the next edition.'

'They say he is writing another story, Mrs Anderson,' Mr Greer put in. 'Do you happen to know if that is so?'

She did and she knew what it was. "Tis called

309

Nicholas Nickleby and 'tis published in monthly parts the same as the *Pickwick Papers* and I'm a-reading of it now.'

'And when 'tis published in book form, she'll have me buy that for her too,' Mr Anderson said, making a grimace.

'Quite right,' his wife said, laughing at him, 'because he'll read it afore I do, which he knows very well.' And that made everybody else laugh.

How good natured they all are, Jane thought, smiling round at them, and how well they chose their topics. She was relaxing more with every minute that passed. But when Mrs Cadwallader's fruit jellies had been served and admired, she was suddenly confronted with a difficult moment. The Andersons had been talking about what an unconscionable time lawyers seemed to take to get anything settled. And Mr Leeman rose to their defence.

'You are quite right, of course,' he said, inclining his serious face towards the two Andersons. 'The law is a cumbersome beast, there is no denying it, but it is the only beast we have for these transactions and if it is to be seen to be just it must, sometimes unfortunately, be allowed to take its time. Like you, I would it were not so, for solicitors can be caught in its toils just as easily as everyone else.'

Mr Anderson found that hard to believe and said so. 'Surely not.'

'I fear so,' Mr Leeman said. 'I will give you a local example of it. George Hudson has been Lord Mayor of York for the last two years. Quite so. However, what most of you will not know is that his election for a second year was unconstitutional.' And when they'd expressed surprise, he went on, 'According to the rules of the corporation's constitution only an alderman can be elected Lord Mayor and Mr Hudson's term as an alderman ceased at the same time as his first term of office as Mayor. He was therefore legally obliged to step aside and make way for another man but he refused to do it and persuaded his friends in the Tory Party to put him up for the second time. All of which would appear to be a straightforward case against him. However, I can tell you that certain members of the corporation, some of whom are in the legal profession, have been trying to test it in the courts since last November and are still no nearer to having the matter decided today than they were then. In fact, I fear the Lord Mayor's second term of office will be over before any decision will be made.'

They were all agreed that it was a most surprising story although Jane noticed that Nathaniel looked uncomfortable to have heard it and the Andersons were puzzled. But then her mother spoke up and put all other thought out of her head.

'Nowt'ud surprise me when it comes to Mr Hudson,' she said. 'I knew him when he were nobbut a child and he were a reet spoilt brat if ever I saw one. Allus had to have his own way. Which he were given, I might tell 'ee, on account of he had such a terrible temper on him.'

Mr Leeman smiled at her. 'I can well believe it,' he said.

'I mind the time,' Mary Jerdon said, 'when...'

311

Jane heart gave a leap of panic. No, she thought, don't, Ma, please. Keep things secret. And as there was no other way she could warn her, she kicked out towards her feet, made contact, and watched as her mother gave a little jump of surprise and stopped in mid sentence. Then she knew she had to say something to turn their attention elsewhere. But what? Her thoughts seemed to be stuck in treacle.

She was rescued by old Mr Greer. 'The one thing we can say with certainty about Mr Hudson,' he said, smiling at them all, 'is that he *does* build railways. They say we shall be able to travel all the way to London on one of his trains in a year or two.'

The wonder of that was discussed around the table and Nathaniel, having recovered his balance, asked his guests what places they would most like to visit 'if you had perfect freedom of choice'. And that kept them very happily occupied until Jane's heart had resumed its normal rhythm. But it had been a nasty moment.

Later that night as they were preparing for bed, she and Nathaniel discussed the evening, almost word for word.

'Mr Leeman seems to share your opinion of Mr Hudson,' Nathaniel said, when they were warmly underneath the blankets.

'Aye,' she said. 'He don't like him much, that's certain sure.'

'Does that please you?' he asked, and there was more curiosity in his voice than reproof so she gave him an honest answer.

'Aye, it does,' she said. 'I don't like him much either. And Ma's right. He does have to have things his own way all the time and that temper is downright ugly.'

'Well, he won't have things all his own way over the Scarborough line,' he said and told her how adamantly Sir Mortimer was opposing him.

She lay beside him in the moonlit quiet of their comfortable bed and wondered. It was gratifying to think that the two men she most disliked were now opposed to one another. 'I must write to Milly about all this tomorrow,' she said. 'Particularly about the party.'

'When they come up to visit us,' Nathaniel promised, 'we will throw another one even bigger and they shall be the guests of honour. How would that be?'

'I wonder how they are,' Jane said, yearning for them again.

'They're as right as ninepence,' he said. 'I'll lay you any money.'

In fact, they were both suffering from indigestion and too uncomfortable to sleep. For the third evening in a row their supper had been so badly cooked it had been barely edible and now they were cross and hungry. Felix said he had half a mind to get up and get dressed again and take a boat across the river and buy them a hot pie.

'You'd be better to speak to Polly and tell her it won't do,' Milly told him tetchily. 'I keep a-telling 'ee. If you don't speak to her, she'll go on feeding us cinders night after night.'

Felix wasn't at all sure he *could* scold a servant.

Mr Glendinning had always seen to that. Not for the first time he knew he was yearning to be back in the comfort of his old home, where life was ordered and predictable and the food was always well cooked. There were altogether too many things that were his responsibility in this new life of his and it was jolly hard work. 'Couldn't you tell her?' he said, rubbing his chest.

'No, I could not,' Milly said. 'You're the master. You tell her and tell her tomorrow afore we dies of starvation.'

'I shall be in court tomorrow.'

'Court!' Milly said, even more crossly. 'You're allus in court.'

'If I were not,' Felix said stiffly, 'we would have no money for food, burnt or otherwise.' His allowance was long gone and now he had to make do with whatever fees he could earn. It was all extremely difficult. 'All the more reason not to let her waste any more of it.'

He turned his back on her. If they went on speaking they would quarrel outright and he couldn't have borne that. But he couldn't sleep even though he closed his eyes. It was all too worrying and on top of everything else the interview with his father was drawing closer and closer and how he would manage to cope with that he simply couldn't think. Especially with no food in his stomach.

Milly lay awake thinking too. If he wouldn't speak to Polly – and she was beginning to suspect that he wouldn't – which was cowardly, there was no other word for it, she would have to do it herself. Perhaps she'd have to dismiss both their

314

servants and do the housework herself. She would certainly make a better job of the cooking. The stove couldn't be all that difficult. If he won't make the effort, I must.

She made it the following morning when Felix had kissed her apologetically and left to catch the ferry. Polly was banging saucepans in the kitchen and looked up cheerfully at her when she walked into the greasy darkness. Why did kitchens always have to be so dark and smell so bad?

'Ah,' she said, 'Polly. We've got to talk about last night's supper.'

'It's this dratted ol' stove, mum,' Polly said. 'I've tried pokin' it and proddin' it an' all sorts, an' all it does is smoke sommink chronic. It won't cook nohow.'

'Then *I* will try what can be done wi' it tonight,' Milly said. 'Buy two mutton chops for us and some spring greens if 'ee please.'

Polly took umbrage at once. 'You won't do no better with the dratted thing than I have, mum,' she said, folding her arms across her chest in a very belligerent way. 'I'll tell yer that fer nothin'. That's a tricky stove and that's all there is to it.'

Milly wouldn't look at her. She turned and left before either of them could say anything else. Really it was too bad to be answered back in such a rude way. She was very angry, with Polly and Felix and herself. A mistress shouldn't have to cook the supper, not when she was paying a servant to do it. Felix should have taken that girl to task. It was his job, not hers. She was still cross when he finally got home that evening, late as always and just as she was dishing up the chops.

'My word,' he said, when he lifted the cover and revealed the meat. It was done to a turn and looked extremely succulent. 'That's more the style.'

'On account of *I* cooked it,' Milly told him, helping herself to greens and potatoes.

'Oh!' he said and was then lost for words. If he praised her for her cooking that might be the wrong thing and he certainly couldn't ask her if she'd spoken to Polly because it was obvious that she had and that it hadn't gone well. Fortunately, he was saved by the arrival of the postman and went to the door with some relief to pay him and receive his letter. It was written in Sarah's beautiful copperplate hand and neatly sealed.

It had a very long preamble, which he didn't expect because his sister usually came straight to the point. He read the first few sentences without making very much sense of them:

'My dearest brother,

I cannot be sure whether what I have to tell you will be welcome to you, given the situation in which you find yourself, or not entirely welcome, or not welcome at all, which might perhaps be the more likely probability given your familial affection. It is hard for me to know what would be the most suitable form of words for me to choose, given the serious nature of the news I have to give you. Believe me, my dear brother, if there were any way in which I could mitigate against the distress you must inevitably feel, I would take it but there is not. I truly wish it were not my task to break this to you howsomever it must be done. The truth is that our father is dead. He was out riding with cousin Henry when his horse bolted and threw

316

him and broke his neck. Henry wrote to tell me at once which was kindly of him. He will be travelling to Foster Manor with the hearse on Tuesday and has asked me to inform the family.'

Milly had been watching his changing expressions. Now she leant across the table and touched his hand. 'What is it, Felix? Is it summat wrong?'

'My father is dead,' he told her bluntly. It surprised him that he was feeling no emotion about it whatever. 'Thrown from his horse. I must go home and arrange the funeral.'

'We shall need mourning clothes,' Milly said, practically. 'I've nowt in black at all. Would 'ee like me to see to it?'

He would. Although he knew he would have to borrow money to pay for it. 'Do what has to be done,' he said. 'Buy the best. Silk, I think, not bombazine. We need to look well or it will be seen as lack of respect. I must let them know in Chambers.'

She got up and walked to the other side of the table to put her arms round his neck and kiss him. 'My poor love,' she said.

It was a very large funeral but a dry-eyed one. Family members had gathered from York and London and Norfolk and the hearse was followed to Scrayingham Church by a procession of very grand carriages. Milly was extremely glad that she'd taken Felix's advice and ordered a fashionable gown and had it made up in silk, because the cousins were all beautifully dressed – although, as she noticed with some satisfaction, rather less fashionably than she was. *If I've to hold my own*

317

with this lot, she thought, I've made a good start, even if that old monster *has* cut us off wi'out a penny.

It felt very strange to be walking in through the front door of the Manor instead of going round to the side and even stranger to be waited on by decorous maids in black and white with a grey-haired Mrs Denman hovering to see that everything was going as it should. There's nowt much changed, she thought, as she nibbled cucumber sandwiches and drank fruit cup and made polite small talk, taking care that she spoke as well as she could. Sarah and Emma swept across the room to kiss her as soon as they came in but to her relief nobody else paid her much attention and none of them asked who she was. She supposed that was because they were all waiting for the will to be read and had their minds on more important things. Now, she thought, as they took their places on the circle of chairs, they will know that my poor Felix has been disinherited and probably why it's been done and, even though she felt extremely apprehensive, she smiled at him to encourage him, poor Felix. It really had been very brave and very dear of him to choose her over all this. And as the lawyer cleared his throat in preparation she wondered which of all these relations would actually inherit.

The will was short and succinct. His wife Elizabeth's jewellery was bequeathed to his two daughters, Sarah and Emma, there were small and equal bequests to all his grandchildren and finally all lands, estates and capital were left to his 'only son Felix'. He hadn't altered his will by

318

so much as a comma.

Felix felt quite sick with relief and Milly was so surprised that she was speechless for more than a minute. Then the lawyer gathered his papers, bowed and left them, and the assembled relations stood up and came across to make their farewells to Sir Felix, who was more than happy to introduce them to 'my wife, Lady Fitzwilliam.' It was dizzying.

'Shall you stay here now?' Sarah wanted to know.

But Felix said not. 'I must be back in London by Friday afternoon,' he told her. 'I have rather an important case coming up.'

'Then we will call on you in Charlotte Square,' Sarah said and turned to kiss her sister-in-law. 'Goodbye for the present, Lady Fitzwilliam,' she said.

It took quite a long time for the rest of the family to leave them for they all had to stop to commiserate with Felix and to be introduced to his new wife but at last she and Felix were on their own in their newly inherited drawing room.

'Could we call in at Shelton House on our way back, do 'ee think?' she asked.

He smiled at her happily. 'Naturally,' he said. It was already planned, for if there were two people he really wanted to hear his good news, those two were Jane and Mr Cartwright.

22

Jane had been worrying ever since she received Milly's hastily written letter telling her of Sir Mortimer's death so she was relieved when her two babies arrived in her drawing room, smiling and looking quite themselves. And when Felix gave them a little formal bow and said 'Mr and Mrs Cartwright, Mrs Jerdon, ma'am, pray allow me to present my wife, Lady Fitzwilliam,' she gave out such a squeal that she made Nathaniel jump.

''Tis the best possible news,' she said when the tale had been told. 'But I don't understand it at all. Did he change his mind, do 'ee think?'

Felix had been pondering that question too. 'I doubt that very much,' he said. 'I've never known him change his mind about anything, once it was made up, and I'm certain you haven't either. No. I think he was waiting for me to come to heel. He was a man who expected to be obeyed, you see. He thought I would give in.'

'And now you've come into your own instead,' Jane said, 'and quite right too. And just think, you'll be living a few miles away instead of being in London all the time.'

'And in that beautiful house,' Mary Jerdon said to Jane. 'Who'd ha' thought *that*, Jane, when we were walkin' in the gardens all those years ago, you and me and our little Milly? Such a thing never entered our heads. And now...'

'Did you visit the house, Mrs Jerdon?' Felix said. 'I never knew that.'

'That's on account of we were allus below stairs,' Mary Jerdon told him, smiling. 'Keeping our place.'

'Well, now you must visit above stairs,' he told her, 'as the grandmother of Lady Fitzwilliam.'

'How this ol' world do change,' Mary Jerdon said, shaking her head in the wonder and bewilderment of it.

'We shall live in London too,' Milly said, grinning at her. 'We have a house in Charlotte Square. We're going there tomorrow. This is just a short visit because we've got a coach to catch.'

'But you'll come back very soon,' Jane said. 'Won't 'ee, my dears?'

'As soon as ever we can,' Felix promised. 'We would stay here now if it were possible. But I have clients to represent and my word is given.'

There was so much to talk about on that journey back to London. It would take time and a great deal of conversation to digest the enormity of the change that had shifted their lives.

'We can tell Polly that we don't need her any more,' Milly said. 'What I'll be uncommon glad to do.'

'We will tell them both that our plans have changed and that we're going to live in Charlotte Square,' Felix said. 'And we must be there by Friday morning because Sarah and Emma are coming to visit us then.'

'But you will be in court, will you not?'

'Indeed I shall, but it is *you* they are coming to

visit. You have to be fitted out with a suitable wardrobe, so they say, and it must all be completed before we return to the Manor, and I can't put that off for there is a lot to be done there and the sooner I start on it the better.' She looked a question at him, so he explained. 'I must inspect the place and see what needs attention. An estate needs a deal of upkeep, you see. You neglect it at your peril. And when that is done I must visit the farm and see what is needed there.'

I never thought an estate would mean so much work, Milly thought. When she'd lived in the house it had always seemed to run itself. Not that Felix was the least bit deterred by everything he would have to do. Quite the reverse in fact. He looked confident and happy, his thick hair positively bushy and his eyes shining. It was as if he was growing into someone else, which was very curious. He was still her dear Felix, of course, that hadn't changed, but he had become suddenly and rather obviously powerful. It was daunting but very attractive. Whatever else, she thought, burnt chops are the least of our worries now.

Sarah and Emma arrived in the Livingston carriage at four on Friday morning and whisked her off at once to visit what they called 'a first-rate house' to choose the materials for her new dresses. It was a very impressive establishment, and far more like a gentleman's townhouse than the sort of draper's shop that Milly was used to. They were greeted at the front door by a footman, who bowed them into what he called 'the *premier magazine*' where an elegant lady in a silk dress and a small lace cap was waiting to greet them. She knew Lady Livingston and Lady Smithson Lumley by name and curtseyed to them at once, saying she hoped she could be of service to Lady Fitzwilliam. Then having settled them into three comfortable chairs she produced a dozen rolls of sumptuous silks and velvets for their inspection. Lady Fitzwilliam had never seen anything so gorgeous in her life but her sisters-in-law took them calmly and set about choosing the most becoming.

'We must consider them in daylight and candlelight,' Sarah said and the silken assistant swayed her head to show how well she agreed.

There were full-length mirrors on every wall of the room, stretching from the sumptuous carpet under their feet to the moulded ceiling above their heads and Milly stood in front of the nearest one while the assistant draped the cloth over her shoulder and arranged it so that it hung in elegant folds that caught the sunlight that streamed in from the long windows. Then they progressed to another mirror at the opposite end of the room where a chandelier full of lighted candles revealed how well the cloth would look 'gracing a supper or a ball', as the assistant put it.

'We will choose three,' Sarah told the assistant, as if it was the easiest thing in the world.

But it took a long time before Milly could make up her mind which three she preferred because they were all so beautiful. And when the choice had finally been made, the entire process began all over again while she picked silks and muslins and figured cottons for half a dozen day gowns and carriage gowns and promenade dresses. And then, while her head was still spinning with colours and textures, she had to choose the styles and trimmings she wanted from a huge pattern book of the most fashionable on offer and, even with Sarah and Emma to help and advise her, it was past twelve o'clock before they left the establishment.

'If this is what it's like being a lady, I'm not so sure I like it,' she said to Felix over their beautifully cooked dinner. And she was only half joking. 'I'm worn out and I've still got chemises and shoes and stockings and bonnets and caps and gloves and pelerines and heaven knows what-all to get.'

'It is important to be well dressed, my darling,' Felix said. 'That is how you will be judged I fear and I mean you to be judged well. You will have a lady's maid to dress you when you get back to Foster Manor and she will notice everything you wear and will report on it to the rest of the house. I want them to think of you as a lady from the first day. Apart from which, you are very beautiful and jewels and velvets will set you off to perfection.'

'But I shan't feel like myself,' Milly complained and then she felt that she was being ungrateful because all these grand clothes were going to cost him a lot of money. 'What happened to Dumma-dumma?'

'She is always there,' he told her seriously. 'Always there and always dear to me. The clothes are merely her adornment. You *do* like them, don't you?'

324

'I'm sure they will be very beautiful,' she told him. 'I only hope I can do them justice.'

She travelled to Foster Manor with a trunk full of new clothes and considerable apprehension and was welcomed like the lady she now was and rather enjoyed it, especially as the lady's maid Mrs Denham had chosen for her was young and shy and very much in awe of her.

'We are back in Foster Manor and getting along very well,' she wrote to her mother the next day. *'I have a lady's maid. Imagine that. Her name is Margaret and she grew up in Scrayingham and is very patient and gentle. When Felix has finished his inspection of the estate, you and Nan and Mr Cartwright must come here and hear what we have planned.'*

It was an extremely thorough inspection. The house was explored from top to bottom and notes made in nearly every room – faded curtains needed replacing, the old-fashioned bed in the master bedroom was to be discarded, the kitchens were too dark and the stove 'downright antiquated', the tiled floor needed considerable repair.

Only the nurseries passed his rigorous test and that was because the nurseries bewitched them. Within seconds of walking through the door, they were back in the days when they'd been children there. They stood together beside their old rocking horse, stroking its mane and running their hands along its flanks.

'All those rides,' Felix said dreamily. 'Do you remember?'

'Every single one,' Milly told him. 'I used to sit up behind you and hold you steady, when you were so little you weren't even walking.'

'Do you think the tops and hoops are still here?' he said, looking towards the schoolroom door.

They were and so were the globes and the child-sized chairs and the little round table where they'd all sat and listened to stories.

'My dear heart alive,' Milly said. 'Not a thing's been changed.'

And there was the old familiar view from the schoolroom window. They walked across the room hand in hand to enjoy it, while Mr Glen-dinning lurked at a discreet distance and kept very still, aware that they were sharing childhood memories and that Lady Fitzwilliam must have been one of the children who visited the house when Sir Felix and his sisters were small.

The next day they inspected the park and Milly admired it all over again, and the day after that they took the dog cart down to the farm and the village where Felix said there was a great deal of work that needed to be done and the bailiff made a note of everything he said.

On the fourth day he decided that they had earned a rest and after a leisurely breakfast he said he thought he would go to the library and answer his letters of condolence. So Milly went with him and settled herself on one side of the library table to write a long letter to her mother, while he sat opposite her, busy with his own correspondence. After a while he looked up and gave her a languid, loving smile.

'Are you happy, Dumma-dumma?' he asked.

They'd been so busy she hadn't stopped to consider whether she was happy or not but now that he'd asked she knew that she was more contented than she'd ever been in her life. 'Uncommon happy,' she said, 'although I still find it hard to believe.' And she got up and walked round the table so that she could kiss him.

He held her about the waist and smiled again. 'I find it hard to believe too,' he said. 'You make an excellent lady of the house, my darling.'

She looked at him thoughtfully. 'In that case, could I suggest summat to 'ee – as lady of the house?'

'Fire away.'

'While you're making changes and alterations,' she said, 'I think you should think about changing the lighting.'

He understood her at once. 'To gas light.'

'Of course,' she said. ''Twould be a much brighter place with gas light – think how good the light is in Charlotte Square – and it would make all the difference in the world to the kitchens, especially on a dark day.'

It was a sensible and obvious idea. 'I will do it,' he told her. 'A letter to the chairman of the gas company, I think.'

He didn't know it, but a letter would not be necessary because one of the directors of the York Union Gas Light Company was already planning to see him.

Mr George Hudson had been very pleased to hear that Sir Mortimer Fitzwilliam was dead and had been succeeded by his young son. 'Happen he'll be more open to a sensible negotiation than his curmudgeon of a father,' he said to Lizzie. 'I

327

shall write to him directly.'

Which he did and got an answer back, remarkably quickly, suggesting that they should meet. It was a satisfactory start.

He dressed for the meeting with more than usual care, knowing how important appearances were when you were dealing with the gentry and his first sight of the new master of the estate showed him how sensible his choice of clothing had been, for the young man into whose presence he was ushered was most elegantly attired, in a green frock coat, very expensive doeskin trousers and the whitest cravat he'd ever seen. He was even better pleased to see what a slender young man he was – tall, yes, but apart from that, there was nothing of him and he was extremely pale, with hair like a girl's and such a silky moustache it was nothing more than a shadow. You could blow him over with a puff of wind. By the end of one swift glance, he was full of his own size and importance and perfectly confident of getting what he wanted.

'I'm glad to make your acquaintance, Sir Felix,' he said, beaming as they shook hands. 'Your father and I were at the point of agreeing a deal when he was so sadly taken from us. A little matter of some land I wished to purchase for the new railway to Scarborough that is currently being planned. I brought the proposal with me, sir, should you care to see it.'

'I am fully cognisant of the details of your proposal, Mr Hudson,' Felix said, smoothly polite. 'I have of course acquainted myself with all such correspondence as was ongoing at the time of my father's death.'

That was a blow. He's not as frail as he looks, George thought, and changed tack at once. 'If that is the case, sir,' he said, 'happen we may proceed to business.'

They proceeded and although he wasn't entirely aware of it at the time, the great Mr Hudson was tied up in legal knots. Such land as was needful for the building of a railway line would be leased to Mr Hudson's company for a term of twenty-five years, with the provision that a 'halt' be built just south of the village and the farm so that his employees could make use of it. The price was declared reasonable by Sir Felix before Mr Hudson could object to it or even begin to barter. It was all over in half an hour and Felix shook hands with the quietly satisfied air of a barrister who has just won his case.

'There is one other, rather lesser matter we might also discuss while you are here,' he said. 'You are a director of the York Union Gas Light Company, I believe.'

George agreed that he was.

'I should like to bring gas light to this house and the surrounding farms and cottages,' Felix told him. 'Could you put the matter in hand for me, perhaps?'

As he was trotted back to York in his smart carriage and four, George Hudson was annoyed to realize that the deal he'd just signed was not as advantageous as he'd expected it to be and certainly not as he'd thought it was when he was putting his signature to it. In fact, if the truth be told, he'd been outwitted by a slip of a boy. The thought was altogether too shaming to be entertained for long so he set about reshaping it. By the time he arrived back at Monkgate, he had decided that he had struck a most advantageous deal and was, as usual, a man to be admired and congratulated.

And so those two great boons to nineteenth-century life, gas light and the railway, were coming to Foster Manor, as Felix was delighted to tell Milly's mother and father and grandmother when they next came visiting.

They were most impressed but Nathaniel laughed when Milly wanted to know if the new railway would be built by the spring.

'Railways take an unconscionable amount of time, what with planning and raising capital and waiting for a bill of approval,' he told her. 'It's possible the first section of track might be up and running by 1842 but earlier than that I couldn't say.'

'What's so special about next spring?' Jane wanted to know, for something about her daughter's face was alerting her to a delicious possibility.

'By next spring,' Milly told her demurely, 'according to Mrs Hardcastle, who knows about these things, you will be a grandmother, Ma, and I thought a railway would be convenient should you want to come and visit the baby at any time.'

'I shall come and visit *that* baby, railway or no railway, even if I have to walk every inch of the way,' her mother told her, springing at her to hug her and kiss her. And then the room disintegrated into a peal of delight and such hearty congratulations that Felix went quite pink. What a good life this was turning out to be.

The great Mr Hudson was dressing for his farewell dinner as Lord Mayor. It was a raw November evening so he was glad he would be wearing his robes and his chain of office. He stood before the long mirror admiring his image, brandy glass in one hand and cigar in the other. There was no doubt he looked the part, solid and wealthy and dependable in his expensive jacket and his white waistcoat, with a white cravat the equal of any cravat he'd ever seen, even the one that young Sir Felix had been wearing and all of it set off by the rich red and thick fur trimming of his mayoral robe. 'Aye,' he said to himself, 'tha's done well, lad.' And now he would be wined and dined and thanked for all the good work he'd done. He was licking his lips at the prospect.

It was a very fine dinner. Excellent fish, roast goose, plenty of wine. And better still, there was a vote of thanks to finish it off. As the master of ceremonies struck the floor with his stave to call for attention, George stroked his waistcoat pocket where his gracious acceptance lay folded, written and ready, and turned his face towards the speaker ready for praise and adulation.

It was a bit of a disappointment to see that it was Mr Leeman who was rising to his feet. The man was a Whig, which was the wrong party for a start, and one of their local solicitors with a reputation for a sharp tongue. But he smiled at the assembled aldermen and counsellors and began well.

'My Lord Mayor, ladies and gentlemen, it has fallen to me to propose the vote of thanks to our outgoing Lord Mayor, Mr George Hudson.' There was a shuffle of interest and a ripple of applause from the Tories. 'Mr Hudson has proved himself to be one of the most notable holders of that office, as all of us here could bear testimony. I feel sure there are many in our company today who have benefited from his endeavours, as I am equally sure he has himself.' That was a bit pointed, George thought. And unnecessary. 'His exploits have brought him fame and renown.' Quite right. Now tell us about them.

It was a list rather than an approbation. He read it from the notes in his hand. And when he'd finished, he laid the paper on the tablecloth and looked round at his listeners. 'Had Mr Hudson stepped down last year, when it was the correct and constitutional time for him to do so,' he said, 'I would have proposed a vote of thanks to him and I would have meant every word. However, Mr Hudson did not step down when it was the constitutional time for him to do so. Mr Hudson contrived to remain in office, unconstitutionally. Now I have to tell you, Mr Hudson, sir, I am delighted to see you go.'

The Whigs were cheering and banging the table but the Tories were on their feet, booing and hissing and shouting 'Shame!', 'Retract, sir!'

Mr Leeman had been prepared to raise hackles but the strength of their opposition was greater than he expected and that, combined with rather too much wine, made him suddenly angry. Within seconds he was too angry for moderation. He turned to face his hecklers, red in the face and shouting back. 'Shame on *you*, sirs,' he yelled. 'Do you think we've not taken your measure? Oh no, sirs, we know you, we know what you are. You are bought men, every one of you. You bow down before the golden calf of Hudson's wealth. You bow down and worship it. Shame on *you!*'

His audience was making such a noise, either booing and shouting or cheering and shouting, that his voice was only intermittently heard. It took nearly five minutes and a great deal of banging before the master of ceremonies could restore order. As soon as there was a hush he proposed the vote of thanks, asked for a show of hands, counted them in an extremely summary fashion and declared it carried. Then, as was customary, he offered the floor to the outgoing Lord Mayor.

George was so angry he was shaking. How dare they do this to him! And at a dinner held in his honour, what's more. Had they no sense of what was proper? It was disgraceful, insupportable, despicable! They should be downright ashamed of themselves to treat a man of his calibre in such a disgusting way. He'd never heard anything to equal it. He wrapped his red cloak around him and stood to face them out, his face puce and his eyes bulging with rage, a bull ready to charge.

'Oh yes, you may mock and bay,' he roared at them. 'Let me tell 'ee, mockery is the mark of un-important men. The mark of unimportant men. I know just the sort of men you are.' And when they roared back at him, 'You are actuated by a little-ness of feeling. A littleness of feeling which, when it is exhibited in its *deformed* state, as it has been this day, is utterly and totally *disgraceful*. Utterly and totally *disgraceful*. For what are you, when all's said and done? Toadies, that's what you are. Toadies who tout for meals and invitations, which is another disgrace, toadies who resort to back-biting when they don't get their own way, toadies who invent conversations which never occurred. Shame on you! You're a disgrace to the name of aldermen and councillors.'

He was still shaking with anger when he and Lizzie got back to Monkgate.

'How could they do such a thing?' he said, slumping into his armchair. He was too distraught to get ready for bed. It was enough just to sit down. 'How could they? After all the good things I've done for this town.'

'Jealous,' Lizzie said, her face full of sympathy for him. Poor George to be shouted out like that. He was right. It was disgraceful. 'That's what. They're nasty jealous. Don't you tek no notice of 'em.'

'They would never have done that to Sir Felix,' George said, remembering how calm and self-assured that young man had been. 'No matter what nasty thoughts they might have had, they'd have stayed polite wi' *him*. But they think they may torment me. Well, they'll have another think coming, that's all. I'll show 'em.'

'Course you will,' Lizzie soothed. 'You're twice the man of any one of *them*.'

'Happen I should buy a country seat,' he said. 'Make myself a landowner, a man of property. That'd show 'em.'

'Yes,' Lizzie agreed, yawning because she was tired after all that to-do. 'So it would.'

'I shall give it thought,' he said.

23

The year 1840 was a bumper year for railway companies, which were springing up everywhere as railway fever spread through the country.

George Hudson had a poor opinion of most of the newcomers, and expressed it forcefully, saying they hadn't got the remotest idea about what was involved in running a railway or how much it would cost and predicting that they would come to grief. On the other hand, by skilful accounting, he made sure his own York and North Midland Railway was doing very well. In the spring, the shareholders were paid their first dividend, which was one guinea and was spoken of approvingly as an excellent return. So it was no surprise that, at their annual general meeting later in the year, they voted to grant £500 for a survey of the proposed line to Scarborough, which provided more work for Nathaniel Cartwright.

'Whatever anyone may think about Mr Hudson,' he said to Jane when he got home from the meeting, 'his railway company is going from strength to strength. The line to London should be up and running by June.'

Jane was sitting in her easy chair sewing a jacket made of the best white lawn for the baby. It was only a matter of weeks before the little thing would be born and she wanted to have everything ready. She put in the last stitch and bit off the thread before she answered. 'So the meeting went well,' she said.

'Yes,' he said. 'It did.'

'No fisticuffs then.'

He smiled at that. 'No. It was all very civilized.' And when she gave him a teasing look, 'Mr Rowntree was anxious about the accounts, but that was all.'

He's been fiddling the accounts, Jane thought, and someone's found out. Hadn't she always known he'd be caught out? Not that she could say anything about it to Nathaniel, given his admiration for the man. It was a continuing sorrow to her that it was impossible to talk to him about the obnoxious Mr Hudson, especially as it was the one and only subject they couldn't discuss, but the habit was established now and not likely to change unless he found out for himself that his god had clay feet up to his haunches. However, if she couldn't ask Nathaniel there were others who would tell her, and the best of them was Mr Leeman, who seemed to know everything that was going on in the city. It wasn't something she could ask him at a dinner party but she often saw him walking in or out of his office when she was out a-marketing. With a bit of luck she could ask him then.

It was several weeks before she got the chance and then it came when she wasn't expecting it. She was walking briskly along Low Petergate enjoying the pale sunshine and so busy thinking about

Milly's baby and wondering if it really would arrive in a week's time the way Mrs Hardcastle seemed to think, that she very nearly bumped into the gentleman himself, who was walking equally briskly in the opposite direction. They jumped back from one another, both laughing, and then he raised his hat to her and gave her good day.

'I was in a dream, Mr Leeman,' she apologized. 'However that's no excuse. I should have been watching where I was going.'

'Mr Cartwright is in Scarborough, I hear,' he said.

'He is,' she said. 'There's a deal to be done on the new Scarborough line, so it seems, if it's to be finished on time.'

'It is like to be up and running next year, I believe.'

'Aye,' she said, thinking how knowledgeable he was. And that reminded her of what she wanted to know. 'There were questions asked of Mr Hudson at the AGM, I believe.' And when he looked rather puzzled, she prompted, 'Mr Rowntree was asking about the accounts.'

'Ah, yes,' he remembered. 'He was indeed.'

She assumed the most innocent expression she could contrive. 'Were they not in order?' she asked.

'Well now, Mrs Cartwright,' Mr Leeman said, giving her his wry smile, as if he knew what she was really thinking, 'the truth of the matter is that we have no way of knowing whether they were or they were not since nobody is allowed to see them. There was a great deal of bluster from Mr Hudson but no offer of disclosure.'

She was too close to the gossip to be cautious. 'Do you have suspicions, Mr Leeman?' she asked.

He answered her seriously. 'We do, ma'am, but suspicions are worthless without proof.'

'And what are your suspicions, Mr Leeman? If I may be so bold as to enquire.'

He considered for a few seconds and then told her. 'We think he paid the first dividend out of company capital, when, as you probably know, they should have been paid from the profits.'

'If my knowledge of the man is anything to go by,' she told him, 'that sounds entirely likely.'

He was remembering the conversation around her dinner table. 'You knew him when he was a child, I believe.'

'Aye, I did.'

'That is extremely interesting,' he said, adding gravely, 'However, for the moment at least, it is incumbent upon us to be discreet in our dealings. For lack of evidence, you understand.'

'I will be discretion itself,' she promised, keeping her face quietly calm, which was difficult because inside her head she was roaring with triumph. Hadn't she always known he would come to grief, always known it and always wanted it, great coarse bully that he was. Serve him right. She was walking so quickly that she was home before her heart had recovered its usual rhythm.

There was an unfamiliar carriage and pair waiting outside her door. For a second she stared at it, wondering who could be visiting at that hour in the morning, then her mind shifted into focus and she recognized the Fitzwilliam crest and knew it must be there because of the baby and ran towards it, half hopeful, half anxious, forgetting all about George Hudson and Mr Leeman and the proprieties and even the proper way to behave, calling as she ran. 'Is it the baby?'

'It is, Mrs Cartwright, ma'am,' the coachman said, catching her excitement and beaming at her. 'Sir Felix sent me. Born last night. He thought you'd want to visit and see him.'

'I should just think I would,' she said. 'My first grandchild!'

He was the most contented baby. When Jane was ushered into the bedroom, he was lying happily fed and blissfully asleep in Milly's arms. And what better place for him, dear little man. For the next hour and a half, they were lost to the delights of baby worship, admiring his exquisite fingers, his soft fair hair – isn't he just exactly like his father? – his dear little snub nose, the delicious smell of him. It was the happiest, easiest occasion and one that was to be repeated every day all through Milly's fourteen-day lying in.

I've never seen her so happy,' Jane said to Nathaniel when he finally came back from Scarborough. 'Not even when Felix asked her to marry him and I thought she was happy then. As she was. But this is different. 'Tis an absolute joy to see.'

'All very natural,' Nathaniel said. 'You were just the same when Nat and Mary were born. You looked like a cat that had had the cream.'

'She's been saying she'll need a nursemaid,' Jane told him. 'She was talking about it again this afternoon. Do you think she would like Audrey? Should I suggest it?'

'What about Nat and Mary? Don't they need her?'

'They're too old for a nursemaid,' Jane said easily. 'Nat will be off to school next year, don't forget.'

That was true. 'In that case,' Nathaniel said, 'you might suggest it.'

Nat and Mary weren't at all sure that they approved of their mother rushing off to see some strange baby every day and when she told them she was sending *their* Audrey to be the baby's nursemaid, they were both decidedly cross.

'I know it's Milly's baby,' Nat said, when he and his sister were sitting together in the empty drawing room, 'but it doesn't have to have our Audrey. That's not fair. And Mama doesn't have to go rushing off to see it every day. I'm beginning to forget what she looks like.'

'*Are* you?' Mary said, blue eyes wide.

'Not really,' Nat admitted. He was aggrieved but he had to be truthful. 'But that's what it feels like. When was the last time she read us a fairy story?'

Mary couldn't remember.

'There you are then.'

'I tell 'ee what,' Mary said, trying to cheer him. 'Let's take Spot out for a walk.'

'Who with?' Nat wanted to know. They always went for walks with Audrey.

There was a lot of the daredevil in Mary. 'Ourselves,' she said.

So they took the dog and went out for a very long walk, across the fields until they came to

Monkgate and then back home through the crowded streets. And as they were strolling along Goodramgate, calling to Spot to keep up with them, who should they meet coming out of the draper's with two fat parcels in her shopping basket but Mrs Hudson. She was rather surprised to see them and stopped to talk.

'You're never on your own,' she said. 'Surely.'

'Oh yes,' Nat said with splendid aplomb. 'We often walk on our own nowadays, don't we, Mary?'

Mary agreed with him, staunchly, nodding her head and giving Mrs Hudson the benefit of her honest blue eyes.

'I thought you had a nursemaid,' Lizzie said.

'We're much too old for nursemaids now,' Nat said grandly. 'I'm going to school next year. You don't need a nursemaid when you're a scholar. She's gone to help our sister Milly with her new baby.'

'Fancy!' Lizzie said, and she was thinking, Just wait till I tell George all this.

He wasn't the least bit interested, although she thought she'd chosen her moment well, between the roast and the sweet, when he was full fed and had drunk a great deal of wine and ought to have been in a good humour. But when she'd told him all about meeting the children and how she was sure the little dog was Dickie's that he used to have, he was the spit and image, if a dog can be the spit and image if you know what I mean, and about Milly's baby and how she could hardly believe it, she truly couldn't, he put down his

341

empty glass and glared at her.

'What are you talking about?' he said.

'Milly's baby,' she told him, quivering a little because he looked so stern.

'Who?' he hooted.

'Milly,' she said and now she was visibly quivering. 'You remember Milly. She was Dickie's nursemaid and a better one you couldn't hope to find. I mean to say, the way she picked him up off the floor when he'd tumbled over that time, poor little man, and kissed it better...'

'Why do you imagine I should be interested in some nursemaid's child?' he said crossly, pouring himself more wine. 'I've got better things to do with my time. It's the grand opening of the York to London railway in a matter of weeks, or have 'ee forgot?' He sighed dramatically. 'There are times when I despair of you, Lizzie, I truly do.'

'She's Jane's daughter,' Lizzie ploughed on. 'You remember Jane. Mrs Smith as was when she was our housekeeper only now she's Mrs Cartwright, of course, on account of marrying Mr Cartwright.'

'If you've nothing more illuminating to talk about than housekeepers and nursemaids, you'd be better to stay silent,' George told her sternly. 'These people are nothing to me. I have a railway to run.' And another to build and profits to watch.

Trade had not been good for the last twelve months, with the price of most shares falling rather too steeply and far too many bankruptcies and far too many shops closing, which was never a good sign. In fact there was a general air of decided gloom pervading the city and something would have to be done to dispel it. I must organize something spectacular for the grand opening, he thought. That should do the trick.

The first train on the York to London line ran on 30 June, exactly as Mr Hudson had promised. Thanks to his extravagant planning, it was a great occasion with bunting fluttering in the summer breeze, a band playing very loudly and occasionally in tune, and magnums of champagne being served to the guests. When the train puffed away from the station there was a chorus of happily contented cheers.

I must push them to get on with the railway hotel, George thought as he looked back along the line. We need Mr Andrews' grand building up and running. Our little station won't do at all now we've got a direct line to London – and that site's been cleared and ready for nearly a year. There's no need for all this shilly-shallying. The council must be made to see it. As always on these occasions, he felt he was equal to anything. Let lesser men go to the wall, he thought, as the engine blew its triumphant whistle. I mean to go from strength to strength.

Young Master Felix Nathaniel Fitzwilliam, having been given the traditional silver spoon and had his name put down for Eton in the traditional way, was going from strength to strength that summer too. He was christened when he was three weeks old, looking angelically pretty in the family christening gown and with his entire and fashionable family gathered about the font in their grand clothes and their most elegant hats and bonnets to welcome him into the clan. His father looked particularly handsome in his fine clothes with a Prince Albert moustache silky on his upper lip and his mother wore her finest day gown, with its seams let out for the occasion, and smiled a welcome to her guests as if she were a lady born.

'We shall expect great things of him,' Lady Sarah told her brother, when the company was back in Foster Manor sipping champagne.

'He won't disappoint you,' Felix promised her. 'He has a splendid spirit.'

'Never a truer word!' Milly laughed. 'I never knew such a determined baby.'

She was right, for despite his angelic appearance, with that soft fair hair and that delicate skin, he was a lusty child and had made it clear, almost from his first day, that he had no intention of being asked to wait for anything, especially his food. By the time he was five months old and was sitting up in his highchair, he had learnt to bang on the table with his spoon and to go on banging until he got the attention he wanted. But he had a smile of such melting sweetness that Milly said she couldn't deny him anything. And his grandmother was bewitched by him and took the carriage to visit him whenever she could.

By this time, Nat and Mary weren't upset by her absences because it left them free to go exploring whenever they wanted to. Over June and July they discovered a water mill, two half-demolished haystacks and a disused clay pit which was the best of all, because it was wonderfully, squashily muddy and they could paddle there without being told not to get wet. Nat said it was almost as good as being at the seaside.

'How do you know?' Mary said. 'You've never been to the seaside.'

'I have so,' her brother told her loftily, 'and I can remember every bit of it.'

'Did I go too?'

'Yes. Course you did.'

'I don't *remember* it.'

'That's on account of you were very little,' Nat said. 'Spot went too, didn't you Spot? I'll bet *he* remembers.' And then he noticed that his sister was looking cast down, so he said, 'Happen we'll go again sometime. Then you'll see.'

'Do you think we will?' Mary said.

'You never know,' her brother told her.

But they were both surprised when their father came home from his latest stint on the railway to tell them he'd booked a cottage by the seaside so that they could all go away for a holiday. It was almost as if he'd been listening to their conversation. And when he told them it was at Whitby and Nat remembered that *that* was where they'd been for that first seaside holiday, they couldn't believe their luck.

It was a wonderful holiday and they enjoyed it so much that Nathaniel said he would take them to some of the other places he had to visit that summer. So they went to Darlington, where they explored the centre of the town and went to see where the new railway station was being built, to Scarborough, where they were impressed by the wide roads and the fine carriages that filled them but much preferred climbing the sea cliffs at the edge of a wild sea, and to Leeds, where their mother showed them round the town, as well as travelling six times to Foster Manor, to see their sister and her baby, who was now called Fill, to distinguish him from his father.

The next year was even better, for this was the year when Nat started at the Quaker school. He came home every day glowing with tales of the new things he was learning and the new friends he was making until Mary grew quite envious and confided to her mother that she didn't see why girls couldn't be scholars too. But although she sighed very sadly, she knew she had to accept the situation. There was no hope of her joining her brother because they only took boys at his school and there were no schools for girls.

But she was wrong. The times were changing. When Nat had been a scholar for two terms and the new year was four months old and Fill had celebrated his second birthday with a great iced cake and eaten so much of it that it gave him hiccups, and big sister Milly was expecting her second baby in two months time, her papa came home one April afternoon with a little booklet in his hand.

'There you are, Miss Mary,' he said, handing it to her. 'What do you think of that?'

He had his teasing face on, so she read the little book at once. It was called 'A Brochure' which seemed an odd sort of title but inside it was all about a new school that was going to be opened in York in September and, wonder of wonders, it

346

was a school for girls.

Her face was a study of surprise and delight.

'Am I to take it that you would like to be put down for a place?' her father said.

Her answer was instant and loving. She bounded towards him, brochure in hand, and threw her arms round his neck. And Jane, watching them from the comfort of her armchair, was suddenly overwhelmed by such happiness that her cheeks grew hot and she had to put up a hand to try to hide her blushes.

These first happy years of the decade had been good to George Hudson too. He'd made sure of it. Just as he'd predicted, some of the small railways companies were struggling within months of coming into existence. So he decided to give them a little canny encouragement. In April 1841, he called a meeting in York for all the companies who were 'interested in forming an east coast link from York to Edinburgh' and, when their directors were gathered together and enjoying his hospitality, he told them he planned to build a line from Darlington to Durham. They were impressed, as he knew they would be, for if *he* built a line, everybody knew it would be up and running in no time and, what is more, it would be successful. One or two of them wondered how such an ambitious project as a line to Edinburgh could possibly be funded and how much it would cost. He told them grandly that it would probably be in the region of half a million pounds and was delighted when one or two of them gasped. Then he told them there would be a second meeting in four months' time, when he would outline his plans in full.

It was no surprise to him when the directors returned in August in a miserably chastened mood. They had made careful estimates of what it would cost to build their section of the line and they knew it was beyond their resources. They weren't rich men, when all was said and done, and potential shareholders were loath to invest when times were so bad. George looked round at their glum faces, as he stood up to address them, and knew they would fall into his lap like ripe apples.

He told them the cost of the project was indeed £500,000 and agreed that that was a sum which was unlikely to be raised on the open market. 'However,' he said, grinning at them, 'that need not disturb us unduly. There are other ways to raise capital. What I propose is this. We have eight companies between us. Very well then, let us join forces and offer these shares to our own share-holders–' He paused so that his next words would have their maximum impact '–with a guaranteed dividend of six per cent.'

There was a frisson of excitement. One man called 'Bravo!', another threw his hat in the air, there was general applause, which George acknowledged with a wave of his fat hand. One bold soul did venture to ask how he could be sure of such a dividend but the answer to that was simple.

'I have given you my word on it,' he said, 'and when George Hudson gives you his word you may depend on it.'

The formation of the new company was ratified by all eight small companies just before Christmas and naturally enough Mr George Hudson was elected chairman and made it his business to have Richard Nicholson as his company treasurer, there being nothing like keeping things in the family. By the time Jane was cuddling her second grandson and telling Milly what a little darling he was and agreeing that the name Jonathan was just perfect for him, the bill for the new Darlington to Newcastle Railway was before parliament. By the following September there was a unified rail network throughout the Midlands with lines stretching from Rugby and Birmingham to York and Newcastle. And the Railway King owned it all.

'There you are, you see,' he said to Lizzie. 'They can carp all they like, but there's no stopping me when I've set my mind to a thing.'

24

George Hudson's spectacular progress was the main topic of conversation at the dinner parties in York during the spring of 1844, that and his ability to pay such high dividends to his shareholders when all the other railway companies were struggling.

Even Nathaniel was beginning to have doubts about his hero. 'What I can't understand,' he said to Mr Leeman, one summer evening, when his particular group of friends and neighbours was gathered about his dining table, 'is how he was able to predict the dividend his new company would pay, even before the line was built and the profits were coming in. He must have had a crystal ball.'

'That has occurred to a good many of us over the last few years,' Mr Leeman said and he gave Jane his quiet smile.

Then they're still keeping an eye on him, Jane thought. She'd grown adept at picking up messages at these dinner parties of hers.

'I can't believe he would be dishonest,' Mr Patterson said, smoothing his whiskers. 'He is a considerable businessman, when all's said and done, and I daresay they have different ways of doing things.'

'So it would appear,' Mr Leeman said – and again that smile at Jane.

'And we mustn't forget he *has* built us the De Grey Rooms,' Mrs Patterson said, 'which are a great adornment to the city. He'd not have done that had he been dishonest, now would he.'

'He'll overreach hisself one of these days,' Mary Jerdon told them all, nodding her head. 'You mark my words. Men like that allus do.'

The company were used to her gloomy predictions about the great Mr Hudson, having heard so many, and took very little notice of her, although her daughter breathed 'Amen' and hoped she would be proved right. Then she looked up at Mrs Anderson and turned the conversation to an easier topic. 'What did you think of Mr Dickens' latest instalment, Mrs Anderson?' she asked.

'That Mr Pecksniff is so *awful*,' Mrs Anderson said happily. 'You really hate him. Leastways, I do. I hated him from the minute he made his first appearance. I do so enjoy Mr Dickens' characters.'

And then they were all off, praising and dissecting, admiring 'that dear Mark Tapley', wondering whether America really was as bad as Mr Dickens painted it, hoping that Mary Graham would marry Martin Chuzzlewit.

'Have you all read the latest instalment?' Mr Greer wanted to know.

'We read it yesterday evening,' Nathaniel told them, adding with pride, 'Our two scholars took it in turns to read it aloud to us.'

'What a blessing it must be to have two scholars in the family,' Mrs Patterson said. 'A son to follow his father into the profession and a clever daughter to keep her mother company.'

Nathaniel agreed that it was indeed a blessing and he and Jane exchanged an amused look because they knew it wasn't a foregone conclusion that Nat would become a railway engineer. His classics master thought he ought to go to Oxford and had told them so, when they'd gone to the school to discuss his future. 'A clever boy,' he'd said to them. 'We feel he should sit the Oxford Entrance if you would be agreeable to it.' They'd agreed at once. What parent would not? It would be such an opportunity and they could well afford it. But they'd decided not to say anything to their neighbours until after the results of the examination were out, just in case he wasn't as clever as his teachers thought. But it was a wonderful secret to hug to themselves.

The dinner party meandered amiably on, the latest news was dissected, the price of cloth deplored, the new railway to Whitby praised and the name of Queen Victoria's latest baby discussed at length. When they parted from one another at a little after eleven o'clock, they were all in very good humour.

'If you have any news of our esteemed friend,' Jane said as she shook Mr Leeman's hand, 'I would be glad to hear it.' Nathaniel was talking to Mrs Leeman and safely out of earshot.

'If and when I have news, Mrs Cartwright,' Mr Leeman promised, 'you shall be the first to hear it. I give you my word. There is much being said, as you can imagine, but nothing to any purpose – as yet.'

But in the event, when news *did* come, it was brought by Lizzie Hudson.

The Railway King was in a temper. 'Look at that!' he shouted, throwing his copy of *The Times* across the breakfast table at his wife. 'Who gave him leave to pontificate? Eh? Tell me that. Damned man. Carping and criticizing. Who asked *him?* Read it.'

Lizzie picked the paper up very gingerly as if it might bite her, looked at it and tried to read it. It was a chilly morning and the fire hadn't taken at all well so she was cold as well as nervous. If only he wouldn't shout so.

'Well, read it!' he shouted. 'Read it.' And he leant across the table and squashed his fat finger against the offending passage.

It was a letter in the correspondence column

and, as Lizzie feared, it was all about him and none too complimentary.

'*I consider Mr Hudson to be a shrewd man,*' the letter writer said, '*but for pity's sake, Sir, call the attention of shareholders to the sway this person is obtaining. Shareholders should be cautious ere they raise a railway autocrat with power greater than the prime minister.*'

'Am I to be told how I'm to run my own business now?' George shouted. 'Is that the size of it? I never heard the like. God damn it, how do they think I can run a railway if I'm not to have any power? That's how the system works. Power and brass. That's the size of it. Power and brass. Which I've earned by t'sweat of my brow, dammit. And now this jumped-up pipsqueak comes along and thinks he can tell me how I'm to spend my own money. He'd not do such a thing if I were gentry. Oh no! It'd be yes sir, no sir, three bags full sir, if I were gentry. I've said this afore, Lizzie, but I'll say it again, I've a damned good mind to buy myself a country estate. That'd show 'em. Summat grand and costly. See how they'd treat me then. What do 'ee think of that? Eh? Shall I buy an estate?'

Lizzie didn't know what to think – or what to say. 'If you think so, George,' she quavered.

'I *do* think so,' he said. 'Should ha' done it years ago. I'll get the opening of the Newcastle and Darlington out the way and arrange the dinner in Gateshead and then I'll set about it.'

'He means it,' Lizzie said to Jane two days later when they were taking tea in Jane's pretty parlour.

'And how we shall mek out in some great house stuck out in the middle of the country I do not know, away from all our friends. I shall never see you and Richard ever again, which I couldn't abide, I mean for to say after all these years. And what's to become of Monkgate? Tell me that. We can hardly live in two places at once, now can we?'

'Plenty do,' Jane told her. 'The gentry have houses all over the place, country estates and town houses in London and all sorts.'

'But we're not gentry,' Lizzie said. 'I mean for to say, gentry are born and bred. You've only to listen to 'em to know that. You should hear young Georgie these days. He speaks so grand I can hardly understand what he's saying half the time what with stuff about the beaks, which is what they call the masters at Harrow seemingly, and capping and shells and yearlings and I don't know what all. Not that I'm saying he's gentry, mind, I'd not presume to that, but he sounds like gentry, there's no gainsaying it, what I suppose I should be glad on. George says 'tis first rate and 'twill stand him in good stead when he gets to Oxford, where he's a-going apparently. He should know, shouldn't he, mixing with the gentry an' all – George, I mean not Georgie, although I suppose he's mixing with the gentry in Harrow, because they all seem to be gentry there. Some of 'em are Honourables. What I can hardly believe, my son hob-nobbing with Honourables. I mean for to say.' Then she paused to gather her thoughts. 'Oh, what if I have to leave York, Jane? I wouldn't see you or Richard ever again.' And she began to cry, the tears running down her long nose and into her mouth.

'Try not to fret, my dear,' Jane said, full of sympathy for her poor weeping friend. 'It might not come to it. He might change his mind.'

'No,' Lizzie said, resignedly, wiping her eyes, 'he won't. Once he's set his heart on a thing he never changes.'

She was right. He bought his first country seat that summer, just after the Newcastle and Darlington Railway had been officially opened. It was a very large estate called Octon and he bought it for £100,000 from the Duke of Devonshire, no less, along with a considerable piece of land at Baldersby near Thirsk.

'Now let 'em criticize me,' he said to Lizzie when he'd shown her round his enormous building. 'This is the style, eh? That'll show 'em.'

'What will happen to Monkgate?' Lizzie ventured. 'Shall we go on living there?'

'We'll live there for the time being,' he said, 'until this is signed and sealed. Then I shall put it on t'market an' this'll be our home and we'll live here. This is just the place for us. Plenty of room. We can hold some rare old parties here. Think on it, Lizzie.'

But Lizzie was thinking of her dear brother Richard and her dear friend Jane and wondering how she would ever get to see them when she had to live in this awful great place, stuck out in the country.

Had she known it, Jane was 'out in the country' that afternoon too. She'd had a letter from Milly that morning that had sent her rushing to catch the first train to Foster Manor. *'Dearest Ma,'* the letter had said, *'I feel so sick and ill I hardly know which way to turn. You would not believe how ill I feel and Felix is worried silly and told me to write to you. Please, dearest Ma, come and see me. I long to see you. Please come as soon as ever you can. Your miserable and loving daughter, Milly.'*

It seemed like a very long train journey and Jane worried through every mile of it. But when she got to Foster Manor and was ushered up to her daughter's bedroom she only had to ask two questions and she relaxed at once, for Milly wasn't in a fever or covered in spots or blisters or anything untoward like that. She was nauseous because she was carrying again.

'Have 'ee been very sick?' Jane asked, sitting herself beside the bed and holding Milly's hand.

'Endlessly,' Milly sighed. 'On and on. You'd never believe it. It starts as soon as I sit up. I can't understand it. I wasn't like this with the other two.'

'Um,' Jane said. 'It does happen sometimes. How far gone are you?'

'Nearly three months,' Milly told her. 'Mrs Hardcastle said everything was coming along well but I don't see how it can be when I'm feeling so ill. I don't understand it.'

''Twill pass when you've reached the third month,' Jane promised. 'And I'll come in and see you every day until it does.'

In fact it took another twenty days and Jane travelled to Foster Manor on every one of them. When Lizzie's unhappy letter arrived to tell her she had moved to '*this awful great house where I shan't see anyone and what will become of me here I cannot think and now he is going to put Monkgate on the market, what I can't see the necessity for, and he is so cross on account of this other railway*', it was nearly a week before she could find time to answer it. And then she couldn't think what to say because it was such a rambling letter she didn't understand a lot of it.

It wasn't until Nathaniel came back from Durham that she found out about 'this other railway'.

'There *is* a new railway being proposed,' he told her. 'The company was formed in May. It's going to be called the London and York Railway because it's to run from London to York. Mr Hudson is furious about it.'

'But we've already got a railway from London to York,' Jane said.

'Exactly so,' Nathaniel said, 'which is why Mr Hudson is so annoyed. This is another one, taking another route. It will run through St Neots, Peterborough, Lincoln, Grantham and Doncaster and it will be a great deal quicker than Mr Hudson's route on account of it being more direct. The MP for Doncaster is backing it, so I believe, and another MP called Astell.'

'Competition,' Mary Jerdon observed, grinning at him. 'Now there'll be ructions.'

'They've started already, Nanna,' he told her. 'According to Mr Leeman, he's asking the Midland to put up two and a half million pounds to build more lines.'

'He spends money like water,' Mary Jerdon sniffed. 'There'll be ructions.'

The ruction, when it came, was so violent and so public that it sent shockwaves all along the route of the proposed new line from York to London.

It happened on a cold January day and in the middle of Derby railway station and its onset was almost accidental. The great George Hudson had just stepped ponderously down from one of his fine, new, first-class carriages, moving carefully because his gout was playing him up, when he found himself precipitously face to face with his arch enemy, Mr Edmund Beckett Denison, MP for Doncaster and co-founder of the London and York Railway. The two men eyed one another for several seconds and then Mr Denison greeted his rival with apparent courtesy but in tones that indicated unmistakable disdain and hostility. 'Your servant, Mr Hudson, sir.'

'Servant be dammed,' George said, instantly in a fury. 'Out of my way, sir. I have no truck with men who raise capital by foul means.'

'Have a care, sir,' Mr Denison warned. 'I'm not a man for foul means, not for any of my endeavours, which is more than can be said for some. You would be well advised to watch your tongue, sir.'

'You watch your own tongue, sir,' George roared. 'God damn it, I won't be spoken to in that way in my own station.'

They were toe to toe and bristling like fighting cocks and their furious voices and hot faces were attracting a crowd.

'You'll be spoken to in any way I choose,' Mr

Denison shouted.

'I will not, God damn it,' George shouted back. 'Foul means I said and foul means I meant. I'm a man as speaks my mind.'

Mr Denison drew himself up to his full height, which was considerably taller than his opponent. 'Have a care, Hudson,' he said, playing to his gathering audience. 'I've warned you before now to restrain your language. You are a blackguard, sir, and I have done with you. Go, go away!'

The attentive eyes switched from the MP to George Hudson, avid to see what he would do next and as he looked back at them he knew he'd been outmanoeuvred and could be made to look a fool if he wasn't careful. He turned on his heel and limped off the platform with as much *sang froid* as he could manage, given his gout and his temper. He was seething with anger but it was the only thing he could do. If he'd stayed where he was there would have been fisticuffs.

'It was an abomination,' he said to Lizzie when he finally got home. 'To be shouted at on my own railway. God damn it. I don't know what the world's coming to. I'm landed gentry now, Lizzie. Landed gentry. I've earned a little respect. He'd no right to treat me so.'

'Nasty jealousy,' Lizzie tried to soothe. 'That's what it is, George. Nasty jealousy. Take no notice.'

But he wasn't soothed in the least and went on raging for nearly half an hour, vowing to be revenged. 'Summat must be done,' he roared over and over again. 'I'll not stand for it.'

Mr Leeman thought the story was all very amusing and showed just what sort of character Mr Hudson was at heart. He told Jane all about it the next time they met and the two of them stood on the pavement in the winter sunshine and enjoyed themselves at Mr Hudson's expense.

'It don't surprise me in the least,' Jane said. 'He were allus a bully.'

'It will be interesting to see what happens next,' Mr Leeman said.

'It will indeed,' Jane said.

What happened next was that her third grandchild was born. She arrived at Easter when the daffodils were in bud and she was called Sarah-Jane after her aunt and her grandmother, to her grandmother's delight. Because the children were on school holiday the entire Cartwright family took the train to Foster Manor to see her as soon as they knew she was born. Mary was most impressed with her and thought she was very pretty. 'Like a little doll,' she said, gazing at her, enraptured. And when she was asked to stand godmother to the baby she was so pleased she was speechless for a full thirty seconds, which her father teased her was a thing unheard of.

Bully-boy Hudson can do what he likes, Jane thought, watching her, but he'll never do anything to equal this.

What he did raised eyebrows wherever his name was mentioned. That summer he bought another two country seats, Newby Park, which stood by the River Swale and was next door to his estate at Baldersby and instantly became his principal residence, and after that, Londesborough Park, which stood in 12,000 acres of prime land in East Yorkshire and cost him half a million pounds.

'The extravagance!' people said to one another. 'He's got one country estate. What does he want with three?' The general opinion was that he was 'flashing his money about and showing off'.

'It makes you wonder what on earth he'll do next,' Jane said to Mr Leeman at her next dinner party.

'It does indeed,' Mr Leeman said.

According to an announcement in *The Times,* what he did next was to put himself up for election as the Member of Parliament for Sunderland.

'Although why he should want to be an MP is beyond me,' Mary Jerdon said, as she and Jane and Nathaniel and the children sat at dinner that evening. 'There's never any end to him. He'll go too far one of these days, you mark my words.'

'He makes me think of the fisherman's wife,' Jane told her.

'Which fisherman was that?' Nathaniel wanted to know.

'The one in the fairy story,' Jane explained. And as he looked puzzled, she retold the tale. 'She and her husband were so poor they only had a hovel to live in and then one day her husband caught a magic flounder that told him it could grant wishes. He was so overawed by it that he simply threw it back but when his wife heard what he'd done she was furious with him for being so foolish. "Go back," she said, "and tell it you want to live in a pretty cottage." So he went back and called to the fish and told it what his wife wanted.

"Go home," the fish said, "she is in the cottage already." And she was. That should have been the end of the story but it wasn't because the fisherman's wife was greedy and no sooner had she had one wish granted than she thought of another even better. First it was to live in a castle, then she wanted to be king, then emperor, then pope. And the fish granted her every wish one after the other until she decided that she wanted to be the lord of the universe. And that time, when the fisherman told the flounder what she wanted it said...' And she paused and looked at her children, who'd been following the story and grinning at one another because they knew what was coming.

'Go home,' they chorused. 'She is back in the hovel already.'

Their father and their grandmother applauded them.

'A very moral story,' Nathaniel said, smiling at Jane. 'You are right. It could be applicable.'

Amen to that, Jane thought. But for the moment she kept the thought to herself. If he was changing his mind about his hero, she must let him do it in his own time and his own way. But you wait, Mr Fisherman's Wife, she thought, I'll be even with you yet.

362

25

Mr George Hudson, parliamentary candidate for the Sunderland constituency, stood on the balcony of the George Inn in the high street with Lizzie and his children ranged obediently behind him and looked down at the crowd which had gathered below him. They weren't a particularly friendly crowd – in fact some of them looked downright surly – but he meant to win them over and the first thing he intended to do was to scotch some of the rumours his opponent was spreading about him.

'I am charged,' he said, in his boldest voice, 'with being a railway speculator and in favour of the Corn Laws.' Then he paused to give them a chance to say things to one another, which they did. 'To both,' he went on, smiling at them, 'I plead in some measure guilty and I'll tell you why. It is all very well to *talk* about the poor–' Another pause '–but I like to *act* for the poor. My opponents *preach* about the poor, while I give *employment* to the poor.' Another pause during which there was a lot of murmuring. 'Without which many of them might starve. Away then with the charge of being a railway speculator! If work a-plenty and food a-plenty flow from the railways to enrich the poor, as they do, then I have been a benefactor to my country.' This time the pause was filled by a slight cheer. 'Is it a charge against me that I have made a fortune?' he went on. 'Is it a bad thing to earn good money and spend it on your fellow men?' And he looked round at them all and waited to hear what they would say next.

The surly expressions were gone. Most of them were looking decidedly attentive, some almost seemed enthusiastic. 'No!' some shouted. 'No!' And one man took up another cry. 'Vote for Mr Hudson! He's the man for us!'

He spoke to them for nearly ten minutes, outlining his plans for the Durham and Sunderland Railway, which he knew they wanted, and speaking about the value of the Wearmouth Docks and how he would rejuvenate them. When he stopped, they cheered and clapped and threw their hats in the air. 'Vote for Hudson! He's the man for us!'

'You're so clever George,' Lizzie said, when they left the balcony.

'Aye,' he said. 'I know.'

The election took place three weeks later and, just as he expected, Mr George Hudson was elected Member of Parliament for Sunderland, having defeated his opponent by 627 votes to 497.

Nathaniel Cartwright was away in Scarborough that week and didn't come home until several days after the election was over but he brought back the relevant copy of *The Times* and passed it across the table to Jane at dinner that evening.

'The fisherman's wife is now an MP, you see,' he said.

'Aye,' she said, rather sourly. 'Lizzie wrote and told me. Much good may it do him.'

'Good may well come of it,' he said, giving her his wry smile. 'He'll be able to push through any railway bill he wants instead of waiting for someone else to condescend to do it. It could speed up the process considerably, which would be no bad thing, you must agree.'

'Aye,' she said, setting aside the paper she'd been reading. 'Happen. But read that.'

It was a copy of their local paper, *The Yorkshireman*, and the article she'd been reading was outspoken in its criticism of the great Mr Hudson, which had given her a rush of satisfaction, as it always did when someone else understood how appalling he was.

'It is quite clear to us,' it said, *'that Mr Hudson's return to Parliament is quite the worst thing that could have happened to that gentleman. Out of Parliament he was a great man, and wielding immense influence. In Parliament he will be nobody, and destitute of all influence. He will discover this himself, by and by. It is quite a different thing to address a meeting of railway speculators panting for 10% and to face the congregated intellect, learning and gentlemanly accomplishments such as the British Parliament contains. Men find their level in the House of Commons and Mr Hudson will find his. Perhaps, too, it may do him some good.'*

'Um,' Nathaniel said thoughtfully. 'It could be true. He does tend to ride roughshod and he'll not be able to do it there. I wonder how he'll make out.'

'He'll get his own way,' Mary Jerdon predicted

dourly. 'On account of he allus does.'

Jane ignored the prediction because she had something more pleasant to talk about. 'And now,' she said, smiling at Nat, 'we've got some really good news for *you*. Wouldn't 'ee say so, Nat?'

'I hope you will consider it so, Papa,' Nat said. At seventeen he had grown into a very personable young man with his father's height and colouring and his mother's fine brown eyes. 'I have been awarded a scholarship to Corpus Christi,' he said. 'To read Philosophy and Theology.'

'That,' his father told him, smiling fit to split his face, 'is the best news I have heard in a long time. The very best. But no more than you deserve, young man, for we all know how diligently you've worked for it, do we not, Jane? We must have a special celebration. A dinner in your honour at the Star and Garter. How would that be?'

Nat was blushing. 'It would be...' he began and then he was lost for the right word to say.

His sister finished for him. 'Just what you deserve,' she said, hugging his arm. 'He's such a clever old stick, ain't he, Pa?'

And at that they all told him how clever he was and how much they admired him and how well deserved this scholarship was so that he blushed even more deeply and held up his hands as if he was warding them off. When the uproar had subsided into laughter, he looked at his parents one after the other, and spoke again, rather hesitantly.

'Could I ask you a favour?' he said, looking at his father.

'Ask away!' Nathaniel said. 'You can have the top brick off the chimney today.'

'It's my friend Toby,' he told them. 'Toby Henderson. He's won a scholarship to Corpus Christi too and he's every bit as deserving as I am, probably more so, only he has no family to praise him – only a grandmother and by all accounts she's so deaf I don't think she hears what he's saying half the time – so what I'm wondering is whether we could include him in the dinner too. He's my very best friend.' Then he paused and waited.

'No sooner asked than granted,' Nathaniel said. 'It's a splendid idea. Now we'll have two scholars to praise.'

Jane didn't know which of her menfolk she admired the most, Nathaniel for his instant generosity – wasn't that just typical of him – or Nat for thinking of his friend and wanting to include him in his celebration – which was typical of him too. They are both such good men, she thought, and Nathaniel has the right of it. This is a splendid idea. What a time we shall have.

Which they did, although not quite in the way she expected. The trouble was that 'my friend Toby' was impossibly shy and extremely gauche. He was shorter than Nat and rather more stocky and that made him look the clumsier of the two, especially as he had large hands and very large feet, and to make matters worse for himself, he blushed and stammered when anyone spoke to him and spent a great deal of the meal earnestly contemplating his plate and clearing his throat. And then, when the family raised their glasses to drink to his success and Nat's, he was so over-come he knocked his own glass of wine all over the tablecloth and was then miserably embar-rassed by the stain he'd caused. Nathaniel assured him that it could have happened to anybody, but he wasn't comforted and blushed so deeply and for such a long time that they all had to look away from him to give him time to recover. But when the meal was over, he surprised them by taking his leave with an unexpected grace, thanking them all for their kindness and telling them he would never forget it.

They were so impressed by his little speech that it wasn't until he'd left them that they realized he was on foot and would probably be walking all the way to Haxby. Jane was concerned and wondered whether they should get the carriage and go after him but Nat said a walk would do him good and in any case by the time they'd got the carriage ready he'd be halfway home, which was true enough.

'He'd not want to inconvenience you,' he told his mother. 'That's the sort of chap he is. Salt of the earth.'

They didn't disabuse him of his opinion, which Jane allowed afterwards was like to have a grain of truth in it, but she and Nathaniel told one another privately that the young man had been extremely hard work. Mary was even more out-spoken.

'He's an oaf,' she said to her mother the next day. 'Staring at his plate all the time and doing that silly coughing and forever pulling at his sleeves. That coat was much too small for him.

He looked an absolute freak. He should get a new one and make sure it fits.'

'Happen he can't afford a new one,' Jane tried to point out. 'He's no family to speak of.'

But Mary wasn't having any of it. 'He's going to Oxford, Mama,' she said, 'and poor boys don't go to Oxford. He could afford it if he wanted to. Or he could have worn summat wi' a bit more style. There was no call for him to come to dinner looking like a tramp. He should have made an effort. *We* did. No, it's like I told you. He's an oaf. And I don't know *what* he thought he was doing with that wine. The cloth was awash. I can't think why you invited him. I hope you won't do it again.'

'He did thank us,' Jane said, trying to stick up for him.

But Mary snorted. 'And so I should think,' she said.

Later that night when she and Nathaniel were in bed and discussing the events of the day, Jane recounted the conversation. 'She's taken against him, poor boy,' she said.

'Aye,' Nathaniel said easily. 'So 'twould seem.'

'I've never known her be so fierce. She said she hoped we wouldn't invite him again.'

'Then she's summat to learn,' her father said. 'If we want to invite him again, and I see no reason why we should not, we will and she will have to accept it.'

'She'll not like it.'

'Doubtless. But that's the size of it. The young have to learn their place, like we did. We do them no favours to let them to think they may run the world. The lad is shy. That's all. He'll improve as he gets to know us.'

The matter seemed to have been decided so Jane let it drop. But she was still puzzled by the strength of Mary's opposition to this poor shy boy and fell asleep thinking about it.

George Hudson was caught up in thought that night too, only in his case his thoughts were furious. He'd been at a civic dinner in York that evening and had been driven home to Newby Park in the early hours of the morning, cheerful with brandy and bonhomie and feeling wonderfully full of himself. As he staggered through the hall he saw the latest copy of *The Yorkshireman* waiting on the silver salver for his attention. He picked it up drunkenly and carried it upstairs with him, thinking he'd glance through it before he settled for the night. Happen they had some news of his latest triumph and praise was always welcome. The article was like a shock of cold water. He charged into the bedroom where Lizzie was peacefully snoring and yelled at her to wake up.

'Have 'ee seen this?' he demanded.

She opened her eyes, still drugged with sleep. 'What?'

'What? What?' he roared, shaking the paper at her. 'This, woman. It's infamous, monstrous, insupportable. How dare they write about me like this? Don't they know who I am?'

Lizzie was trying to pull herself back to wakefulness and finding it difficult. 'What time is it?' she trembled.

'Time!' he roared. 'Time! Time I taught them

all a lesson. That's what time it is. They need teaching a lesson, dammit. Jumped up scribblers writing about me. How dare they! Very well then, I'll show 'em. I'll be the biggest success London has ever seen. That's what I'll be. I'll buy the biggest house in London, you see if I don't, and I'll give the grandest parties. I'll have all the big-wigs standing in line begging for an invitation, that's what I'll do. I'll be the most successful MP they've ever seen. It'll be a different story then. God damn it! How dare they treat me like this? I'll get on to it directly.'

'Yes, George,' Lizzie said dutifully. 'Happen it could wait till morning though?'

'We will go to London on the first train,' he told her. 'I'll not stand for this. Move over. You're taking up all the bed.'

And he lumbered into the bed and fell asleep at once.

They caught the second train, because he'd overslept, but he set about finding a suitable house as soon as they'd booked in at their hotel. The one he chose was called Albert Gate East and was absolutely enormous. It stood on the north side of Knightsbridge, beside Hyde Park, and was one of a pair newly built by Mr Cubitt who was the most renowned builder in the capital. They had stood empty for rather a long time, so long, in fact, that the locals had nicknamed them the two Gibraltars because 'nobody would ever take them' and they were extremely expensive. Not that George worried about a thing like that. The more expensive his new house was known to be, the better. Albert Gate East would suit his pur-

371

poses to perfection and he made up his mind to buy it as soon as he saw it.

Lizzie was overwhelmed by it, although naturally she didn't say so. But really she had never seen anything so grand. It was built in the Italianate style and was five storeys high, with a splendid staircase that rose from the entrance hall to the third floor and was topped by a dome made of wrought iron and glass. There were marble fireplaces in all the principal rooms and more bedrooms than she could count and the moulded ceilings were a wonder to behold. It was built for entertainment on the grand scale.

'As soon as it is legally mine, I will have it decorated in the very latest style,' George said as they walked back to their hotel.

'We shan't have to live in it straightaway, shall we?' Lizzie asked. She'd only just got accustomed to living in Newby Park and she really couldn't face another move.

'We'll tek up residence in January when I tek my seat in t'House,' he told her. 'And we'll hold our first ball the week before. I shall see to it. Then we'll stay here until the end of t'Season and set our Ann on t'road to a handsome husband. And then we'll go back to Newby Park and stay there till t'next Season. I've got it all planned.'

It made poor Lizzie feel exhausted simply to hear it being talked about but she said 'Yes, George' and accepted that she would have to put up with it. Oh, if only they could go back to the old days in Monkgate. She'd been so happy there with Jane and Richard just a walk away. I'll write to them as soon as I get a minute, she decided, and tell them what's been happening.

Richard Nicholson was very impressed by his brother-in-law's latest acquisition and spent the next three or four days bragging to his acquaintances about how wonderful it was. Jane sniffed at it.

'High time the magic flounder put him back in his hovel,' she said to her mother.

'He'll do it come the finish,' Mary Jerdon said. 'Pride allus comes afore a fall. Isn't it today we're going to collect our Nat's new jacket?'

New jacket, new trousers, new shirts, new boots, a whole wardrobe full of clothes, hats, socks, chemises, under breeches, pocket handkerchiefs, silk cravats – nothing had been left out for Jane had made her mind to have everything done to perfection, even though Nathaniel teased her for making such a fuss. Now that her son was leaving home, he was going to do it in style.

He left at the beginning of October, wearing his new brown frock coat, his new cream-coloured trousers and his new scarlet cravat and looking so handsome and so very like his father that she was near to tears just at the sight of him.

'Write to me as soon as you can,' she urged, as he and Toby were climbing aboard the Rugby train.

He stood in the doorway and looked down at her, grimacing and rolling his eyes to show her she was fussing. But Toby understood her anxiety and tried to reassure her.

'I'll look after him, Mrs Cartwright,' he said. 'He won't come to any harm, I promise you, an'' he'll write to you the minute he's arrived or I'll pull his ears for him.'

He may be aw'kard, Jane thought, and nowt to look at, but he has a good heart. I'll say that for him. And he's uncommon fond of our Nat.

He was also as good as his word. Nat's first letter arrived the very next day to say that he and Toby had had an easy journey and were quite settled in. Their rooms were very grand, he said, they'd explored the college, met up with lots of others scholars and were looking forward to their new life. *'Oxford,'* he wrote, *'is a truly beautiful place. It's old and settled and full of colleges, yet all contained within a single square mile. I've never seen anything to equal it. You and Pa must come and visit me and see it too. I know you will like it as much as I do. I will write again at the end of my first week and then I will have more to tell you.'*

It was very reassuring. And although he didn't write to her every week – she could hardly expect that – he wrote at regular intervals to tell her about his lecturers and his first tutorial and how he'd joined the debating society and the natural history society and had taken up rowing.

'Now,' Nathaniel said, 'you can stop worrying. He's settled in, he's enjoying life, all's well with the world.'

'Aye,' she said. 'So it is.'

'Which is just as well,' her husband told her, 'on account of I've to be in Sunderland and thereabouts for the next three weeks – or even four. Now I can leave with a stout heart and a clear conscience.'

That autumn was damp, dark and miserable. There were too many fogs to clog their lungs and reduce them to coughing, too many early morning mists to chill the day and their spirits, too many fires that wouldn't take in the damp or smoked when the wind finally blew, too many runny noses, too many cold hands, too many feet stinging with chilblains.

'We shall all be ill if this goes on,' Mary Jerdon predicted. She'd taken a cold on her chest during the first thick fog and was finding it hard to shift. 'I been hacking and coughing for three weeks now an' I tell 'ee I'm sick to death of it.'

Jane tried to comfort her. 'Better weather's coming, Ma,' she said. 'Bound to be. It can't keep on like this for ever. November's allus foggy. We all know that.'

'But not like this,' her mother said. 'Not on and on and on.'

Jane was glad that Mary had left school and was at home to help her, for when everyone else was coughing and spluttering she was blessedly healthy and even more blessedly cheerful. 'Not to worry about Nanna,' she said. 'I'll make a bread poultice for her. That'll do the trick.'

But even *she* was worried when Toby Henderson's letter came, particularly as her father was away working on some distant railway line out in the countryside and they couldn't get in touch with him.

Toby had written extremely carefully so as not to alarm them but the message was too bad to be disguised. Nat was ill. He'd had a cold for several days but although Toby had nursed him '*to the*

375

very best of my ability, I do assure you', he had got steadily worse and was now, *'so the doctor says'*, suffering from congestion of the lungs. *'I felt you should know,'* Toby wrote. *'I am so sorry to be the bearer of such tidings.'*

'We must go there at once,' Jane said, putting the letter beside her plate. 'On the first train. Congestion of the lungs is serious. We must bring him home.'

But when they finally reached his rooms, having been escorted there from the station by Toby, it was obvious that he was much too ill to travel, racked by the most ugly cough and plainly in a fever.

'We must nurse him here,' Jane said to Mary, and she set about it at once, turning to Toby for information and answers to her questions. The fire was inadequate and would need stoking up and keeping in day and night. Extra coals must be ordered at once. Could that be done? His feet were icy. Did he have a hot-water bottle? And a kettle? Had he had anything to eat or was he too fevered for food? Had anyone tried him with gruel? Was there a saucepan in the place and a wooden spoon? Where was the chamber pot? Had the authorities been told what was going on?

'Indeed they have, ma'am,' Toby told her. 'It was the first thing I did when he was taken bad.'

'You're a good friend, Toby,' she said. 'Are they agreeable to him being nursed here?'

'Yes, ma'am.'

'Then we will get on with it,' Jane said, 'but I must warn you it is going to take a long time. I've nursed sick children afore so I know. The only thing we can do at the moment is to watch over him very carefully and keep him warm and see that he drinks as much water as he can until he reaches what they call the crisis – for that's what happens wi' congestion of the lungs – and that could take days or even weeks. So for a start,' she said, turning to Mary, 'you and I will need to find somewhere to stay, where we can sleep and take our meals when we're not sitting up with him. I will stay with him tonight and after that we will take it in turns, one night on, one night off.'

'Or perhaps one night on, two nights off,' Toby offered, 'if I were to take turns too. I mean, I wouldn't want to push in if you'd rather I didn't but I'm more than willing.' And then he stopped because he wasn't at all sure he'd said the right thing.

'You,' Jane told him, unconsciously bending her body towards him as if she were going to kiss him or hug him, 'are the best friend my Nat could possibly have. And we will take you up on your offer. We shall need all the help we can get on account of nursing the sick is a wearying business, especially when you love your patient the way we love him.'

'Thank 'ee kindly,' he said. 'And if I may make bold again, should I go out and find an inn for you? There are several hereabouts and I know where they are. It would be no trouble.'

She accepted that offer too, suggesting that Mary should go with him so that if she found 'summat what would suit she can tek it, there and then, instead of traipsing all the way back here'. Then when her two young helpers had gone she turned the gas down to a glimmer and settled to her first vigil.

It was a long, anxious night, for although she tried to push the memory from her mind, she couldn't help thinking of the way she and Lizzie had nursed poor little Matthew and their darling Dickie and how dreadful it had been when they died. 'Please God,' she prayed, over and over again, 'let me keep my Nat.' Towards midnight Toby returned to say that Mary had found a comfortable inn and had taken a room there and that he'd promised to go and collect her in the morning to escort her back, so that she wouldn't lose her way, and that his room was just across the stairs if she needed him. Jane thanked him and meant every word. But when he'd gone she was on her own with her thoughts and her vigil. The minutes ticked past very, very slowly and her poor fevered son stayed the same.

As he did for four fraught days and five anguished nights but on the morning of the fifth day, just as Jane and Toby had come back into the room to relieve his sister, who'd been sitting with him all night, he opened his eyes and asked for a drink of water and struggled to sit up to drink it.

'Praise be!' Jane said, trying not to cry. 'I think he's passed the crisis.' He was certainly much cooler than he'd been since they arrived and although he went back to sleep after about a quarter of an hour, he was a better colour and breathing more easily. 'Praise be!'

Two days later he was so much better that he was sitting up in bed, eating bread and butter and asking if there was any possibility of a glass of beer, and at that point she decided he was well enough to travel home.

They all went home together, she, Mary, Nat and Toby, who found them a cab to take them all to the station, virtually carried their patient down the stairs to the courtyard – and then went back for the bags – and escorted them gently and attentively all the way back to Shelton House.

'I don't know what we'd have done without him,' Jane said to Nathaniel when he finally came home to his first family dinner in weeks and discovered what had been going on while he'd been away. 'He was a true friend in need.'

'We will invite him to come and stay with us over Christmas,' Nathaniel decided, and looked at his daughter to see what she would say about it.

'A very good idea,' she said.

So the invitation was sent and accepted and they all spent a very happy and blessedly healthy Christmas together.

26

The Hudsons moved into their prestigious London address as soon as Christmas was over and George threw his first London party two weeks later. It was the biggest and most extravagant event he'd ever organized and he made sure that everybody who was anybody was there. Gilded carriages jostled for position all along Knightsbridge, dukes and duchesses climbed his splendid staircase, the house was ablaze with gas-lit chandeliers, the crush in his flamboyant reception room was the most gratifying thing he'd ever experienced. He'd even prevailed upon an equerry to the Queen to attend and spent several happy minutes during the evening telling him that, 'if I may make so bold as to offer a little advice', Her Majesty should be considering a new and truly comfortable way to travel, and that, if she were of a mind to use a train on occasions, he would be happy to commission a special carriage for her which would, of course, be furnished to the highest standards and kept for her exclusive use.

Oh yes, he thought, as his noble guests clamoured to speak to him, I've come a long way since I were a lad. A reet long way. I were nowt but a poor farm boy when I set out, an outcast wi'out a penny to my name, and now I'm t'Railway King an' t'richest man in England an' I've done it all wi'out a soul to help me. I mix wi' lords and ladies an' I've a son at Harrow and two at Oxford an' I'll marry my daughter to one of their high-born sons, just see if I don't, an' he'll be happy to have her. They'll sit up an' tek notice when I tek my seat in t'House. I've made sure of *that*.'

But, as *The Yorkshireman* had predicted, the great Mr Hudson was to discover that life as a Member of Parliament was a great deal more difficult than he expected. After a few weeks, he realized that he had become a member of a club whose rules he didn't understand and whose behaviour was completely incomprehensible. It seemed a lot of nonsense to him that you weren't allowed to speak unless you were wearing a top hat, and that you had to refer to your fellow MPs as Honourable Gentlemen when they were plainly no such thing.

But far worse was the way these drawling, 'honourable' gentlemen could deliver an insult. He endured it fairly soberly for a week or two but as it showed no signs of abating and, if anything, seemed to be getting worse, he eventually took fright and brandy, and started to arrive at the House in a state of cheerful inebriation to boom and bellow when he came under attack. His aggressive behaviour made him feel better but in fact it was no help to him. It wasn't long before an MP called Mr Brotherton stood up to suggest – to hoots of delighted laughter – that 'the House would beget additional respectability if Mr Hudson would join a temperance society' and another called Mr Joseph Hume complained that 'Mr Hudson has a nightly habit of coming down to the House, *flushed*', which the fools applauded. Why couldn't the beggar talk English? In Yorkshire they'd have said 'You're drunk, sir' and they'd have done it good humoured and given him a chance to stand up for himself, which these drawling dandies never did.

'God damn it!' he said to Lizzie after one particularly virulent exchange. 'I'm not putting up wi' this. Don't they know who I am? I'm the richest man in England, God damn it, and not because I was born to money like them but because I've earned it by the sweat of my brow. By the sweat of my brow, damn it. They've no right to abuse me the way they do. They were hurling insults at me, and yet *I* was the one who was called to order. It's insufferable. I'll not stand for it.'

Lizzie didn't really know what to say so she murmured that he was quite right and stood back to let the diatribe burn itself out.

'I'll show 'em,' he said. 'They needn't think they can ride roughshod over *me*. What's wrong wi' taking a drink now and then? Tell me that? I've seen plenty of *them* the worse for wear. Well I'll show 'em, that's all. I'll not let 'em get away wi' it. They'll dance to my tune come the finish.'

He showed them by holding another extravagant party even larger and grander than the first and, when *that* didn't silence them, he held a third and a fourth and crowned the fourth by welcoming Prince Albert, no less.

He was drunk with popularity and excess. 'I'm the talk of the town,' he boasted to Lizzie.

Which he was, although not quite in the way he imagined.

'The man's a buffoon,' Lady Livingston said. 'I've never seen anyone so overblown nor so ugly. He looks like a toad in a suit.'

'You are a trifle hard on him,' Felix said mildly. 'After all, he *has* built a prodigious number of railways, which most people would say is something to be thankful for.'

'He's a buffoon,' Sarah repeated. 'He never talks about anybody but himself and how rich he is, which is the height of bad taste, and how he's going to run railways the length and breadth of the country, which is the most boring topic of conversation you can imagine, and how he's going to find a rich husband for his ugly daughter, which ain't a thing for a man to brag about. And as to that wife of his, well, really, my dear, she beggars description. She seems half-witted to me and I declare I never saw such deplorable dress sense in all my life.'

Milly had been listening and saying nothing but now she sprang to the defence of her poor Lizzie, speaking before she could stop to think that it might not be proper to contradict her sister-in-law. 'She means well,' she said. 'She was always very kind to me – and to Ma, as I'm sure she would tell you. We were talking about it only t'other day sitting in this very room. I'll grant she's scatty – no one could deny *that* – and she does say silly things sometimes but I think that's because she has such a mortal hard time of it with Mr Hudson.' Then she stopped and wondered if she'd gone too far.

Sarah wasn't put out in the least and she didn't change her opinion either. 'That may well be so,' she conceded, 'but she looks an absolute fright. The gown she wore at their last party was in purple and orange, if you can imagine such a thing, and so hung about with bows and flounces and ribbons you could hardly see the cloth. And it's not as if either colour suits her. You will see for yourself if you come to town for the Season. Is that still planned, Felix?'

'It is,' Felix told her. 'I must pay some attention to Charlotte Square – it's high time – and there are one or two cases I should like to take, just to keep my hand in. But maybe I should be more accurate and say it is planned as far as it is possible to plan when you have three small children.'

'But you will leave them here, surely,' Sarah said.

'No,' Milly told her firmly and a little tetchily for really Sarah shouldn't be allowed to think she was right on every single matter. 'We most certainly will not. If I'm to go to London, they will come with me.'

'You amaze me, my dear,' Sarah said, raising her eyebrows. 'I've always been only too glad to leave my children for someone else to look after, which they do perfectly adequately. One needs a rest from time to time, wouldn't you say?'

'We all have our different ways,' Felix said mildly. 'And of course our Sarah-Jane is young yet to be parted from her mother.'

And as if to prove him right, Audrey came tapping at the door, in her timid way, to say, 'Not meanin' for to bother 'ee, sir, but Baby's took a little tumble. Nowt to worry about, ma'am, but she wants her mama.'

'Quite right too,' Milly said, getting to her feet at once. 'I can't have my little one crying.' And she left her sister-in-law to digest *that*.

Mr Hudson's marriage-broking kept London society entertained all through that Season. 'The effrontery of the man,' they said to one another, enjoying themselves immensely. 'All this talk of money is so vulgar. I wonder he don't hang a placard round his daughter's neck and have done with it: *Going with half a million pounds*.' Nevertheless, despite Mr Hudson's deplorable behaviour, they went to all his parties because Albert Gate East was absolutely *the* place to be that Season and flashed their diamonds at one another and drank his champagne and ate his rich food and amused themselves by watching as Miss Ann Hudson flirted gauchely with every man her father brought her way. 'So vulgar,' they said. 'So utterly, utterly vulgar. Selling her off like that. Dreadful little man.'

George was in his element, playing the host in his costly clothes, decking Lizzie with diamonds, booming greetings to the great and good, as though they were old friends, fawned on by members of the aristocracy – and why not? – flirted with by titled ladies, the centre of attraction and attention, powerful as a prize bull, the lord of all he surveyed. True, Ann couldn't make up her mind which of her many suitors she would choose, except for some useless foreign count called Suminski, and he wouldn't do at all, as he'd told her, but she was young yet and would come round to it next Season. No, the only problem was that he was spending a deal more money than was actually coming in and he'd be seriously out of pocket if he didn't do something about it. He'd already taken out a sizeable loan from Mr Glyn's London bank in order to cover part of the cost of his London house. As soon as t'Season's over, he promised himself, I'll put my mind to it and see what can be done. Meantime he would go on enjoying the grand life at Albert Gate and put in the occasional appearance at the House, just to show willing, and let those fool MPs go hang.

Milly enjoyed her Season as much as the great Mr Hudson, and wrote full reports of it to her mother, and Fill, who was seven and quite the scholar, wrote a postscript on the end of her letters. *'We have been to the Tower Nanna and seen the B Feeters'*. *'St Pols is very big. I like our church better. So does Jonathan.'* *'There are lots of horses in London. The streets are full of dung. You shood see it. Audrey says to look out for our feet because she does not want to be cleening our boots all the time.'*

Jane treasured every note and laughed out loud at most of them. 'Dear little man,' she said. 'What style he has.'

The seventh letter contained a snippet of news that delighted her as much as Fill's postscripts had done. *'I think I had best let you know this,'* Milly had written, *'or you will wonder at how fat I am become since I came to London. By the end of the year, God willing, you will be a grandmother again.'*

'So many babies,' Nathaniel said. 'I declare she is rivalling the Queen.' Then he noticed that Nat had had a letter too and that he was reading it with more than usual concentration. He was instantly concerned. 'Who is your letter from, Nat,' he said, 'if I may ask?'

'It's from Toby,' Nat said. 'His grandmother has just died. He's in a bit of a state. He says he doesn't know what to do. I think I should go to Haxby and help him.' And he passed the letter across the table to his father.

Nathaniel read it carefully. 'Yes,' he said. 'You are right. I think you *should* go and as soon as you can. Grief is hard to contend with, especially when you are young.'

'I'll come with you,' Mary said to her brother, her face full of sympathy. 'Two would be better than one.'

So the carriage was ordered for ten o'clock and the two of them set out, with a list from their father of things that would have to be done and a hamper of food from Mrs Cadwallader, for as their mother said, 'I'll wager he's had nothing to eat. You forget about food when you're grieving.'

It was the first time either of them had visited Toby's home and although neither of them passed any comment on it, even at first glance they found it a shocking place, for it was a labourer's cramped cottage and the living room was dark and dank. It had an earth floor, a rickety stove and very little furniture that they could see apart from a battered rocking chair by the fireside and two plain wooden chairs beside a plain wooden table in the centre of the room. And it smelt of dust and decay.

'Oh Toby!' Mary said, when he opened the door to them. 'I'm so very, very sorry.' And she put her arms round his neck and burst into tears. At which he cried too and the two of them stood with their arms around each other and sobbed together, wet cheek against wet cheek. It took quite a while for them to recover and in the meantime Nat had carried in the hamper and set it on the table and had then gone out to the coachman and told him they might be quite a time and suggested that he might like to water the horses and take some refreshment in the local inn, being careful to provide the money to pay for it.

Mary found plates and beakers in the kitchen

and they did what they could to coax their smitten friend to eat. But he was stuck in grief and shock and couldn't manage more than a mouthful.

'She was sitting in her chair,' he told them, over and over again. 'Sitting there, bolt upright and stone dead and I wasn't there. I was upstairs asleep and she died in her chair. Sitting there bolt upright, stone dead and all alone. I wasn't there and I should have been. Oh Mary, what am I to do?'

It was Nat who provided the answers, checking his father's instructions point by point. 'Have you seen the undertakers?'

Toby waved towards his grandmother's rocking chair. 'They took the – er – er...' Then he was overcome and wept again.

'Of course,' Nat soothed. 'Has the funeral been arranged?'

'Funeral?' Toby said vaguely, wiping his eyes on his sleeve.

'I will arrange it for you,' Nat said and put a tick on his list. 'Do you have any relations that ought to be told?'

'No. It was just us,' Toby said and added wildly, 'I left her on her own to die, Nat. How could I have done such a thing after the way she's looked after me all these years? She was all the mother I ever had.'

It took until late afternoon to make all the necessary arrangements and by then Toby had wept himself into a state of stunned calm. When Mary suggested that he should come home with them he simply nodded. And when she asked if she should help him pack a few things to take with him he nodded again and followed her up the dark stairs like a child.

The journey home was unnaturally quiet. Toby never made a sound even though Nat smiled at him from time to time to try to encourage him and Mary held his hand all the way. He just sat and looked at his boots. It was quite a relief to reach Shelton House and hand him over to their mother. She would know what was to be done with him. Which she did, easing him into the house with her arm round his shoulders, providing hot water for him so that he could go upstairs to the spare room and have a wash, and then persuading him to lie down and take a little nap. 'You must be worn out with all you've been through,' she said, 'and sleep is healing.'

He slept until dinner time and wouldn't have woken then if Jane hadn't gone upstairs to call him for the meal. But he sat at the table looking thoroughly shamefaced and staring at his plate.

'You are so good to me,' he said, apologetically, when Nathaniel served him a gentle helping of Mrs Cadwallader's meat pie.

Jane smiled at him. 'And why should we not be?' she said. 'I seem to remember you sitting up all night with our Nat when he was so ill and carrying him down those terrible stairs when he could barely stand up and bringing us all home, which we'd never have managed without you. I'll never forget it. We owe you a great deal.'

'But I...'

'We're glad to have you,' Nathaniel told him. 'You are company for Nat and Mary.'

Although in fact in those first fraught weeks after the funeral *they* were company for *him.* Gradually and with a lot of patience, they turned him into one of the family, taking picnics with them, going to church with them and to the theatre, reading their books and discovering Charles Dickens, walking out into the fields with Nat and Mary. By the time he and Nat went back to Corpus Christi he felt as if he'd never lived anywhere else. 'Although,' he told Nat, 'I shall have to look for a place of my own next vacation.'

'Time enough,' Nat said easily. 'In any case you can't desert us at Christmas.'

'Why not?'

'Milly's expecting another baby,' Nat explained, 'and when *that's* born Ma will be off to Foster Manor all the time and Mary and I will be orphans of the storm.'

That made Toby laugh. 'You won't.'

'You watch,' Nat said. 'We shan't see hide nor hair of her. Lost and lorn, that's what we'll be.'

'Oh well,' Toby said, laughing at him, 'I can't have you lost and lorn so I'd better stay and look after you.'

'Good,' Nat said. 'Have you written an essay on Aristotle?' And when Toby nodded. 'Oh good! Could I see what you had to say?'

That Christmas was the best Toby had ever spent. Nathaniel came home on Christmas Eve with a fir tree in a huge pot, just like the Queen had in her castle at Christmas time and they stood it in the window of their holly-hung drawing room, dressed it with miniature candles and stars cut from gold paper and piled their presents

390

at its feet, the way they'd seen it done in the pictures of the royal family. Toby was bewitched by it, as he told Mary as they were walking to church for midnight mass.

'Your family are extraordinary,' he said.

'Yes,' she agreed, tucking her gloved hand into the crook of his elbow for warmth. 'I know.'

'Your father is so calm,' he said. 'I've never seen anyone with such an equable temperament. I can't imagine him ever getting ruffled by anything – look at the way he took me into the family – and your mother is so loving and so busy looking after folk, she makes my head spin and Nat... Well, Nat is the most brilliant person I've ever met.'

She wondered what opinion he had of her but didn't think it would be proper to ask. But after a few seconds, he answered her anyway.

'And as for you, Miss Mary Cartwright, you are the most forthright girl I've even known.'

'Is that a good thing or a bad one?' she asked, teasing him.

'Oh, a good thing,' he told her earnestly. 'There's such strength in knowing your own mind and being prepared to speak out. I wish I could do it.'

'Come along, you two laggards,' Nat called back to them, 'or the service will be over before we get there.'

'Oh dear!' Toby said. 'Perhaps we'd better run.'

She laughed at him, her bright eyes shining in the gas light and her breath streaming before her like smoke, warm and forthright and alive to her pretty finger tips. Dear, darling Mary.

And what a joy it was to stand in the ancient church in that packed congregation, under the golden glow of the candles, side by chaste side, singing the old hymns. Oh my dearest, he thought, as they held the hymn book between them, I do love you. Not that he could tell her so. That wouldn't do at all. After all, they were like brother and sister. Dear, darling Mary.

At that moment, Jane was glancing along the pew in their direction and she saw the expression on his gilded face and knew what he was thinking. I'll wager you've not said anything to her, she thought, great shy critter that you are, and she made up her mind to do something about it. She didn't quite know what it would be because there was a lot to do just at the moment with Milly's new baby, who was an absolute joy, dear little man, and the christening coming and her mother ill and crabby with another cold, but she would do it as soon as the occasion arose. It would be a perfect match.

George Hudson was giving thought to his affairs that Christmas too and as always his thoughts led to action. He was even further into debt than he'd been in the summer, many thousands of pounds short if the truth be told, and something would have to be done about it. As soon as Christmas is over, he decided, sitting by the fire in his huge drawing room at Newby Park, I will look for some solutions.

They were easy enough to find, especially to a man with his energy and determination. Within days he had discovered a new railway company that needed rails, which was most fortuitous when he had several tons of that very article lying in his stockyards. He sold them a thousand tons and made a very healthy profit. Then there were several thousand pounds that had been allotted to him by his various companies to pay the land-owners whose land he had either bought or rented, and that could stay in his coffers for the time being, or at least until the new railways began to make money for him. But there was still a sizeable shortfall and he knew it would require something rather out of the ordinary to fill it.

It took him nearly a week to think what it could be and then he was astonished by his imagination and the strength of his daring. For it was daring. There was no denying it. He would print more shares for one of his companies, probably the Great North of England, and set the price at the highest rate that would be acceptable to new shareholders – and why not, they were his companies and his shares – and then he would persuade the new shareholders that he was offering them an exclusive bargain, which being a greedy lot and not particularly wise in the ways of the business world, they would jump at. A fool and his money are soon parted. Just to be on the safe side – because it was risky, he had to face that – he would get brother-in-law Richard on board to give it respectability. After all, he *was* the treasurer and he'd be glad of a few thousand to buy more pictures for that collection of his – and he wasn't a man to think things through. I'll go to York this afternoon and put it to him.

Brother-in-law Richard was in a happy mood

that afternoon. He'd just heard from his art dealer that a rather special picture had come into the gallery and he was checking his accounts to see whether he had enough capital to buy it when George came breezing in with his proposal.

'Capital idea,' he said. 'Count me in.'

'I'll buy an' sell 'em for you,' George offered. 'Then all you've got to do is sit back and wait for a nice fat cheque to arrive.' *And I can take my cut which you don't need to know about.*

So the matter was settled and over three and a half thousand shares were bought from the Great North of England Railway at £15 a time and sold to the York, Newcastle and Berwick for £23.10s, which was a very handsome profit indeed.

'We shall have our best Season yet,' George said to Lizzie, when the money had all been gathered in, 'and by the end of it I'll have married our daughter to the best catch in society. You mark my words.' He was George Hudson, the richest man in England, the King of the Railways and anything was possible.

But not quite everything, for there were doubts niggling in more minds than ever that year and one particularly disturbing one was troubling Richard Nicholson. He worried about it until it was keeping him awake at night. He'd heard too many disquieting things about share dealing since railway mania began and although he enjoyed living in a rich house and buying beautiful pictures, he didn't want to think he was doing it illegally. He needed a good friend who would understand the situation and could advise him about what he was doing. But whom could he ask? His friends were good company but they knew as little as he did. In the end he wrote a long letter to Lizzie, who read it twice, couldn't understand what he was talking about and decided she would have to go and see him.

Her visit didn't do either of them much good, for even when they were face to face she couldn't understand half of what he was saying, as she told her dear friend Jane later on in the morning.

'It's not like my Richard to fret hisself for nowt,' she said, as the two of them took tea. 'You know that, I'm sure, I don't need to tell 'ee, but really, my dear, I mean for to say, he was so upset I had to come to York to see him. He said he had no idea which way to turn, what I'm sure I don't either, although I might if I knew which the ways were, if 'ee teks my meaning.'

Over the years, Jane had learnt how to sift through the muddle of her friend's utterances so she set about picking her way to the heart of this one. 'What is troubling him?' she asked.

'It's these shares,' Lizzie confessed. 'He's got it into his head that they were sold for too much money although I told him that weren't a bit likely, seeing it were my George who sold them and he's allus had such a good head for business – George, I mean, not Richard, although I daresay he can handle *some* business well enough. He buys the most beautiful paintings.'

Her explanation made Jane's heart skip a beat. Shares, she thought, and there's summat wrong wi' 'em or he'd not be fretting. And George is behind it. He's been up to summat crooked and Richard knows what it is, or suspects summat.

'What shares were those?' she asked, keeping her voice calm with an effort.

'I don't know the ins and outs of it,' Lizzie confessed. ''Tis all mumbo jumbo to me.'

Jane persisted. 'But it's shares he's fretting over.'

'Aye.'

'Railway shares would it be?'

'Aye. They were,' Lizzie said.

'And rather a lot of them you said.'

'Aye,' Lizzie admitted. 'Over three and a half thousand so he said. Although, like I told him, if George wants to sell shares from one of his companies to another one it must surely be fair and above board, or he'd not do it, and anyroad he owns 'em both so what harm could there possibly be in it, if 'ee teks my meaning.'

Jane was taking her meaning with greater and greater understanding. He's been share trading, she thought, and making a profit out of it. 'And they were Mr Hudson's companies, you say?'

'Aye they were, so that meks it right, wouldn't 'ee say? My George wouldn't do anything wrong, I'm certain sure of that.'

'No,' Jane said, noncommittally. 'Not if they were his companies, which they were, I'm sure.'

'Oh yes,' Lizzie told her eagerly. 'They were the Great North of England and the York, Newcastle and Berwick. They're both his.'

'Well, there you are then,' Jane said. 'You've got nothing to worry about.'

'Tha'rt such a comfort to me,' Lizzie said, setting down her empty tea cup. 'I knew tha'd see the rights and wrongs of it straightaway if I told 'ee. Oh Jane, I *do* wish I could see thee more often.' And she sighed. 'But there 'tis.'

'Tek some more tea,' Jane offered. She was feeling guilty at the way she'd questioned her poor friend and tea was one way to make amends.

Lizzie shook her head. 'I daren't stay any longer,' she said. 'We're off to London in a day or two for the Season, and tha knows what a stickler George is for everything running to plan. I must go for there's things to be packed and if I'm not there it'll be done anyhow, which wouldn't do at all.'

After she'd gone, Jane sat in her parlour on her own, with her heart beating in the most deliciously tremulous way and gave herself up to her thoughts. For the first time in her life she had no time or desire to consider other people – not her husband nor her children nor her grandchildren, not even the latest baby or Toby's love for Mary – for she was caught up in a moment of total and triumphant self-absorption, knowing beyond any doubt that her chance to take revenge had come, just as she'd always hoped it would. It had taken long enough in all conscience. She'd waited years for it. Thirty-three years now she came to count it. A lifetime. And yet here it was at long, long last. She knew it as surely as she knew that her name was Jane Cartwright. I shall tell Mr Leeman, she thought, the first chance I get.

27

'Oh dear,' Toby Henderson said, as he walked into the parlour at Shelton House the next morning. 'Are you orphans of the storm again?'

Nat and Mary were sitting by the window, playing Bezique. 'Where have you been?' Nat said. It wasn't like Toby to go sneaking off on his own. They usually all did things together. He'd been quite put out to find that he'd breakfasted early and gone.

'Out,' Toby said, trying to look mysterious and failing. 'Is Mrs Cartwright not here?'

'No idea where she is,' Nat told him. 'She's as bad as you. She's been out as long as you have and she can't be at Foster Manor because they've all gone to London. Went yesterday.'

'That's a pity,' Toby said. 'I wanted her to be the first to hear my news.'

They were instantly intrigued and Mary asked, 'What news? Is it something special?'

'I've taken rooms,' Toby told her. 'In Coppergate.'

Neither of his friends reacted in the way he expected. Mary was open-mouthed with surprise and Nat was cross. 'What do you mean, rooms?' he said.

Toby blushed but persevered. 'To live in,' he said. 'Lodgings. Rooms of my own.'

'What nonsense!' Nat said. 'What do you want

with a room of your own? You've got a perfectly good room here.'

'I know that,' Toby said, his blush spreading like fire, 'and you mustn't think I'm not grateful...'

'That's exactly what I *do* think,' Nat said and he stood up and left his cards to prowl about the room. 'There's no call for it.'

'No, truly, Nat,' Toby said, trying to follow him. 'I'm uncommon grateful. Always have been, always will be. I don't know what I'd have done if Mr Cartwright hadn't taken me in. I'd have been lost. I *was* lost. I know that. But I must make shift to support myself. You *can* see that, can't you? I'll not be much of a priest if I can't support myself.'

Nat snorted. 'I can't see any such thing,' he said. 'There's no call for it.' But Mary was speaking too, almost at the same time. *'Are* you going to be a priest?'

Toby looked from one to the other, not sure who to answer first. He chose Mary because her question was answerable. 'I should like to be,' he told her, 'if the Church will have me.'

'I'm sure they will,' she said, trying to comfort him. He looked so uncomfortable and Nat was glowering as if he was going to lash out at him at any moment. 'You'll make a very good priest. You're so gentle.'

The blush was burning his neck. 'Well, as to that...' he said. 'What I mean to say...' But then he stopped because he didn't know *what* he meant to say – except for the words that were roaring in his head and he couldn't say them and certainly not in the middle of a row.

Mary was upset by his confusion. 'Why were

you asking for Mama?' she said.

'I thought she might like to come and see them,' Toby confessed. 'The rooms, I mean. Do you know when she'll be back?'

'We might if we knew where she was,' Mary said. 'Would I do instead?'

Oh she would, she would. 'Yes, please,' he said.

'I'll get my bonnet,' she said.

'Ridiculous nonsense,' Nat said as they left the room. 'First Mama cutting off without telling us and now this. I don't know what the world's coming to, I truly don't. It's just a puzzle.'

He would have been even more puzzled if he'd known where his mother was and could have heard what she was saying.

Mr Leeman's office was a wide, well-lit room above the corn chandlers and the chairs he kept for his clients were well upholstered and very comfortable. So many of the people who came to consult him had difficult matters to discuss and he'd found it made things easier for them if they were at least sitting comfortably. Mrs Cartwright had settled into her chair like a nesting bird.

'Well now, Mrs Cartwright,' he said encouragingly. 'What can I do for you?'

'Actually,' Jane said, enjoying herself. ''Tis more a matter of what I can do for you.'

'Is it so?'

'You will doubtless know the rights and wrongs of what is called share-dealing?'

'Indeed.'

'And you are still interested in the business affairs of a certain Mr George Hudson.'

'Indeed.'

'Then I can tell you that one place where you might care to look would be the accounts of the Great North of England and the York, Newcastle and Berwick.'

He sat up in his chair, smiled at her and waited.

She told him everything she had found out, being careful not to accuse the odious Mr Hudson of anything but simply letting the facts speak for themselves. As they did, extremely loudly.

'It seems to me,' Mr Leeman said, when the tale was told, 'that there has been, shall we say, some illegal trading here but it may take a case in Chancery to prove it. With your permission I will pass on your information to a gentleman called Robert Prance who, I should tell you, is a shareholder of the York, Newcastle and Berwick and a member of the Stock Exchange, and will know better than I what sort of malfeasance we have here.'

'Of course,' she said, staying composed, although her cheeks were flushed and her eyes unnaturally bright.

'I will keep you informed as to any progress,' Mr Leeman promised as they shook hands.

And then she was out in the crowded street among the unknowing shoppers with their workaday bonnets and their dust-hemmed skirts and their laden baskets, under a sky full of scudding cloud and with the beautiful stone tracery of the Minster rising high and dependable above the rooftops, and she was trembling with excitement because the moment of her revenge had come at last.

Mary and Toby were walking in the fields beyond the city walls. They'd visited Toby's rooms and Mary had found the right things to say about them, although secretly she hadn't been impressed because they were rather cramped, and now they were taking a stroll in the sunshine.

'Now then,' Mary said, when they were well away from the town, 'you must tell me what's the matter with Nat. He's been like a bear with a sore head ever since he got up. And don't say you don't know for I can see you do.'

'It's not really my business,' Toby said uncomfortably. 'I mean, he might not want me to say anything.'

Mary wouldn't accept that. 'If you know you must tell me,' Mary said. 'We can't put things right for him if we don't know what's wrong.'

He was caught between loyalty to his friend and love for his lady. 'Well...' he said. 'If I tell you, you must give me your word it will go no further.'

'You have it. Naturally.'

'He's worried.'

'Worried?' he sister said in disbelief. 'What about, for pity's sake?'

'He doesn't know what he wants to do when he comes down,' Toby explained. 'I've made it worse for him, I'm afraid, on account of I've known all along.'

'Well, how silly,' Mary said trenchantly. 'He can do anything he wants. He'll have a degree and Papa to encourage him. If you ask me, he's making a fuss about nothing. He should try being a girl. We only have *three* choices open to us.'

He wasn't sure whether she meant him to laugh or to take it seriously so he decided to be serious. 'Which are?' he asked.

'To be a servant or a governess or a wife,' she said, succinctly. 'He should try that.'

'That's very...' he said and then stopped to find the right word. He could see how strongly she felt about it and he didn't want to annoy her. 'Confining.'

'Exactly so,' she approved. 'Confining. That's exactly what it is. We might as well be tied up in swaddling all our lives.'

'Does it truly seem so bad?'

'To be a servant?' she asked. 'Up all hours at everybody's beck and call. I can't think of anything worse.'

'But the other two might be...' And then he stopped in alarm, with his heart racing, because if he went on they would be talking about marriage.

She ignored the possibility of being a governess. ''Twould depend entirely upon what sort of man were asking you to marry him,' she said. 'Some would be totally impossible. I'd rather be married to a pig.'

She looked so pretty and so cross with her cheeks so pink and her eyes so bright, he was emboldened to take the conversation further. 'I can see you wouldn't like a pig,' he said. 'But what sort of man would you prefer?'

'He would have to be gentle,' she told him. 'I couldn't stand a bully. Gentle and sensible like Papa. And trustworthy and clever. I wouldn't want to be married to a dunderhead. Think how

403

boring that would be.' And she grinned at him. 'I don't want much, you see.'

The grin ripped away his restraint. 'Would I fit the bill?' he asked.

'You?' she said and she sounded so surprised he gave up hope on the instant.

'No, no,' he backtracked, suffused with blushes. 'I was joking.'

'Never joke about marriage,' she told him sternly. ''Tis too serious a matter.'

'No,' he said again. 'You are quite right. It is.' And he quoted the marriage service: *'An honourable estate ... not to be enterprised, nor taken in hand, unadvisedly, lightly or wantonly.'*

Their conversation had moved on to quite another level. They had forgotten to walk but stood quite still, facing one another beside the newly green fields under the turbulent clouds. 'If you were to marry,' she said, 'would you take your vows seriously?'

'I would mean every word,' he said.

'And so would I,' she told him. *'For better for worse, for richer for poorer, in sickness and in health, till death do us part.* Every single word.' They were caught up in the magic of the old well-tried vows and standing so close together it was as if they were bound by invisible threads.

'I love you,' he said.

She bit her lip but said nothing.

Having come so far, he simply had to go on. 'If I thought you would accept me,' he said, 'I would ask you to marry me.'

'Yes,' she said. 'I know.' And she *did* know. She'd known for a very long time – without realizing what she knew.

He caught her hands and kissed her fingers, but very gently so as not to alarm her. 'And if I were to ask you now, would you say yes?'

'Yes,' she said, 'I think I would.'

He held her hands between his own and bent his head to kiss her on the lips. It was a clumsy kiss for neither of them was quite sure how to go about it but they were both well pleased with themselves.

'Now you will have to ask Papa,' she told him.

'Now,' he said, venturing to tease her a little, 'we must go home or your mama will be wondering what has happened to us.'

Her mama was wondering what had happened to all of them, for she'd come home to an empty house and all she got out of the parlour maid was that Mr Toby and Miss Mary had gone out to look at 'some rooms or other' and that Mr Nat had gone storming out two minutes later 'what I've no idea where to, ma'am'.

'I turn my back for five minutes,' Jane said, 'and the sky falls.'

But their absence brought her back to her senses. By the time Mary and Toby came ambling back towards Bootham Bar, deep in conversation and arm in arm, as she noticed with great satisfaction from the parlour window, she was ready to receive them and hear their news. Which was just as well, for Mary was calling her as soon as she set foot in the parlour.

'Mama! Mama!' she cried, running towards her mother. 'What do 'ee think? Toby's asked me to marry him.'

'I think 'tis the finest thing for the both of you,' Jane said, and added, teasing, 'If you've accepted him.'

Toby did his best to be formal, asking, 'When will Mr Cartwright be home? I mean ... I should have spoken to him first. I *do* know that.'

But Jane dismissed all formality and swept them both into her arms to be kissed and congratulated. Oh, what a day this was turning out to be.

It took a change of mood when Nat came sloping back to the house wearing his thunderous face. He did his best to take the news as graciously as he could, kissing his sister and thumping his friend between the shoulders and telling them both he was very happy for them, but his mood was dark nevertheless. It reminded Jane of how he'd been when Felix had first visited them with Milly. I must do summat about it, she thought, but not now. Later, when Nathaniel is back home. Mary knows what's the matter, if that odd expression she gave him is anything to go by. But Mary kept her knowledge about her brother to herself, as she'd given her word to her fiancé.

In London, George Hudson's second Season was even more dazzling than the first had been. Prince Albert had become a regular guest at his extravagant parties and, once again, Albert Gate East was the place to see and be seen. Even his fiercest critics had to admit that a party thrown by the Railway King was sure to be a major event, although some of them *did* wonder privately how he could spend so much money and still remain solvent. But the money was being well spent. By the time the Season was half over, he had persuaded his daughter to accept the hand of the most prestigious suitor in the capital. His name was George Dundas and he was twenty-eight, which was a highly suitable age for marriage, and splendidly wealthy since he was a member of the renowned Zetland dynasty, no less. And as if that weren't enough, there was his occupation, which was Member of Parliament for Linlithgowshire, and that was not only socially commendable but politically useful.

'He couldn't be bettered,' he said to Lizzie on the morning the engagement was announced in *The Times*. 'I've done well for our little girl. It cost but it was worth it.' It had been a moment of pure triumph when Mr Dundas came calling to ask for his consent. 'Let all those carping fools say what they like, we've really arrived now.'

Some of those carping fools were actually very influential men. Two of them were writers who had a wide following and a considerable reputation and what they said was outspoken and cruelly to the point. Macaulay called him *'a bloated, vulgar, insolent, purse-proud, greedy, drunken blackguard'* and Charles Dickens said he wanted to *'throw up my head and howl whenever I hear Mr Hudson mentioned'*.

'Unnecessary!' George said to Lizzie, when he read it. 'But who is he when all's said and done? I'm the one wi' t'brass. I own half the railways in England, I've a son who's a barrister, an' another who'll be a doctor when t'year's out, an' a

407

daughter marrying into the aristocracy. Let him beat that. They may say what they please, Lizzie.' And he quoted the old proverb. *'Sticks an' stones may break my bones but names'll never hurt me.'*

But even as he spoke, another less well-known writer was producing a pamphlet that would have more impact than he could have imagined as he sat in state in his prestigious house. It was called *The Bubble of the Age* or *The Fallacies of Railway Investments, Accounts and Railway Dividends* and it was written by a man called Arthur Smith.

Mr Leeman brought a copy of it to Shelton House and gave it to Jane on the morning it was published. 'I think you may find this somewhat to your taste,' he said.

She read it at once, while he sat in one of her easy chairs and watched the changing expressions on her face.

It was quite a short pamphlet but what it contained was as powerful as dynamite for Mr Smith's argument was that dividends in George Hudson's companies had indeed been paid out of capital rather than revenue, exactly as Mr Leeman had suspected all those years ago. It ended with a call for Mr Hudson to open his accounts to public scrutiny.

'Heavens!' she said, when she finally looked up from the page. 'What will happen now?'

'The shareholders of his various companies will ask to see the accounts,' Mr Leeman said. 'Which they have every right to do.'

'I should like to be a fly on the wall when that happens,' she said. 'When do they meet?'

'Not until February,' Mr Leeman told her. 'But

408

that may be all to the good. It will give them time to prepare their case. And we all have plenty to do in the meantime. You and Mr Cartwright have a wedding to arrange, I believe.'

'Aye,' she said happily. 'We have. Our daughter Mary is marrying Mr Henderson, providing he gets a living, that is. We shall have to wait until that's settled.'

'There are new churches being built at every turning,' Mr Leeman said, 'which is only to be expected as our towns and cities expand. You have only to take a stroll outside our city walls to see that. I'm sure a suitable living will present no problems.'

Nathaniel held much the same opinion and expressed it cheerfully when they were enjoying their last family dinner together before Nat and Toby went back to Oxford to start their final year. 'By this time next year,' he predicted, when the first course had been cleared and they were waiting for Mrs Cadwallader's fruit pies, 'Toby will have a parish and Mary will be an old married woman.' And he raised his glass to them. 'Here's a health to you both.'

'And what of me, Papa?' Nat said, his face darkening.

'That is indeed a question,' Nathaniel told him, speaking seriously but with deliberate gentleness. 'However I have no doubt you will tell us what your plans are as soon as you know them yourself, which you do not at present, am I not right?'

There was a pause while Nathaniel waited and Jane held her breath and watched him and Nat glowered. Then Mary the bold spoke into the silence.

'Tell them,' she said to her brother. 'Don't just sit there looking like thunder. Tell them or I will.'

He glared at her.

'And don't make that face at me or I'll do it straight.'

He sighed and frowned, gathering his thoughts and his courage and finally confessed. 'I've no idea what I'm going to do, Papa. That's the truth of it. Absolutely no idea. It's all very well for you, Toby. You've got the girl you want and you'll have the job you want as soon as you've graduated. And don't misunderstand me, I'm truly glad that's how it is. Glad for both of you. But it's different for me. I can't think of a single thing I could do. Not one single thing.' And he sighed like a bellows.

'Which naturally makes you feel unhappy and inadequate,' his father said.

Nat caught at the word. 'Inadequate,' he said. 'Yes, that's exactly it. Good for nothing.' And as they were all looking at him with a variety of expressions, his mother's face full of sympathy, Toby uncomfortable, his father listening patiently, Mary daring him to go on, he tried to justify what he was saying. 'I used to think I wanted to go into the church like Toby,' he said, 'but I know now that I couldn't do it because I can't stand up in front of a crowd of people and say what I think and make sense of it. I learned that in the union debates. So that rules out the Church and teaching. And I don't really want to be an engineer. I don't think I'd have the aptitude for it. And for the life of me I can't think of anything else.'

They all looked at Nathaniel and saw that he was thinking – and waited for him. It seemed like a long wait but eventually he looked at Nat and asked him a question.

'What have you enjoyed most about your life at Corpus Christi?'

The answer was immediate and heartfelt. 'Oh, the essays. That was something I *could* do.'

'And he did it very well,' Toby put in. 'He was renowned for it. You've got to admit it, Nat.'

'Yes,' Nat admitted. 'I do have a flair for essays. That's true. But that's not the sort of thing to fit me for a profession.'

There was another pause while they all digested what he'd said. Then Nathaniel spoke again in his considered way.

'What I would suggest to you,' he said, 'is that you look for a position as a reporter on one of our local newspapers.' And when Nat opened his mouth ready to tell him it wasn't possible, he went on quickly, 'Hear me out before you condemn the idea out of hand. Reporters need to be able to write well, which on your own admission you can already do, and to write quickly and honestly, both of which I am certain you could manage given the sort of young man you are.'

'Well...' Nat said, giving it thought. 'I suppose it might be possible.'

'What I would suggest to you,' Nathaniel said, 'is that you should write to *The Yorkshireman* or one of our other local newspapers and ask if they have a vacancy in their office and if they have, offer them your services. Oh, now here comes

411

our pie and uncommon good it looks, wouldn't you say?'

The pie put an end to any further conversation but it didn't prevent continuing thought and at the end of the meal when they were all walking up to the drawing room to sit round the fire, Nat drew his father aside.

'I will do it, Papa,' he said. 'I can't promise anything will come of it, mind you, but I will do it.'

'Very wise of you,' Nathaniel said. 'We will take a glass of brandy to celebrate your wisdom. You will join us, Toby, I trust.'

'Do 'ee think he'll really do it?' Jane asked later that night when Nathaniel had told her what had been said.

'We must wait and see,' Nathaniel said. 'He's got plenty of sense despite the occasional black mood.'

They waited for more than two weeks until Jane had begun to think that nothing would come of it after all. But then she had an excited letter.

'*I wrote to* The Yorkshireman, *as I promised, Papa,*'Nat had written, '*although I had little hope of a reply. But, lo and behold, they have offered to take me on as a junior reporter for what they call a three months trial. The shareholders of the Midland Railway will be holding their half-yearly general meeting in Derby on February 15th and they want me to cover it. Please tell Papa how sound his advice has turned out to be.*

'*Your most loving and happy son, Nat.*'

Thank the Lord for that, Jane thought as she set the letter aside. Nathaniel *will* be pleased when he comes home and sees this. And it occurred to her that she would have a fly on the wall at Mr Hudson's meeting after all. It almost made her believe in the wheel of fortune.

28

Nat Cartwright dressed with great care for his first assignment as a newspaper reporter, choosing the brown frock coat and cream-coloured trousers his mother had bought him when he first went up to Oxford nearly three years ago – what a long time it seemed – and finishing it off with a sky-blue cravat. He had a notebook in his hand, a local map of Derby and three well-sharpened pencils in his coat pocket and he felt he was ready for anything. All he needed was a meeting that was worth reporting.

It was being held in the City Hall, which was easy to find because it was an imposing building. Smiling to himself because he was undeniably excited now, he strode up the stairs to the room which had been allocated to the shareholders and walked straight into a crush. Every seat was taken and the room was crowded to the walls with obviously angry men. The air was hazy with the smoke from their cigars and booming with the fury of their voices. Oh yes, Nat thought, this is going to be a meeting well worth reporting. There was a baize-covered table at one end of the room with its customary glass and decanter, a gavel on its wooden stand and an ornate seat set ready for the chairman but no sign of the man. Nat squeezed through the throng until he'd made himself a space by the back wall where he would have a good view, took his notebook in hand, licked his pencil and waited.

He didn't have to wait long. There was a stir at the far end of the room, the door was opened and the great Mr Hudson bellied into the assembly.

It was the first time Nat had seen the man on his feet and at such close quarters. He'd seen him several times out in the streets of York, of course, but always sitting in a carriage, usually waving to the crowd as if he were royalty. Now, having such a very close view, he cast around in his mind for a way to describe the man so that his readers could see him too. Powerful. Yes, there was no doubt about that. He oozed power. And grossly fat with that belly and that thick neck, those ugly jowls, those little piggy eyes. But not a pig. An animal with more strength and aggression than a pig. And then Hudson turned his head and glared at the crowd and Nat saw what it was and made his first note: *bull in the bull ring facing hostile crowd*. Then he too looked at the crowd and wondered who the matador was going to be.

Mr Hudson called the meeting to order by shouting at them for attention. 'Gentlemen! Gentlemen! If you please.' Then he sat down to deliver his address.

The shareholders were growlingly unimpressed by the size of their dividend that half-year and shouted their disapproval: 'Five per cent!' they yelled. 'Shame on you, Hudson! It's a disgrace!'

George Hudson stood his ground. 'Share values rise and fall, gentlemen,' he said. 'We all know that. 'Tis a bad year. They'll rise again. You have my word on it.'

There was more growling but they had to accept his figure. He was right about share values. They *did* fluctuate. But when the growling had subsided, a man sitting in the body of the hall stood up and announced his name which instantly commanded an expectant silence. The matador? Nat wondered. Or just a picador? And he made a note of his name. '*Mr Wylie.*'

'I have to say, sir,' Mr Wylie began, 'I find the company statement you have just read to us most unsatisfactory. Most unsatisfactory.' Then he paused to allow the audience time to respond, which they did, angrily. 'A more bald account,' he went on, 'I have never seen issued by any public body. It contrasts most unfavourable with the accounts of the London and North Western, which were open to all the shareholders and complete in every detail. 'Tis my opinion, Mr Chairman, that *this* company's accounts should be thrown open for inspection by all *this* company's shareholders, in the same manner.'

The bull barely flinched. 'Oh aye, I've no doubt that is your opinion, Mr Wylie. However, in *my* opinion there's no call for it.'

At that, there was so much shouting in the hall that for a few seconds he couldn't make himself heard above the din and after two attempts to call the meeting to order, which were both totally ignored, he gave up the effort and decided to sit it out.

Then another man rose from the body of the hall and looked round at the angry faces with obvious satisfaction, and this one, as Nat saw at once, was important enough to be granted silence as soon as he was on his feet. The matador without a doubt.

'Brankner,' he announced. 'As a major shareholder of this company, I would like to propose that a committee of investigation be set up to look into the company's affairs.'

'Yes!' his audience shouted. 'Quite right, sir. A committee of investigation. That's what we want. Yes.'

And they looked at Mr Hudson to see what he would say to that.

George was furiously angry but he kept his control. 'Tha can have my resignation if that's what tha wants,' he said, speaking as if he was daring them and he blew cigar smoke in their direction, contemptuously, and then sat back to see how they would respond to *that*. God damn it. How dare they treat him in this way? Didn't they know who he was? Couldn't they remember how well he'd treated them all these years? There wasn't another man alive who gave such high dividends.

'No, Mr Hudson,' Mr Brankner shouted above the uproar. 'Disabuse yourself of that idea, sir. That is not what we want. What we want is a committee of investigation. I propose that one be set up here and now and I put it to the vote. All those in favour?'

There was another roar. 'Aye,' they shouted. 'Aye.'

'This is irregular, sir,' George shouted back. 'All proposals must go through the chair.'

'They may go through the chair if you wish,' Mr Brankner told him coolly, to renewed cheers. 'Either way you'll get the same result.' And he turned to look round at the crowd. 'Against?' he asked.

There was silence, then a cheer.

'In that case,' Mr Brankner declared. 'I would say the proposal is carried. Wouldn't you agree, Mr Chairman?'

George Hudson rose to his feet. 'In *that* case,' he said with as much dignity as he could muster, 'there being no further business, *I* declare this meeting closed.'

He was jeered from the room. And Nat put his notebook in his pocket and caught the last train back to Oxford.

He spent the journey writing the first draft of his article, keeping the bull-fighting analogy because it seemed more apt than anything else he could think of, and finishing with a flourish. *'This evening in Derby we have seen a triumph of English democracy. A man who believed that his power was so absolute that he was above the law has been voted into submission by the will of the majority.'* That night he sat up and transcribed a fair copy to send to the editor the next morning, and, because he was feeling proud of what he'd written, he wrote a second copy for his parents.

Two days later he had a letter from his mother telling him how accurate she thought his writing was, and another from the editor to tell him that his article had been published in that day's

417

edition, that he had been appointed to the paper as a junior reporter as from the day of the meeting in Derby, and that, in that capacity, he was to attend the next two shareholders' meetings of Mr Hudson's companies which were to be held in the Grey Rooms in York in three days' time. It was very hard to settle to mere study after that.

Toby Henderson travelled up to York with Nat two days later. He said he had some news but that he would like to keep it until they were at table that evening and he could tell them all at once. It was very good news indeed. He was going to be ordained in York Minster in May as soon as he'd finished his finals and, what was even better, the dean had found him a living.

'It's in a little village called Snodwortham,' he told them, 'which is about twenty miles away and not on the railway, I'm rather sorry to say. But I shall run a carriage of some kind so there will be plenty of visiting.'

'Have 'ee seen it?' Jane asked.

He had and was hoping to take Mary there the next day so that she could see it too and take a look round the vicarage, 'which is a bit ramshackle at the moment, I must confess, but they have promised me I may make alterations and improvements and I'm sure Mary will advise me.'

'I shall take a notebook,' Mary told him, 'and make a careful note of everything that needs to be done. Depend on it.'

'I think we should have champagne tomorrow evening to celebrate,' Nathaniel said.

George Hudson was drinking champagne that evening too, although in his case he drank morosely and took little pleasure in it. He'd been pouring wine and spirits down his throat since early afternoon and he was maudlin with drink and self-pity.

'I can't understand it,' he said to Lizzie, over and over again. 'After all I've done for 'em all these years. I've paid out bigger dividends than any man alive or dead. *You* know that, don't 'ee, Lizzie. Much bigger dividends. You never heard a one of 'em complaining when the going was good. Oh no! They took the money when the going was good. Took it an' glad to have it. It's downright ingratitude. That's what it is. Downright ingratitude.'

'They're nasty jealous,' Lizzie tried to comfort. 'Don't tek no notice of 'em, George dear. They're not worth it.'

By that time, he was weeping so miserably he barely heard her. ''Tis like being set on by a swarm of wasps,' he cried. 'That's how 'tis. A swarm of nasty, little, low-grade, ungrateful wasps. Sting, sting, sting. On an' on an' on.'

But cry as he might, he couldn't stop the swarms and they were gathering for their next attack.

After the fireworks at Derby, Nat was rather disappointed by the half-yearly meeting of the York and North Midland Railway Company, for it all went off rather tamely. The shareholders groaned when they heard that their dividend was only going to be six per cent, but there was no demand for a committee of investigation and no need for anybody to be called to order. However, the meeting that followed later that day was an entirely different matter.

The shareholders of the York, Newcastle and Berwick were well primed and had a powerful pair of leaders in two quietly spoken gentlemen called Horatio Love and Robert Prance, who were much in evidence as the crowd gathered, moving from group to group, greeting and talking. There was no sign of the chairman as yet, so Nat moved through the crowd too. It didn't take him long to establish that, as well as being shareholders, the two gentlemen were also members of the Stock Exchange and had been looking into the company affairs for what his informant said was a considerable time. 'I think you'll find Mr Hudson is in for a bit of a scrap, like,' the man said.

And a bit of a scrap it was. As soon as the company report had been read, Mr Prance rose to his feet and announced that there was something puzzling him about the company accounts. Then he paused, smiled and expressed the hope that the chairman could enlighten him.

The chairman looked disconcerted but grunted that he had leave to proceed.

'I have discovered,' Mr Prance said in his gentle voice, 'that shares that were valued at £15 and *bought* for £15 have been sold to this company at a price of £23.10s.' There was a frisson of excitement but no interruption. 'The total number of such shares bought by the York, Newcastle and Berwick,' Mr Prance went on, 'was 3,790. I am

420

sure that no more than the odd hundred were bought by the public, so someone has received great benefit by selling them at this extravagant price to the company. We should like to know who that person was.' Then he looked up from his notes and smiled at Mr Hudson.

The chairman was caught red-faced and red-handed. 'Well now,' he said. 'This is all very curious, Mr Prance. I cannot account for it, sir, leastways, I cannot account for it directly, you understand, on account of not having the full facts and figures in front of me. However, I shall certainly look into it for you. You have my word on it.'

But that wasn't the answer Mr Prance wanted and he wasn't going to allow Mr Hudson to get away with it. 'I can hardly believe that the chairman of a great company like ours would attend the half-yearly meeting of his shareholders without bringing the company accounts with him,' he said smoothly. 'We would be prepared to wait until you have perused them to refresh your mind.' And he turned to address the meeting. 'Would we not, gentlemen?' He waited for their murmured agreement before speaking to Mr Hudson again. 'I need hardly point out that this is a very large sum of money. The transaction could hardly have escaped your notice, for as we all know you oversee all the company's business, personally.'

'Naturally,' George had to admit. This man was a deal too oily. 'I just didn't recall it to mind when you asked about it. Now I come to think about it, there was some business over share prices. Mr Nathaniel Plews had charge of valuing shares at that time, as I recall, and I suppose there might have been some overcharge. If he were here, he could answer you directly but unfortunately he was not able to attend. However I will personally guarantee to do whatever the shareholders think will be most just and fair.'

'*Fortuitous absence of chosen scapegoat*,' Nat wrote in his notebook, thinking, This man gets more unpleasant by the minute.

His guarantee didn't wash with Mr Prance any more than his excuses had. 'That, sir,' he said, 'is not satisfactory to me and I doubt if it is satisfactory to the other shareholders here.' There was vociferous agreement. 'Therefore I wish to propose that a committee of enquiry be set up to investigate this company's affairs.'

'*Caught*', Nat wrote.

The motion for a committee of enquiry was passed unanimously, there and then, and to everybody's satisfaction Mr Robert Prance was chosen to chair it. Nat couldn't wait to get home to tell his parents.

'Splendid,' his grandmother said, when the tale was told. 'That'll larn him.'

And his mother said, 'I've heard of your Mr Prance. By all accounts, he's a very good man.'

'After what I've seen of him this evening,' Nat said, 'that would be my opinion of him too.'

'He's writing a report on Mr Hudson's doings,' Jane told him. 'It should make good reading.'

'Is he so?' Nat said. 'When will it be published? Do you know? I'd like to get hold of a copy. Maybe I could interview him about it, if he were agreeable. Any revelation about Mr Hudson's activities would be newsworthy. My editor would love it. He can't stand Mr Hudson at any price.'

'Hold your horses,' Toby said, laughing at his eagerness. 'You've got finals to sit before you can start reading reports.'

'Finals,' Nat told him happily, 'will be easy after this.'

As it turned out, for neither of them had any real problems with any of the papers and earned themselves double firsts and what Nathaniel called 'well-deserved praise'. And when the academic slog was over, there was the May ball, to which Mary was invited, and which they all enjoyed uproariously, and then a week of parties and fireworks and gallons of champagne to drink, so that although Mr Prance's report was published none of them noticed it.

It had actually come out in April and it was incendiary. Mr Hudson's wrongdoings were listed and examined, calmly and inexorably, one after the other. It was established that *he* was the one who had fixed the price of the Great North of England shares which he had then sold to the York, Newcastle and Berwick Railway at an exorbitant profit, exactly as Mr Prance had said at the company meeting. In addition to that, there were other charges. Rails had been bought cheaply and sold for huge profits, compensation cheques had been withheld from landowners and left in Mr Hudson's account to accumulate more profit for him and shares in the Bradbury Junction Railway Company had been illegally appropriated. It was unanswerable and it had to be answered.

By the time Nat and Toby came down for the last time – Nat to begin full-time work with *The Yorkshireman,* Toby to start his life as a clergyman and to set about redecorating and modernizing his shabby vicarage, according to Mary's detailed requirements – the York, Newcastle and Berwick Railway had sued their chairman for £30,000 and the citizens of York were agog with gossip, either shaking their heads at the news or rubbing their hands, according to their opinion of the man, but all of them telling one another that his downfall was imminent. By the beginning of May, the rumours reached Richard Nicholson's elegant house in Clifton Green.

At first he tried to tell himself that it was a storm in a teacup and would soon pass over but the rumours persisted and when he read that his brother-in-law was being sued by the York, Newcastle and Berwick for illegal share-dealing, he remembered the shares they had bought and sold together and was seriously alarmed. Painful though it most certainly would be, he would have to buy this dreadful report that everyone was talking about and read it for himself.

He found a copy in the bookseller's beside the Minster and bought it, which took a moment of courage because he felt that everybody in the shop was staring at him accusingly and it was a struggle not to look shamefaced. Then he hid it in his pocket and took it home to see what it contained. It shocked him so much that he couldn't speak for the rest of the day. He couldn't, wouldn't believe it. I may be a bit of a fool, he told himself – that was undeniable, everybody knew it

424

– but I'm not dishonest. Never have been, never will be. And yet there it was. In print. The shares were crooked. He and George had broken the law. Oh dear God, how *could* it have happened?

He lay awake all night, in a state of terror, worrying and fretting and feeling sick and utterly at a loss to know what he could do. It wasn't until dawn was breaking at slow last that he remembered Lizzie. That was the answer. He would write to his sister and ask her what he ought to do. She knew George better than anyone else. She could tell him.

The letter was sent as soon as he'd eaten what breakfast he could. And twenty-four hours later Lizzie arrived in his parlour, her face full of concern.

'Now don't you go a-worritting your poor old head about all this nonsense,' she said. 'I mean for to say, what is it? I'll tell 'ee. 'Tis just nonsense. Folk being jealous, that's all. What does that Mr Prance know about running railways? You tell me that. Nowt, that's what he knows. Pay him no mind, that's my advice to 'ee. Pay him no mind at all. I mean for to say, who is he? He's a nobody, that's who he is.'

In his terror-heightened state, Richard had acquired a peculiar sharp-sightedness. She doesn't know what's been going on, he thought. This is all George talking, not her. I can hear his voice. And she's taken it all in and believes him. Oh my poor Lizzie. 'He's a member of the Stock Exchange,' he said, wearily. 'He knows about shares.'

'Well, let him,' Lizzie said stoutly. 'What's that got to do with us? My George wouldn't do anything dishonest. You know that. Never in this world. So don't you worry your head. It fair makes my blood boil the way he's upsetting folk. Not my George, I don't mean. The other one. That Mr Prance. I'd prance him if I could get my hands on him. Upsetting folk. Saying things. And in print too. I don't know what the world's a-coming to. I truly don't. My George is a fine, up-standing God-fearing man and as honest as the day. Don't you go worrying your head. That's my advice to 'ee.'

Your George cuts corners and goes in for shady deals, Richard thought. He's done it for years, if Mr Prance is to be believed and I see no reason to disbelieve him, and you don't know. You've never known. I've had a sneaking suspicion sometimes but you've never known. She was still prattling on, so he looked away from her and sighed as deeply as he dared, accepting the fact that she was no help to him at all and feeling achingly sorry for her, because she thought she was doing her best for him. Then he served her tea and tempted her with the sugar cakes he couldn't possibly eat himself. And when she left, he kissed her goodbye and thanked her for com-ing over so quickly and, as a loving afterthought, told her he would take her advice.

'Much the best thing,' she said and trotted across the path to her carriage, waving to him quite gaily. It was the last time she would ever see him.

That evening, when he'd toyed with his dinner for nearly an hour, he put on his hat and his second-best jacket, because the best one was too recognizable, and walked down to the river to think. His misery had deepened during the day and the chill air and ominous gloom of the evening made it worse. He was finished. He knew it as surely as he knew he was standing by the river. It wouldn't be long before he and George were arrested and taken to court to face their crimes. Oh dear God, arrested and taken to court. How could he bear it? He had no idea what sort of sentence they would have to serve but that was immaterial. He couldn't face a court case, let alone a prison sentence. It was insupportable.

The rank smell of the river rose to fill his nostrils and he looked down at it, licking at the banks, and noted vaguely that it was moving at a greater speed than usual. If I were to fall in, he thought, I would drown because I can't swim. I would drown and it would all be over. The thought was suddenly extremely tempting, filling his mind and pulsing along his veins. I would drown and it would all be over.

He took off his jacket and his boots and held his nose and jumped into the running water. It struck so cold it took his breath away, so cold that it filled his mouth, so cold it clogged his nose, so cold it blanked his eyes and made his ears roar. Somewhere at the back of his frozen mind he knew he was slipping away downstream. I shall drown, he thought, but the words were taking a long time to enter his mind and he felt peculiarly calm.

They fished his body out of the river the next morning and his death was reported in the evening papers, the reporter saying that there were no marks of a struggle on the body and that it was to be presumed that Mr Nicholson had taken his own life.

Nathaniel had been working on a complicated engineering design in the library for most of the day. He carried the paper into the parlour and gave it to Jane as soon as he'd read it.

'I think you'd better see this,' he said and waited anxiously while she read it too.

She was very upset. 'Suicide?' she said. 'No, surely not. Whatever got into him to do such a thing? It's not like him. Not suicide. He was always so light-hearted. Wouldn't 'ee say so?'

'He found us this house,' Nathaniel remembered. 'He said it was rare sport to take me house-hunting. But as to suicide...' And he paused. 'Happen it was something to do with Mr Prance's report.'

She was struck by a shock of the most uncomfortable conscience. 'Surely not,' she said again. 'I mean to say, the report was about Mr Hudson, not him. It couldn't apply to *him* surely.'

'It could if he was buying and selling the same shares.'

'But that's dreadful,' she said. And yet even as she spoke she knew it could be possible. Oh, poor Mr Nicholson. What a fearful thing for him to have done. He must have been desperate.

'Yes,' Nathaniel agreed. 'It is. I wonder how poor Mrs Hudson is taking it. It will be a parlous shock to *her*.'

Mrs Hudson was screaming abuse at her husband. It had been a totally awful day. First her poor Ann had come weeping into her bedroom before she was dressed, to tell her she'd had a terrible letter from Mr Dundas informing her that 'in view of the present situation' he was 'releasing' her from their engagement.

'I'm to be shamed before the whole of society,' she wept. 'The whole of society. It's not fair, Ma. *I* didn't sell any shares. Why should I have to be shamed because of what my father's done? It's not fair.'

'Happen you could marry someone else,' Lizzie said, trying to comfort her.

'No one'll have me,' Ann wept. 'Not after this. I'm ruined. Oh, Ma, it's not fair.'

It had been well into the afternoon before she stopped crying and then she went off to her bedroom and locked herself in and the housekeeper came storming into the parlour to complain to Lizzie because the maids couldn't get in to clean the room. As if *that* mattered when her daughter's heart was broken.

Then the newspaper arrived and the stupid housekeeper brought it in to her at teatime as if she were doing her a favour. *'I thought you ought to see this, ma'am.'* What a thing to say. She'd had to read it twice because she couldn't bear to believe it the first time. He couldn't have done such a dreadful, awful, appalling, sinful thing. Not her Richard. Not her darling Richard. And to have it all in the papers for everyone to read. It made her want to scream that it wasn't true, that it couldn't be true.

And then as if all that weren't bad enough and

just as she'd stopped wanting to scream, a second letter had arrived and that one was from William to say that he was *'going to take the Queen's shilling and join the army, on account of it is impossible to stay at school now there is all this fuss over Papa.'*

'I can't bear it!' she shouted when George came whistling into the house. Whistling! As if there were nothing the matter, when her world was falling to pieces. 'Don't you understand? I can't bear it. First my poor Ann and how she'll get over a blow like that I really don't know, she were crying fit to break her heart, and then that awful newspaper – what I mean to say, she didn't have to bring it up to me like that. She must have known what was in it. And William gone for a soldier, when he should have been going up to Oxford like his brothers. It's enough to drive anyone distracted.' And she started to howl.

'Stow that row!' George shouted at her. 'Do you hear me? Just stow it! I've not come home to listen to all this rubbish.'

'Rubbish!' she screamed. 'My brother's dead.'

'Yes,' he said shortly. 'I've heard.'

That stopped her for a second – but only a second and then she was screaming at him again. 'What are you going to do about it?'

'Do?' he roared. 'What are you *on* about, woman? The man's dead. Can't you understand? He took the easy way out and he's dead. You can't bring the dead back to life.'

By that time, she'd reached spitting fury. 'Easy way out!' she shouted at him. 'Easy way out! How can 'ee stand there an' say such a vile, hateful thing? You're ... you're...' What was the word she wanted? 'You're heartless, George Hudson. That's what you are. Heartless. You're the most heartless, abominable wretch I ever clapped eyes on – and the most selfish and the most unkind, and, and... And here's my Ann been jilted and my William gone for a soldier and all you can do is stand there and say easy way out. You should be ashamed of yourself! Downright ashamed!'

He drew himself up to his full dominant height, red in the face and hot with fury. 'I will not be spoken to like this in my own house!' he roared. 'Make your mind up to it. I've enough on my plate wi' court cases an' people bellowing at me to resign and threatening to take away my estates and all my capital, wi'out having to listen to your stupid nonsense. If you go on, I'll have you sent to an asylum for the insane. Do you hear me?'

'The whole house can hear you!' she shouted at him. 'The whole world.' Then she ran from him, sobbing wildly.

Heartless and foul tempered he might be, but what he was telling her was correct in every detail. He was being beleaguered on all sides. The bank had foreclosed on his mortgage, which meant he would have to sell Albert Gate, he'd already resigned his chairmanship of the York, Newcastle and Berwick and all his other railway companies were demanding his resignation too, he had three court cases pending, all of them in Chancery, and in seven days' time he had to appear before the House of Commons to answer charges that he'd been bribing MPs. His life couldn't have been at a lower ebb. But he had no intention of sinking into self-pity. He was George Hudson, the Railway King. They'd not see *him* taking the easy way out. He'd stand up to 'em. He'd show 'em. If he couldn't beat 'em, he'd go down fighting, God damn it.

His daughter Ann had much the same fighting spirit. Within three days of her uncle's suicide, she announced to her mother that she was going to marry Count Suminski. 'I'll not let folk mock me,' she said. 'Not when I've a suitor ready and willing.'

'But I thought you told me no one would have you,' Lizzie said. 'How did you...?'

'I wrote to him,' Ann said. 'He asked me by return of post.'

'But he's foreign,' Lizzie objected. 'You'll have to live abroad.'

'Aye, I will,' Ann said. 'And a good job too. I've no intention of staying here to be a laughing stock.'

She was married and gone within three weeks. Poor Lizzie was distraught. 'First Richard and now my Ann,' she grieved.

But George wasn't listening. He had battles to fight.

Jane Cartwright had spent a happy summer preparing for her daughter's wedding, supervising the making of the bridal gown which was to be in white like Queen Victoria's wedding dress, sending out invitations, and watching the transformation of the vicarage, but she took time off now and then to check on her adversary's downfall because it gave her such a wonderful sense of satisfaction. It really was so exactly what should be happening to him. Poor Richard hadn't deserved his terrible fate at all but George most certainly had. Now that Nat was working with *The Yorkshireman*, she had an almost daily source of gossip, although for the most reliable news she had to wait to read the reports in *The Times* like everybody else in York. There was only one thing that troubled her and that was what would become of the people Hudson employed – and in particular of her Nathaniel.

She worried for more than a week before she decided she must talk to him about it, for if he were to lose his job, they might have to move from their lovely house, which would be extremely sad, especially with the wedding coming.

He was instantly reassuring. 'There are plenty of railways,' he told her, 'and more being built or at the planning stage. Hudson may be gone but his companies are still up and running and they can't build railways without the engineers to design them and build the bridges and the viaducts and all the other things they need.' Then he noticed her expression and asked, 'Were you worried about it?'

'I was,' she confessed, 'but I'm not now.' And she was thinking, those courts can do what they like with George Hudson, if that's the case.

What they did, as the months passed, was to strip him of all his assets, ordering him to pay back all the money he owed, to every company he had cheated. One by one his expensive properties were sold and naturally, given the situation he was in, all of them went cheaply. Albert Gate was sold to the French government for a mere £21,000. By August, even Newby Park was lost and by the time he and Lizzie had to leave it, he had no property left and precious little money. And to make matters worse he was still heavily in debt.

'I shall have to go abroad now we've lost this place,' he said to Lizzie, as he closed the door for the last time. 'There's nowt else for it.'

'Abroad?' she said. She was finding all these changes very hard to contend with but the thought of leaving the country was the worst thing she could imagine. 'How will I see my boys if I'm not in t'country? I mean for to say. Bad enough losing Ann and William wi'out being cut off from the others.'

'You're not going,' he told her. ''Tis just me.' And he tried to explain. 'If I stay in this country, I shall be arrested for debt and sent to prison. That's the long and short of it. I'll find you somewhere in London until I get myself an appointment. Don't 'ee fret. 'Twill all work out. I know more about railways than any man alive. I'll find some government that wants a railway built. They'll jump at me. You'll see.'

'Where are we going now?' she asked, waddling after him.

'To t'station,' he said.

29

There was a harsh rain falling when the Hudsons arrived in Euston on that August afternoon and Lizzie was tired and miserable. She'd had a most uncomfortable journey because something seemed to have happened to their usual coach and they'd had to travel in an ordinary one, which was none too clean and crowded with people. Now she trudged along the narrow streets between the most ugly soot-black houses she'd ever seen, damp with rain and burdened by a great bag full of shoes and clothes and all sorts of things that he *would* have her bring, and wondered where on earth they were going.

'Is it much further, George?' she said as they turned down yet another street of poverty-stricken houses. They really were hideous, with their peeling paintwork and their rickety doors standing askew and all those windows caked with such thick dust it looked as if it had been there for centuries. She pitied anyone who had to live in houses like this, she truly did, but then the people they were passing were a rough-looking lot and probably didn't notice how bad they were. The women wore men's flat caps and filthy shawls and broken-down boots and the children were in rags. There was a group of them lurking about on the corner with no shoes on their feet. One of them was smoking a clay pipe as if he were a man. It made her shudder to look at them. 'Is it much further?'

'This'll do,' George said, stopping in front of one of the houses. There was a clumsily written notice propped up against the filthy window and, peering at it through the rain, she saw that it said *Rooms to let*. Surely he's not going to take a room here?

'Wait here,' he said. 'I'll not be a minute.' And he walked in through the squiffy door, calling as he went, 'Anyone at home?'

She waited awkwardly, standing on the pavement in the rain but at a distance from the house, because she wouldn't want any of the passers-by to think she had anything to do with a place like that, and keeping a wary eye on the dirty children who were eyeing her up and down. What if one of them were to jump out on her and attack her? They looked capable of anything and that one with the pipe was downright ugly. Oh, do hurry up, George, she thought, looking at the blank face of the house. I don't like it here.

The boy with the pipe sauntered towards her. 'You waitin' for summink, missus?' he said.

'No, no,' she said in confusion. ''Tis all right.'

'Not from round these parts, are yer?' the boy said.

'No,' she said, looking round rather wildly for George. And there he was, striding out of the door towards her. Praise be!

'That's settled,' he said. 'Come on.'

He was leading her into the house. Why was he leading her into the house? 'I've got you a couple of rooms,' he said. 'First floor front. Best in the

436

house so the landlady says.' He was leading her up the stairs, and nasty rickety stairs they were. It was a wonder they didn't fall headlong. They reached the landing. 'There you are,' he said, opening a door and inclining his head to show her that she should step inside. 'This one's the bedroom. 'Tis all paid up and reg'lar. You've got it for six months.'

It was a dreadful room, dark and gloomy and very scantily furnished, with no curtains at the windows and only very dirty boards on the floor. There was a lumpy-looking bed against one wall with a decidedly dirty coverlet pulled clumsily across the top of it and a chamber pot rather horribly visible beneath it, a chipped wash stand with a plain jug and basin lurking in a corner and a plain deal table and one plain deal chair standing forlornly in the middle of the room. But if the bedroom was bad, the sitting room was worse. It smelt sour and every item of furniture in it seemed to be suffering from a sort of palsy. There were two chairs that were leaning on one another like a pair of drunks, the table had one of its legs propped up by an old book, there was a filthy dresser and a sofa that was so lumpy she could see the bumps in it from where she stood. The grate was empty and showed no signs of ever having been used. A dreadful, dreadful room. 'I can't stay here,' she said. 'It's a foul place.'

'You've no choice,' he told her brusquely. 'It's either this or live on the streets.'

'But it's a hovel, George.'

'Don't fuss,' he said. 'There are pie shops just round the corner so you'll not go hungry, and they do a good ale at the Pig and Whistle, which you'll be able to find easy enough, so Mrs Grimshawe says, and there's a baker's, and a butcher's and you've got your things. You'll mek out.'

She was tired and hungry and her coat was soaking wet and her hat was wrecked and her back ached and her feet were sore and she didn't want to make out. 'I can't stay here,' she said.

'Like I said, you've no choice,' George said. 'I've not got the money for owt else. You'll just have to make do wi' this till I can find a job and start making money again. You'll be fine here with Mrs Grimshawe. She comes from Leeds.' And he kissed her forehead, once and perfunctorily, and left her.

She sat on the bed and cried for a very long time. But there was nobody to hear her and nobody to take any notice of her, so in the end she dried her eyes as well as she could on her damp sleeve, took off her coat and hung it on a nail that was sticking out of the door, and unpacked her bag. Almost the first things she found were the pen, ink and paper he'd told her to pack that morning. That's it, she thought. I'll write to my boys. They'll look after me. And she sat down at her nasty cheap table and began to write.

'My dear George, You will be shocked to know that I am living in a very small room in a dreadful place called Burton Street, which is somewhere near Euston Station. Please, please come and visit me. Your father has gone abroad and for the life of me I don't know what to do or where to turn.'

Two days later the sun was shining and Shelton

House was heady with the scent of roses because it was Mary's wedding day and her bouquet lay ready for her on the dining room table. The guests had been arriving all morning and the excitement was increasing with every arrival. Milly and Felix had brought Audrey and her two nursery maids with them because Milly said she didn't think young Albert could be trusted not to disgrace himself, which he duly did, being suddenly sick all over his pretty new dress so that he had to be carried away upstairs to be cleaned up and changed, while his mother sighed. Sarah-Jane was being angelic and looking extremely pretty in her blue bridesmaid's gown with a chaplet of rosebuds on her fair hair. She was very conscious of being part of an occasion and stood between the two other bridesmaids, who were school friends of Mary's and had been commissioned to look after her, holding their hands and watching the comings and goings, owl-eyed.

What with friends and family and neighbours, there were so many people come to wish the young pair well that they made a noticeable procession as they all set off together for the church, laughing and chatting through the crowded streets, as passers-by waved and nodded at them and the church bells rang above their heads. Jane felt quite dizzy with the success of it all.

And then there they were, gathered in the cool and quiet of the church and there was the vicar waiting for them and Toby and Nat in their fine clothes standing before the altar rail and they were barely settled in their pews before Nathaniel and Mary were walking down the aisle towards them with the three bridesmaids behind them, Mary looking more beautiful than Jane had ever seen her, in her white dress with its fashionable bell-shaped skirt – the Queen was right, white was the perfect colour for a bride – and Nathaniel even more proud than he'd been at Milly's wedding. And the congregation hushed as Mary handed her bouquet to Sarah-Jane and the age-old ceremony began. 'Dearly beloved...'

'I've never been as happy as this in the whole of my life,' Jane said, as she and Nathaniel were walking back to the house at the head of their guests.

'Not even at our wedding?' he teased. 'I thought that was rather good myself.'

'This is different,' she said and when he pretended to look crestfallen, 'that was just us. This is our entire family, every single one of them and all our friends and neighbours. This is simply perfect.'

'That I will allow,' he said. 'So it is.' And he led the way into the house.

But there is a price to pay for perfection. Later that afternoon when the newlyweds had been driven off to the station, dappled with rose petals, and the guests had made their farewells and drifted away group by group and even Nat had left them to go off with his friends from the newspaper, she and Nathaniel were suddenly alone in a house that felt decidedly empty and lonely.

'I shall miss them,' Jane said. 'It's going to be odd in this house without them.'

'Get your bonnet on,' Nathaniel told her, 'and

we will go for one of our walks. I could do with some fresh air after all that crush.'

They followed the familiar pathways under the familiar sun, arm in arm, and for the first mile they talked about the wedding, reliving its moments and enjoying them all over again. Then Nathaniel surprised her by saying he had a bit of news he thought she would enjoy. 'Time for a breather, I think,' he said. 'Under that oak tree would be the perfect place.'

They sat together on the grassy knoll beneath the tree and Jane took off her bonnet, closed her eyes and raised her face towards the sun like a country girl. 'So what is it, this news of yours?' she said. She wasn't particularly interested. News was trivial after such a wedding.

'Have you read the newspaper today?'

No, she hadn't. 'Newspapers were the last thing I were thinking about this morning.'

'Then I will tell you,' he said. 'Mr Hudson has gone into exile.'

She opened her eyes at once. 'Left the country, do 'ee mean?'

'Left the country,' he told her. 'There are too many creditors after him and if he stays here, he's like to be arrested and sent to debtors' prison.'

She was delighted. 'Well, good riddance,' she said. 'Good riddance to bad rubbish.'

He thought for a minute before he spoke again and then he said, 'You really do hate him, don't you?'

'Aye,' she said easily. 'I do.'

'I think I've always known it,' he told her, 'but I've never really understood why it should be.

441

There must be a reason for a passion as strong as that.'

'Aye,' she said again, 'there is. I've known him a long time.' And then *she* spent a minute thinking. 'Happen I should tell you a story.'

'A fairy story on a wedding day,' he said. 'What could be better?'

'No,' she told him seriously. 'This is no fairy story. I only wish it were. This is true.' She paused again, only briefly this time, for he was looking at her so lovingly. 'When he were nobbut a lad,' she said, 'the great Mr Hudson fathered a child. He were just a village lad in those days and village lads were expected to stand by the babies they fathered and marry the girl and make an honest woman of her. But that wouldn't do for the great Mr Hudson. Oh no. He was above taking responsibility. Responsibility was for *other* people. He was all for himself, even then. Me, me, me, all the time. That was the great Mr Hudson. So he paid a bastardy fee and walked away from the village and left the girl to bring up her baby on her own. Which were mortal hard work.'

He finished the story for her. 'But the child grew up into a fine young woman, did she not, and now she is Lady Fitzwilliam and has four fine children of her own.'

It should have been a shock that he knew but in an odd way it was what she expected. 'How long have 'ee known?'

'For about three minutes. Possibly less.'

That made her smile.

'Why didn't you tell me before?' he asked, and his voice was gentle and loving.

'It wasn't the sort of thing I could tell anybody. Folk are uncommon cruel to a mother wi' no wedding ring on her finger. I thought you would think less of me if I told you.'

'Less of you?'

'Aye,' she admitted.

'Oh my dear girl,' he said. 'You were quite, quite wrong. I would have thought more of you, not less. I would have loved you even more than I already did. As I do now.'

She was close to tears. 'Truly?'

'Truly,' he said and stood up, brushing the twigs and dead leaves from his trousers. 'Time for us to go on with our walk, I think.'

She wiped her eyes, put on her bonnet and held out her hands so that he could lift her to her feet. 'Aye,' she said. 'You're right. 'Tis time for us to go on.'

The publishers hope that this book has given you enjoyable reading. Large Print Books are especially designed to be as easy to see and hold as possible. If you wish a complete list of our books please ask at your local library or write directly to:

Magna Large Print Books
Magna House, Long Preston,
Skipton, North Yorkshire.
BD23 4ND

This Large Print Book for the partially sighted, who cannot read normal print, is published under the auspices of

THE ULVERSCROFT FOUNDATION